JEAN KEATHLEY
Age of Broken Lives

An Epic of Triumph and Tragedy

The Tennessee Publishing House
496 Mountain View Drive
Mosheim, Tennessee 37818-3524

Age of Broken Lives

An Epic of Triumph
and Tragedy

by

Jean Keathley

Published in the United States
By
The Tennessee Publishing House
Mosheim, Tennessee March 2010
First Edition, First Printing

Cover Design: Kellie Warren-
Underwood

Disclaimer:

This document is an original work of the author. It may include reference to information commonly known or freely available to the general public. Any resemblance to other published information is purely coincidental. The author has in no way attempted to use material not of his own original unless such information has been cited, documented or given some other properly recognized written form of credit for such work The Tennessee Publishing House disclaims any association with or responsibility for the ideas, opinions or facts as expressed by the author of this book.

Printed in the Unites States of America
Cataloging-in-Publication
ISBN: 978-1-58275-217-4 Paperback

Copyright by Jean Keathley

ALL RIGHTS RESERVED

PROLOGUE

The misery of Ireland in 1845 was deeply engraved in the memory of Daniel Shaw Carrick and his dark brooding eyes held a tired, haunting look because of it. Whatever else he was denied; they could not take away his stubborn spirit and crusty pride.

It was a mean life on the day Daniel first smelled the rotting decay coming from his field of potatoes. The overpowering stench gagged him. Half running, half stumbling, he ran into the field. The round plump potatoes he'd dug a few days ago now came out of the earth black and shriveled.

As the total failure of the potato brought starvation throughout the land, Daniel was favored by luck. His tenement farm sat on a broad shelf up above the craggy cliffs in the shadow of the ocean, where all varieties of fish, shellfish and seabirds kept food on their table. Often he hunted, bagging an occasional wild fowl or hare, selling fish to buy oats, barley and meal.

The roads were filled with hungry, ragged swarms of humanity, pale and gaunt with feeble gait. The pitiful starving children with hair thinned and bald patches with wild, hollow-eyes and bare feet begging for food was a sight Daniel could hardly stand. On a day when he was returning from the parish church, sitting tiredly on his horse, he came across a mass of bodies, buried without coffins, half-eaten by rats and starving dogs.

That was the last time he went into Galway by way of the road, nor did he allow his wife Doreen to attend Mass from that day on. But Doreen whose heart of gold clouded her good judgment insisted on sharing what little they had with their neighbors. Blessed with food, though scanty as it was, she believed they were protected in God's love and they must share what they could spare.

The horror of fever in the land was an added worry and Daniel begged Doreen to stop visiting the neighboring households. "We canna' feed the whole county, Doreen. Sure and ye're takin' the food from the mouth of ye're son, and it's the fever ye'll be bringin' onto us."

It was Doreen's stubbornness that killed her. She died of the dreaded typhus fever on Christmas Eve. Every day for weeks after her death, Daniel stiffened his spine waiting for the time he and Morgan would be joining her. But as time passed, he came to accept that it was not to be. The truth of Doreen's words were fresh in his mind that he and his son were indeed saved by God's hand.

Losing his wife was a terrible thing but Daniel had his son and they were free of the fever. His heart was sore, but he kept his face from being hard for his son's sak, saying to himself over and over "I can abide it, for his sake." Bitterness was a waste of time and strength, and it was strength he needed to fortify himself to carry on. Gradually, the quiet dim shadows of Doreen faded and long with it his sorrow. With all his heart he loved this child who had the beguiling, endearing smile and optimism of his mother and the fear of losing him was forever with him. Because of this, he dared to bargain with God."

"God above, if ye'll keep me alive to raise me boy, ye'll have me promise I'll sing ye're praises at mass agin, and I'll see to it me son is raised to do the same."

As a returned sinner, Daniel's faith was strengthened all the more when he and Morgan were saved from death one day when caught in a squall out in the ocean. The high winds and choppy seas tossed them about for hours until they were pulled into the bay by a trawler. Daniel was heartily reproached by the parish priest who chided him for venturing out into the high seas with a lad of ten.

"Twas the luck of the Irish that saved us, Father."

"Luck me eye, Daniel, it twas the hand of God that spared the two of ye. Ye've no right to be venturin' out into the unpredictable sea with the lad, knowing the foul nature of it."

When the weather and calm seas allowed, Daniel and his son followed a trail across the mountain over the craggy rocks, flecked with dark green moss rising up from the sea to where their curragh was moored to the quay wall below. Settling into the curragh with net and tackle, they fished for rockfish in the calm blue waters of the cove. No more did Daniel face the danger of the open sea where the best fishing was found until he himself signed on with a fishing fleet while Morgan was in school. Working on a trawler was a meager livelihood when fishing depended on the sea and weather. On those days when the weather was foul, and there was no fish to catch, Daniel never paused a day or an instant in idleness, but spent his spare time plowing the fields of his tenant farm.

It was something to be glad of, not that he was the bragging type, but proud he was of the job he had done of raising Morgan without the soft hand of a woman to guide him.

It was from the big house on a quiet lane in Cappagh, she left as a servant girl to marry Morgan Carrick, with her parents long gone of the fever. Coming as a bride to the little thatched cottage on the side of the hill with a view of the sea, brought Mary Frances Dimity the blessings of her own home, an adoring husband, and the accepting arms of an honest welcome from a father-in-law she soon came to love.

With the death of Morgan's father, all rights reverted to the landowner, Lord Leroy Dudsworth, one of the most powerful landlords in the county. Morgan was forced by law to vacate the tenant farm. No land in Ireland was more cared for than this farm rented by Daniel Carrick, who paid out the rent money faithfully year after year for thirty acres of stony soil cleared with great labor into a field of cultured land by him and his son. Sheltered by the hills on the far side of the valley facing the sea was their three room cottage neatly thatched and whitewashed.

"You must vacate," the agent for the Lord of the Manor informed him. ; He was a bitter, tyrant of a man who did his Lord's bidding.

Morgan stood stiffly in the doorway of the cottage. "And if I don't vacate?' he asked, looking into the agent's blazing eyes.

"It's the law. When the tenant dies, the land is turned back to the landlord."

Morgan felt helpless. "But I am the tenant's son. Me father was too ill to work. It's the work I've done these past five years that has paid the rent. I'll be asking ye once agin, "he pleaded, "and if I don't be leavin?" He knew no words could persuade this tight featured man to show any forbearance.

"It's the civil law. If ye refuse to abide by it, the torches will be lit, and ye'll be burned out by sundown tomorrow. Take only what is ye'rs," he warned, spitting in the dust. With a set, determined jaw, he turned on his heel, lifted himself into the stirrup and rode off.

Morgan's heart sank, the blood draining from his face. All too often he'd seen glowing torches touch thatched roofs at the signal of a raised hand, torches held by hired thugs. The unfamiliar faces of the armed horsemen rode in the black of night, hired to demolish the cottage of the tenant farmer in arrears. It was a formidable sight, at first the light of the flaming torches, the blue smoke of the smoldering turf, the glow of the shooting flames, stripping naked the surrounding land with one stroke of the torch. It was happening all through the country.

Closing the door, Morgan drew in a breath at the light touch of Mary Frances' hand on his sleeve.

"Oh Morgan, what will we do?"

"May he roast in hell, but the devil himself will be disappointed when he arrives in hell, the bastard."

"He's too mean to die, Morgan, as is Lord Dudsworth. It's his orders he enforces," she said, her pale hazel eyes narrowed and sad. She looked into the fear filled eyes of her children clutching her skirts, Dimity and Daniel, their six year old twins.

It became real to Morgan when he closed the door of the cottage behind him for the last time he was closing the door on their sheltered security. In a matter of days, the family boarded the ship Alberta to sail for America.

CHAPTER ONE

It was early April in 1850, when Morgan Carrick and his family were herded along with the mass of humanity onto the ship, Alberta. This ship carried double t'gallant sails on fore and main, and single on the mizzen, large and deep. All their worldly possessions tied in two canvas sacks were slung on the shoulders of this tall, burley man, but for the small cloth bundle borne on the back of Mary Frances. Clicking her tongue in annoyance at Dimity and Daniel who lingered behind, their mother urged them to keep up. "Sure and ye'll be left behind. The both of you now, grab onto me skirts."

Stumbling up the gangplank, the family paused momentarily while Morgan handed over the four numbered tickets. Stepping on board the freshly washed decks, the truth suddenly struck Mary Frances. Making a brave effort to fight back her tears, she turned for one last look, for one more glimpse of the misty green dewy brambles and gorse bushes springing alive with yellow blossoms.

Morgan eyed Mary Frances sympathetically, sensing her apprehension and worry for her unborn child and her fear of the long journey. "Come now darlin' the Lord is smilin' down on us on this glorious, happy day," he proclaimed with infectious cheerfulness

Mary Frances shook her head in agreement, her heart contracting with an ache in her throat, she managed a few steps forward as Morgan grasped her hand.

"Step along, step along," the pockmarked First Mate urged. At his side Captain Stuart Lang stood stiffly with arms folded over his broad chest. There were no welcoming words of greeting from his lips, only a look of impatience at the delay for he was anxious to get underway.

"Come along, step lively," the Second Mate snapped, waving the crowd of steerage passengers on, down the hatchway.

The Captain's heavily bearded face contorted as his deep, resonant voice shouted a frantic note of urgency. "Good God, Mr. Bennett, it's about time that's the last of the livestock." He pointed a crooked finger to the two uniform figures bearing a crate of chickens, the livestock intended for the officers' mess.

"Aye, Aye, Captain sir." Mr. Bennett paused to study the cargo manifests.

"Give it here, man," the captain shouted angrily. "The wind's southwesterly and we're already two hours past sailing time. If those contrary winds off the heads hadn't delayed our departure yesterday, we'd be long gone. I'd hoped your cargo was already set in place, Mr. Bennett."

"Aye, this is the last of it, sir." Mr. Bennett turned away dismissing the captain with an indifferent shrug all but pleased with himself at his good fortune at this last minute purchase.

Crowded on board the Alberta were two hundred passengers and a crew of twenty-eight seamen. The group of noisy passengers, who seemed half-drunk with excitement, now catching a first glimpse of their home to be for the next six weeks, became a silent apathetic crowd.

Entering the steerage deck with his family close behind, Morgan eyed his surroundings skeptically. Biting his lip, he smiled thinly.

"Well now, we can make do," he sighed. Quickly claiming an area for his family, he shifted the weight of his two bundles onto a lower and upper bunk. It was not what he had expected. It was a barracks of bunks on top of bunks lined up, two feet apart, noisy with human life at a cost of $20.00 per head with food for the privilege of sailing in steerage.

Morgan turned to lift the calico drawstring bag of personal possessions from Mary Frances' shoulder.

Remembering her children and the need to dispel their fears, Mary Frances echoed his smile, momentarily stifling her uneasiness; she went on gaily, "Indeed, we will make do." She collected the twins within the circle of her arms, their sturdy bodies now healthy and strong.

"Mama," Dimity cried in wide-eyed innocent delight, plopping herself down on the ticking covered straw, "Is this where we will sleep?"

"Yes, darlin'," Mary Frances avoided Morgan's eyes.

Reading her thoughts, Morgan rested his cheek on her head, willing the stir and rumble of voices out of their heads to shut out reality, shielding their privacy if only for a moment.

"Me, too? Will I sleep here with Dimity?" Daniel asked, seating himself beside her.

"Of course, boy." Morgan eyed his son with pride, lifting him to the upper bunk. "Here it is ye'll be sleeping, ye and Dimity."

Abandoning the lower bunk, Dimity struggled to climb up to the upper bunk. Morgan gave her a quick boost. Their smiling faces glowed with joy at the wonder of this new adventure.

Mary Frances leaned back in the bunk and closed her eyes, her thoughts and her heart echoing the words she'd said to Morgan. It was her persuasion, chiding and pleading to seek the fortunes of America still ringing in her ears. "We must escape to the blessed land of freedom, a land of sunlight and plenty, Morgan." She wondered now where providence would lead them.

But for his worn and patched waistcoat, Morgan looked almost dapper with his high buttoned collar, Mary Frances thought as he slid in beside her. Urged by a compulsive desire to shield her from all hardships, he gathered her in his arms. Watching her fondly, he brushed the wisps of windblown hair off her forehead. With an edge to his voice, he whispered, "It's not what we thought is it darlin'?"

Making a visible effort to hide her disappointment, she grasped his hand, "We canna' turn back, me love. Twill be our home for only a short while. We've made our choice. We must be strong, my darlin', and turn a blind eye to all but our vision of a new life and the promise of a future without hunger, without injustice.

It was a cloud of canvas, a lovely full rigger in the fair wind that embraced the Alberta sailing out of the harbor into the open sea. The ship continued to sail with light headwinds the first three days. The warm wash of the sea air cleansed Morgan's soul of hate. Were it not for Mary Frances' pleading, he would have carried out his overpowering wish to seek revenge with a smoking gun to the man who'd driven them out of their home, but now he was comforted and grateful for his wife, and a blessed hot excitement replaced his gloom and somberness in the first days of the voyage.

Under sail with anxious faces pressed to the wind, the steerage passengers soon became infatuated with the sea as the Alberta swished along in her own suds. Discovering one of the mysteries of nature, the sailing of a ship, Morgan and his family in good spirits and good health joined in the holiday atmosphere high-stepping to the Irish jig to the tune of the fiddle and flute. For a time they forgot they were homeless and the strength of their optimism took over. In a fine Irish tenor, Morgan burst into song, with a chorus of droning rhythmic voices joining in. If they weren't singing and dancing, the steerage passengers were sitting around the open brick fireplace telling tales or playing games. Because there was room for only four or five pots on the grill at a time, the remaining women sat by patiently awaiting their turn to cook the few vegetables and rationed meat into a stirabout. In the meantime, the older group of women passed the time sewing or knitting and listening to the tales told by the men while the young mothers played with their children.

In just the early stages of her pregnancy, Mary Frances feeling well and content was able to put aside the many inconveniences of steerage passage for the time being. The delicate look of her was transformed into a radiant healthful glow amid her lightness of heart returned during those first glorious days of sailing with the feel of the delicious sweet smelling sea air on her face.

"Me brother says they eat like Christmas everyday," John Duffy went on, pleased with himself at revealing a tidbit of news that only he could know about.

"It's a lovely vision ye've got John Duffy, but if I were ye, I wouldn't be having such high notions," Mrs. Mulroon chided him, snapping off her words like pistol shots.

"No, 'tis true. And work is there for every able man," he pointed out.

Coming startling to life with all its implications, his group of listeners sat wide-eyed, their belief in his tales weaving a thread of hope of things to come.

"Ladies, ye'll be dressed in silk with jewels hanging from ye're neck."

With a sharp eye, Mrs. Mulroon pointed a finger, "Sure and it's a lose tongue full of the old blarney ye have, Mr. Duffy, sir."

"It comes to me secondhand from words written on paper by me beloved brother in America and I tell it in truth. If it helps to keep ye're hearts up, what harm?"

Doling out the stir about to her family, Mary Frances laughed never knowing of such luxuries and wondering if it could be true.

At the end of the prayer, the twins watched their Mother's face before beginning their meal. Dimity and Daniel dug in at the nod of her head and after their Dada's first bite. Sopping up the last of her stir about with a crust of bread, Dimity hesitated before putting it in her mouth. She took a small bite, and then placed the remaining piece of sopped bread into a crevice of the brick fireplace.

"And what do ye think ye're doing, my girl?" Morgan asked, objecting to the waste of food, albeit one bite.

"I shall leave that for the wee people," she chirped gleefully.

Mary Frances smiled a knowing smile, placing her hand on Morgan's arm. "Ye know, Morgan, I've taught her the Irish Lore. Whenever we milked the cow, a bit of milk was spilt for the wee people. It's only something she's done all her life."

"It appears Daniel is too hungry to leave a morsel for the wee people, and Dimity may have to allow the wee people to find their food elsewhere in the days to come," he warned.

The days of laughter and warm camaraderie soon ended along with fair weather and favorable light headwinds when the weather became squally and threatening with a howling northwest gale blowing in the prospect of a stormy night. With the weather worsening rapidly and showing all signs of becoming dirty and freshening to a hard gale,

Captain Lang had the lifelines stretched fore and aft. The Captain then reduced sail to a main lower topsail and mizzen staysail, ordering extra gaskets to be put on all sails. As the storm grappled the ocean in anger, the sea and the sky became one. The big ship's lee rails plunged under water with water high on the lee side of the poop, with tons of water sweeping her decks.

The seamen manned their stations, ready to carry out the Captain's orders to take in sail when the gale first started to blow, and the quartermaster's orders to man the braces.

"Batten down the hatches," the Captain bellowed through the speaking horn. "If you want to see the end of this voyage," he warned, "step lively."

The surging seas doused and flooded the decks with ocean spray. With the water seeping down into steerage, a chill of prickling terror closed in about them. There was no escape. No escape from the roar of the breaking waves and howling winds or the continuous pitching and lurching of the vessel, or the sound of the creaking ship, or the sound of crying children, or the moans and retching of the sick.

"It's clear to be Jaysus she's taking us," John Duffy roared in fright.

The damp cold whistled through the drafty ship gnawing at their bones. The few passengers not reduced to seasickness lay shivering, huddled together in prayer in the semi-darkness with the only light from the kerosene lantern that swayed back and forth with the rocking of the ship, sending off a faint yellow glow in the airless, dark shadows of the steerage deck.

Morgan sat upright and wide awake in the tiny cramped space ducking his head to avoid the overhanging half-timbered bunk. His dark sad eyes traveled to the gentle, delicate face of Mary Frances whose once blooming pink-cheeked and healthy complexion was now changed to the gray color of an overcast sky.

Morgan looked at her thinking what a beauty she was at eighteen when God blessed their wedding day with the sun smiling down on them, and the day the twins were born. "Tis blessed by God himself, we are Mory, to send us two beautiful babies," her happiness overflowing.

Long after the storm had passed and most of the passengers were recovered, Mary Frances still suffered the miseries of seasickness, her weakened condition eventually causing a miscarriage. She fell into black despair at the loss of her baby, and as the days dragged on, she developed a high fever and a racking cough.

Dangling, dirt-encrusted feet hung over the edge of the wooden planked bunk as four grubby hands clutched the lump of hardtack to their mouths. Though not identical, Dimity and Daniel both had their mother's soft hazel eyes and delicate features, and both had hair of burnished gold. With the length of Daniel's hair matching Dimity's, he looked like a girl but for his ragged pantaloons rolled halfway up his skinny dirty legs. Devouring each bite in half-starved gulps, the meager bits of food gradually soothed the discomfort in their bellies.

Studying the pale faces of his children whose tattered, dirty clothing now hung on their shrunken bodies, Morgan dabbed at his eyes with a foul smelling rag. Raising his eyebrows, he shouted at them with alarm, "here now, you little mutts, easy, easy, or ye'll be fillin' the chamber pot with ye're vomit."

Fearing the scanty portion of food would be taken from them; both children studied his face anxiously.

Reminding himself his tone was too sharp, Morgan smiled a slow, gentle smile, and then tousled both heads of soft fair hair, shining gold in the early morning sunlight escaping through the open hatch. In wordless gratitude for the warmth of the sun and pure sea air creeping into the dark confines of the hold, he drew in great gulps of blessed fresh air. Oh, he thought, for a taste of one of Mary Frances' meat pies, or a bite of roast goose, or a nip of whiskey to soothe his jangled being. Devil take it! It had been a long voyage.

Imprisoned in this dismal tomb of misery all these weeks, Morgan was beginning to worry his mind was slipping. At twenty-five, all dignity and youth was gone from him.

Daniel chuckled, "ye look like a weasel, Dimity," he giggled, pulling her braid. First, ye smell the biscuit like a weasel, and then ye take a wee weasel bite."

"I do na'," Dimity pouted. With a swift twist of her body in an attempt to move away from her brother's teasing, she dropped her last remaining piece of biscuit. Reaching out to grasp the treasured morsel, Dimity fell headfirst out of the top berth onto the deck planking.

A high-pitched shriek escaped from Dimity, more of fear than of hurt as Morgan slid off the bunk and gathered her in his arms.

"Ye're not hurt now, are ye wee one?" He lightly touched the reddened area on her forehead. "Just a bump, love."

"I didna' push her," Daniel spoke up guiltily.

Morgan waved him to silence with a raised hand. He cringed at the sound of Mary Frances' cry of pain from the lower berth.

With the weight of Dimity no more than a sack of twigs, Morgan hoisted her up to the upper berth and handed her the few remaining crumbs of her biscuit.

"Shh!" he held his forefinger to his lips. "Be good ya ' little pixies while I tend to ye're Mama."

Clutching the precious biscuit in her tiny fist, Dimity's sobs gradually softened.

Seeing the naked, unrelenting pain on his wife's contorted face, Morgan's pale eyes watered as he sat on the bunk beside her. He touched his lips to her feverish cheek.

"Tis it my darlin', Dimity, that's doin' the cryin'? Mary Frances asked in a weak voice.

"She's fine, darlin'. Nothin' to worry your pretty head about."

Mary Frances' eyes followed the sunlight. "At last, the heavenly white dawn of America. God bless America!" She tried vainly to lift her head to the side of the berth, her eyes following the path of sunlight.

"No, darlin', not yet. But soon," Daniel stroked her forehead, his hand soothingly cool.

Just four weeks at sea, and the beautiful green of Ireland seemed a dream, but the dream of America and a new life was the dream that demanded the ultimate sacrifice, abandonment of their beloved homeland, a land rooted in their hearts.

At Mrs. Mulroon's kind offer, Morgan turned the twins over to her care while he nursed Mary Frances. "Tis' not for their young innocent eyes to see their mother suffering so," she chided, her lined, haggard face troubled with a gnawing doubt and a fear that Mary Frances was past getting well.

During the night as the ship pitched and rocked, once or twice Mary Frances began to retch, each time Morgan held a basin to her. As she tried to sit up, her face twisted into an expression of agony. Morgan's fear mounted when he noticed the streaks of blood in the basin. She tried to speak, moving about in a constant motion, throwing off the ragged quilt, her face and neck was flushed, her skin hot and dry. Her quickened pulse and rapid shallow gasps of air and spasms of pain exhausted her.

Growing more frantic, Morgan dropped down on his kees beside her, the tears flowing freely down his cheeks. "Mary Frances! Mary Frances! Oh God, please dona' take her from me," he prayed. Smoothing the bronze strands of hair away from her face, he bathed her face with a wet cloth, moistening her parched, split lips with his ration of water.

Her full, feverish eyes looked at him in recognition. With an agonized effort she lifted her hand momentarily to touch his face; she uttered slurred words, barely above a whisper, "Mory."

Morgan leaned closer to hear her.

"Take care of the twi." her chest rising with the last gasp of labored breath.

It seemed an eternity that he knelt there staring into her angelic face, unbelieving, unmoving, his shoulders sagging under the weight of his grief.

The touch of a hand on his shoulder sending a convulsive tremble through him brought him out of his momentary apoplexy. "Come now, Morgan," Mr. Mulroon urged, "It's with God she is. See the quiet look of her now at peace." His strong hands lifted Morgan to his feet. Putting an arm around his shaking shoulders Mr. Mulroon led him away.

It was several hours before the sun rose bright in a cloudless sky, a cruel mockery to the death of Mary Frances Carrick. No longer would Morgan hear her soft spoken voice or feel the soothing balm of her hands on his flesh, or see the graceful elegance of her, or see the sparkle in her warm hazel eyes.

While on their way to the water closets, to take care of the call of nature, the sober faces of the awakening steerage passengers passed by the corpse of the young woman. Conscious of yet another death in their midst, each of them paused   to bow their heads and mutter a prayer.

Trusting no one else to see to the final ministration of her, Morgan used his last bit of rationed water and the remaining piece of soap to clean the body of his beloved wife for the burial. He gave no indication of awareness when the first mate came to order the removal of the body. Because of the fever, the steward and hands refused to touch her, so it was Morgan and Mr. Mulroon who lifted the body out of the dark hole of the steerage. Laying her in the mummy bag of canvas, Morgan grabbed hold of the Steward's hand holding the needle and thread. "I want to brush her hair."

"Are you daft, man?" shouted the sailor over the wind with a coldness that cut into Morgan's heart. "When she hits the water it won't make much difference now, will it?"

Morgan's eye caught the glimmer of gold as the needle and thread worked its way upward. Once more, he put his hand on the sailor's arm to stop him. "Wait."

"The devil take you, man. Matey," he called to one of the seaman standing by, "Haul him away."

"No wait," Morgan pleaded, "It's her ring. Please. Let me remove her ring." He gently slipped the gold wedding ring from her stiffened icy finger.

The tolling of the forward bell sounded, drowning out the words of the Captain, "Into the depths of the sea, we commend the soul of Mary Frances Carrick to go forth and meet her maker."

Morgan was inconsolable as the body was lowered into the sea. His pitiful incoherent babblings were heard below deck by his children who began to cry, squirming to be free from the arms that kept their young eyes from the frightening sight of their mother's burial.

CHAPTER TWO

During the last week of the sorrowful voyage, Morgan totally surrendered to hopelessness, leaving the care of his two children to Mrs. Mulroon whose barren life had clouded her good judgment when it came to children.

She attended to their needs, lovingly mending their ragged clothing, doing their laundry, even to the point of sparing a few bites of her rations. At the urging of Mr. Mulroon, she finally gave into his reasoning that Morgan needed to return to the living and accept the responsibility of his children.

"But I've tried, Mr. Mulroon," she insisted to the kindly, gentle giant of the man that was her husband.

"It's talking sense to the man. That's what I aim to do," he said, determined. He walked to Morgan's bunk where he stood for a moment before speaking, looking down at the painful sight of him, disheveled and unkempt, his face turned to the wall. Morgan stirred, his eyes fastening on Mr. Mulroon.

"It's time Morgan lad; you begin acting like a father. Tomorrow is the day of landing and the Mrs. and I will be going our way, God willing, and ye'll be going ye'er way."

Morgan muttered a half-heard reply, "Yes sir."

"Just a kind word of encouragement to them, Morgan. Sure and Mary Frances trusted ye to take care of the little ones."

Morgan's fix stare softened at the mention of her name. He swung his legs over the edge of the bunk, sat there rubbing the stubble of his russet beard.

"Go now lad to ye're children and pray for strength. Ye must know in ye're heart lad, ye're prayers will be heard with ye're beloved Mary Frances up there to pass on the word. Keep ye're promise to her man. Take care of the treasures God has left with ye."

Mr. Mulroon helped him to his feet. Morgan faltered as he stood, grabbing hold of the bunk.

"Ye're legs are a bit rickety, lad. Ye must be eat in' some-thin' to get ye're strength back," Mr. Mulroon said, with an arm around him to steady him.

The children came running to him when they saw him.

"Dada," they cried in unison.

He gathered them in his arms. "Have ye been good children? Daniel, have ye not teased ye're sister?"

"No, Dada," Daniel replied.

Their faces brightened in the warmth of his caress.

Awakening to the pink, rosy dawn, Morgan laid there for awhile half-awake knowing to his intense relief that the unhappy voyage was close to being over. Unable to stand the unbearable foul smelling stench any longer, he quickly gathered their few belongings together. Morgan gently nudged the children awake and helped them dress in the clothes they had worn when they departed Ireland. Pulling on Dimity's long black stockings, he smiled a slow gentle smile as she lovingly fingered his ginger bristly beard.

"Is it the devil that took our Mama away, Dada?" Daniel asked tearfully, his little mind knowing only evil and meanness was connected with the devil, and knowing nothing of the path of sickness and death.

"No! No, indeed, boy. Sure and the devil had no hand in it."

How indeed, could he explain when goodness was God and evil was the devil? He pressed his bearded cheek to Daniel's dimpled cheek. "It's an angel she is in heaven at God's side, to watch over ye and Dimity and me self."

Remembering the wedding ring in his pocket, he drew it out. "Ye're mama left her ring for the both of yeu to remember her by."

"But Dada, there's only one ring and two of us, "Dimity reminded him."Who will wear it?"

Pulling out a chisel from his sack, his work worn roughened hands began sawing on the ring with a practiced skill. Before long, the ring broke in two. He then proceeded to press both ends together into two tiny rings, bringing the circles of shiny gold close to their faces so they could better see the inscription.

"Ye see," Morgan pointed to the inscription, "Dimity's ring has "Two Hearts" imprinted and ye,

Daniel, have the side with "One Soul." He placed Dimity's on her middle finger and Daniel's on his.

Dimity fingered the ring lovingly, smiled a wide smile, and then reached up to plant a kiss on Morgan's cheek.

"Always wear her ring and ye'll remember ye're dear sweet mama every time you look at it. When ye're fingers grow as you grow, ye'll move the ring to the next finger."

Standing to demonstrate, holding his arms over his head, "then when ye are as high as ye're Dada, and ye're fingers are as fat as ye're Dada's, ye must pull a string through the ring and wear it around your neck. Will ye promise to remember all that I've said and vow to never take it off?"

"Oh never," cried Dimity. "I shall never take it off?"

"Nor shall I," Daniel agreed.

"And," Daniel went on, "Ye both must always remember, because ye were born on the same day, and been' twins ye have two hearts," Daniel pointed to their chests, "but one soul."

The twins looked at him with wide eyes.

"Can you remember that?"

"Oh yes, Dada, " Dimity and Daniel agreed.

"Two hearts and one soul," Daniel repeated.

Hanging excitedly to their bundles, the toddlers followed their father up to the main deck, where the sun was rising in a splendor of unexpected glory. Those passengers who were not too weak to struggle up the stairs were gathering with their belongings, and eating the last ghastly meal to be doled out to them on the Alberta.

Morgan's spirits lifted a little at the children's open excitement.

A lump gathered in the boatswain's throat when he saw the poor wretches without their Mama. "Good morning to you, Mr. Carrick, and to the wee lassie and laddy," he lifted his dirty wool cap in greeting.

"Sir," Morgan acknowledged, bowing his head to the youthful Shamus McInnis, not much younger than himself, who had been especially kind, offering extra biscuits from his pocket to the children from time to time.

"They know of their mother, do they not?" he asked, patting each head gently, and then turning his head to fasten his eye on the wailing toddler sitting atop the shoulders of his father.

"Yes," Morgan whispered, dropping his eyes.

"They be a sweet laddy and lassie."

Morgan had a warm liking for him. He was a hard working sailor with a sense of duty, and plagued with concern for the steerage passengers.

'Twas the first sign of conversation coming from the lips of Morgan Carrick. "And do ye intend to spend ye're young life on a ship?" he asked.

"I do, sir, and me old one too. The sea is me love," he answered, stooping to pick up Morgan's canvas sack of belongings. "Ye best come with me, sir, out of the way."

They followed Shamus to the after part of the main deck, where there were few eyes to see.

Shamus, with an air of authority directed the family to a cluster of empty casks where they could rest away from prying eyes.

"Here ye be, little ones, sit ye'reself down. I've a bit of lime if ye can stand the sour of it." He reached into his pocket for two halves of lime covered with pocket fuzz. Picking it off, he handed one to each child, then dried his hands on his pantaloons. "By the look o' ye, ye could do wi' some fattenin'." He pinched each child's cheek spattered with freckles.

It was pitiful watching them greedily suck in the juice, these two innocent waifs now puny and undersized, showing the signs of their bodily suffering. Shamus was saddened at the injustice suffered by the steerage passengers, especially for the little children.

"Here now," Morgan halted them, "Can ye not offer a word of thanks to the kind gentleman?"

"Thank you, kind sir." Daniel said with puckered lips.

"Yes sir, thank you," Dimity chimed in after one more swallow, then dropping the rind long enough to hitch up her flannel drawers.

When they had finished eating rind and all, Shamus pulled out a piece of salt meat wrapped in a dirty piece of clothe. "There be enough for the three of ye," he said, handing it to Morgan. "T'would make a suggestion sir, that ye stash it away until later as they're handin' out the porridge, and that'll be the last of the grub ye'll be gettin' onboard."

The expression on Shamus' face revealed nothing of his feelings, but Morgan sensed that beneath this talkative lad's carefree demeanor he had a big caring heart.

Shamus wondered how Morgan planned to manage without a mother for the children. Sure and the man didn't appear to be tower of strength. Shamus felt it was the least he could do to give them a helping hand.

"Do ye have family and work waitin' for ye in America, Mr. Carrick?"

Morgan looked about him avoiding the boatswain mate's eyes, his voice flat and bleak, "No, no family." He ran his fingers through his hair. "No work."

"I've a friend in the dockyard. If ye tell him Shamus sent ye, I have a mind he'll put ye to work. The name is John Driscoll. And if you need a place to stay, I know of a boarding house on 1200 Chatham Street. Shamus handed him a piece of torn sailcloth with the address scrawled on it.

Morgan repeated the name John Driscoll, then the Chatham Street address. Morgan could read but remembering the name and the street address is what he had in mind in case he lost the piece of sailcloth.

"Do not think me out after ye're money, Mr. Carrick, sir, but is it pounds or dollars ye're carryin' with ya?"

"Why do ya ask?" Morgan eyed him warily.

"If 'tis pounds, the moneychangers will be after ye. When ye step ye're foot on America's soil, it'll be dollars ye'll be a needin'. I'd oblige ye with dollars for ye're pounds until ye can change the rest at the bank later on."

A rush of color flooded Morgan's cheeks as he drew out the coins from the pouch he carried around his waist. It was that bit of kindness that endeared Shamus to him.

When Shamus had finished counting out the dollars he could spare in exchange for Morgan's pounds, he pressed an extra silver dollar into Morgan's palm. Twasn't much, but Shamus felt the better for it.

At the sound of the bell, the children rushed eagerly to claim their bowl of porridge.

The tall, dignified figure of Captain Lang bawled out orders in his deep baritone voice, "Man your stations," he shouted, removing his eyeglass, and then replacing it quickly. "Land ho! Land ho!"

"Thank you, Shamus," Morgan held out his hand.

"God be with you and the little ones, sir." Shamus turned to answer the order of the bullhorn. He couldn't be found neglecting his duty.

The catcalling mob on deck let loose a whoop of triumphant joy. With that reassuring sound, there was a rush of the poor souls to the leeward side where land was sighted. Those passengers still below swarmed aloft in a swift stirring of heightened voices of excitement.

The day dragged on. It was midday when the Alberta left behind the wide expanse of the sky blue waters of the open sea to sluggishly maneuver her way into the becalmed, glassy, murky waters of the New York harbor.

CHAPTER THREE

Ships laden with provisions and passengers were docked alongside the public wharf when at last the Alberta was tied up to her larboard chains and the ship finally dropped anchor. Preparations to disembark began and a chorus of happy shouts arose at the sight of the gangplank being lowered to the wharf.

The Irish immigrants, who disembarked that day in June 1860, bore their packs, their sacks, their bundles, and their babies. All had experienced the same share of misery, all were united in a common plight, and all were homeless and poor. Tired, hungry and sick, and minds whirling with two many questions, their eyes were full of suspicion.

Though happy they were to be off the ship, the arrival and facing the immigration authorities was one more cause for mental anguish. The steady stream of bodies were lead into Castle Garden, a massive structure built in 1807 as a fort on the west side of the Battery where they were met by government immigration officers and then surrendered to the demoralizing examinations of the cold unfeeling nurses and doctors whose duty it was to exclude the sick and contagious, lunatics and idiots, and any immigrant who was unable to care for himself.

Mrs. Mulroon took Dimity and Daniel aside with her while Mr. Mulroon and Morgan were herded in the line of men who were told to drop their pantaloons. Knowing not what was in store for them, Morgan accommodated the doctor, but the set of his mouth and the squareness of his jaw told of his distaste at the examination of his genitalia. He emerged from the examination feeling violated. No explanation was given to the men for this personal invasion. The majority of them had no notion of venereal disease and that that was the reason for the unfamiliar fondling they experienced. It was demeaning and emotionally shattering to Morgan.

Each child's head was examined for the loathsome ringworm disease, the deaf and dumb and the half-witted were weeded out, and all children over the age of two were observed for their ability to walk without assistance.

Those found to be breathing heavily with a racking cough, or fever, or those unable to walk without assistance were set aside for rejection and sent back. America did not want the burden of an unhealthy citizen.

At last, Morgan and his family, and the Mulroon's were given a stamp of approval with a mark of colored chalk on their shirts. They were handed a piece of cheese and bread and allowed to leave. "You are free to go." The door to America was open to them.

Understandably frightened by the government officials, the ordeal was a grim reminder of the tyranny they had left behind. Exhausted physically and emotionally, like dazed bullocks, the two families walked with an unhurried gait into the dirt street of America, the look of it far from being a paradise.

"Do ye have a place in mind to go, Morgan?" Mr. Mulroon asked.

"Yes sir. I have the address here. It's a rooming house at 1200 Chatham Street," Morgan handed the crumbled piece of paper to him. "Do ye'reself and the Mrs. have a place to spend the night?"

No, but there's a crowd of good wishers holding up signs for lodgings. Sure and we can find a place for the night."

"I've been warned, Mr. Mulroon, not to go with any who seem so willing. They're not the softhearted generous people they make out to be. Ye and Mrs. Mulroon best go with me. I've been told this is a reputable rooming house."

"If ye're sure ye don't mind, Morgan lad, we'll do just that," Mr. Mulroon agreed, patting him on the back.

"It's grateful we are to ye, Morgan," Mrs. Mulroon gathered Dimity and Daniel to her, whose sleepy eyes did not go unnoticed. "The little ones need to be put down. And Morgan, I'll be glad to take care of them for ye when you find work, that is, until it's time for us to move on to Philadelphia where Mr. Mulroon's brother lives." Thinking of how he intended to manage working and take care of them at the same time saddened her.

No sooner than they were out of the shipyard, they were met by the moneychangers, a stream of hawkers, and the shysters who pretended to be friendly, ready to guide them to an Irish boardinghouse near the waterfront. These lodgings were usually neglected ruins for which the immigrants paid dearly, and then soon found themselves at the mercy of an unscrupulous landlord. From these temporary lodgings, the immigrants moved to tenements, old warehouses or they became squatters in a shantytown where outside privies were not far enough away from the water supply which contributed to disease.

Ignoring them, Morgan and the Mulroons set off down the dusty road facing the new world with a sense of urgency and a fierce resolution to survive. It was hot and the air was alive with mosquitoes. Morgan could see nothing that fit the descriptions told to him of lush green grass or deep black fertile soil or verdant wooded areas. It was a wild unbelievable metropolis with a rhythm of activity impossibly crowded with thronging vehicles of horse drawn trolleys, wagons and carriages rushing helter skelter in confusion through the streets, lined with the dismal, gray stone walls of the tenements. It was a neighborhood of paupers.

From the Battery on, Morgan stopped to ask directions from anyone who would stop, showing them the address. Bowery Street was a street with the most vivid contrasts in the world where the highest respectability was elbowed by the lowest degradation and the headquartered the likes of vagabondry, thievery and prostitution.

"Hot corn! Hot corn!" the cries of the night street peddlers reached their ears. Hot corn on the cob fished out of a cedar pail of hot water was a favorite snack of the street crowd for two cents an ear.

It was close to midnight when the group reached the Chatham Street address, a three story frame house, not as shabby as some seen on the way, but a stones throw from a slaughterhouse. The coarse bloated face of the half-awake landlady wearing a filthy yellow stained nightgown scowled at them through the open door.

"It was Shamus McInnis who sent me," Morgan explained, "'Tis sorry we are for the late hour. Would ye be having a room to rent?"

"That I do. That I do, for a friend of Shamus. That scaly-wag!" She looked down at the sleeping children, one in Morgan's arms and one in Mr. Mulroon's. "It's not the best room in the house, but for you comin' off the boat it'll do. It's seventy-five cents a week with meals."

Morgan looked at Mr. Mulroon who shook his head in agreement.

Lighting the way with a kerosene lamp, she led them through a maze of doors and passages to the back of the house up a dark narrow stairway. The room was furnished scantily with four cots, a wooden table and four chairs, and a small table with spindly legs holding an empty pitcher.

Scratching her frowsy hair, the landlady pointed to the pitcher, "Water is down there in the back, out of the pump."

After the hardships of the desolate voyage, Morgan dared not think. Already disillusioned with America, his disappointment was written on his face.

"Things will look better in the daylight, Morgan, after a good night's sleep," Mrs. Mulroon consoled him, helping him to put the whining children to bed on one of the cots with Dimity aimed in one direction, and Daniel aimed in the other direction.

It was late the next evening when Morgan returned to his children; his eyes alight with fresh dreams and new hope and purpose. He'd been hired on the spot as a dockhand by the man who was Shamus friend. In America only the fit can survive, and Morgan knew it was every man for him with conscience and honor gone.

Only when they'd accustomed themselves to the sights surrounding them and the loud unfamiliar sounds from the street did the children agree to go outside with Mrs. Mulroon to wait for their father. After supper, they waited anxiously, sitting close to Mrs. Mulroon on the front steps watching for a sign of him coming down the street each day still wearing his canvas apron and the sleeves of his blue work shirt rolled up to his elbows.

During the day the children watched the droves of cattle, sheep and hogs that were, driven through the streets, leaving their droppings on the way to the slaughterhouse next door. The entrails of the animals were cleaned, bones boiled, fats melted and hides cured outside of the slaughterhouse exuding pestiferous fumes. Between that and the smell of the overflowing backyard privy, the garbage heap and manure pile, the stench was unbearable.

With Morgan's strength slow in returning, he was very tired each day when he returned from a day's work, although inspired by a new personal ambition to make a better life for his children.

Dimity and Daniel let out a yell when they spotted him.

"Dada," they called, running to him.

He lifted first Dimity into the air, then Daniel. "And how was your day?" His russet hair hung in clinging dirty strands. Feeling a twinge of conscience at leaving them, he tucked both children under his arms, his last precious link to Mary Frances. He stood there for a moment succumbing to a wave of nostalgia for his homeland.

Morgan set the children down, and tipped his cap to Mrs. Mulroon. "I trust they've been good children, Mrs. Mulroon."

"That they have the darlins', though they've been a bit squeamish watching the drove of cattle coming down the street to the slaughterhouse all the day."

Morgan put the children down.

"I'm not afraid, Dada," Daniel cried, "but Dimity, she be afraid." The child's eye caught the sight of the chickens clucking and pecking contentedly about the yard. He took off after them in a flash. With feathers flying, he caught a small hen, whose wings flapped wildly.

"Put the hen down, Daniel. She'll be pecking your eyes out."

Morgan turned his attention to Dimity. She clung to his dirty shirt as he sat down on the stone steps with her on his lap. Putting her tiny fingers to her nose to prove her point, "Ooh Dada, it stinks so bad here."

"She's telling the truth there, Morgan.'Tis not a fit place for the children. It's of no matter to Mr. Mulroon and me self. We'll be leaving in a day or two, but when you've had a chance to put a little money aside ye best look for better lodgings. I know it's dog cheap here, but it's their safety I fear. Have ye spoken to the landlady about the care of the children when we're gone?" She gave him a pensive look. He was a level-headed, methodical fellow, and responsible too, finding a job when Mr. Mulroon said jobs were hard to find.

"Yes Ma'am, I'll be asking her, and this weekend I do not work so it's then I plan to look for another place."

"And how's the job?" Mrs. Mulroon asked. "Hard work, I take it. Ye look worn out. Ye're supper is put aside. She turned to the children, "let ye're father come in and have his supper, children," she said, taking each child's hand. Now that he had work, Mrs. Mulroon could see his spirits were up. He needs to find a new wife and mother for the little ones, she thought. Knowing that Morgan Carrick was facing his responsibility, the worry of them was somewhat eased in her mind.

On a warm morning two weeks after they left the ship, and one week after the Mulroon's left, Morgan left for work as usual. He walked down South Street in the soft glow of the early morning sunlight. His head was in a whirl; at last he found a decent place to live and the money to pay for it. Morgan breathed in a deep breath of free air. He'd given the new landlady three dollars the day before, a month's rent for two clean rooms with a window.

When he saw the kindness in her eyes, and her willingness to care for the children, he snatched it up. They'd be moving in tonight after work. Fired up by this promise of a new life, Morgan stepped up his pace through the dirt encrusted streets, and smiled to himself at the happiness of his thoughts.

So, on this Friday morning, Morgan looked forward to working a full day, and the pay at the end of it. He'd thrown himself into his work with a new found strength, but quite aside from his work, his hands were full at night soothing the children's hurts, and comforting their fears. He had cause to worry about them the past week in the care of the present landlady for they were fretful and tearful when he came home at night. It wasn't that she laid a hand on them, but the unkind words and hateful way of her had a deleterious affect on them emotionally. From her peculiar ways, and by instinct, Morgan came to believe she had a definite dislike towards the children. She did it for the money and no other reason. Not only that, but the children had little or no space to play with the backyard overgrown and stacked with garbage and trash and piles of horse manure. They were afraid to use the backyard privy with the horse running lose, and sometimes her reluctance caused Dimity to have an accident, and wet her drawers with the landlady severely chastising her. Out of spite the child was not allowed to change them and to Morgan's disgust Dimity was still wearing the wet, smelly drawers at the end of the day, an indignity that truly upset the child. Morgan was eager to move them to their new home away from her.

Making his way to the waterfront, the hum of commerce and the bustle of business was alive with early morning activity. The foot of South Street lined with stables, breweries, foundries and coopers and buildings housing the grain merchants who prospered from the cargoes coming in off the ships. The clamor of drays and wagons on the cobblestones could be heard for blocks, and the odor of manure and the stench of rotting fish from the Fulton Fish Market were an assault of smells that carried for blocks. The fishmongers and greengrocers were already leaving the area, their carts loaded with produce and fish. The horse-drawn drays and wagons stood ready at the warehouses waiting to be loaded.

As Morgan approached the warehouse where he worked, Mr. Hirsch, his boss, stood mopping his brow, barking out orders to the dockhand named Curley.

Curley yelled back at him. "It's not seven yet. I'll not be workin' 'til seven." He turned his back on his boss and walked away.

Ignoring the bold-faced muscle-bound man as though from fear, Mr. Hirsch turned to Morgan, "You," he said, rolling his cheroot to one side of his mouth, "you, Morgan Carrick, load those barrels onto the dray."

"Yes sir." Morgan had no intention of incurring his displeasure. He needed the job and he tackled it with a vigorous gusto.

Hearing this, Curley began a slow walk towards Morgan, his lips set in a thin line, the muscles in his face tightened "Damn the likes of ya' ya' greenhorn, with ye're thoughts in the air," he shouted. His words became more venomous with each step. Curley was known to be a sturdy fighter and one who picked a fight for the love of it.

Morgan found himself opposite a man whose dark eyes burned with a fiery hate. It was evident a conflict was imminent.

Quick as a flash Curley's clenched fist struck Morgan a staggering blow.

Morgan swung a blow to the man's jaw, the whack of his huge fist knocking him against the rope on the pier.

The fight went on long after the bell clanged to start work. The men's fists continued waving with blood oozing down their faces. Suddenly, Curiey bowed his head, and in a dead run butted Morgan in the stomach sending him flying over the rope and into the frothing, scuddy water. Morgan's head hit the side of the ship anchored there with a sickening thud and Morgan went under. Attempts to pull him out in time failed.

Morgan's body was put on a wagon and carried to Potter's field. Little was known of Morgan's private life, only his name. Mr. Hirsch had no address listed and knew of no immediate family. It was judged to be an accident by the onlookers who were all Curley's friends, and no charges were made against the man who caused Morgan's death.

CHAPTER FOUR

After four days when Morgan failed to return to the boarding house, Mrs. Chambers, the landlady grew suspicious that he had dumped the children on her. She walked to the wharf making inquiries along the way, when finally she was told by Mr. Hirsch that Morgan Carrick had died. He offered no details and no assistance for the children left behind.

Under a summer cloud the children were told of their father's death. They were too young to know the raw sadness of it, but soon they began to realize he was never coming back to them and they were bewildered, subdued and broken, pining after their father.

Mrs. Chambers' brain was in a tumult as she held no affection for Dimity and Daniel, and she was incapable of sympathizing or comforting them in their grief. Unable to endure their presence any longer, and knowing there was no money for their keep, she proceeded with the irksome task of pawning them off on the Sisters at the Mercy Orphanage.

When Dimity and Daniel were told to gather up their few belongings, fear gripped them. Her tears blinded her as Dimity helped her brother pack their few belongings.

"But Daniel, where is she packing us off to?" she asked in a quivering voice, "to see our

Dada?" The vision of seeing her father was all she lived for.

Daniel stuffed their remaining ragged clothing into the calico sack then turned to look at his sister, speaking to her in a grownup way. "It's dead, he is, Dimity.with Mama in heaven ."

Dimity's power to fathom this news was too much for her little mind until it was repeated to her by her brother. She crumpled in a heap on the cot, sobbing her little heart out.

They were at the mercy of Dora Chambers who cared nothing for them. Everyone they loved and who loved them had been taken away, and the soothing protection and security of loving arms they had known in their short lives was gone.

"Where are you taking us," Daniel asked.

"To the orphanage," Dora Chambers answered gruffly, with no pity in her heart. "You be orphans with your father dead. Tis' charity cases you are now."

The children remained silent and somber on the long walk to the orphanage. The simple truth that they were orphans held no significance in their small child's minds as their understanding and conception of life's turmoils was underdeveloped and held no real meaning to them.

When they set out, a light blanket of mist covered the streets which quickly changed into a downpour. The children, dowdily dressed were soon rain soaked and looked more forlorn than ever by the time they reached the orphanage. As they came in sight of the twenty year old three-story frame house, the clouds broke away into the distance opening up the sky to the awakened sun which cast a crimson glow over the shabby building.

Thirty some odd children were packed into this house at the end of a narrow lane far from neighbors as though forsaken by the rest of the human race. The property was indeed in a sorry state when taken over from a farmer who demanded his money in cash in six monthly installments, installments hard to come by until the Sisters' benefactor was blown in by a sainted wind. This the nuns firmly believed. Their ardent patron supplied them with large quantities of meats and vegetables, and with the chickens, pigs and cows they housed in their barn, they made out fairly well. The nuns also took in sewing, washing and ironing from the uptown wealthy in their effort to provide for the orphans.

Dimity and Daniel followed the impassive woman with faltering steps up the pathway to the house girdled by a tall wooden fence and shadowed by huge oak trees. A large, stout nun in the blue serge habit of the Sisters of Mercy greeted them at the door. The haunted look on the two pale faces of the children standing behind the skirts of the hard-featured woman touched her heart.

"And what is it I can do for you?" Sister Veronica asked.

"I've two orphans for you, sister," Dora Chambers pushed Dimity and Daniel towards her through the door.

"Come in! Come in! And what do we have here? Is it twins I see? A boy and a girl?"

"Yes'um, a boy and a girl."

"I'm afraid we take only girls. You'll have to take the boy to the Boys Home across town." Sister Veronica quickly closed the door behind them, blocking any attempt at flight when she saw the wild-eyed fear in the childrens' eyes.

Their comprehension of what was happening wasn't at all clear in the children's minds up to that point, but the mention of a separation melted Dimity's courage. Although Daniel stood straight with a proud indifference, Dimity clung firmly to her brother in desperation fear with a powerful urge to cry. Dimity, once the pretty romping child with bouncing golden red curls, the delight to all who laid eyes on her, stood with beseeching eyes to the nun who seemed inclined toward an affectionate heart.

With only one singular purpose, Dora Chambers proceeded to explain how she was left with the two children whose father was killed on the docks this past week. "I cannot be bound to two strange children, Sister. It's lucky they are I did not send them out into the streets after their father's death. I've little enough to eat on my own table."

Sister Veronica's narrowed gaze focused on the dirty, unkempt woman. She could see there was no redeeming attributes or sterling worth about her. "And what of their mother?"

"'Tis buried at sea, she is."

Daniel's lips twitched as the image of his mama swam before him. With the memory almost too great a burden for the little tyke to bear, a tear trickled down his cheek.

Dora Chambers dropped two bundles at the nun's feet, one rapped in a length of calico, and the other in a canvas sack, and reached for Daniel's hand. "It's off we'll be then, Sister."

Angered at her bullied treatment, Daniel's unbelieving eyes traveled over Dora's twisted, weathered face. Momentarily his courage sank with a gathering dread, but every nerve in his body cried out at the injustice. With quickness, in the space of a heartbeat, Daniel succeeded wrenching free and pushing her against the wall. In his desperation, he continued to lash out at her kicking her with the toe of his high-topped shoe.

With a screeching cry of alarm, Dora raised her hand to strike Daniel, whose teeth were imbedded in her arm. "You wicked, evil boy." She clouted him on the head with her grubby fist.

"Here now," Sister Veronica rescued the child, believing his mutinous behavior was not from wickedness but from the fear of separation from his sister. "There's a good lad," holding him firmly within her arms, soothing his shaking sobs, protecting him from Dora Chambers and this large and uncaring world that had left them wholly dependent, friendless and forsaken.

As if in answer to a silent prayer, Sister Veronica knew in her heart as she gazed into the face cold as stone she could not turn this child over to Dora Chambers who stood with arms folded over her buxom breasts muttering to herself.

"The rain is settling in again," Sister Veronica remarked, looking out of the window. "It's a dripping, gloomy evening for you to be going clear across town with the boy, and t'will be dark before you get there. We'll take care of the children, Mrs. Chambers." She had no intention of explaining in front of the children that she would see that Daniel was taken to the Boys Home. Sister Veronica moved quickly to the door, staring down at Dimity and Daniel. "You go on now, Mrs. Chambers."

Without a word, Dora Chambers bounded for the open door with not a glance backward.

A tiny spark of relief flickered in the childrens' trustful eyes with their fate solely in the hands of this kindly nun. Daniel put his arm around Dimity. They were together.

Sister Veronica read their thoughts. Knowing she would have to betray their trust when the boy was taken away the next day, she felt numb and her head throbbed as the sadness of it washed through her.

Sister Veronica blinked a tear away behind her thick glasses.

"Dimity and Daniel," she said with a sweet smile, "if you pick up your bundles and follow me, we'll have a quick wash before you eat supper."

Blotting away the picture of the evil face of Dora Chambers, the twins eagerly watched Sister Veronica light the kerosene lamp on the table in the reception hall. Curiosity stirred through them at the sound of the chattering voices within the closed oaken double doors, which Sister Veronica opened to the smell of cooked cabbage and the sound of the noisy, high-pitched voices of giggling girls. Girls of various ages sat at long wooden tables eyeing the twins with inquisitive, quizzical looks.

"Girls! Girls! This is Dimity and Daniel," Sister Veronica said, "will you say a good evening to them?"

"Good evening to you, Dimity and Daniel," the girls shouted, echoing the nun's words.

The twins shyly lowered their heads.

Sister Veronica marched Dimity and Daniel back to the kitchen where she washed them with yellow soap, and gave them their supper.

"And where will we be sleepin' Missus?" Daniel asked, looking up from his plate of cabbage and potatoes, worried that they would be separated.

"You may call me Sister, Daniel, and you'll sleep together in a nice clean bed upstairs."

'Twas not too soon for Dimity, she fell asleep with her head on the table next to her half-eaten plate of food.

It was long before daylight three days later when Sister Veronica with a saddened heart walked to the bedside of Daniel who was sleeping soundly alongside his sister. She stood stiffly erect beside Father Nathaniel who had come to fetch Daniel.

Gazing down at the child, she motioned to Father Nathaniel to lift Daniel.

"Please Father, hurry before Dimity awakes," she whispered in a choked voice. It was almost more than she could bear, this terrible cruel thing she was doing, separating these children. The dread of it was the reason she postponed the separation, and the sadness of it was revealed in her haunted face.

When Father Nathaniel lifted the child into his arms, Daniel awoke blinking in the yellowish dim light of the lantern Sister Veronica held, and then quickly closed his eyes in sleep once more.

"There's a good lad," Father said softly, patting him gently as Daniel stirred in his arms.

Sister Veronica led the way through the darkened hallway down the stairs to the horse-drawn wagon waiting in front. Father Nathaniel placed the child on the hard boards of the wagon. Half asleep, Daniel popped up in a sitting position only to fall back down; curling himself in a ball under the worn quilted coverlet Sister Veronica had placed over him. The child was clad only in threadbare underwear. Against Sister Veronica's protestations, Father Nathaniel thought it best not to dress Daniel for fear of waking both children in the process.

The journey across town to the Jesuit Fathers' Boys' Home was a little less than ten miles and Father Nathaniel wanted to be off and away before Daniel awoke with the jogging of the wagon. Climbing up into the seat, Father Nathaniel reached for the reins. He gave Sister Veronica a knowing nod, the reins lax in his hands. "The lad will be in good hands, Sister. You're not to blame. Tell yourself that. The great black cloud hanging over these children was not of your doing. We'll pray to God that their little hearts and minds will heal." He gave the horses a cluck, turning them north up the narrow rutty lane, over the hill into the bright glare of the rising sun.

Sister Veronica stood watching the wagon until it was out of sight. The thought that the wound left by their parents' death was to be further deepened, jabbed at her heart like a knife. Her only comfort was in knowing Daniel would be cared for by the good fathers. It was far better than being a victim at the hands of the Children's' Aid Society where she had seen children ragged and dirty who were forced to fend for themselves by stealing and begging on the streets, or sent out West on orphans' trains to work on farms.

"Mother of Mercy, heal their little hearts of this sorrow," she prayed with a bowed head.

CHAPTER FIVE

U p she sat, flinging the thin worn quilt off of her, hastily glancing sideways to the empty spot where her brother laid next to her when she fell asleep last night.

Still half-asleep Dimity rubbed her eyes with her balled up fist, looking about her at the sleeping girls in beds lined up in neat rows. Her eyes traveled to the chair where Daniel's ragged pantaloons and shirt were placed with her dress the night before. She leaped out of bed, lifting her dress to see if Daniel's clothes might be underneath. His clothes were gone.

Dimity called out sleepily, "Daniel! Daniel, where are you? Daniel?"

He did not answer and was nowhere in sight. Her screams of terror not only alarmed the girls who were asleep but was heard by the nuns who hurried down the corridor from the chapel where they were gathered for morning prayers.

The nuns entered the dormitory, Sister Emily tending to the girls now awake and Sister Veronica sitting on Dimity's bed intent on comforting the child in her distress. Drawing Dimity into her arms, she spoke softly, "Hush! Hush, child!"

"Where is Daniel?" Dimity choked between sobs, tears streaming down her cheeks.

"Now, now, Dimity, don't cry." Sister Veronica spoke in soft soothing tones, rocking Dimity back and forth, pressing the child's tear stained face against the white starched wimple. At this moment, Sister Veronica felt inhuman. There was not enough love in the world to make up for this child's heartbreak. If there was a cure for the nameless horror of abandonment that had touched Dimity, it was a lasting enduring love of a family environment. This was a security that was not in Sister Veronica's power to provide unless the child was adopted by a loving couple.

"You see, dear, because Daniel is a boy, he must live in a home with boys and you must live here where there are all girls. He will learn the things that are important for a boy, and you, Dimity, will learn the things that are important for a girl. You will learn to sew and to cook. Won't you like that?" she asked.

"No! No! I want my brother," she screamed, wailing pitifully into Sister Veronica's habit.

Oh how much Sister Veronica wanted to be honest with the child, but knowing that she was too young to understand and that her misery would not be assuaged by either the truth or a false explanation, the nun told her a white lie. "Forgive me, Lord," she prayed to herself.

"You will see your brother," Sister lied, knowing in her heart Dimity would probably never see him, hoping time would erase the memory of him. There was no consoling her. It was that way for days, weeks and months.

Once the beautiful, carefree, romping child, Dimity became somber, her hazel eyes glassy and unseeing, staring into space with a disturbingly blank face that was usually stained with tears. She was pale-faced and skinny. With searching, silent eyes, Dimity stood for hours peering out between the wooden slats of the gate, clutching her only remnant of the past, a dirty rag doll. There was one exception; she still wore the gold ring on her finger. She watched and waited for God knows what, possibly a glimpse of the familiar face of her brother Daniel. Often she was discovered sitting under the dark stairway listless and tearful, or seated aloof on a hill above the play yard away from the other girls, or standing behind the starched white curtains gazing forlornly out the window.

"When will Daniel come back?" This was a question she continually asked and the only words she spoke.

At first, she reacted with an uncontrollable wild anxiety, and then succumbed to a mute suffering, fighting a mental battle as well as a physical illness. In her troubled child's mind she seemed to forsake her natural instinct for life with an all-knowing will.

The four nuns of the Order of Sisters of Mercy and Nellie O'Grady, their cook and housekeeper, cared for Dimity with a tender devoted affection, especially Mrs. O'Grady. She was a woman of robust, solid frame with a sound, healthy constitution who was prone to lifting Dimity up into the air into her arms to give her a tight squeeze in a show of affection.

On such a morning, Dimity's feverish eyes did not go unnoticed. "Dear heart," Nellie cooed, "ye're lookin' a bit peeked." She held her cool palm to the child's forehead. "And sure if ye're not with a fever."

As the day progressed, Dimity's breathing became labored and her fever soared. It was Mrs. O'Grady who summoned the doctor and sat up with her bathing her with cool cloths to bring down the cursed devil's fire.

The narrative of facts told to her by Sister Veronica opened Nellie's eyes to the sad truth of Dimity's illness. Nellie's love of children and the need of motherhood, which was denied her when she lost her husband before she could bear children, was the lure that brought her to the Orphans' Home.

In soft, lilting words, Nellie pried open the dried, parched lips with a broth filled spoon. "Taste it darlin'," she urged, lifting Dimity's head from the pillow.

Dimity looked into Nellie's face with searching, silent eyes. The kind voice stirred memories within her, memories of another voice which vibrated like music, a mother's voice. Dimity sipped the warm soothing broth, and as her taste buds opened up, she soon began savoring the delicious chicken flavor. Suddenly, her whole being was awakened to the world around her. Her sad hazel eyes rested on the patch of sunlight on the polished floor. Hearing the sound of the exuberant voices at play outside, she gazed forlornly out the window while she sipped the next spoonful Nellie held to her lips.

"That's the way, ye're doin' jest fine, angel," Nellie smiled. To her surprise, the child was showing the first signs of interest in food as well as her surroundings. Nellie felt encouraged. What sorrowful eyes! Nellie pressed Dimity further for a few more bites, offering a bite of biscuit smeared with jam and a sip of tea. Nellie's chubby hand tenderly touched the child's forehead. "At last, dear child, ye're fevers broke."

Feeling the protecting security of this kindly woman, Dimity seized Nellie's hand. Holding it tight, she asked. "Are you my friend, Miss Nellie?"

Realizing the depth of anguish this question revealed, Nellie gathered Dimity into her arms, offering her the comfort of belonging, if only from a friend. "Yes, Dimity, my darlin' child, by all that's holy, Nellie's ye're friend."

Nellie helped Dimity to stand at the side of her bed.

"Why do I feel so funny?" Dimity asked, looking down at her shaking legs.

"Well now, little one, ye've been that sick for too long a time, and ye're a might weak. Ye'll start to feel ye're old self now that ye can eat. Let Nellie give you a good wash and change ye're nighty, and ye'll perk right up."

Dimity sank back down onto the bed, clutching her rag doll to her, doubting that a 'good wash' would perk her up. But as Nellie removed her flannel nighty and gently touched her skin with the warm soapy water and toweled her dry, a soothing warmth spread through her.

Sitting on the edge of the bed, Nellie hummed a cheerful tune as she brushed Dimity's mass of tangled curls, interweaving the reddish blond tresses into two fat braids.

"Sure, and if ye're not a pretty picture. Do ya not feel better; love.all fresh and clean?

"Yes, Miss Nellie," Dimity smiled a wan smile, the first ever Nellie had seen coming from the child.

"After ye've had a nice rest, we'll take you out into the fresh air this afternoon. Would ya like that, darlin'?"

"Yes," Dimity choked as a paroxysm of coughing overtook her.

"See there," Nellie said, pouring cough medicine into a spoon, ye've still got that bad of a cough. She waited until Dimity stopped trembling. "Open wide," she urged. There was no sight so sad to her than to see a sick child.

Dimity screwed up her little face as the liquid went down.

Nellie's eyes twinkled. "That's the girl."

In the months following her illness, Dimity finally settled into the convent routine, into this new phase of existence. Her pale, wizened face had become less somber, her listlessness and tearfulness gradually disappeared.

Dimity's plight was no different from the other girls, indeed, nor more painful. They all shared the same fate of how to go on with life when grownups let you down, and the strong bond of love was gone. This tragic uprooting reduced the orphans to mute resignation.

All were not Catholic at Mercy Orphanage. The religious question was not the core of their struggle to reorder their lives. Some were of Jewish heritage, German, Italian and Balkan, and of course, Irish, as was Dimity. She was among the youngest to be taken in by the nuns. Most of the girls were children of the streets, thirteen and fourteen year olds, dispossessed by parents who abandoned them, or who were left alone when a widowed mother or father died of the fever. With the help of the policemen patrolling the streets, the nuns were able to rescue these girls from a crime befouled life on the East Side, all innocent victims of prostitution and thievery. The cry of a hungry, homeless child haunted and drove the nuns to make it better for them. Although some proved to be rebellious at first, they were eager to escape the abominable conditions of life they came from, and showed signs of hopefulness that their constant struggle to survive was over. With patience and kindness, the sisters gradually won them over, establishing a firm foundation of integrity, and honesty. Before long, with persistent teachings of goodness, the nuns were able to convince their charges that crime was a source of shame, and most importantly, a sinful existence, punishable in this life, as well as, the next.

There was no idleness in the convent. Dimity learned to keep herself neat and tidy, to lace and tie her high toppers. She was taught to mend and sew, to help the older girls with assigned kitchen tasks, and to her delight, she was allowed to attend classes. She was quick to learn her numbers and letters, and proudly recited the prayers she learned.

When the bell awoke the girls at 6:00 *A.M.*, they quickly dressed, tended to their morning toilet, made their beds, put their room in order, lined up behind Sister Justine, and proceeded to the chapel for morning mass.

The chapel, normally a high ceiling, gloomy room, became most inviting at morning Mass when the candlelight gave off a divine aura of heavenly presence. Dimity loved the pungent fragrance of the burning candle wax, and the best part of the Mass was when the priest swung the gold container of burning incense and the kind feminine face of Sister Veronica looked out from her constraining wimple and gave the signal for the prayer 'mea culpa, mea culpa'.

Dimity responded with great enthusiasm while beating her chest with her doubled-up fist. Being told she was too young to partake in Holy Communion was Dimity's greatest disappointment, and waiting a whole year to make her First Holy Communion was an eternity to her. After Mass, the whispering, giggling girls were forced into silence by a policing nun while they assembled in the dining room for their breakfast, a breakfast supplied by benefactors with charitable hearts. One of the most faithful of these was the good hearted milkman, who left a can of milk at the back door each morning.

The harsh sound of two hands clapping together was the signal for quiet. "Quiet! I say, quiet!" Sister Justine clapped again, determined that talk and eating did not go together.

Standing by the table where Dimity sat, the nun's eyes caught the quick hand of Callie lifting a muffin from Dimity's plate.

Dimity's cry of alarm echoed throughout the dining room. "It's mine," she cried out, jerking it away from the fourteen year old, who was a newly appointed monitor over Dimity.

By giving the older girls the responsibility of two or three younger girls, the nuns hoped to see the girls develop some semblance of kindness to the little ones who soon came to depend on them for companionship, love and guidance. In most cases, the belligerent, selfish behavior they'd adopted to survive on the streets dissolved under the admiration of their charges.

"I didn't take it," Callie lied.

"You did! You did!" Dimity accused her, a tear forming in her eye.

"Callie," Sister Justine ordered, "kindly follow me."

The nun had clearly seen the girl take the muffin. She wondered if Callie was resorting to her old ways. She had proved to be on her good behavior, and that was the reason she'd been appointed monitor.

Outside the dining room, Sister Justine fixed her eyes on the tall fourteen year old, whose busy dark hair was an uncombed, tangled mess.

"Could you not see fit to run a comb through your hair this morning, Callie?"

"I did, Sister," Callie responded.

"That's now the second lie you've told me today young lady, and breakfast not yet over."

The girl frowned, looking down at her unpolished shabby shoes.

Sister Justine, knowing that discipline needed to be rigidly enforced, added, "For the bold-faced lies you told, you'll go without breakfast this day, and you're to blacken the shoes of all your charges."

"Yes Sister." Callie stood there dry eyed and silent, fearful of missing another meal if she sassed the nun.

As the loud dismissal bell sounded, Sister Justine warned her with a few last words. "If I ever see you taking the food of the little ones again young lady, you'll no longer be a monitor. I shall assign a monitor for you."

Perched high on a stack of hay in the barn, Dimity sat howling in a high yapping voice, with cheeks aflame, her screeches barely drowned out by the yowling of the cat being twirled in circles by its tail. With a hard edge smirk, Callie fastened her eye on Dimity as she sped the half-dead animal in circles.

The wailing of Dimity was heard by Nellie who followed the sound into the barn.

Rushing forward in a gasp of horror, Nellie struck Callie full in the face with the back of her hand. The girl immediately dropped the cat, which was blessedly left with enough strength to run for cover.

"Ye bloody beast of a girl," Nellie raged. "Ye're eyes are black with meanness," she said, grabbing a handful of hair as she pulled her through the barn door. "Come darlin'," she called to Dimity.

Standing at the back door, a finely dressed gentleman turned his head to see the sorry sight of Nellie dragging a girl by her hair up the back steps, and her yipping at the top of her voice, pretending hurt that was not there.

His eyes of condemnation for the child's treatment quickly shifted to the lovely little lamb of a girl whose upturned nose was dripping, along with hurtful tears dripping down her cheeks.

Nellie stopped her headlong march up the stairs, and released her hold on Callie. "Good day to you Mr. Durant, sir. It's a sad occurrence caused by this girl," she croaked, in a vain attempt to defend herself.

"That bad, eh?" he said, resting his hand on Dimity's head whose untidy hair felt silky soft under his fingers. "And this little lamb, what might be your name?"

"Dimity." she sniffed, looking up at him with big sorrowful eyes, and then shifting her gaze to Nellie O'Grady."Please, Miss Nellie, may I go see to Tabby?"

"As soon as I take this one to Sister Veronica," she said, staring into the scowling face of Callie. Nellie was torn between her duty to see that the girl was punished for her despicable act, and wanting to calm Dimity.

"But." Dimity insisted, "The kitty might be hurt."

Albert Durant spoke up. "May I take the child to see the cat, since you seem to have your hands full at the moment?"

"I hate to put ye to all that bother, Mr. Durant," Nellie said, loosening her hold on Callie, "but Dimity's that worried the cat was hurt with the hateful treatment this girl gave it."

"No bother! Dimity is it?" he asked, taking her little hand in his. "Shall we see about Tabby?

"Yes sir!"

"Oh, by the way, Mrs. O'Grady, that box of groceries is for you," he said, pointing to the large crate sitting on the back porch. Albert Durant never came to the orphanage empty-handed. The towering giant of a man was one of the orphanage's most generous benefactors.

Albert Francis Durant lowered his dark cavernous eyes to the tragic little figure whose tears were still wet on her cheeks. The sight of this delicate frail child tugged at his heart. In his usual deliberate manner he lifted a clean white linen handkerchief from the pocket of his Chesterfield coat.

"Here now, little one, let's dry those tears," he said, in his heavy bass voice, dabbing at her eyes.

Dimity hardly dared to raise her eyes to look at this mountain of a man who was giving her such close attention, but at this signal of kindness, she peered up into a face gentle and wise and smiled wanly.

His eyes grew soft. "Would you like to keep this hanker-chief?" he said, holding it out to her.

"For me? Truly?" she asked, fingering the soft material wonderingly. The thin pale lips trembled. "It's too pretty for me," she said, handing it back to him.

"Of course it's for you. And it's not as pretty as you," he said, lifting her chin, tweaking a fiery red curl, and then tying the memento around her neck. "The Lord must have had a big smile on his face the day you were born, Dimity."

Dimity flowered under his word of praise, her happy steps meeting his as he whacked each step with his knotty walking stick with its silver-knobbed head. The feel of this great chunk of a man's hand recalled a scene painted in her memory when her Dada used to hold her hand. His long hairy fingers opened and closed on Dimity's tiny hand as he spoke, waving his cane at the clucking chickens in their path. "Out of the way, you chickens or you'll be swimming in my stew pot." He laughed out loud, looking down at Dimity for her reaction.

Doing her best to keep up with his long strides, Dimity's smile widened, thinking he was a funny man that made her feel warm all over.

The flies were thick when they stepped inside the airless barn, and the thread of pestering insects began buzzing around their heads until Mr. Durant waved his arms around, swatting at them. The sound of the creaking barn door broke the stillness and started the cow bawling.

"That's Belinda," Dimity informed him.

"Belinda, you say?" His eyes narrowed at the sound of the faint meow coming from the corner of the barn. Hoping the animal was not hurt, he instructed Dimity, "You stay here Dimity while I take a look see over there." If the cat was too far gone, he didn't want the child to see it.

The coal black, shiny cat stayed in one spot, sitting on the woodpile, his beady black eyes half shut. But the moment Mr. Durant moved towards him to grab him, he let out a screechy yowl, and shot pass him knocking over the water pail with a loud clatter. He ran into the safety of Dimity's arms.

Dimity sat on the low milking stool cradling the ball of fur in her arms.

Mr. Durant smiled down at her, showing his white teeth through his shaggy mustache. "He must like you, Dimity," he said, petting the cat.

"He does. I help Mrs. O'Grady feed him every day. I'm his friend." Her large hazel eyes were fixed on the gold watch chain dangling from Mr. Durant ' s vest pocket, a chain as thick as her finger.

"I declare, he's no worse for wear. His tail hairs look like they've been plucked, but other than that, he's right perky." He couldn't help but notice her fascination with his watch fob. He pulled the shiny gold watch out of his pocket and held it to her ear.

She listened with an exaggerated attention.

"Can you tell time, Dimity?"

The small contours of her little face screwed up in a puzzled look.

It was plain she hadn't the slightest notion what he was talking about. "Well, my dear, some day I'll teach you how to tell time."

At that moment, Mrs. O'Grady pushed open the barn door. She moved inside the door warily, expecting the worse, but seeing Dimity sitting with the contented cat on her lap, she was relieved. She caught Mr. Durant's eye and smiled.

"And how is Tabby?"

"Oh Miss Nellie, Tabby is feeling much better," she said clutching the cat to her, "and Mr. Durant is going to teach me to tell time."

In spite of the pleasant look about the man, Nellie couldn't believe he planned to spend more time with the child. He was one of New York's most wealthy, influential men, whose kind heart was the good fortune of the sisters. For some unexplained reason he seemed to be taken with the child. Nellie could certainly understand why. Now that Dimity was coming out of her grief, she was a pure delight. Nellie could see Dimity was thrilled half to death having this fine gentleman paying her all this attention.

"Dimity child, Mr. Durant is a very busy man. He can't be takin' the time out of his busy day to instruct you on tellin' time.

The child's smile slipped away. "But.Miss Nellie, he said. Dimity's eyes questioned him. He was the shadow of the man she had tucked away in her memory, the father she would never see again.

"Of course, I can take time to teach Dimity how to tell time," he said, putting his arm around her shoulders. "Everybody's got to learn new things, and you shall learn how to tell time, little Dimity." This child was one of the injustices of this world, one of the little innocents who were left to suffer alone without the love of a mother and father.

Dimity fairly glowed with his words.

Albert Durant was as good as his word, arriving at the back door of the orphanage at around nine o'clock every Saturday morning at the heels of his weekly charitable donations of fresh vegetables and freshly cut meat.

In the first few weeks of Mr. Durant's visits, Dimity's everyday question, "Is this Saturday yet, Miss Nellie?" finally prompted Nellie to mark off the days on a piece of paper for her. As Dimity became accustomed to crossing off each day and counting her fingers, she came to know that each day crossed off brought her nearer to Saturday.

Dimity's vigil at the kitchen door on Saturday mornings began soon after morning Mass after she d gobbled down her breakfast in huge anxious gulps, and becoming panic stricken should the big hand on the clock pass number twelve, if only by seconds. On one such day Dimity was dissolved in tears when the big hand on the clock reached three before the big hulk of the figure of Mr. Durant knocked on the door. Smiling through her tears, she clapped her hands, and jumped up and down, and ran to meet him.

"What's this, little lady? Tears?" His compassionate streak was awakened at the sight of the child's tears. "Here now," he said, brushing away a tear that trickled down her cheek. "No need for tears."

Nellie smiled, happy for the child. "And she was that worried, her eyes glued to that clock, worried you weren't coming today, Mr. Durant, sir."

He took Dimity's hand, leading her to the corner of the kitchen, away from the outburst of giggles coming from the girls standing in the doorway to catch a glimpse of the man who came each Saturday to see Dimity. For some of the girls, it was pure envy and jealousy at Dimity's good fortune for they were not so lucky. For the other girls, it was just a normal curiosity.

Nellie shooed them away, closing the door. Circling the large oak table where they were sitting, Nellie cleared her throat, "I've a nice fresh pot of coffee, Mr. Durant, sir. Would ye be liken' a cup to take away the chill on this fall day?"

Mr. Durant raised his head. "I expect I would at that, Nellie," he said, accepting the cup with a large hand speckled with stiff dark hairs.

Studying the child's intent young face, he dropped his heavy hand affectionately on her folded hands she held dutifully on the table in front of her. "Are you ready to begin, Dimity?"

Nellie stood kneading her bread at the other end of the long table, listening at his patient words to the child as he spoke slowly and precisely.

As he moved the hands on an old worn-out railroad clock, he was amazed to find that she was indeed at the point of mastering the skill of telling time.

Dimity gloried in his approving eyes when her answer was correct, but realizing her lessons would soon be coming to an end, she began making mistakes deliberately.

One day when this was happening repeatedly, he suddenly realized why when she asked him, "What will happen, Mr. Durant, when I know how to tell time? Will you still come to see me?" Dimity had a shrewd head on her shoulders for a little girl of seven, already reasoning in her own little mind that teaching her to tell time was Mr. Durant's only reason for visiting her each week.

His face was solemn, but anxious to allay her fears, he chuckled in an attempt to assure her. He felt like a sentimental blathering fool when it came to this child. "Why of course, I'll still come to see you, Dimity." He glanced over his shoulder at Nellie who was moodily scowling over her lump of unbaked dough. "You will be a fine scholar some day, Dimity, if you keep at your lessons, and I aim to point you in that direction.

Dimity smiled widely, relieved at his words. "But what will we do when you come to visit?" she asked, with marked curiosity and interest.

"Oh," he tilted his head in thought, plunging in, eager to convince her. "Reading books together, helping you with your homework.I," he hesitated, looking down at her high-tops "could teach you how to tie your high-tops."

She sucked in a deep breath, contented to know he would be coming to visit for a long time, knowing that more than one person gave up trying to teach her how to tie her high-tops.

Yes, she thought, that would be the best new reason to keep Mr. Durant coming for many more Saturdays.

He could see how much these visits meant to Dimity, and he wasn't about to discontinue them. It was clear to him that her little human spirit had been bolstered by his visits and the thought of not seeing him again was all too threatening for her. This blighted orphan's life she was forced into was no fault of her own according to the information he had gleaned from Nellie O'Grady, and it was his fervent wish to see her freed from this servitude of an orphan's life.

These Saturday visits were a semblance of reason and order to Albert Durant's life, although at times he couldn't help but feel that the relationship he'd developed with Dimity was more meaningful than his relationship with his own daughter. And he sometimes felt guilty because of it.

Nagging questions tugged at Albert Durant's heart. For many weeks he kept his private thoughts to himself, thoughts about adopting Dimity. Convincing his wife that another child in the house may be the answer to their daughter's hateful, spoiled ways may take time. Knowing that his wife's deep desire for another child could never be a reality, he hoped she'd welcome the idea when he broached the subject. Because Mercedes could never bear more children, she had lavished her love on her only child, spoiling her to the point where she was blind to Clarice's misbehavior, always excusing her mischievous pranks and her uncontrollable temper tantrums.

The issue of his wife's constant pampering of their daughter had long been a source of many arguments between them and having another child in the house may force her to share that attention she bestowed on Clarice. He truly believed that having Dimity would prove to make a marked influence on his daughter and his wife and that Clarice's inexhaustible wickedness would cease with a little sister to keep her company.

Though his wife was the soul of correctness in most things, she turned a deaf ear when he confronted her with Clarice's antics and the need for discipline and possibly a heavy hand. To Mercedes, Clarice was one of God's blessings, and she could do no wrong. To Albert Durant, his child of ten was a holy terror who had a special knack for deceiving her mother. She had an oh so sorrowful look when scolded for a wrongdoing.

Albert Durant had a thoughtful look on his face when he said goodbye to Dimity that day, promising to see her next Saturday.

"Next week, Dimity, we'll have a little test to see how much you've remembered." He patted her gently on the shoulder.

Nellie walked Mr. Durant to the door, admiring his fancy manners, and believing he was the kindest man never coming empty-handed.

"She's pure come out of her shell, Mr. Durant," Nellie whispered, following him outside. "It was that full of sadness she was before you brought the smile back on her face. There was little comfort the sisters and I could offer her when her brother was taken away."

"That's good to hear, Nellie," he smiled. "See you next week," he said buttoning his coat and pointing his cane he was never without towards the first step. His heart was sore at the thought of the brother and sister's separation, but there was no hope in hell that he could persuade his wife to take on the boy. He'd be mighty lucky if she'd agree to have Dimity. He'd have to make it plain that it was for his daughter's own good as well as his wife's. It wouldn't do to let either of them know of the deep attachment he held for the child, he speculated. But the thought of uprooting the child again may be another obstacle he'd have to face. She seemed so attached to Nellie O'Grady, and she to the child. Dimity was so defenseless and helpless, he thought, and facing one more change in her life without the familiar arms of Nellie O'Grady may prove to be too much for her. He'd have to think about that.

CHAPTER SIX

It was almost dark when the carriage pulled up in front of the orphanage at the end of the lane where the cobbled street ended. Albert Durant climbed down from his seat, stepping onto the dirt road. "Shouldn't be too long, Isaiah," he said, glancing over his shoulder at his black driver, who held the two lively black horses with a firm hand.

He made his way briskly through the gate, turning to the side of the house, hoping he could slip past the front windows before any of the sisters saw him. They should be in chapel for evening prayers, he thought. His business had to do with Nellie O'Grady. It was no concern of the nuns; leastways, not unless Nellie agreed to his proposition.

He paused at the back door, puffing thoughtfully at his cheroot before knocking. He looked up through the denuded trees to the eastern sky turning purple in the twilight. The smell of autumn pervaded the air tempering the smell of his cheroot.

Dressed in a clerical black waistcoat and black silk cravat, he could have passed for a clergyman was it not for his gray-striped pantaloons. He kicked the dust off his polished boots and stood reflecting on the turn of events that brought him here, the words of his cook. "It's off to be married. I'll be needin' to leave before the weeks out." That announcement was a prologue to chaos in his household, a pure crisis. The news fairly put his wife into a fit of apoplexy. He could not envision his wife of impeccable Manhattan heritage who had never had to lift a finger, dirtying her hands, or soiling her gowns toiling in the kitchen. It would not only be improper for a woman of her standing but utterly impossible, for he knew he must live by her rules and exigencies if he were to keep peace and maintain her high spirits. When he seized the opportunity and told her their dilemma could be easily remedied if he could hire Nellie O'Grady away from the sisters, her face brightened. And if it so happened that Nellie wouldn't leave without the child, then he'd have the excuse he needed, and his wife would be hard pressed not to agree to the adoption of Dimity. It only meant his plans to tell his wife about the child had somewhat speeded up now that they were faced with replacing their cook. What a godsend!

He dropped his cheroot, stamping it out on the wooden floor of the porch, and then knocked.

The door swung open to the smell of cinnamon and cloves. Nellie 0'Grady looked at Mr. Durant with open surprise. "Mr. Durant, sir!"

"Good evening, Nellie," he said, tipping his hat. "I wonder if I may have a few words with you?"

"If it's Sister Veronica ye're here to see, she's this minute at chapel prayers. It'll be a wait."

"No, it's you, Nellie. I've come to speak to you."

"Me sir?" Her eyes were wide with curiosity and faintly gleaming in the diffused light. "Will you step inside out of the chill?"

She stood in the middle of the room holding a wooden spoon, staring at this man with authority and importance. In an attempt to look more presentable, she reached up with her free hand and began tucking the few straggly ends of gray hair into the tight twisted bun at the nape of her neck. Pointing stiffly with her spoon, she motioned, "Do have ye'reslf a seat, sir."

In the dimly lighted kitchen lit by a coal oil lamp, with flickering flames from the fireplace, Mr. Durant sat down at the table squinting his eyes. Following the smell of freshly baked cookies on the wood stove, he asked, "Could you spare one of those cookies to a man who's not had his supper and is fairly starving, Nellie?"

She laughed, putting down her spoon, brushing her hands on her flour spattered apron. "Sure and I'd be that pleased to serve you a cup of tea with your cookies."

While she put on the kettle, Mr. Durant began with his mission. "I'm here to ask you to come to work for me, Nellie, to be my cook," he blurted out. "It seems our present cook is leaving." As an afterthought, he said, "I'd pay you well."

Nellie's mouth fell open in absolute surprise. She was flattered at his offer. Her heart beat hard. The thought of working for the Durants, one of New York's most prominent families was almost too much for her to comprehend. "Aach! Holy Saints!" She was speechless.

"You would be responsible for the cooking only," Mr. Durant said persuasively; "We have two maids who take care of the cleaning, and your wages would be seven dollars a

Thinking of it threw her head in a whirl of confusion for the hard work at the orphanage was nearly doing her in at her age, but. Setting his cup of tea and plate of cookies before him, she sat down with her hands folded in her lap. "But, Mr. Durant, I cannot leave the wee one. She's come to depend on me. And the sisters. Then with a deliberate finality, "I'm that pleased that you asked me, but." She moistened her dry lips, and with her words heavily measured, she said, "her little heart would be broken if I left."

He could see she was interested but for her worry of Dimity. "What if I were to tell you, Nellie, that I was considering adopting Dimity?"

Her hands trembled in her lap. "For a fact?"

"For a fact," he assured her. "That little girl has wound herself around my heart and with the Missus wanting more children and not able to give our daughter a brother or sister, Dimity could bring the smile back onto her face."

Nellie smiled timidly, nodding her head. "I cook plain, Mr. Durant. It's not a fancy cook ye'll be gettin'. Do ya think I could cook proper enough for ye're Missus?"

Mr. Durant sipped the last bit of the tea in his cup and rose to leave. Replacing his hat on his head, he drew in a deep breath. "That's not a thing to worry about, Nellie. I'm sure the Missus will have some instructions along that way. You are not to mention a word of this you understand, until I've had a chance to visit with Sister Veronica. Do I have your word on that?"

"Oh yes, indeed, sir."

Albert Durant suspected Nellie O'Grady would be more than happy to leave the drudgery work of the orphanage. The only problem was finding a replacement for the sisters.

"There is one other thing I've been meaning to ask you, Nellie.

"Yes sir?"

"It's about Dimity's twin brother. Does she speak of him often?"

Her eyes rested blankly on him.

"Mr. Durant, sir," she said, clutching her breast, "it's like Christ himself the little thing has suffered, losing both mother and father and then her brother." She looked at him with sorrowful eyes. "But would ye believe the yearning of him all of a sudden has passed, like the bleeding fragments of her little suffering heart are at last healed. It's that queer, sir, she's not uttered his name for the longest time like she's locked the memory of him away. She speaks readily enough about her Dada and the ring she wears." Nellie gave a weary sigh, looking at him and shaking her head.

"The ring?" he asked curiously. "Can't say as I noticed a ring."

"Oh yes, sir, it's her mother's ring cut in half made into two rings by her father. The boy wears the other ring.

"I see," his voice trailed off, thinking that some day he'd try to locate the boy and make sure he was taken care of.

Mr. Durant spoke sternly, struggling with his guilt. "I'm afraid Mrs. Durant would not agree to have the boy as well.

As he stood in the open doorway, he remarked, "If your cookies are an example of your cooking, Nellie, I look forward to more of the same."

Well into his fortieth year, Albert Francis Durant was a stern and bearded master of his financial and industrial empire, not allowing his soft heart to show through when it came to the business world. He did not inherit his wealth, and his formal education ended at age sixteen when his father died. Forced into the responsibility of supporting his mother, he began his business career as a junior accountant with his father's employers, Dillard, Sheriton and Company, private bankers in downtown Manhattan. He seized every opportunity to learn, to study. He investigated the shipping business by visiting various seaports to find out how the imports and exports were handled. He studied the market, then bought up cargos, and sold at a profit. Even though his ideas for making money often conflicted with his superiors, it was these bold, but prudent transactions that made money for the bank as well as for himself. His business success largely came from the driving force of his ambitious enterprising spirit and his instincts, which were the instincts of a genius when it came to making money. As a result, fortune favored him, and lucrative sizeable profits followed. When his finances allowed, Albert Durant branched out on his own, involving himself in the speculation of gold, buying gold then shipping part of it abroad in order to raise the price, then selling the gold he kept at a profit. This was a brave scheme, but it worked, as did his gambling on the stock market with his successful short sales of securities.

Albert Durant prospered under these various undertakings, continually battling for control among the nation's expanding and growing industries. He was in his thirties and already realizing great wealth with interests in shipbuilding railroads, steel, munitions manufacturing, and the sleeping giant of oil exploitation.

Although he truly felt men did not get rich by honest labor, he had no desire to imperil his soul with dishonesty while achieving his wealth. In justifying his control over politicians, he attributed this phenomenon to the power of money. Money was power and he had earned that power.

"And it's all right with you, Mercedes dear?" Albert, asked, dropping his hand affectionately on her shoulder.

"I had hoped for another daughter," she said, sighing, looking hard at him, "and as you say.Albert, it may be good for Clarice to have a sister."

With his wife's approval of the adoption, Albert Durant was able to settle matters with the sisters before the week ended.

When Mercedes Durant made it clear to her husband that she would not accompany him to fetch the child, his usual composure gave way. "But Mercedes how will that look to the sisters? You are the adopted mother. I'm afraid they may hesitate to release the child to our custody without you being there," he argued.

"I do not wish to see my new daughter in those surroundings, Albert," she insisted, knowing that the self-doubt she harbored might deepen should her first glimpse of the child be in the repulsive atmosphere of the orphanage. "I ask that you indulge me, Albert, in this request."

"As you wish, my dear," he agreed, failing to comprehend his wife's reasoning at first, but then recalling her reluctance to accompany him on his visits to the orphanage with the excuse that it was too painful for her to see the wretchedness of these homeless children.

Mercedes Durant deeply felt that her self-worth had long been wounded in her husband's eyes by her inability to bear more children, and she was more than willing to bow to his wishes for this adoption if it would relieve her from the guilt she had been burdened with. What beclouded this adoption for Mercedes was the doubt that her hunger for another child would be satisfied by a little orphan waif. She would have little choice to change her mind once the deed was done.

Dimity gave Nellie O'Grady a steady, puzzled look when Nellie ended her discourse. Dimity didn't exactly know what it meant.adoption. "Is this adops.sin a good thing, Miss Nellie?"

Nellie had convinced Albert Durant that it would be less of a shock to the child if she were allowed to break the news to her.

Nellie leaned over with pleasure on her face and patted her cheek, "Oh my yes, Dimity! It's a mother and father ye'll be havin' and a beautiful house to live in, and servants, and a new big sister to play with," she babbled on. "Ye'll be the little girl of the fine gentleman, Mr. Durant, and his wife. Ye'll not ever again be cold and hungry, or have to wear raggedy clothes and rundown shoes.

Dimity smiled. To have all these good things happening to her must be good, but then the smile left her. In her heart the emptiness still hurt from the bitter memory that came at odd times, the memory of her family, which she'd squeezed out of her brain even though their spirits still hovered about her. For a moment she shrank back into herself when the thought of leaving Nellie surfaced. Nellie had been the miracle that had guided her out of her emptiness.

Seeing the worried look, Nellie asked, "What is it, child?"

Dimity's voice quivered. "Does adops.sin mean I have to leave you, Miss Nellie?"

The clear meaning of Dimity's distress rushed through Nellie as she looked into this little suffering face still in the evil shadow of abandonment, and fear of once again being uprooted from the familiar, and from loving arms.

Nellie's eyes grew soft as she lifted Dimity onto her lap. "I'll be going with you, Dimity," she assured her, hoping her words would appease and comfort her. To further explain at this time that her place would be that of a servant in the Durant home, would not serve any purpose. No point to fill the child's head with more than she could handle, she thought, as she combed the tangles out of her hair, thinking the child was like a tumbleweed who was being blown through life through no fault of her own.

"Oh, Miss Nellie, I like it," she cried happily.

"What do you like, Dimity?"

"Adops.sin." It was a lilting, magical word now that Nellie O'Grady would be with her for this adops.sin. Her child eyes held a look of hope.

CHAPTER SEVEN

aniel awoke to the noise of the rattle of the traffic and the horse drawn trams clashing past them. As he was rocked awake out of the darkness into the glowing splendor of the rising sun, he instinctively reached out to feel the nearness of his sister. A shadow of fear gripped him when he discovered he was alone. A half-remembered nightmare of being hoisted into the wagon without her crept into his foggy memory. The threadbare quilt covering him fell away as he sat up. Listing to the starboard, Daniel gripped the sides of the wagon with his small hands, his eyes following the dark figure of a stranger who sat stiffly in the driver's seat.

Clad only in his summer weight drawers, he shivered now that his skinny bare legs were bared. In an excited, high-pitched yapping voice, he cried out over the noise of the clanking of the iron-rimmed wheels passing over the hunchbacked cobbles.

Daniel's sobbing was a woeful sound like a wailing wind coming from this innocent child he had snatched away in the night. The old priest crushed the leather reins in his hands and drew the horse to a halt in front of an old dry-stone wall which marked the boundary of the institution. The abrupt stop forced Daniel forward, face down.

Father Nathaniel was a man of tender heart and feelings. He knew well of this childhood terror he'd seen so often. He climbed down and hitched the horse to the hitching post.

In a quiet gentle voice the priest urged, "Come now, lad."

Daniel scooted to the edge of the wagon, rubbing his runny nose with a knuckle.

"Now, now, Daniel," he said, reaching into a potato sack and pulling out a shirt and a ragged pair of pants, "you must be a brave little soldier." Father Nathaniel looked sorrowfully at the boy's worn shoes.

Tense with fear, Daniel stiffened as the priest helped him dress. "I want my sister. Where's Dimity?" he asked, shivering, as he crouched over to look in the priest's face as he put on his shoes.

"Your sister has a nice home with the sisters, and you, Daniel will have a home with other boys. It's quite nice. You'll see!" he said, lifting him down from the wagon.

As soon as they turned up the path and had taken a few steps, Daniel felt a fierce fear darting down his spine, the fear of never seeing his sister again. Rage of the injustice of it gripped him. She was all he had in life. He screamed. "No!" Struggling against the priest, he broke away with a wiry strength.

The priest quickly thrust an arm out to catch him, dragging him up the path. Stopping at the stone stairs leading up to the large plain, solid brick building, Father Nathaniel turned to face the boy, holding him in the vise of his two hands.

"Daniel, if you run away, there's no place for you to go.

"I'm goin', Daniel cried, the tears glittering in his eyes, "to find my sister."

The child's threat worried him. He'd seen it before. The priest hugged the child to him. Oh, the way of man's inhumanity to man, he thought.

He sat down on the stone steps with the boy beside him. "Daniel," he said sighing, taking the child's hand in his, "it's a cruel thing that's happened to you, losing your family, but I'm here to take care of you. There is nobody else to do that, and the sisters will take care of your sister. If you run away, you'll not have anything to eat, or a place to sleep, and you won't be able to find your sister. We're too far away. And Daniel," he said, flicking the soft, russet curls off Daniel's forehead, "you're too little to go wandering about the streets with strangers."

Father Nathaniel was a red-cheeked man of God in his sixties who had a trace of merriment in his eyes and Daniel felt his kindness. With a dazed look in his eyes, the child settled against him.

The location of the boys' home on a narrow cul-de-sac on Rivington Street was just east of the Bowery. With this close proximity to the sordid conditions in that area where the homeless ran wild, the Jesuit Fathers were able to offer a refuge to the homeless, oftentimes rescuing them from a life of crime, from gangs who used them to rob and steal for them.

Within a mile of the home was a saddlery, a pharmacy, a poulterer shop, clothing, dry goods and millinery stores, livery stables, candy and peanut stands, a hardware store, a tailor and hat store, a furniture store, a barber shop and a bank. The Jesuits enlisted the help of these merchants to provide employment for their boys as they came of age.

The Jesuits were not without their enemies for the majority of Native Americans were not only anti-Irish, but anti-Catholic. It was often said that when they came to America, the Jesuits arrived in disguise, putting aside their priests' garb until they were established and accepted.

The good fathers were scholars and taught the boys well in the classroom. Their sympathy for the unfortunate dispossessed boys of New York City did not result in a weak indulgence towards them. Indeed, it only fortified their desire to provide a religious upbringing, giving them a sense of belonging and worth, and to teach them good, honorable habits, and of course, laced with discipline.

Daniel, in his institution garb of drab dark brown pants and gray woolen shirt, was defiant and bitter. He did not suffer his loss mutely, but reacted with rebellious behavior. His numbing sadness and haunting emptiness lasted into the winter months.

"He needs time to adjust to his surroundings," Father Nathaniel said, excusing him to the other four priests who were losing patience with him. "He's too young to understand his loss or to realize he's been rescued."

"Is there no one Daniel has grown attached to?" Father Lassiter asked, "To help rid him of the hidden hurt in his heart?" As though a flash of inspiration passed before him, his voice mellowed as he smiled. Placing his hopes on another child, he offered his solution to the fathers, "What if Jake would befriend him?" Jake was a good-natured sixteen year old whose laughter was a healing balm to the entire household.

"It's worth a try," Father Nathaniel agreed. "I'll have a talk with Jake."

Two weeks later, the fathers could already see a marked difference in Daniel, who trailed after Jake like a puppy. Daniel seemed almost human again as though the strain of sorrow had melted away in his veins. All the scoldings, reproaches, upbraiding and even kindnesses the fathers had heaped on Daniel had no effect. Only Jake's genuine friendly interest and companionship brought the child out of his grief imposed isolation. Jake was someone for Daniel to hold onto. Jake had a cock-sureness that soon brought a worshipping gaze to Daniel's face.

Grasping his shabby old woolen cap in his hand, Jake stood looking curiously at Daniel, who was perched on the barnyard fence watching the cattle grazing. After Father Nathaniel spoke to him about Daniel, Jake had willingly agreed to befriend him. "Treat him like a little brother, Jake," Father Nathaniel had prompted. "He's a sad little boy who's lost his sister. The good Lord will smile down on you.

But Jake took his good old sweet time before he approached Daniel, watching him from a distance, pondering why he was so different than the rest of the orphans, and why he didn't wish to speak or join in the games or take notice of anyone. He guessed it was a sign of his great sadness.

Daniel jumped down off the fence when he saw Jake.

Jake pushed an apple towards him. "Here," he said, "I saved it from lunch. You can have it."

Daniel watched him as he bit into the juicy fruit, thrilled at the touch of friendliness. His face glowed. None of the other boys had paid him any mind, only this tall freckled-face boy who saved his apple for him.

Jake began to whistle a tune as he walked away without a word, past him to the barn where he threw himself onto the haystack in a running leap.

"Well," he said to Daniel who had followed him, "hit it."

Daniel looked at him oddly. In one swift deliberate aim, he flung himself into the haystack. Only then did the laughter escape his throat as he buried his face in the straw.

Jake put his hand on his arm in a friendly gesture. "I don't have a mother or father either, Daniel, he said, cracking his bony fingers as he drew his hand away."I'm just like you. An orphan!"

From that day on, Daniel was Jake's shadow, and the little brother Jake never had. He provided in his own way the loving support of another human being the child had been denied.

The dreary days of winter passed quickly. Jake's assistance with his school work encouraged Daniel's intense desire to learn.

The unnatural way Daniel first held a pencil gripping it like a fork brought forth a burst of laughter from Jake, who quickly formed the child's clumsy fingers around the pencil in the proper way. Daniel enthusiastically studied his letters with a concentrated absorption, and was visibly pleased with himself when he was correct.

At sixteen Jake was old enough to get his working papers and was off to work at a grocery store around the corner and a livery stable on Hester Street. At last, Jake was a man. Of the dozen boys housed in the home, Jake was the oldest and was by far the most ambitious, always willing to help the fathers with odd jobs. He was likely to be seen doing most anything, sweeping the floor, helping Father Emmanuel with the cooking, milking the two cows, and gathering eggs. The priests would miss his help, but it was time he was striking out on his own. He knew he couldn't stay forever.

On the first day Jake reported to work at the grocery store heavy snow clouds swept the sky over New York City. There was a good six inches on the ground when he left for work after school. As Jake turned the corner, he caught a glimpse of Daniel who was bundled against the sweeping wind in a long woolen coat sizes too big for him with his woolen cap pulled down over his face.

Jake stopped to face him before entering the store. "Go home, Daniel. You can't come to work with me."

"But Jake, I can help you work." It seemed very natural to Daniel that he should be with Jake who had become his idol.

"No!" Jake shouted impatiently. "You can't!"

Daniel had no intention of going home. He turned away slowly pretending to obey, but skirted around the corner and there he waited until he thought enough time had passed. He waded through the snow back to the front of the store where he stood watching through the frosted window, watching Jake who was busily sweeping the floor. Daniel stood there for what seemed like hours in the blizzardy wind gazing inside, holding fast to the window edge until his fingers were too stiff to hold on. Overcome by an overwhelming tiredness, he slowly sank into the foot deep snow, clutching his coat around him.

When Father Nathaniel's search of the house did not uncover Daniel's whereabouts, the priest immediately departed for the grocery store, trusting his judgment that Daniel very likely followed Jake to work.

His eyes were dazzled by the falling snow as he approached the store, and in his eager haste he very nearly stumbled over the huddled form.

"Dear Jesus," he cried, bending over the little figure. He lifted the child in his arms and carried him home.

It was a mental terror for Father Nathaniel until Daniel opened his eyes and spoke after he was undressed and in the warmth of his bed.

"I was awful cold, Father, waiting for Jake." He rubbed his eyes sleepily with a balled-up fist.

"Daniel," the priest scolded in a firm voice, "you are never to follow Jake to work again. You could have frozen to death." He held a cup of tea to his lips. "Take some of this nice tea, now."

The wide-eyed boys collected in the doorway of the dormitory, at first to observe all the commotion connected with Daniel's rescue, and then they lingered to witness his chastisement. Except for bits and pieces of the conversation, Father Nathaniel's soft words were inaudible, but their curiosity kept them there.

Soon after Daniel was put to bed, Jake appeared, clutching a sour pickle in his fist. He was unaware of Daniel's escapade. He pushed his way through the throng of boys, whose whisperings and the sight of Daniel in bed gave him a clue to what had happened.

Ignoring the scowl on the priest's face, he handed Daniel the pickle. "Feel like eating a nice big pickle, Dannie?"

Daniel's face lit up with pleasure at the unexpected gift. Without a word, he grabbed the pickle and stuffed it in his mouth and began sucking on it loudly.

"And how do you come by a sour pickle, my boy?" the priest asked with a direct gaze.

"Mr. Levy says that's part of my pay cuz he knows I like pickles. Three cents a day and a pickle!"

Father Nathaniel looked at the two boys in amazement, thinking theirs was a curious friendship. In such a short time, they had grown so close.

At the sound of the supper bell, Father Nathaniel turned his attention to the boys milling around. "Be off with you boys, for your supper!"

At his command, they scattered down the stairs.

As Jake turned to go, Father Nathaniel raised a hand.

"Wait up, Jake."

Daniel propped up in bed against two pillows eyed them while he nibbled on his pickle.

"Jake, didn't you know Daniel followed you to work this afternoon?"

"Yes, father."

"And you did not bring him home?" "No, father."

"Jake," Daniel interrupted, swallowing a mouthful of pickle, "told me to go home." He could see that Jake was in trouble because of him.

"Is that true, Jake?"

Jake sat there shivering. "Yes, father. I thought Daniel went on home."

Father Nathaniel felt the chill in the room. He rose from his chair, picked up the poker, opened the door of the pot-bellied stove and stirred the fire. The shovelful of coal he added sparked the flames.

"Should that ever happen again, Jake," he said, closing the iron door of the stove, "you are to bring Daniel home yourself."

"But father, what happened to Daniel?" he asked, dreading the answer.

"I found him lying in the snow. I know he's a tough little fella, but he's sure to fall sick from this."

Jake hung his head. "I'm sorry, father."

The priest endeavored to be firm. "Because of the seriousness of this, you will have to be punished. Father Lassiter will see you both in the morning. After Mass."

Daniel was a little puzzled at his reprimand, not quite understanding why they had to be punished.

For the next two weeks, Daniel and Jake were confined within the walls of the institution except for their daily trip to the barn to clean up the horse and cow dung in the stable. The first day at their unpleasant task Daniel whined and gagged and vanished out of the door, leaving Jake with the shovel in hand. Jake quickly dragged him back by the collar and tied his scarf over his nose. Obediently, Daniel pitched in to do his part, as much as his small size would allow. After a few days, the odor didn't bother him.

One day was very like another in the past two weeks, but having completed their forced confinement, Jake and Daniel were filled with a fiery gladness to put that everydayness behind them. They were early out of bed on their first free Saturday morning and waiting for Father Emmanuel out in front of the home, bundled up against the cold in their second-hand woolens from Hester Street.

With a quivering excitement at being allowed to go, Daniel busily stacked loaves of bread into the wooden wagon.

"No, no, Daniel, you'll crack the eggs," Jake directed, removing the bread he'd placed on top of the eggs and rearranged the loaves. "Father Emmanuel will tan your hide if you break Mr. Schneemeier's eggs before we deliver them." Jake reached over to pull Daniel's woolen cap over his ears.

Their eyes shifted to follow the beam of light coming from the lantern the stocky priest was carrying as he descended the stairs.

"We'll need some light until daylight breaks," Father Emmanuel said, handing Jake a blanket. "Lay this blanket over the eggs. We don't want to deliver frozen eggs to Mr. Schneerneier.

Jake carefully placed the blanket in the wagon.

"Good morning, Daniel," Father Emmanuel greeted him, setting his lantern down, winding Daniel's dangling scarf around his neck. "Are you awake, lad?"

"Oh yes, Father," Daniel chirped, "But Father, Jake and I didn't have our breakfast."

"I know that lad, but you had a nice cup of hot tea with sugar," he laughed. The cook for the orphans had a jolly manner and it was his earnest desire to keep the boys fed, and selling his freshly baked bread and the eggs from his henhouse once a week helped it along.

"Besides, the hungrier you get, the quicker you'll make your deliveries and get home to eat so Jake can go to his other job and I can be there to feed my other boys."

Father Emmanuel grunted, "Let's get on, boys. We don't want our eggs to freeze. We'll deliver the eggs first thing, and then we'll try our luck at selling the bread. Remember now, it won't do to let Mr. Schneemeier see the bread. He'll quit buying our eggs if he finds out we're competing against his bakery," he sniffed, taking a wrinkled handkerchief from his pocket to blow his nose. "And Jake, pay attention carefully which streets I turn down and where I stop. Next Saturday, you'll be on your own." The priest gave a light tap against the side of the wagon, a signal for them to proceed.

"Getting an early start is most important," he reminded them.

Winter had an icy grip on the city as they trudged down the dark frosted street. The cold morning air was laden with the sickening smells of the streets, of putrefaction, pig swill, of rotted garbage and fresh manure.

The street was desolate in the darkness of the early morning, but ever so often, they came across a group of homeless men who had lit a fire in a can or a drum.

"Warm your hands a bit," Father Emmanuel coaxed the boys, stopping at a street corner.

Both boys held their hands towards the warmth. It felt good in the ten degree weather, but they quickly backed away when it began spewing smoke and sparks from the barrel.

At the German bakery, Father Emmanuel lifted the basket of eggs out of the wagon. Handing them to Jake, he said, "You boys bring them in. Mr. Schneemeier has a soft heart when it comes to our orphans."

When the boys returned, they were both munching on a heel of bread. Jake handed over the egg money to Father Emmanuel.

"What! Is that all you could squeeze out of him, a heel of bread?"

"It's good, Father," Jake said, "isn't it, Daniel?"

"Sure is," Daniel agreed. "It's most gone," he said, swallowing a big bite.

They stood in front of the bakery until the boys finished their bread, and then headed down Hester Street.

The orphanage was within a stone's throw of the southernmost part of the Bowery. It was neighborhood of filthy vagrants, thieves and prostitutes. It was a perpetual kaleidoscope in this wild metropolis, of a noisome cesspool of humanity.

Father Emmanuel put out the flame in the lantern as daylight spread slowly in the sky. Daylight brought the sounds of shouting children, barking dogs, and bellowing cows, and a stream of neighborhood activity with the roll of carriages and the clop-clop of the horses' hoofs.

Daniel danced and jigged about in the street ahead of them, jostling about on a low slung bare branch of a tree like an intoxicated squirrel. Among the dirt and disorder, Daniel saw beauty working among the peddlers who now thronged the streets.

Jake was too absorbed to pay attention to Daniel, taking seriously his bread-selling enterprise. "Here's your fresh baked bread, ho!" he called out, bringing housewives to their doors. "Will you buy a loaf of bread from we two orphans who've got no home, but for the good fathers who feed us?"

Father Emmanuel grinned at Jake's bold and vigorous pitch.

They halted at the call of one such housewife who came out of a tenement, leaning over the banister on the top floor.

"What's your price?" she yelled.

"Five cents a loaf," Jake answered.

With a nod of her head and the point of one finger, Jake took it as a sale. With the loaf of bread Father Emmanuel handed him, Jake proceeded to take it to her.

Running after Jake, Daniel cried, "Let me! Let me!"

Jake handed him the bread as they made their way up the rickety outside flight of stairs, the noise of their footsteps on the landings forcing the dislodged rats to cross their path and forcing a scream from Daniel's throat.

Father Emmanuel looked up at the patched, broken windows and the rotten beams supporting the stairs and shook his head wondering how many people were living in the indescribable squalor of this broken down tenement. When the smelly vapors from the outside privy reached his nostrils, he covered his nose with his handkerchief.

Daniel held out his hand proudly, his cheeks glowing pink from the cold, "Jake says this is five whole cents, Father."

"Thank you, Daniel. You and Jake are quite the hucksters," he said, quickly pulling him out of the way of the panting team hitched to the streetcar galloping towards them.

Daniel pointed to the crowded streetcar, watching it pass by, "I'd like to ride on that sometime, Father," he said, longingly.

"I'm sure some day you will, lad," he smiled.

They continued to thread their way through the crowded streets. Among the hucksters and peddlers that lined the streets was a tottering rag picker who had pulled his bony horse to the side.

Father Emmanuel stopped to speak to him and to look through his wagon piled high with junk and old clothing. Inspecting a long overcoat which was somewhat worn but still serviceable, he lifted it out of the rubble and held it up to himself. It might fit. One of the older boys, he thought, feeling the material thoughtfully, and raising the garment up and down in the air to determine the weight of it for its warmth.

"How much?" he asked.

The old man climbed down from his wagon seat. He noisily snuffed a pinch of tobacco that he pulled from his oversized coat pocket. Grinning a toothless grin, he answered, "a dollar?"

Father Emmanuel chuckled, replaced the coat and began walking away.

"Fifty cents then?" the man croaked, quickly changing his mind.

"Twenty-five! Not a cent more," the priest countered, not planning to haggle with the shiftless shyster any further for a coat more than likely stolen from a corpse.

The old man nodded his head, handing over the coat and holding out his scrawny, dirty hand. "You rob a poor citizen trying to make an honest living."

The priest dug in his pocket pulling out four nickels and five pennies and dropped them one by one into the grimy outstretched hand.

With two last loaves of bread to be sold, Daniel raised his voice to a high pitch, "Fresh baked bread here," attempting to drown out the hucksters who were shouting, "Hot yams! Ho! Hot yams!" With stomachs empty, the boys' mouths watered at the tempting smell of the hot yams roasting in the brazier as they passed a corner stand.

Children eleven and twelve hurried before them with brooms at the street crossing, sweeping aside the offal, hoping for a penny.

Father Emmanuel glanced over his shoulder, at the sad sight of these dirty, ragged boys who tugged at his heart. It wasn't uncommon to see hordes of children begging on the streets and sleeping in dingy hallways in cardboard boxes at night. These were the dispossessed of New York City.

Clamping a hand on the shoulder of one of the older boys, he reached in the wagon for a loaf of bread, leaving one last loaf. He held it out to him.

"If I give you this bread, will you promise to share it with the other children?" he asked, vowing to stop by the New York Children's Aid Society to inform the authorities of the begging youngsters. If only they had more room at the home to take in more boys.

The boy grinned at the relief of the offer and that the hand of the stranger was not a Children's Aid Society official. The harsh treatment suffered at the hands of the attendants working there was one of the reasons the boy was now roaming the streets. He had barely escaped the last orphan train sent out west.

"Oh, yes sir!" he agreed, yanking the loaf of bread out of the priest's hands, greedily stealing a quick bite.

"I said share," the priest called to him as he stood watching the boy encircled by his street companions.

"Only one left, boys," Father Emmanuel said as they passed an all-night dance hall.

Curious at the loud tinkling piano coming within, Daniel stopped to peak inside.

"Glor.ee be," a skeletal woman with highly rouged cheeks chirped, recognizing the man she bumped into to be a man of the cloth. "If it ain't the bible totin', holier than thou good father," she bawled, shimmying directly in front of them, spitting the ground before him.

Taking the cue, Father Emmanuel shouted, "Out! Out of our way, you woman of immoral purposes. You're a disgrace parading yourself before these two innocent boys."

The boys stood rooted to the spot, looking upon her with a mixture of fear and awe.

The haggard stern faced woman held her ground, the joy of living long gone from her with the life of poverty.

"Is it just gettin out of someone's bed you are, or have you not been to bed yet like decent folks?" Father Emmanuel asked, admitting to himself that the sorry state of her and the blighted life she led may not be of her own doing but her only means of putting food on her table and a roof over her head. Though, by the skinny look of her, her meals were few and far between, he guessed.

He pulled the last loaf of bread out from under the blanket, shoving it at her. "Here," he said, "fresh baked this morning."

A tear trickled down her rosy cheek. "Thanks," she choked, turning away, too embarrassed to face this kindness direct. She sidled past them, a shrinking spirit, right now wishing she was more ladylike. Glancing over her shoulder, she saw the priest make the sign of a cross in her direction.

The sky was lightened with the promise of sunshine as Daniel pulled the empty wagon. He walked happily behind Jake and Father Emmanuel knowing all the bread was gone and that they were headed towards home and would soon has something to eat.

"Is it far 'til we get home?" Daniel asked, dragging farther behind them, his legs too tired to go any faster.

Father Emmanuel, realizing the child was weary, stopped and grasped the handle of the wagon from Daniel. "I'll tug it along for awhile, Daniel."

Walking ahead at an unhurried pace, Jake's breath formed a continuous cloud in the cold air as he went along whistling a snappy tune.

Daniel fell in step with Jake. "Will you teach me how to whistle sometime, Jake?" Daniel asked, puckering his lips in a mocking gesture.

Jake looked at him and grinned, hearing no sound coming forth. "Now, blow the air through your lips, Daniel," Jake instructed him, "See," he demonstrated, whistling a clear tone.

With the steady stream of newly awakened, disgorged citizens crowding the streets, coming and going, they did not see the boy who streaked across their path running from the police until the second boy slammed into Daniel as though he'd been shot out of a cannon.

Daniel was knocked flat.

Daniel let out a blood curdling scream.

Father Emmanuel abandoned the wagon and in one swift leap, he had the vagrant boy by the scruff of his neck and quickly turned him over to the policeman. The policeman gave the priest a surly nod as he clutched the boy reeking with the grime of neglect. The thief sneaked a look over his shoulder at the boy on the ground shrieking with pain. Remaining silent, he pouted grotesquely, dropping the stolen blood-smeared switchblade at his feet.

The hair on the nape of the Father Emmanuel's neck bristled when he saw the dreadful gash in Daniel's leg. He immediately tied his handkerchief around the wound, but the blood rapidly soaked through. "There, there, Daniel," he tried to comfort the sobbing boy whose head rested on Jake's shoulder. At the sight of the gushing leg wound, Jake was experiencing a strange tight sensation in the pit of his stomach and his face was growing paler by the minute. He'd never seen so much blood. His fingers opened and closed on Daniel's shoulder, nervously kneading. "You'll be all right, Daniel."

Daniel was beyond comforting, his trembling body and pitiful ripping sobs testimony to his pain.

"It hurts so much, Jake," he cried, his small hands clenching his upper leg.

The policeman offered his handkerchief while still holding on to the boy who was suddenly turning gloomy, and beginning to soften from his militant behavior, releasing a tear, saying, "I didn't mean it. Honest!"

"For the love of St. Peter," Father Emmanuel said, absorbed in his effort to stop the bleeding by using his belt as a tourniquet. When the bleeding slowed, he hoisted Daniel into the wagon, "It's a bad wound. We must get him home."

In the blur of confusion Father Emmanuel forgot about the skinny rascal who'd caused Daniel's injury. Father Emmanuel covered Daniel with the blanket, and then raised his eyes to study the poor wretch. He looked like a hard-headed young upstart. It was the boy's face that caught the priest's heart, his look, the look of abuse he'd seen in so many of the boys' faces. But his eyes.dark and penetrating, the eyes of someone who despised authority, with wickedness showing through, a boy twisted by poverty.

"How old are you, lad?"

"Don't rightly know for sure. Fifteen, maybe?"

This victim of despair was hardly more than thirteen, Father Emmanuel thought.

"Your name?" the priest asked his eyes boring into him.

"Hiram's me name."

Father Emmanuel faced the policeman. "What'll become of him, officer?"

"Too young to jail," he answered, "most likely off to an orphans' farm out west."

Father Emmanuel had heard tales of those farms. The priest's kindness had often caused him to indulge in poor judgment. Few people would understand after what Hiram had done, but this was one of those times.

"How would you like to go home with us, to St. Joseph's home for boys?"

"Yeh!"

"God Almighty, Father, you're talkin' about takin' in a hard-core criminal here," he warned.

Father Emmanuel gave him an exasperated look. He's only a boy, officer."

Hiram stood cowering, his head bowed in silence, looking purposely timid.

"By God, boy, devil that you are," he warned, shaking his forefinger at him, "if you don't behave for the good fathers, you're a bigger fool than I thought. It's only by the goodness of his heart that you're not on the next orphan train headin' out."

Hiram frowned. He was tired of listening to the officer's wagging tongue. The more he thought of it, the better he liked the idea.to have something to eat without having to steal it, and a place to sleep out of the cold. And not being shipped to the orphans' farm was the best part of it. He could sure live with that.

Hiram drew in a deep breath of relief.

The policeman nodded his head in affirmation. 'If you're sure you want to take him, Father, he's all yours."

The boys at the home were all eyes and cringing as Daniel was carried upstairs. The priests were disbelieving when told what happened and that the new boy strutting in with a certain superiority was the cause of it. They didn't question Father Emmanuel about his judgment for they had all been guilty of bringing home thieves and misfits. He would have to be watched, Father Lassiter thought, but didn't they all at first.

Once Daniel was tucked in bed, Father Lassiter sent for the doctor, who promptly told them it wasn't as bad as they all thought. With the gentlest touch, the doctor cleaned the wound, but quickly halted his ministrations when a murderous scream escaped from Daniel's throat.

Daniel's reaction prompted Jake to come running into the room to calm him. "Show the doctor what a big boy you are, Daniel," he said softly, holding his hand. "Don't cry!" he said, lifting a finger to flick away a tear.

The doctor started in again, swabbing the area with an antiseptic, knowing the vicious, biting pain of it was more than a little boy could stand. After he dressed the wound, Daniel laid back exhausted.

"Are we still friends, Daniel?" the doctor asked.

"You're not my friend." he pouted, rolling his eyes.

Dr. Logan smiled. "Maybe this will help," he said, handing Daniel a peppermint stick.

Puffed up with his importance, Daniel sat up in bed perfectly content the rest of the week, fully enjoying the attention he was getting, especially from Jake whose company was all he cared about. Their loneliness and the deep intense devotion between them had pulled them closer together.

Though hammered into defeat in the crushing weight of life, Daniel was too young to question the injustice of such a world, or to revolt or avenge himself against it, but the passing of time and Jake was the healing force that changed his life.

Tied to Jake in friendship in the past year, Daniel's little boy look disappeared as he grew in height and matured in temperament.

"I'm seventeen," Jake explained, buttoning his jacket. "I need to leave so as to make a life for myself." Jake had dreaded this moment. He'd deliberately put off telling Daniel his news against Father's Lassiter's wishes until he was ready to leave, thinking it would be easier.

"Easier for you!" Father Lassiter had tried to make him understand, "but not for Daniel. You should prepare him. You two have fairly been braided together. Give Daniel time to get used to the idea, Jake." But Jake wouldn't listen, and did it his way.

Jake's words quickly wiped the grin off of Daniel's face.

Fiddling with his sack of possessions Jake went on, "When I went to work in the livery stable I was told I'd be put in charge when I was seventeen. I'm seventeen now, Daniel. I'll be in charge."

"I'm going with you, Jake."

"You can't, Daniel. You're not big enough to leave." he said in a tired voice, all six feet of him squatting down to hug him. "Daniel, you knew I'd be going away before long.

Daniel nodded. He tried to untangle the meaning of Jake's explanation, but the news brought back the painful memory of another separation. Ever since Dimity, he'd had Jake.

Daniel's soft hazel eyes looked into Jake's face adoringly, "Oh, I wish I was big enough, Jake," he choked, his nose stuffed up with backed-up tears clutching at him as Jake left.

It was a stinging blow to see Jake leave. Miserable and dejected, Daniel chewed his lips. He sat there for only a few minutes before he bounded out of there to follow him.

CHAPTER EIGHT

Though daylight still lingered, it was close to tea time when the carriage turned off the wide street, and swung through the wrought-iron gateposts. A powdery dust of snow was beginning to settle on the gravel driveway winding up to the mansion. The formidable French Renaissance structure with its distinct air of wealth looked like a fairytale castle to Dimity, who had never seen anything like it.

"Posh!" exclaimed Nellie, grabbing hold of the side of the carriage when her heel caught in the hem of her skirt.

"Here now, Miss Nellie, take care," Albert Durant said, putting his hand on her arm to steady her.

Feeling embarrassed, she lowered her head. "It's that clumsy I be," she clucked, reaching up for Dimity.

Gently moving Nellie aside, he lifted Dimity out of the carriage. "You're home, little one," he smiled into Dimity's sober face. He looked down at the child's dowdy clothes, at her dirty worn boots and raggedy shawl, thinking he should have brought her new clothes to the orphanage for her to wear. He took her little hand in his and guided her up the wide rose brick steps.

The door flew open, and a little girl with dark hair flung herself into Mr. Durant's arms.

"Papa!" she said, laughing.

Dimity lifted her eyes with interest to the girl who was inches taller than herself. She quickly perceived that the two of them standing side by side were ever so different, she with a beautiful green rich velvet dress and lovely shiny shoes and herself with an ugly dress and worn out high toppers.

"Come inside out of the cold," he said.

Nellie nodded, swallowing at the beauty of it all when they entered the main entry hall, her eyes following the staircase of highly polished oak and the glittering chandelier overhead.

Albert Durant put his arms around the two little girls and turned them in to face one another. "Clarice, this is your new little sister, Dimity. Do welcome her," he directed, reminding her of their little talk when he told her she would be having a new little sister."

At first, Clarice stood stone-faced resisting her father's suggestion, but then reluctantly gave Dimity a quick half-hearted smile.

"Did you not forget something, Clarice?" Albert Durant prompted her.

"Oh yes! Welcome to the Durant family," she said in a stilted manner, examining Dimity from head to foot.

"Thank you!" Dimity replied with a bowed head.

Seeing Dimity's gracious reply, Nellie's grey eyes twinkled, but inside she fretted for Dimity for she was afraid that angelic look of Clarice was deceiving.

They were ushered into the drawing room where the cheerful warmth of the fireplace greeted them and where Mercedes Durant sat waiting in a high-backed armchair.

"Mercedes, dear," Albert Durant said, signaling their presence. "Our little daughter has arrived." He quickly attempted to smooth out Dimity's tangled hair as the shawl slid away from her head. "This is our little Dimity."

The black-haired woman sat tight-lipped and stiff, eyeing Dimity for what seemed the longest time before she held out her arms. "Come child, let me look at you."

Dimity stepped slowly towards her, feeling insecure and fearful. Looking into the plain, unsmiling face, she thought, this new mother was not like the old mother she remembered. Dimity stopped short, hesitating to come within reach of the woman's outstretched arms.

Mercedes' eyes grew soft at the pitiful state of the child and the loveliness of her. She wished most intensely that her own daughter was as naturally pretty.

Mercedes summoned her closer. "Come here to me, Dimity."

Dimity, with eight pairs of eyes on her, moved shyly towards the lady who smelled of lavender.

Mercedes gently removed Dimity's shawl, recoiling from the touch of it, and then fingering the child's hair gingerly.

"I think that after we've had a good wash, we'll try on your new clothes. Would you like that, Dimity?

"Yes'um!"

Mercedes lifted Dimity's chin to raise her eyes to meet hers, "Do you have a middle name, Dimity?"

"Dimity Mary," she answered softly.

"Well now," Mercedes said thoughtfully, "Mary is a much prettier name. Yes, that suits you far better. We shall call you Mary." Mercedes looked at her husband. "Don't you think so Albert?" Not waiting for his response, she went on, "Mary Dimity Durant."

"If that is agreeable to Dimity," Albert Durant said, offering Dimity an out for what seemed too profound a decision for a little girl to make.

Dimity was trembling at the intimidation, and saved from answering when the remains of her afternoon snack came up sourly from her stomach and the vomit spattered the burgundy silk of her new mother's gown.

Clarice snickered behind her hands as Nellie rushed to Dimity's rescue. "It's too much for the little darlin'," she said, wiping Dimity's mouth with a rag of a handkerchief she'd dug out of her coat pocket.

Realizing that the prolonged scrutiny from his wife was indeed too much for the child, Albert Durant instantly gathered Dimity up into his arms and carried her upstairs to her new room where he gently undressed her and put her to bed.

It was Albert Durant's wish that the two little girls share a room, but when Clarice threw a tantrum, refusing to accept a roommate, he promptly gave in.

"There now, little one, have a nice rest and you'll feel better," he comforted her.

Dimity shivered, knowing the bad thing she'd done to her new mother. "Oh, Mr. Durant, sir," she said, her teary eyes peering out of a sad face, "I'm that sorry."

"You'll not be calling me Mr. Durant, Dimity, now that you're my little girl. You shall call me Papa, and you're not to worry you were sick," he assured her. "Can you say Papa?" He smiled warmly, feeling closeness to his little daughter.

"Papa," she repeated after him.

"That's right, Dimity."

"But Papa, my new mother said my name is to be Mary."

"Is that all right with you, Mary Dimity?"

"Yes sir!" she agreed, her eyes growing heavy.

After Nellie cleaned up the mess with the help of the maid called Lilly, Mrs. Durant reappeared in a different gown.

"I see you've met Lilly," Mrs. Durant said, bending over to examine the wet spot on the carpet. Satisfied with the cleanup, she lifted a pointing finger, "if you'll follow me, Nellie, I'll show you the kitchen."

Mrs. Durant led her through the door of the large oval dining room where she stepped down three steps to the kitchen which was on a lower level. The mistress of the house introduced Nellie to Lucinda who stood by the gleaming gas range preparing tea. "And you've already met Lilly."

The two maids smiled a welcoming smile, more than happy to be relieved of the cooking chores they'd shared in the past week.

After explaining each minute detail of the household to Nellie and instructing her on the type of food preparation that was expected of her, Mrs. Durant suddenly realized that the uniform left by the former cook may not fit.

"Oh dear," she said, holding up the gray and white striped uniform she'd retrieved from the pantry door. "You'll need to try this on, Nellie. If it doesn't fit, I'll have two new ones made for you."

"Yes ma'am, Mrs. Durant," Nellie said, holding the long calico dress up close to her. "Near to my size, it is."

"Good! Now then, it's past tea time. Please see to it, Nellie." She lifted a white starched apron off of the pantry door, handing it to the pleasant-faced cook.

"Yes ma'am," Nellie nodded her head respectfully, but her pulse quickened as she looked around her not knowing just where to begin. Nellie had already forgotten the words of instruction. Her fingers fumbled clumsily with the apron strings.

"On second thought, Nellie," Mrs. Durant said, seeing her nervousness, "I'd prefer you observe for the next day or two. Lucinda and Lilly will show you what is expected of you.

Turning to leave, Mrs. Durant paused in the doorway. "Oh yes, and Nellie, after tea, Lilly will show you your room. I'm sure you want to unpack."

A look of surprise crossed Nellie's face. It only that minute dawned on her that she'd left her meager belongings in the carriage.

"Beg ye're pardon, ma'am, but I've gone and left me satchel in the carriage. It's that forgetful I be."

"I'll have Isaiah bring it in. Now for tea."

The roar of the gale lasted through the night, but by the next morning, the wind had gone on and the snowstorm with it, leaving behind steep white banks of snow.

"It's a great sight, isn't it dear?" Albert Durant stood looking out at the gray frosty morning of the snow-covered world.

"It is that," Mercedes agreed, glancing past him out the bay window, "if you don't have to go out in it."

"That we do, I'm afraid."

Sitting in the chair he held for her, she asked excitedly, "Oh Albert, could we go to church in the sleigh? We have plenty of time," she pointed out, checking the time on her pendant watch. "It's now only eight thirty."

"Why, of course, my dear. I'll have Isaiah get it ready. He's had it polished and shining for days, just waiting for the first snow."

The Durants loved having a leisurely early morning breakfast on Sundays when Albert did not have to rush off to the office. This was a time they kept to themselves for private conversations, free from their daughter's chatter, whose breakfast was taken with her governess in the schoolroom on Sunday mornings.

Mercedes looked up at Lucinda who stood in the doorway.

"Please serve us from the sideboard Lucinda," she instructed her. "Mr. Durant will have a little of everything. I'll have a biscuit and jam, please."

They had not taken the first bite when they were jolted out of their reverie by a paroxysm of high-pitched screams.

The dining room door flew open. "It's Dimity," Nellie informed them as if they didn't know.

Yes, Nellie," Mrs. Durant acknowledged calmly, rising from her chair. "What a bore! The child should be happy away from that horrid orphans' home."

"I'll see to her, ma'am. It's a cry of fear of finding herself in a strange place."

"No need to be irritated, Mercedes. The child may have fallen out of bed or it could be as Nellie says. She's so small and frail and being shut up in a dark empty room may be frightening for her." Albert Durant put his napkin down after dabbing at is mouth.

"Come with me, Nellie. You are the familiar face she needs to see."

The three of them started up the stairs. Another loud piercing screech greeted them as they reached the door of the child's bedroom.

"Cry baby! Cry baby!" Clarice cried, and then quickly hushed when she heard the door open. She shivered when she saw the look her father gave her.

"Enough!" Albert Durant scolded her, "how shameful of you, Clarice, taunting her like that."

Clarice ran to her mother, hiding her head in her bosom.

Dimity sat in the bed confused and bewildered, her reddened skin taking on the color of her vibrant hair. The charming surroundings of her new room held no interest for her. Her only interest at the moment was her perplexity at being left alone. When Nellie sat on the bed beside her, Dimity threw her arms around her neck.

"Oh Miss Nellie, why did you leave me? Am I going to live in here all by myself?"

"No darlin'," Nellie comforted her, "this is where ye'll be sleepin'."

"Not by myself!"

Albert Durant sat on the other side of the bed. He hadn't given it a thought that the child had never been alone. It was well-nigh too inhuman to have put her away all alone in a room by herself.

"You'll not have to be by yourself, Dimity. We love you and we want you to be happy," he said, kissing her on the cheek feeling the wetness of the gossamer lashes wet with tears.

The blessing of her new Papa's words and thinking she'd be sleeping with Nellie was all she needed to bring a smile on her face.

The sight of her Papa taking on so with this new little person they called her sister brought a hot madness within Clarice as her mother left her side to go to Dimity.

"Nellie, if you'll tend to Mary Dimity, we'll finish our breakfast, and then she can breakfast with Miss Tyson and Clarice."

"And Mary Dimity," after you and Clarice have had your breakfast we'll be off to church in the sleigh," she said, giving her a kindly look. "Would you like that?" Mercedes decided to call her by both names for awhile until she was accustomed to it.

"Yes'um! Is Nellie goin' too?"

"No dear, Nellie will be busy cooking our dinner."

At the doorway, Mercedes turned, "Nellie, do give the child a good wash and put on one of her new frocks hanging in the armoire.the dark blue one will do nicely, and by all means, the new boots. I do hope they'll fit."

"Clarice, run along dear, and eat the nice breakfast Nellie's prepared for you. Miss Tyson is waiting."

Albert Durant fingered his gold watch-chain thoughtfully as they sat at the dining room table waiting for their food to be reheated. "I should have realized the child would be frightened all alone."

"And what do you propose, Albert, telling the child she will not have to be by herself?"

"Why, we'll move her in with Miss Tyson."

"Do you think the governess will be agreeable to such an arrangement? After all, she's with the children all day. She needs some time to herself," Mercedes pointed out, looking up at Lucinda who was pouring her a cup of steaming coffee.

"Thank you, Lucinda."

"No doubt about it when I tell her she's to be paid extra," he answered her, waiting until Lucinda passed through the door.

"There is one other problem, Albert. Mary Dimity's attachment to Nellie must be severed. She's much too dependent on her. "

Thinking that the child had already been deprived of the unselfish love of a mother and father and her twin brother now gone from her, he hesitated before answering her. He could not give his wife the answer she expected.

"In time! In time, Mercedes, but not just yet."

"Gracious Albert, why not?"

"I've told you what the child has suffered, losing her mother, her twin whisked away from her in the night, and now she's been handed over to strangers." He shook his head. "Surely, you can feel some pity in your heart and allow her the comfort of having Nellie close by."

"It is dreadful, I agree." She knew there was no use in pressing the matter any further. "I'm sure in time she will adapt to her new family."

Soon after breakfast, the household was in a frenzy preparing to leave for Mass and the excitement of having the first sleigh ride of the season added to their high spirits. Clarice was especially eager to get started.

Mercedes raised her head as Clarice burst into the room. Though prettily dressed in a red figured woolen dress, Clarice's ankle-length full skirt only added to her chubbiness.

"Mama!" she cried with a mouth full of her Sunday breakfast. "She's got a new dress, and I have to wear this old thing." Clarice pulled at her skirt to make a point.

"Clarice dear, do not speak with a mouth full of food," Mercedes scolded. "Are you speaking of your step-sister?"

"Yes, she's.

"Mary Dimity is not to be called a step-sister in this house," Albert Durant commanded, putting down his paper. "Mercedes, do I need to remind you that Mary Dimity is our little daughter as is Clarice, and Clarice," he directed his gaze to her, "she is your little sister. Is that understood? I do not want Mary Dimity to feel she is an outsider."

"As you wish, Albert." Mercedes Durant was far from happy at her husband's outburst but his freezing look told her to leave well enough alone.

"Come dear," she reached out to her daughter, fluffing the child's dark straight hair in place. "You must understand, Clarice, Mary Dimity did not have any pretty clothes like you."

The moody scowl Clarice wore gave her plump face the quality of an old woman. "But Mama, she could wear my old clothes," Clarice offered, her dark wide-set eyes brooding.

"No dear, your clothes wouldn't fit Mary Dimity."

"But Mama, I want some new clothes like her," she insisted with a note of jealousy in her voice.

Suddenly, Albert Durant's reserve snapped. "Clarice, come here," he beckoned, his arms outstretched.

Clarice seated herself on her father's knee.

"I want you to be nice to Mary Dimity. When your mama and I spoke to you about your little sister, you seemed eager to meet her. Now that she's here, you've shown little kindness towards her."

"But she wore ugly raggedy clothes and she smelled when she arrived yesterday," she said in an attempt to defend herself.

He gave his daughter a severe look of reproach. "Shame on you, Clarice. Mary Dimity cannot help that she was a poor orphan. That's reason enough for you to treat her kindly. Why," he paused, "you're the big sister and big sisters take care of their little sisters. Will you do that, Clarice dear, and help to take care of her?"

She sucked in her breath, and bobbed her head, pretending to be on her good behavior, "Yes Papa."

"Good girl!" he kissed her on the cheek. "Run along now. We'll be leaving shortly."

It was like sitting in the middle of a dream for Dimity with her self-identity so disconnected from the old world. Looking back at herself in the large gilt mirror, she smiled.

"Is that me?" she asked, looking at Nellie and Miss Tyson, who had come to help Nellie dress her.

"Yes, Mary Dimity," Miss Tyson said, looking past the child in the mirror's image, "that pretty little girl dressed in that lovely blue dress is you."

The warm, gentle nature of the child had already touched the heart of the governess the moment Dimity lifted her pretty face to greet her. "Good morning, Miss Tyson," she said, having been prompted by Nellie.

Dimity let her mind wander. Everything seemed unnatural, unreal. As awareness of her surroundings took over, she realized she had passed into a world of beauty and she was absorbed by it. The spell of awe went unbroken for days and weeks.

This big house to Dimity had wonderful smells of an unfamiliar life of tempting cooking, of aromatic spices, of sweet smelling soap, of her new mama's lavender smell and the overpowering smell of cheroot around her new papa. And sounds, sounds which made dins against the silence, of the crackling fires, of the hissing of the jet gas lamps, of the many clocks striking the hour throughout the house, of voices and laughter, all the sounds of living in the Durant house.

Dimity explored with her eyes the multitude of beautiful objects which she dared not touch, the bisques, the delicate porcelain figurines, the hand-painted plates, the ormolu clocks on the mantelpieces. The rooms were all filled with priceless collectibles and oil paintings and portraits in gold frames.

Everything was done on a grand scale in the Durant home, the Italian marble flooring in the entryway and the imported bronze sculptures and oriental rugs all added to the beauty and grandeur of the Fifth Avenue mansion.

"Gracious, it's cold," Mercedes said, tucking the tartan rug around the two girls and Miss Tyson who sat between them.

Clarice whooped delightedly as her father gave the signal to Isaiah, her moody resentment gone.

"Yo!" he shouted in a booming voice. "Let's be off."

Isaiah clucked to the horses and they took off down the snow covered street.

Dimity sat tight-lipped as the swirling cold air rushed by, but a faint smile crossed her face as the sleigh went gliding along past the fancy brownstone houses on Fifth Avenue, the center of polite society.

As they crossed Thirty-fourth Street, a horse car lumbered by with only two passengers who were huddled together in the front seat. The driver gave them a wave.

Albert Durant gave him a stiff-handed salute in greeting as they bobbed along, the dying echoes of the horses' hoofs on the ice-bound streets shattering the silence.

The bearded hoarfrost sprouting from the trees and buildings created an artful beauty of new sculptured forms as the harshness of winter softened before their eyes, yielding to them a favor of nature and of God.

This was an all-right world this Sunday morning, Dimity thought, as she waved a woolen, mittened hand to the driver, a shy smile lighting her face.

Not to be outdone by Dimity, Clarice quickly withdrew a hand from her beaver muff and waved also.

Isaiah on his lofty perch spurred the horses on, touching their shining haunches lightly with the tip of his whip. The Durant's coachman sat straight and proud. To some, this gentlemanly black man with the perpetual smile on his face may have appeared sorely impressed with his importance. In truth, driving this family of privilege and the two handsome bays with their manes and tails swishing in the wind, and their brasses gleaming, Isaiah was the picture of contentment.

Though the smoking, thriving industries of the city were shut down for a Sunday, the streets soon became crowded with carriages and sleighs, mostly of Sunday morning churchgoers. Following an omnibus, the Durants' progress was slow until Isaiah clucked to the horses and they sailed past it.

While driving through a crowded East Side slum area where the garbage lay rotted in the streets, Mercedes Durant held a lacy handkerchief to her nose. "Gracious! It's a veritable stink bag," she complained, refusing to suffer in silence, "Albert, certainly there is another route we could take."

"My dear, I know it is a round-about way we've come, but I instructed Isaiah to follow the tracks where the snow is somewhat cleared. I had no idea the street cleaners had neglected their duty hereabouts. I must say, this street is deplorable," he agreed, raising his gloved hand to his nose to block out the stench. "I will speak to the mayor the first thing Monday morning. Why, the debris is knee deep."

It was not Albert Durant's temperament to accept such conditions with patient resignation. Had this been all of the problems in the city, he would have been less concerned, but other signs of neglect were apparent due to the well-known graft throughout city hall. If rumor were to be believed, the graft was growing more riotous every day and any indecent or swindling schemes could operate openly provided they paid for protection. Albert Durant knew that the street cleaning was contracted out to a contractor who was receiving an outrageous sum of money to keep the city clean.

Albert Durant and several of his business associates who held equal disdain for the government workings were now serving with distinction on a self-appointed committee of wealthy respected and concerned citizens. As chairman of this citizens' group, it was his aim to merit the honor conferred on him. The burden of ever increasing taxes had aroused a considerable outcry among all of New York's citizens and it was time the situation was taken in hand.

At Mulberry Street Isaiah turned the corner and brought the team to a halt in front of St. Patrick's Cathedral where the New York City Catholics were alighting from their carriages and sleighs, some giving curt nods of greeting, others shouting exuberant good mornings.

Though few words had passed between their lips to one another on the way to church, the girls' eyes met and held as they were lifted out of the sleigh.

It was evident to Miss Tyson from Clarice's expression that beneath the surface she clearly harbored resentment towards Dimity. The governess knew from that moment on that this wretched child would work diligently to sabotage any happiness in Dimity's future. Miss Tyson vowed to be the obstacle in Clarice's path. She had very nearly decided to give up her position with the Durants when Albert Durant had broached the subject of her staying with Dimity at night. But then there was the additional money, and now with her concern for the child she was suddenly resolute and would agree to the arrangement.

"You must be frozen," Miss Tyson remarked, tucking the girls close to her as they walked ahead into the cathedral, marching up the aisle to the very first pew reserved for them.

"Do you think Archbishop Hughes is out of his sick bed and will be saying Mass this morning, Albert?" Mercedes whispered to her husband as he ushered her into the pew.

"I'm sure he has recovered by now."

Crawling over Dimity who was sitting on the end, Mercedes seated herself in between the two girls.

When Albert sat beside Dimity, the child looked up at him with a touching gratitude, giving him a shy smile to match his.

Albert Durant had firm views as to the kind of respect due the church and how his family should act in church. This was the reason Mercedes made it a point to be seated next to Clarice who was known to fidget and whisper and sometimes exhibit a giggling fit.

Turning her attention to the people around her, Dimity thought, it's a world of grownups and so different from the chapel at the orphanage. While the parishioners sat in their pews waiting for Mass to begin, the Durants joined in singing a hymn with gusto.

Unbuttoning her red mohair coat, Dimity slipped the black buttons through the buttonholes piped with black braiding. She looked down at her new black boots and grinned, remembering the look of herself in the mirror. She opened her small fist and gazed wonderingly at the pennies her new papa had placed in her hand.

At the entrance of the archbishop the people stood and the medley of sound ceased.

"Shh! Shh!" Albert Durant whispered a warning to Clarice, whose voice had grown louder and louder with a constant irritating banter to her mother.

Instantly contrite, Clarice bowed her head, at the same time wishing it had been Dimity who had been chastised.

At the offertory when the collection basket was passed, Albert Durant prompted Dimity by holding her clasped fist directly over the basket, separating her fingers to allow the pennies to spill freely into the basket. She watched wide-eyed as the other members of the family did the same.

Seeing her disappointment and realizing the child thought the coins were for her, Albert reached into his pocket and pulled out two pennies. "These are for you, Dimity," he said, whispering in her ear. "Put them in your coat pocket, dear."

By the time Mass ended, the day had turned raw, and long before they'd turned up Fifth Avenue the vast grayness of the sky turned white with falling snow. In spite of the cold, the family chatted gaily all the way home while Albert amused the children by blowing smoke rings over their heads.

Clarice reached up to grasp one in her chubby hand.

"Oh papa, I've caught one," she cried, giggling with delight, opening her fist to discover there was nothing there. "Where did it go?"

Dimity, who was sitting beside Clarice, looked into Clarice's hand as well, and she too was surprised the puff of smoke was not there. Seeing Clarice's exuberance in the game, Dimity decided to join in the fun, and extended her arm to catch one of the suspended particles of vapor. In doing so, she knocked Clarice's bonnet off her head.

Clarice jumped to her feet and with an incongruously booted foot; she aimed a kick at Dimity's leg.

Dimity instinctively let out a fierce yowl for the entire world to hear, but quickly twisted herself to face her attacker and returned the kick. The hurt in her leg was forgotten when she looked into Clarice's shocked eyes.

"Here now," Albert said, giving his cheroot a pitch in the snow. "There will be no more of that, either from you Clarice," who was clinging to her mother, sobbing fearfully, "or from you, Mary Dimity."

"She started it," Clarice cried through a mist of tears while Mercedes retied her bonnet.

"No, you kicked me first," Dimity retorted.

Miss Tyson pulled her shawl around her thinking, however tenuous the children's relationship might be she was sure that Dimity's quick assertive action left a lasting impression on Clarice. No doubt, she would think twice before she tangled with Dimity again.

Indeed, Miss Tyson thought, patting Dimity under the rug, the child has spunk after all.

That was the beginning of Dimity's years as a member of the Durant family. At first she was in a nameless limbo when a new name was forced on her, but in time, the name of Dimity was all but forgotten and the snug security of her new life settled in.

CHAPTER NINE

In the early spring of 1861, a wave of patriotism swept over New York City with the newspapers calling for recruits. Though Mayor Fernando Wood had actually suggested the separation of New York City from the Union, an action which proved he did not share the sentiments of the Lincoln administration, he quickly jumped on the band wagon and organized the Mozart Regiment. When Fort Sumter was fired upon in April, Lincoln called for 75,000 volunteers to protect the Stars and Stripes. In the following weeks in New York City there were continuous parades and ceremonies in honor of departing regiments.

Jake sniffed the warm morning air, breathing in a whiff of fresh manure that mingled in with the sweet flower smell of the spring blooms sprouting throughout as he marched slowly up the cobbled street behind a horse and wagon. The faraway look in his eye deepened and a frown creased his brow as he thought of Daniel.

At the sound of the blaring band playing 'Rock of Ages' he paused, his fingers closing around his sack of belongings.

Up ahead was a regiment of marching soldiers. Jake went tearing after them, past the horse and wagon to catch up with them. He lost all count of time following them up Broadway to Union

Square where the buildings and store fronts were decorated with gay, colorful bunting.

Jake came to a stop when the marching regiment halted in front of St. Patrick's Cathedral. It was a melodramatic scene to watch these men fused together and full of the spirit of patriotism swearing to uphold the flag. The ceremony was complete when Archbishop Hughes gave his blessing over the sea of bowed heads.

After the ceremony an ear piercing din erupted amid a tumult of uproarious shouting onlookers. It was a scene of wild excitement and Jake's spirits lifted as he watched the soldiers amid the clatter of swords and muskets march off to the awaiting ferry. With shoulders back and heads up, they proudly marched with an uprightness befitting their soldier status. Jake was greatly impressed by the scene. He stood and watched them until they were out of sight. He sighed regretfully that he was not going with them.

By the time Jake reached the livery stable it was well past noon. Knowing he was a good three hours late, he quickly stashed his belongings in the tack room, picked up the curry brush and began currying his favorite mare, moving over the sleek coat in sweeping motions. He was thinking about what he had seen when the booming voice of Mickey Eagan, known as "Big Mick" lifted above the sounds of the lively, noisy busyness of the stable, over the clanking of the blacksmith's anvil, and the rattle of loaded wagons and carriages.

"Jake, boy! Look what I got here."

Jake looked back over his shoulder into the florid, personable face of his boss who was holding the hand of Daniel.

"Look who followed you, this rag tag young'un. He looks like he's done for. Too tired to move another step he is.

"Daniel!" Jake cried, not believing his eyes, "how did you get here?'"

"I followed close behind you, Jake."

"Well, I'm sorry Daniel, but you can't stay here."

The dark freckles stood out on Daniel's nose and cheeks, his eyes hurtfully glaring. "I will so!" Jake looked up at Mr. Eagan. "I'm all he's got. "Well now, come along Daniel, and you too, Jake," he said, guiding Daniel back to the tack room where old cast off buggy parts were stored and where he'd set up a cot for Jake.

"How's about taking a little rest here on the cot?" he coaxed, knowing the child was sorely exhausted.

"Will Jake stay here with me?" Daniel asked worriedly, giving the man with the flowing walrus mustache a pleading look.

"You betcha!"

Mr. Eagan waited until Daniel was asleep. "You know, Jake, this ain't no hotel."

"No sir, I know. It's just that he's that attached to me. I can take him back to the orphanage, but I'm afraid he'll keep running away."

"You don't say!" Mr. Eagan rolled a cigar around in his mouth thoughtfully. Mickey Eagan was a man without a family, and whose charitable heart went out to the orphans being an orphan himself. "If the little feller stays, he'll be the youngest boy I've ever had working for me."

Purely astonished at his words, Jake squeaked out a question, "You mean it? He can stay?"

"I don't see why not, if you promise to look after him."

Jake broke into an eager grin. "Oh yes, Mr. Eagan. That I will. That I will promise."

"I'll speak to the good Fathers," he said, patting Daniel on the head. "He's a cute little rascal, ain't he?"

Although they were somewhat aware of Mickey Eagan's shady business, it was Mickey Eagan's promise to the Jesuits that he would send Daniel to school and as an afterthought, promptly professed his desire to adopt Daniel.

"You know, Father, when I saw the little fella yesterday, I thought of myself growing up without a mother and father." He narrowed his dark eyes thoughtfully. "I'd like to give the kid a home."

Father Lassiter knew very little of the man who called himself Mickey Eagan, only that he was the Alderman of the Sixth Ward and he owned a livery stable. The priest looked more closely at him. Not only did he have great height, but very broad-shoulders which added to the strong look of him. This man in his late forties, whose wide girth was proof that he did not go hungry, or without, was flamboyantly prosperous looking wearing an emerald green waistcoat and a diamond stickpin in his white silk cravat.

"And your wife, Mr. Eagan, how does she feel?" Father Lassiter asked.

"My wife is with the angels, Father. She left me with no children," he said, reaching in his pocket. "I'd like a son. A son like Daniel." He held out a roll of bills to Father Lassiter. "For the boys here at the home."

"Why, Mr. Eagan, you're very generous," the priest smiled, looking at the wad of green bills in his hand. "It appears you are quite capable of providing a home for Daniel. I see no reason why the adoption cannot be arranged." He certainly has a kind heart, the priest thought.

Seeing the distrust in Father Lassiter's eyes disappear, and noting his quick change of heart, Mickey Eagan was amused to see that the feel of money in the palm was not that far removed from holiness.

'Big Mick' Eagan suffered no inconvenience with his new status of adopted father, nor did he intend to be put upon with this added responsibility. Giving Daniel a home as the priest said, did not mean his own home, which was upstairs from the stable, and shared by a woman named Sophie, who prepared his meals and kept the apartment clean and his bed warm. For the time being, Daniel would stay with Jake in the tack room and eat his meals upstairs. Mickey Eagan hadn't quite decided when he would be a father to his new adopted son, or when he'd tell the boy of the adoption.

Thinking of him with a smiling gentleness, Mickey Eagan wasn't quite sure what made him do it. His lips were set in a hard, thin line when he thought about this new responsibility and wondered if he should keep Daniel sheltered from his Empire of crime. The goal of his whole life was to have a son to follow in his footsteps, but Daniel was only a little boy. Meanwhile, it could wait.

Breaking off a great hunk of bread, Mickey handed it to Daniel, who had taken up the soup bone in his hands and was hungrily sucking the marrow out of the hole with loud slurping sounds.

In the name of God, son, there's more to eat," Mickey chided him, at the same time enjoying the spectacle of the boy's utmost content as he impaled the bony morsel with his teeth eating the meat clinging to it.

Jake appeared in the doorway, holding a dirty rag up to his eye.

"What's kept you, Jake? Your supper's cold."

"I delivered the gelding to Mr. Franklin," he replied, seating himself next to Daniel.

"And the reward money? Did you get it?"

"No sir! Jake eyed him with a fearful timidity, knowing what he had to tell him would result in violence." He said he wouldn't pay out money to the likes of you who stole his horse from him in the first place."

Running a quavering hand through his shock of stiff black hair, Mickey's face grew florid, and his jaw tightened. He jumped to his feet and snatched the rag covering Jake's eye away, revealing a blackened, swollen eye.

"And who did that?" he asked in a harsh tone, realizing it was his own fault for sending Jake without one of his henchman. But it was a way of getting Jake's feet wet and he needed to do it alone.

"Mr. Franklin!"

"Oh he did, did he? He'll wish he'd never been born when I get through with him."

Mickey's body shook with anger. There was fire in his eyes and fire in his blood. "He'll be a piece of petrified wood," his throaty, hoarse voice shouted.

"What's petrified wood, Jake?" Daniel asked.

"Means he'll be dead."

Daniel's innocent eyes grew larger and inquisitive as his gaze followed Mickey Eagan.

Mickey's voice rang out in the next room where Quincy, one of his bodyguards, sat at the kitchen table eating his supper. Mickey made his way into the kitchen, stumbling over Quincy's boots. He was jolted against the pointed edge of hearth, cracking his shin. Barking out a string of curse words, "You damn piss ass! Damn your hide, Quincy." His flailing arms knocked the pots and pans free from their hanging nails. The clattering as they hit the floor brought Sophie running to what was causing the commotion. She stood wringing her hands, screaming, "Oh dear, oh dear," in a shrill, prattling tongue.

Mickey lifted himself from a kneeling position, and stood leaning against the brick fireplace. He bit his lip, pushing Sophie away as she tried to help him.

Quincy's face reddened. He dropped his fork, wiping his mouth with the back of his gigantic hand. He jumped up, running to Mickey's side.

"Pour me a whiskey," Mickey croaked, as he sat down, looking with disfavor at Quincy. He sat with eyes closed, rubbing his leg.

Quincy quickly poured a finger of whiskey into a glass.

Mickey drank it down in one gulp, holding the glass out to Quincy, "Nuther."

Jake and Daniel stood in the doorway all eyes.

"Quincy," Mickey said in a voice of reason, his senses calmed by the whiskey, "I sent a boy to do a man's job." He pointed to Jake. "Look what happened to him. That sonofabitch gave him a black eye. I want you and Ira to take care of Franklin. The old fart refused to pay Jake the reward money."

Quincy grinned knowingly. "Sure thing, boss."

"Give him some good jolts. Knock him about so's he'll remember us." As an afterthought, he said, "But first, get his horse. This time, he won't get it back."

Daniel had been all ears and the thought of the petrified man puzzled him. He gingerly went forward to where Mickey was sitting. Daniel stood before him, gripping the man's fleshy knee with his fingers.

"Mr. Mickey, if I pray to God, he'll do you a favor and the man won't get petrified dead."

Mickey Eagan chuckled, tenderly lifting Daniel onto his lap. Mickey wasn't a man who wanted goodness from another's prayers when in truth he wanted to kill that sonofabitch Franklin. But realizing religion had been an integral part of the boy's life; he vowed to watch his tongue around the boy.

"Petrified dead? And where did you come by that, Danny boy?" he asked, laughing amusedly.

"You, Mr. Mickey! You said it! He'd be a piece of petrified wood."

"Petrified wood, son, not petrified dead."

"Means dead. Jake said so."

"Drivel! Plain drivel! Franklin ain't goin' to be dead."

"But you said."

"No! No! No need to pray for somethin' that ain't gonna happen," he insisted, pulling out a long cigar, biting off the end, and then circling it around in his mouth.

Jake stood there listening to every word. His instincts told him Mickey Eagan was a man who had little regard for right or wrong, a man to be feared. Jake didn't understand all that went on in the livery stable, or know exactly what the other boys did who were in an out all hours of the night. But he was awakening to the fact that Mickey Eagan was involved in dishonest dealings and surely breaking the law. No doubt, he thought, he too, would be a part of it. But Mickey had been kind to him, and now to Daniel. Jake stood staring at him, wondering where he would fit in.

Jake was right. Hiding under the honest cloak of his political position as Alderman and his charitable and religious causes, the livery stable was a front for much of Mickey Eagan's criminal activities. He was the indisputable leader of the Irish gang called "The Lions." Mickey picked this name because he fully intended to 'get his lion's share'. The livery stable was not only the headquarters for election repeaters, but the training ground for Mickey's lawbreakers who learned the fine arts of theft, of pick pocketing, of armed robbery. The course of instruction they were required to master before they were a part of the secret squad was how to crack a safe, how to wield a stiletto with such expertise that you could slice up a man without killing him, or in one swift well-planted stab, kill him. Stable grooms were trained to be expert horse thieves. The horses were stolen from distant neighborhoods in the night. A few days later the horse would be miraculously found and returned to the owner for a hefty reward. The premises were a sanctuary where the police never set foot. It was under their full protection for a price.

The livery stable was not Mickey's only enterprise. He owned a saloon, a poor man's club where for the price of five cents his customer could get a beer and a free lunch of hardboiled eggs, pickled fish and lunch meats. In the back room, Mickey ran a gambling casino, and in the adjoining house, he trafficked in prostitutes. Mickey was proud of his fancy ladies whose earnings continued to soar.

It was not his worry that the police would shake him down, but that the Italian gang would invade his territory, a threat which put him constantly on guard. When some of his customers were assaulted by the Italian gang because they were not patronizing the Italian gambling casino, Mickey felt a complete contempt for the Italians. Late one night when Mickey was informed that the Italian gang leader could be found in his house with only one bodyguard, Mickey and his men broke into the house. Mickey cornered Pasquali, seizing him by his bushy mustache and lifted him off the ground while Mickey's man Ira killed the gang leader's bodyguard in front of him.

Antagonism grew between the two factions and the undercurrent of a gang war was always there, always an ongoing, constant threat keeping Mickey Eagan on his toes.

Though a scoundrel in his own right, Mickey Eagan commanded the loyalty of his gang, who obeyed him in all matters without question. Most of his wants were within his power. Rarely, were his wishes denied him, but losing Jake and some of his gang to the Zouaves Regiment that summer was an unwanted blow, both to himself and to Daniel.

Mickey held Daniel's hand as Jake took the oath to serve his country at Tammany Hall. Witnessing the departure of Jake marching off to war made the little boy's spine tingle with fear. He was trembling when he bolted forth to latch onto Jake as he marched past.

"No! Go back, Daniel," Jake shook off the boy's hand clutching at his sleeve, with a pleading look to Mickey Eagan who had grabbed Daniel with a whip hand force out of the way of the rowdy marching soldiers.

"You'll not go chasing after him, Daniel," Mickey held him closely. "I tell you, they'll trample you to the ground." Daniel pulled away from Mickey, his hands doubled in fists; he began beating them against Mickey's chest.

"I hate him! I hate him!" Daniel cried, his face dark with defiance, his lips trembling.

Mickey shook his head. His mouth was a hard, angry line at the injustice of it. Once more the kid was losing the one person he loved. It was a crazy, wicked world.

Daniel's sobs could not be heard over the harsh baritone voices of General Billy Wilson's Zouaves Regiment, who belted out in song "Get Out of the Way, Old Dan Tucker." This regiment was made up largely of crooks, gangsters and the scouring of the worst slums in New York, but they were all aflame with war spirit, all in a hodgepodge of dress, frock coats, pea jackets, firemen's red shirts and plug hats. Unknowingly, they would be receiving their baptism under fire at Bull Run, and would suffer some of the heaviest losses of any New York regiment.

Daniel stood by Mickey in Union Square amidst the swarm of excited well-wishers in silent bewilderment, his eyes following the last of the regiment as they rounded the corner. All the faces in the crowd reflected excitement, especially those of the young women who stood waving to boyfriends and husbands. Carriages of the polite society also halted to watch the departing regiment.

In a carriage on the other side of the street just passing by, sat a stately prosperous looking man accompanied by two little girls, one dark-haired, and one with a shock of russet curls, much the same color as Daniel's.

If Daniel had only given one quick glance in that direction, he would have seen his sister, Dimity. Or had she looked past the glaring sun, over the heads of the uproarious crowd, she would have seen her brother.

The cobbled street resounded with the heavy booted marching of the soldiers, and the clanging wheels of the Durant carriage moving on down the street.

Daniel sighed, squinting in the bright glare of the sun, holding back his tears. "I don't see why Jake has to go to war, Mr. Mickey."

Now that Daniel was his child, Mickey realized it was his duty to ease the grave worries on the boy's mind. Yet, there was no way he could explain any sense of justice to the boy when he's lost, his best friend to war. He was too young to understand.

Mickey smiled faintly. He spoke with the same liquid accent all too familiar to Daniel, his words lilting upward as he remembered the voice of his Dada. "It's that dreadful a thing, war is, Danny boy," he said as they walked on. "We can't hear the guns and cannons sounding off from here, but where Jake's goin', down South there, where the war is, he'll be hearin' 'em. And God Almighty let him stay out of the path of the gunshot."

"Will Jake be back soon?" Daniel started to cry. Big watery tears slid down his face.

"Ain't gonna be tomorrow, son, but I'll be here for you," he assured him, feeling a pang of pity for the boy.

Mickey tucked Daniel's hand in his pocket and they walked towards home.

In the following months, Daniel became Mickey's shadow, and in time Mickey drew him out to find his identity. It was as though the boy's feelings were locked up in a vault. Mickey was curious to know how much Daniel remembered of his folks. He was especially puzzled when one day he noticed the swelling of Daniel's middle finger.

"Danny boy, let me see that hand of yours," he motioned to him to sit on his lap.

Daniel held out his hand.

"No," Mickey said, grasping the child's left hand, "this one." He carefully touched the swollen area around the ring, where the flesh was bulging and red. "Christ," he bellowed, rolling his eyes in disbelief, "are you blind, boy?" Holding Daniel's hand in his, he tried to slide the little gold band off his finger, but abruptly stopped when Daniel winced with pain.

"Pretty, ain't it?" Daniel smiled, eyeing it s luster shining in the golden sunlight as though it was the first time he'd really looked at it.

Mickey shrugged. "Reckon it ain't gonna' be a pretty sight if we have to cut the finger off to get that piece of gold off it."

Daniel looked up at him with a look of mistrust, shaking his head violently, his shaggy mass of russet hair falling freely over his freckled face. "No! No, Mr. Mickey. I can't take it off."

Daniel was not prepared to remove the ring, much less, his finger. He bowed his head stubbornly.

"Holy Jaysus, boy, and why not?"

"It's my dead Mama's," he choked in a weak voice, looking into Mickey's enormously rosy face. "I promised my Dada I'd always wear it. My sister Dimity has the other half of Mama's ring. When I find her, you'll see.

Mickey sat there full of silent, sad bewilderment.

He wondered where God was when this boy was plagued with the unhappiness of a cruel world. Mickey's face softened. The boy's been robbed of his childhood. He reminded him of himself.

Daniel looked up at him with sorrowful eyes.

Staring down at Daniel's finger with an increasing uneasiness, Mickey could see the boy would be tortured with an overpowering guilt should he cut the ring off. The man that could be ruthless suddenly found himself beguiled by the trusting eyes of a little boy. He laid his hand on Daniel's shoulder and vowed to save him from further unhappiness. He was the son he'd always wanted.

"Hmm!" Nodding his head, he guided Daniel to the commode and poured cold water into the china bowl and held Daniel's finger in the water, soaping it down around the swollen roll of flesh.

To Daniel, it seemed the longest time that his hand soaked in the soapy water, with the skin all wrinkled and crinkled before Mickey finally freed the gold band off his finger.

Pleased with himself, Mickey dried Daniel's hand vigorously with a fresh towel. Lifting the ring out of the water, he dried it, then handed it to Daniel. "There now. Wasn't as tight as I thought."

Mickey grumbled loudly when a few moments later he raised his eyes to see Daniel putting the ring back on.

"We'll have none of that," he said, frowning. "Ain't you got an ounce of sense, boy?" Mickey pursed his lips, letting out a loud whistle. "I thought you was smart."

"See," Daniel held out his hand. "It's not too tight on my little finger."

"God bless it, Daniel, havin' all five fingers is more important than wearin' that ring. Mickey held his beefy face up close to Daniel's. "Before you know it, it'll be squeezing that finger," he said, sliding the ring off.

"But I promised."

Mickey could not help smiling. Putting his arm affectionately around Daniel, he leaned back in his chair lifting him onto his lap.

"And the promise to your dead Dada you'll be keepin', Danny boy." Mickey pulled out a piece of string from his pantaloons pocket. He gave Daniel a wink and slipped the string through the ring, then tied it loosely around his neck. "This here ain't long enough, but it'll do for now."

Fingering the circle of gold dangling from his neck, Daniel beamed happily, and raised his hand to touch the bearded chin of his benefactor.

Mickey chuckled. The pleasure of this boy and his deep hunger for a son softened the hardness in his heart. That night, he moved Daniel's meager belongings upstairs.

CHAPTER TEN

The black clouds of war raced across the city in a hot tempered voice of confusion and dissent, a city disembodied by citizens whose allegiances avowed to the most pragmatic of denominators, money.

Among the merchants of New York City, there was a mutual feeling that the conflict between the North and South would surely sever trade with the southern states. And so, with their investments at risk, and with no passion for justice, patriotism was seen sparingly. The New York merchants sent petition after petition to Congress, urging conciliation with the South. And when they had already freed their own slaves in New York City nearly a quarter century earlier, they were of the opinion that the end of slavery in the South would naturally follow without war.

The end of serfdom came about in New York in 1856 when a slave girl was auctioned from the pulpit of the Brooklyn Plymouth Church. In using the language of the slave market, Pastor Henry Ward Beecher opened the bidding for the freedom of a slave girl named Sarah. For her freedom, men's purses were thrown into the collection plate along with women's jewels. This event went far toward freeing other slaves in New York.

Albert Durant was not in agreement with Mayor Fernando Wood when he suggested to the

Common Council that Long Island, Staten Island and Manhattan should secede from the Union and form an independent state called "Tri-Insula."

To counteract this movement, Albert Durant gathered together a group of men of wealth, Wall Street brokers, business men and bankers to thwart such secession. With his power of persuasion and with the help of the members of the Union League Club, the group did their patriotic share by giving willingly and generously to the cause. It was a joyous pilgrimage for Albert when they were able to outfit the Seventh Regiment for active duty.

There was about Albert Durant the aura of a man with a vision. It was well known that this was a man with an astute mathematical mind, and coupled with his ready made power in the banking world power he commanded the respect of the financial world.

Albert Durant was one of the first to shy away from the romantic lure of the clipper ship and build a steamship. The age demanded a faster communication link, and with his foresight, he was confident the steamship would take over the supremacy of the clipper ship. And it did. And wealth once again poured into Albert Durant's coffers.

In 1863, the National Bank Act made New York a money reservoir for the government, and it was then that all available troops were sent from the city to the front, leaving a lawless element in control of New York City. The passage of the Draft Act permitted men to purchase exemption from military service. This proved prejudicial to the poor, and the fury of the vicious element was directed against the innocent Negroes in the city.

Towards noon on the morning of July 13th, Isaiah came running breathless and bleeding into Albert Durant's office.

"Mr. Albert, suh, it's a riot in the city and the Missus is at the armory," he bellowed.

Seeing the blood trickling down Isaiah's cheek, Albert Durant's facial muscles contracted. "Here now, easy," he gestured, pulling out a chair. "Sit down, Isaiah."

Isaiah instinctively obeyed.

Albert Durant pulled a linen handkerchief from his pocket, and began dabbing at the crimson flow. The Negro's little dark eyes squinted at his touch. He could see his servant needed more than words to calm him. He lifted the decanter of whiskey from his desk, and poured a good two fingers into the glass. "Drink this, Isaiah. It'll stop your shaking."

Feeling embarrassed at being waited on, Isaiah took a few sips then put the glass down.

"All of it!" Albert Durant urged.

After gulping the remaining brown liquid, the warmth of it soon calmed him down enough to tell the tale.

"Now! Tell me! What happened?" Albert Durant asked, anxious to know what caused the vicious attack against his servant and if his wife was truly in danger.

"It's on my way to pick up the Missus at the armory." He stopped to clear his throat.

"And? Go on." Albert Durant was becoming impatient.

"Yes suh! It's comin' around the corner there by the armory when I sees the mob waving clubs and breaking store windows. They came at me with a club." He narrowed his eyes thoughtfully as he fingered his cut. "Then I wupped the bays and raced 'em on ahead before they cud catch me."

"And you say Mrs. Durant is still at the armory?"

"Yes suh! She and the chillun."

You mean the girls are with her?" he asked unbelieving, knowing it was not Mercedes custom to take the girls along on the days she volunteered to roll bandages.

"Isaiah, Mrs. Durant never takes the girls."

"The Missus, she say it time the girls do their part."

Albert Durant was aware of the dissention caused by the Draft Act, but he couldn't believe it had come to this. It appeared the mob was taking out its anger against the Negroes.

The casualties of war were housed at the Thompkins Market armory, which was located at Sixth and Bowery. The wounded and dying were tended by the overworked and uncomplaining Daughters of Charity, whose first pleadings for help to the affluent society women went unheeded. Because it was the common consensus that the terrible rigors of war were only felt by the South, reality did not set in until the armory was half-filled with wounded men. This myth was quickly dispelled and the sullen apathy of the Northerners suddenly unraveled.

Not altogether insensitive to the needs of the suffering men, but mostly coerced into service by members of her prestigious ladies' club, Mercedes dutifully offered her services. However, her nervous system was such that at her first attempt at nursing, and at her first glimpse of a blood-soaked bandage and at hearing the sounds of the gasping last breaths of the dying, she fled in terror with a quivering, bared psyche. Sister Mary Margaret promptly delegated her to the back room to prepare bandages, bed pads, and medicine trays.

It was a warm, humid day with the first signs of storm clouds gathering, together with the rumbling storm of emotions and fear within Albert Durant. He had gone but a few blocks when he spotted the mob of cursed, lethal disturbers of peace waving placards and clubs. He quickly wrenched on the reins to make a hasty retreat down a side street. The carriage slithered through the narrow back streets within the shadow of warehouses and dilapidated factories now deserted. The clatter of the carriage wheels on the cobbles was the only sound in the hollow emptiness of the streets. As he neared the armory, the faint ripples of sound first heard from a distance became louder and louder. As he pulled up the horses to a stop at the back entrance of the armory, the hair on his neck bristled as the din of noise from the restless, stomping feet and shouting, of the angry mob was but a stones throw away.

He hitched the horses to the hitching post, then examined his huge gold watch. Two hours late, he whispered to himself. Mercedes would surely be suffering a fit of apoplexy. He walked quickly to the back entrance, which he found locked. After pounding unceasingly, the door secured by a chain, slowly opened. An obviously frightened nun peered through the crack.

"Sister, Albert Durant here. I've come for my family."

"Yes, yes, of course, Mr. Durant!" she acknowledged, hastily unfastening the lock, allowing him to enter.

"It's that afraid we are of the meanness invading our peace. The war has come clear to the North to plague us."

"Now! Now, Sister! Do not be alarmed. It's only a show that a group of blustering thugs are putting on. It'll not last the night," he assured her, not for a minute believing it in his own heart. Albert Durant was not a man to be intimidated easily, but his sixth sense told him that this defiant group of embittered men was not to be reckoned with. He was certain he had seen muskets flashing in the crowd, and they were not beyond using the weapons. At the very moment he spoke those words there were booming echoes of gunfire outside.

The nun nodded indulgently. "This way, Mr. Durant."

Mercedes was prancing back and forth, twisting her hand; when Albert entered the room. She was not one to adjust easily to any set of circumstances and with the steadily increasing violence outside and Isaiah's failure to come for them at the scheduled time, she was visibly shaken.

"Albert," she cried, running to him, flinging her arms about him. "Oh Albert, what possesses them to act in this hideous manner?"

"Why my dear," he said sympathetically, holding her close, "You're trembling."

"Yes, and my head aches so," she said in a strained, faint voice.

"Papa," the girls cried, running to him.

He moved to include the girls in the circle of his arms.

"What happened to Isaiah? Why did he not come for us?" Mercedes asked, perplexed at their servant's thoughtless behavior.

"He did, my dear, but was turned back." Albert had no intention of adding to his wife's fear by telling her the whole truth.

"We must leave, and quickly," he said, squeezing his wife's hand.

Mercedes cringed. Sniffing, she held back the tears.

Seeing the fear in her eyes, he tried to reassure her. "We'll be fine, my dear. I have the carriage out back. No harm will come to us."

The nun watched them leave, then silently closed the door.

"Hurry! Hurry," Albert urged, lifting the reins off the hitching post. Mercedes and the girls scrambled into the carriage. He quickly jumped up into the driver's seat. Without wasting a second, he touched the whip to the bays and they plodded off. His mouth tightened. Fear nibbled away at him when he heard the running of feet. Mercedes and the girls sat stiffly in paralyzed fear, afraid to breathe.

Mercedes uttered a faint cry when a large stone struck her on the back of the head. At the sound of her cry, Albert whirled about, staring with unbelieving horror into his wife's face contorted with pain. She pitched forward, slumping to the carriage floor.

"For Christ's sake,' Albert screeched, twisting his body grotesquely around, "you cold-blooded cowards, you've struck down a woman." He stood half-crouched, shaking his fist. The crowd of angry men knotted together stood frozen in their tracks as the carriage rattled furiously down the cobbles.

The girls sat in breathless silence, in one blur of confusion, stealing quick stiff-necked glances behind them as the carriage took off at high speed. But when the maniacal attack of the unruly crowd felled their mother, both girls let out piercing screams. They were clearly crazed with fear.

At the sight of blood oozing from her Mother's head wound, Dimity was catapulted into action by the pressure of her Mother's immediate need. She bent down and quickly tore off the flounce from her Mother's petticoat. With an instinctive, calm gesture, Dimity pressed the wadded-up cloth to her Mother's head. Dimity swallowed a sob. Her lips were trembling.

In comparison, Clarice, tore her eyes away, meeting the desperate scene with wild, frightful wails.

When Albert turned in his seat to calm his daughter's wailing sobs, and to see to his wife, he realized it was Dimity, who was ministering to Mercedes. It was a queer picture to see Dimity taking over when his oldest child sat by in a helpless daze, screaming, and making no effort to assist in her Mother's care. His eyes grew tender, for his own reserve had clearly snapped, and to see this little noble soul bravely tending to his stricken wife warmed his heart.

"Clarice, calm yourself," he pleaded, "your Mother will be all right."

She looked at her Father, shaking her head helplessly.

He could see his wife's condition was grave. Grim-faced, with jaws locked, he cracked the whip. Clarice's continuous wailing sobs drowned out the bedlam of the drays, carriages, and horse cars as they drove wildly through the spidery tangle of streets. Finally, they reached the familiar, 5th Avenue.

"Clarice, quickly," he called, reining in the horses, "run inside for Isaiah. He must go for the doctor."

He took the blood-soaked cloth Dimity had dutifully pressed against the bleeding wound. "You're a brave little girl, Mary Dimity." He lifted his unconscious wife into his arms and carried her into the house.

Mercedes regained consciousness shortly after the doctor arrived. When he had completed his examination and dressed her wound, he assured Albert that she would recover.

"Nothing solid to eat, Mr. Durant," he instructed.

Mercedes made a soft sound, a groan. Her eyes opened. "Albert," she moaned weakly, "what happened?"

"You've had a nasty blow on the head, darling," he explained, bringing his face close to hers which was ghastly pale.

She nodded her head weakly, then closed her eyes again.

"Rest is what she needs," Dr. Pennington sighed, closing his satchel, his eye following the ministrations of Lilly who was busily washing the blood out of her mistress's hair "Here now, gentle. She's got headache enough."

"Yes doctor," Lilly said sheepishly, withdrawing the blood-soaked rag and quickly rinsing it in the basin of water.

Albert's tore his eyes away from his wife for a moment. It was too painful for him to look upon the bandaged spot where the doctor had cut away her beautiful hair. He grabbed his wife's hand and kissed it. Her hand was limp and icy cold. His eyes teared as he turned to watch Lilly remove the globs of caked blood from his wife's thick black hair showering over her pillow.

"She should sleep the night through," Dr. Pennington said, turning to leave.

"But Doctor," Albert said, focusing his burning black eyes out from shaggy brows, "you can't be leaving. My wife needs you," he pleaded, rising from his chair.

Resting his hand on Albert's arm, the doctor reassured him. "Believe me, Mr. Durant, your wife will be as good as new in a day or two, but if it would give you peace of mind, I'll send a nurse in to care for her."

Looking down at his sleeping wife, Albert shook his head in agreement. In a gentle voice, he said, "Yes, by all means we must have a nurse."

At the same moment in the house, Clarice sat at the dining table sullenly picking at her food under the watchful eye of Allison Tyson, whose patience with Clarice had finally snapped. The child was utterly impossible at times and this was one of them. Always, Clarice's wrath seemed to be aimed at her adopted sister, and when Dimity uttered the merest echo of triumph to Miss Tyson that her father had commended her for her bravery for tending her mother's wound, it was indeed, one more reason for Clarice's hatred of Dimity to deepen.

Using exaggerated words with absolutely no truth, Clarice broke in at Dimity's explanation, "It was I who stopped the bleeding, not Mary Dimity." She smiled scornfully with satisfaction.

"You did not!" Dimity shouted back at her. "You bellowed the whole time. You fraidy cat!"

Miss Tyson could see the evidence of who was deceitful and who was truthful. While Dimity's frilly dress of peacock blue was blood-soaked, the pristine cleanness of Clarice's buttercup yellow dress told the true story.

Clarice's pale brow knitted into a frown. In a gesture of fury, she flicked the peas and carrots she had on her fork directly in Dimity's face.

"Enough!" commanded Miss Tyson. "That will be enough, young lady." The governess picked up the silver bell, ringing it furiously.

With both maids busy with the Missus, Nellie came running in answer to the bell. "Ma'am?" she said, standing in the open doorway.

"Nellie, will you take Mary Dimity into the kitchen with you." Her voice carried a note of irritation. "So that she may eat her dinner in peace."

The pale cheeks of Clarice flushed slightly. And suddenly, the girl began to weep hysterically. "I want my mother."

Nellie took Dimity by the hand. "Come darling,' Nellie'll warm up your dinner."

For a moment Dimity stood by Nellie's side. "I didn't do anything, Miss Nellie." Dimity couldn't understand why she was being banished to the kitchen. A lone tear fell to her cheek.

"Dimity," Miss Tyson called to her. "You did nothing wrong, child. It's Clarice's bad manners that's keeping you from eating your dinner. Oh, and Nellie, please remove Mary Dimity's dress." The governess's eyes gravitated towards Dimity. "Those stains are likely to set and ruin the dress. And Clarice."

Clarice looked up, sniffling in great gulps.

"I want you to apologize to Mary Dimity. I know you are upset about your mother. But that is no reason to behave in this ugly manner. Now!"

Seldom was there a kind word spoken between the two children for it was Clarice's passionate resentment that was the barrier. After a reluctant pause with eyes lowered, Clarice blurted out words which were almost impossible for her to utter and were barely audible, "I'm sorry!" That was all she said. Her real feelings toward Dimity remained hidden, deep within her. She'd do what she was told to do, but some day..

Dimity's lips twisted in a hopeful smile. She was content to have Clarice's apology, not fully realizing how halfhearted it was. She turned to give Clarice one last look as Nellie guided her into the kitchen.

"That one," Nellie shook her head, muttering to herself, "Hers is a fairly mean heart." Humming a catchy tune, Nellie untied Dimity's sash, unbuttoned the tiny buttons trailing down the back and lifted the soiled dress over Dimity's head of tangled curls. "We'll give it a good soak, darlin'.

Nellie kissed Dimity on the forehead. "Sit yourself down here and have ye're dinner, luv." Seeing the troubled look on the child's face, as though lost in some profound worry, Nellie sighed and sat down beside her. "Ye're a good girl that ye are."

Focusing her hazel eyes on Nellie, Dimity said quietly, "But Kiss Nellie, Clarice.she's mean to me."

Fixing her smile, she lifted the child's chin in her chubby fingers to speak directly to her. "Give it back to her, luv. It's a terrible thing to give tit for tat, but sometimes it's the only way to stifle such meanness. Mind though," Nellie touched her cheek affectionately, "ye don't take on her mean ways. She's got a fierce struggle of envy towards you darlin'"

Dimity looked into the kind, leathery face. "But why, Miss Nellie? I'm not mean to her."

"Because Dimity, ye're you, a beautiful little girl who everybody loves, and now she must share her mother and father with you."

Relieved and content at Nellie's words, Dimity sat there in the stillness of the kitchen with it's wonderful smells of cinnamon and rising bread, happily eating the sugared blueberries Nellie placed before her.

It was a long night of vigil for Albert, sitting by his wife's bedside in the gloomy gaslight with the nurse who arrived shortly after the doctor left.

"The doctor says your wife will be fine, Mr. Durant. Why don't you get some sleep?" she urged.

Images of Mercedes calling for him leapt into his mind. He cleared his throat. His throat constricted when he spoke, "But she may need me."

The nurse stared down at her patient. "She's sleeping peacefully, Mr. Durant," she said, smoothing back the stray hairs on Mercedes forehead. A look of encouragement crossed the kindly nurse's face. "You go on to bed now."

With an air of great weariness he rose to his feet and leaned over his wife, giving her a gentle kiss. "Sleep well, my darling." He paused for a moment, leaning back wearily against the four poster looking down at Mercedes who had thrown off her covers in a restless frenzy. He straightened the quilt with gentle, caressing fingers, tucking it in around her bare white throat and exposed shoulders.

"I'll leave her in your good hands, Miss.?"

"Folsum, sir," the nurse said, "Ernestine Folsum."

"Yes, Miss Folsum, thank you," he said, fumbling with his watch chain to check the time. His usual manner of sureness and domination of all circumstances was clearly undermined by his wife's injury. Harboring guilt within him, he seemed compelled to make amends by his obsequious behavior towards her.

Dimity was speechless with delight when Albert hoisted her onto the trotting pony. "Oh Papa, is he my very own pony?" she whooped delightedly.

"Yes, of course, he's your pony," Albert chuckled, placing the reins in her chubby hands.

"He is not your pony," Clarice shouted.

Albert looked over at Clarice who was sitting her new pony with a heavy frown, her arms folded stubbornly."

"Clarice! You have a new pony. Puddin' is Dimity's pony now."

"But Papa, I like Puddin' best."

"Clarice, Puddin' is too small for you. You're getting too big to ride Puddin'.

"Papa," Dimity offered, "I'll change to the new pony if Clarice wants Puddin'." It was a pity; Dimity thought that Clarice always seemed to be unhappy. Why, riding a horse was just about the happiest thing anybody could do.

"You'll do no such thing, Dimity. Clarice must ride the larger pony." Sometimes Clarice was so exasperating, especially when it came to Dimity, who was warmer, gentler and prettier than his own daughter. He wondered if Clarice would ever accept Dimity. "And Clarice, you've not yet given your pony a name. He must have a name."

Clarice sat mumbling. "Why on earth must I ride this stup*i*d pony?"

Albert did not answer. He quickly swung his powerful thighs over the back of his stallion held in place by Isaiah. "Let's ride, my girls," he shouted in a commanding voice, tapping his horse on the rump lightly with his crop.

Clarice grasped her reins with shaky fingers. Shifting her weight in the side saddle, her head spun around to give Dimity a calculating stare. Noting the pleasure on Dimity's face, Clarice realized that she'd have to change her feelings about riding. It was clear that Dimity would soon take her place at her Papa's side if she didn't. I'll never let that happen, she told herself. To keep that from happening, I'll pretend I love it as much as Dimity. She looked sideways with contempt at Dimity who was giggling joyously, her brilliant red curls waving in the breeze.

Albert jerked his stallion's leads to hold him at a slow trot to keep pace with the ponies. Following alongside, he coached Dimity. "Show your pony who's boss, Dimity. Tighten your reins, dear." Teaching Clarice to ride was a mission he'd undertaken a year ago. Although she had finally conquered her terrifying fear, it was plain the little minx had no great love for the sport. She's like her mother. She'll never be a horsewoman and ride the hunt with me.

Studying Dimity whose dancing, hazel eyes flashed excitement, he knew she was a born horsewoman. She's a natural. He was delighted. Before long, she'll be riding a real horse.

Dimity gripped the reins as they approached a wooded area. Breathless and wide-eyed her eyes followed every action of her Papa. When he set his heels to his mount's sides, she did likewise with her tiny heel touching her pony's loins lightly. When he pulled in the reins, she copied him.

No longer able to hold Falcon in check, Albert abruptly broke off in a gallop. Giving the stallion his head, he aimed Falcon toward the open field. Turning in his saddle, he yelled out instructions to Clarice. "Guide the ponies away from that steep slope."

As soon as her Papa was out of sight, Clarice seized the opportunity by giving Puddin' a swift whack on his hindquarters. The frightened pony responded by frantically lurching forward, toppling Dimity from its back and thrusting her small body down the steep slope, headlong into a bush.

Having gone a short distance, Albert had already turned around and was close by when he heard Dimity's screams.

At hearing the sound of the horse's hooves, Clarice quickly dismounted. Fear of being discovered was foremost in her thoughts and Clarice wondered if her step-sister realized that she was the one who had spooked Puddin'.

"Mary Dimity, Mary Dimity," Clarice cried shrewdly in a pretext of concern. Running down the slope with an expression of rigid resolution on her face, she was determined that if there was to be a heroine in her Papa's eyes, she vowed it would be herself.

When Albert came charging out of the woods in a wild fury to see the two rider less ponies, his usual calm and steadfast demeanor gave way to terror. Terrified of what he would find, his imagination filled his mind with frightful images of both daughters lying in a lifeless heap. He sprang free of his mount and peered warily over the edge of the cliff. The early morning mist swirled and twisted over the hollow where Dimity, shivering and trembling, clung desperately to a hawthorn hedge.

"What the devil?" he exclaimed as he picked his way swiftly down the steep incline. A sudden smile crossed his face, restoring his good humor when he saw that the child sprawled in the hedge, disheveled and dirty, was unhurt with the exception of a few bruises and scratches.

Clarice's cool gray eyes glowed with hostility as she stood over Dimity tugging at her to free her from the entanglement of the hedge. The more Clarice yanked at her, the more Dimity let out a screeching yell.

"Stop that yelpin'. You're not hurt. You cry baby," Clarice croaked crossly, glancing over her shoulder as her Papa drew near.

"Puddin' got spooked," Clarice said in a loud clear voice with a calculated look of complete astonishment.

The ruggedness of Albert's stern features softened when he saw the tears on Dimity's cheeks glisten in the gauzy sunlight.

There were no tears when the paralyzing fear coursed through Dimity as she tumbled over and over, and down, down to what seemed the devil's pit when the ground roared up in a rush to meet her. Deep inside, Dimity was filled with a bewildering suspicion that Clarice was the cause of her fall, and her tears were mostly for the pain in her heart rather than the pain from her hurt body.

Dimity smiled faintly as her Papa lifted her into his arms. "There, there now, Mary Dimity," he cooed soothingly, while he felt gently over her arms and legs, asking, "does this hurt, little one? Or this?"

"No Papa," she said, touching the deep scratch on her neck, "only here."

"We'll fix you up when we get home," he said, gently moving her head towards him to have a better look.

As they started up the hill, he turned towards Clarice. "And you, Clarice, I'm proud to see you at Dimity's side to help her."

Though wrapped in the arms of warmth and safety, Dimity's heart thumped sickeningly, for when she turned to meet Clarice's eyes, it was a sneering look of hatred she saw. Dimity's suspicions swelled inside her. She could see her step-sister possessed the savagery of a tigress.

Oh, how she wished she could tell him. Dimity looked up into her Papa's bearded face wistfully. But no! She would keep her suspicions to herself she vowed with a silent strength. The fear of being sent back to the orphanage was always with her and if she told on Clarice, she was afraid no one would believe her, especially her step-mother.

As they made their way home over a wet rutted road in a soft misty rain, Clarice sat her pony stiffly, pouting in anger. "Papa, my new riding frock is getting wet," she cried, wide-eyed and breathless, fingering the fawn-colored broadcloth skirt, "and my hair." She brushed the wet strands of hair out of her eyes.

Albert glanced at his daughter. "Clarice dear, it's only a fine mist. We're almost home." What a difference there was between the two girls. Dimity sat her pony, uncomplaining, her glittering hazel eyes dancing. But then Clarice always managed to portray the tragic figure.

Albert gave his horse a smart smack on the rump, whizzing past the two ponies, which broke into a run after him.

When they entered the mansion, Mercedes was sitting in the drawing room, staring stonily out the window, her ghastly emaciated white features rigid and tormented. Since her injury, her mental anguish had progressed steadily. She was vague and forgetful, speaking rarely unless spoken to. Most of the time she was in a dreamy, half-conscious state, retreating into a witless shell. Time seemed suspended for her. But there were times when she would fly into meaningless outbursts of violent temper which seemed to be aimed at Dimity.

The worry of his wife's alarming behavior was a tremendous weight on Albert's shoulders. In his arms at night she lay limply, cold and unfeeling. Despite the doctor's assurance that his wife would be her old self in time, Albert was beginning to digest the hard cold fact that she would never be the same.

It was agonizing for him to watch her. He closed his eyes for a moment remembering her past exuberance and good health. He gritted his teeth, opening his eyes to reality. He stood staring down at Mercedes who was regally gowned, not by her own hand, but by the hand of her devoted maid Lilly. She wore a short-sleeved, plainly cut, lilac silk morning gown. Dropping to his knees, he tenderly grasped her hand and held it to his lips.

"And how are you feeling today, my dear? You are a lovely sight," he said, looking searchingly into her eyes.

Mercedes nodded. She looked at her husband with an artificial attention, her face an expressionless blur.

With Dimity close behind, Clarice burst across the room flinging herself in her mother's lap completely ignoring her mother's secret torment. It was Dimity who sensed the foreboding change in her stepmother's unsmiling eyes. Clarice chose to ignore it.

Smothering her mother with hugs and kisses, Clarice cooed in a trilling gushy voice, "Oh, Mama,

I missed you so this morning. It was horrid riding in the rain."

Mercedes eyes lit up. She responded with a kiss on her daughter's cheek. "There, there, baby, I'm here," she said, in a clear and concise voice, speaking the first words out of her mouth that day.

Where Albert had failed to spur any interest in the world around her, Clarice had succeeded in separating her mother from her tortuous inner self, if only briefly.

And there inside Mercedes was still that absorbed devotion to her daughter.

"And Mama," Clarice pointed, "would you just look at what Mary Dimity has done to her new riding habit?"

A screech burst forth from Mercedes lips. Trembling with temper and raised eyebrow, she coiled her hands in a tight fist. "What a dirty, ugly child," she screamed, shuddering in repulsion. "You've been wallowing in the cinder path and you've ruined your frock."

Dimity breathed deeply, holding back the tears. Her new gray broadcloth riding habit was crumpled and streaked with caked mud. Her little face burned scarlet.

Suddenly, Albert's reserve snapped like a thread. "Enough, enough, Mercedes," he choked, "the child was not at fault. She fell from her pony when he spooked."

"But Papa," Clarice began.

"Clarice, be quiet," he commanded angrily. "You know very well it was no fault of Dimity's."

He gathered Dimity into the circle of his arms. "It's all right, Mary Dimity."

Clarice shut her mouth stubbornly.

"Oh dear, oh dear," Mercedes moaned, holding her head in her hands, "I have a frightful headache."

"What does it matter?" Dimity told herself. She could endure it for her Papa had the biggest, most tender heart and she knew he loved her. And then there was Nellie, whose immense broad face beamed at her with love. She touched the gold band on her finger. It was times like this that her heart ached for her brother.

DANIEL

CHAPTER ELEVEN

Mickey Eagan swore under his breath. It wasn't bad enough he was operating short-handed after losing four of his men to the war, but now he was forced to make his own collections. Impatiently, he twisted the lever of the door chime.

A tall woman in a gaudy, flimsy red and black dressing gown opened the door. "Why Mr. Eagan, sir," she said with a lilting accent. Tossing her unruly red hair out of her eyes, "do you not have your key?"

"Forgot it, Dory," he said, removing his tall hat.

Dory was the proprietress of the brothel on 108th Street. Mickey Eagan had rescued her, half-starving, from a hovel not far from his livery stable, and to this day, Dory's gratefulness sang in her heart whenever she set eyes on Mickey.

"Cover yourself up, Dory," he ordered, the muscles in his jaw tightening like cords. "Can't you see I got the boy with me?"

Daniel clutched his step-father's hairy, powerful hand as they stepped inside to a cavernous house, dark with shades drawn. The usual blaze of light and clangor of activity of the night customers was missing. Dory's customers stood around, drink in hand, waiting for a whore to free up. Among them were a few in blue-coated uniforms with gilt sparkling buttons.

Dory quickly clutched her dressing gown to her with one hand and with the other she tweaked Daniel's cheek. "So this is Daniel?"

Daniel looked up into Dory's face. Matching the smile on her scarlet lips, he smiled back.

"Well?" Mickey's tone was impatient. "Me and Daniel have got things to do, Dory. Get on with it."

Dory sidled up to Mickey, her face inches away from his. "You mean you got no time to cuddle up with little ole ' Dory?" she said, smiling sweetly, draping her arm around him. "I'll get one of the girls to stay with the youngun'."

There was a slight scowl on Mickey's reddened face for the offer was tempting. "This here's a business call, Dory," objecting in an attempt to quell his mounting desire as his eye caught a glimpse of the voluptuous white breast protruding from her gown.

Glancing downwards Dory could see he was softening by the bulge in his pants. She smiled with a silent enjoyment as she lifted out a roll of bills from beneath her camisole and handed the wad to Mickey.

Mickey quickly flipped through the bills, and nodded, pleased at the weeks take. The world was filled with vultures, but Dory wasn't one of them. Grinning, he stuffed the bills in his inside coat pocket.

"Nothin' like an afternoon of lovin' to get your motor hummin'," Dory whispered discreetly, smiling knowingly. "Shall we?" Dory hooked her hand through Mickey's arm.

It momentarily annoyed Mickey that this sensual creature held such a power over him, but glancing down at her cleavage with a reverence of appreciation, his resolve to collect his profit and leave quickly left him. His dark eyes narrowed. With a forehead beaded with moisture, he closed his gigantic hand around Dory's waist and gave her a squeeze.

Dory crooked her finger, motioning to one of her whores lounging against the piano.

"Frederica, take Daniel here and play a few tunes for him," she instructed, patting the boy on the head. "And. crack open that jar of candy."

Daniel hesitated. Looking up at Mickey, he protested, "But Mr. Mickey, you promised we'd ride the horsecar."

Mickey shook his head angrily. "What did I tell you, Danny? Can you not call me Papa? Did you so soon forget our little talk," he whispered, bending down low to look into the boy's face.

"No sir," Daniel said.

"No, you can't call me Papa. .or no, you didn't forget?"

"Yes, Papa, I forgot." He gave Mickey a forlorn look. Mickey pulled Daniel towards him, into the softness of his huge belly.

"And the horsecar will be awaitin' for us, Danny boy, just as soon as I take care of this business," he assured him, humming under his breath as he took two stairs at a time with Dory breathlessly keeping in step with him. At the top of the stairs Mickey turned. "Off with ya now."

Mickey was getting impatient. "Go with the pretty lady, Danny."

"There then," Fredericka said, taking Daniel's hand in hers. "You can call me Freddie."

For the first hour Daniel sat on the piano bench with Freddie enthusiastically tapping his toes to the rhythm of the lighthearted music she played, and sucking noisily on a peppermint candy. But as the time wore on and the novelty wore off, Daniel began fidgeting impatiently.

"When is Papa's business goin' to be done?" he asked, rising from the piano bench and backing towards the stairs. "I'll go see."

"No you don't, Danny," Freddie said excitedly, rushing to his side.

"But why?" he asked, pouting.

Finding her voice between giggles, she said, "Whatever could a little boy like you do to carry on such business. It's a big man you have to be, Daniel, before you can go up those stairs.like your Papa." Freddie gripped his hand to steer him away.

Danny looked around at the other painted ladies that broke into a feverish laughter. He'd never seen so many different colors of hair, and the dresses they wore were ablaze in a rainbow of colors.

Seeing all eyes on him, Daniel stood silent and unmoving with eyes downcast. Then at the sound of Mickey's laughter his eyes wondered upwards. When he looked up to see that familiar, reddened, face smile in his direction, the uneasiness he'd felt for being left behind quickly vanished.

Out of the corner of his eye Mickey saw Daniel's face light up. At first, Mickey had second thoughts about having Daniel accompany him on his bawdy house rounds, but after that initial rush of conscience, he knew that he wanted the boy's education to begin. The younger, the better. But knowing about the inner workings of his vast operations would follow later when he was old enough to understand.

"My business has been satisfactorily concluded, Danny boy," Mickey chuckled knowingly, lighting a cheroot. He saw the flicker of satisfied delight cross Dora's face.

Mickey and Daniel left the bawdy house, walking out into the heat of the late afternoon, and the wild metropolis crowded with pedestrians, soldiers, and thronging vehicles. They walked down the street lined with stately Lombardy poplars alive with caterpillars.

Daniel skipped happily along, ahead of Mickey, dragging a stick in his path. His lively eagerness amused Mickey. When Daniel suddenly stopped and began poking at something with his stick, Mickey wondered what the boy was up to.

"What's that you got there, Danny boy?" he asked, blowing out a cloud of cheroot smoke.

"Look, Papa," he said, jabbing at one of the fuzzy worms until a green oozy juice exuded, "he's got green blood." His cheeks were aglow with color and excitement.

Mickey chuckled. "One thing, Daniel, you ain't got a squeamish stomach like no girl." He smacked him on the backside lovingly.

They crossed at Sixth Street to catch the horsecar at Cooper Square. Busy traffic choked the bald, dirt thoroughfare. With the savage struggle of city life swooping down on them, Mickey and Daniel wove their way through the military wagons, carriages drawn by lively horses, speeding hacks and carts and wagons filled with filth and garbage, throwing out pestiferous fumes.

They clamored aboard the horse car amidst a grumbling crowd of passengers. Mickey and Daniel sat back on the red lacquered, hard seat, a seat that was somehow lacking in comfort. Inside it was dank and grimy, the floors covered with layers of foul smelling straw spattered with tobacco juice, and the air stunk of stale cigars and unwashed bodies. To Mickey, riding the horse cars was repulsive, and the ugliness of it disgusted him. But when Daniel who rarely expressed emotion lit up with his excited chatter, Mickey's thick lips parted in a wide smile. He puffed on his cheroot contentedly.

There was no doubt the boy was sorely tortured from the loss of his twin and his loneliness for Jake. The pain of Daniel's plight stirred the hard-nosed Irishman who had long ago put away all sentimentality. When all the doors were closed to him because he was Irish, Mickey was forced to resort to beggary. After enduring such hardships, he had no regrets he'd turned to crime. His once gentle eyes grew hard with a cold determination as his life of crime progressed.

As for Daniel. Mickey vowed to see to it that the boy would not be a witless weakling. Under his wing, Daniel would learn the trade. He'd be a man of strength like himself, untouched by useless sensibilities. There would be no hurt in his life. He would not be indebted to any man. As his son he would be an Irishman respected as he himself was in these tormented times of war.

Daniel drew in a deep breath. His freckled brow wrinkled, and his nose puckered at the stench coming from the two fluttering, squawking fowls held in place by the skinny, squirrely old codger sitting in the seat across from them. He was dirtier than his snow white chickens.

"Whoo!" Mickey bellowed, pointing a finger at the chicken droppings clinging to his grimy pants, "you need a chamber pot there old man."

Patting the hens with approval, the old man gave Mickey a toothless grin. He wasn't used to seeing a cavalier figure in fancy duds riding the horsecar. He watched as Mickey removed his coat and loosened his silk cravat. Hanging from his waistcoat hung a braided chain the size of a ship's rope. He oozed self-importance.

Suddenly, the horsecar came to an abrupt stop. Daniel twisted in his seat, pointing to the back of the car.

"Look Papa!"

Mickey turned to see a half-dozen men lead by a thickset man with a scraggy beard staggering onto the horsecar. The leader stood smoking a cigar with the air of a monarch looking over his subjects.

Startled by the sudden intrusion, those passengers dosing peacefully behind their newspapers dropped their papers and quickly sat up at attention. Shock spread across their faces.

"We need some warm bodies to join us in our march," the leader said matter-of-factly, motioning to Mickey and three other men."

"Are ya daft, man?" Mickey stood up to face him square in his beefy face. Mickey Eagan had heard that as soon as the draft offices opened the day before, a group of embittered men shouted in protest, refusing to go to war for a lot of "dirty Naygers." But Mickey had no idea it was this serious.

"This is a folly I don't intend to be a part of," said one gentleman. The other men passengers nodded wordlessly.

"Out!" One of the rioters motioned, sliding his lead pipe across the top of the seats menacingly. The threatening gesture brought about the reaction he counted on with the three men following him stealthily along the aisle to the back of the car. But Mickey Eagan stood his ground.

"I know ya," the leader said, staring directly at Mickey. "Ye're Mickey Eagan." Turning around, he shouted, "Hey guys, this here's Mickey Eagan, the big shot from the Bowery."

Mickey's face broadened with a smile of satisfaction. Now that he was recognized, he felt certain he wouldn't be pressured into joining the mobsters.

"You ready, big shot?" the burley man said, nudging him with his musket.

"I ain't goin' with ya," Mickey said, never taking his eyes from him. "Ye're madder than a hornet who's lost his queen. I can't have my boy here marchin' with the likes of ya and get tin' hurt." Mickey gently drew his hand around Daniel who sat trembling in fear.

"Not the big brave man I've heard so much about, I see. Made of porcelain, are ya?" he sneered, waving his fat red hand to two of his men. "If ya have a mind to keep ye're property from a flamin' torch, Mickey Eagan, ye'll do as ye're told."

Mickey's face wore a skeptical expression. Then his eyes turned hard, believing the man meant what he said. Weighing the situation and knowing he was outnumbered, Mickey wasn't dumb enough to protest too loudly. He wasn't one to run purposely to danger but then he'd not run from it either. He grabbed Daniel's hand and followed the sleazy thugs out of the car.

With Daniel's hand held tight in his, Mickey, muttering under his breath, marched alongside the howling, blaspheming rioters infuriated with bad liquor. They passed through the giant belly of the city, over cobbled streets, viaducts and bridges, brandishing clubs, knives and muskets, walking boldly past the gaping, useless policeman who remained idle onlookers. Along the route they proceeded to assault everybody in sight, clearing the streets of citizens who locked themselves in their houses in terror.

By the time the ruffians reached Fifth Avenue they were a mob of two hundred. The barricade erected by Albert Durant and his neighbors at the entrance of the palatial residential area did not stop the rioters in their excited zeal to cause havoc in the highly respectable neighborhood.

As the rioters marched down Fifth Avenue, they were momentarily blocked by a line of police officers who were called in to protect New York's influential citizens. The officers on duty in that area knew better than to ignore the threat to this residential area, which included the Mayor who resided on the posh street. At first the police tried to push the mob back with their Billy clubs, but when they were stopped by a rain of stones, the police sergeant standing in the middle of the block with a force of officers gave the order to fire. When the rioters were met with a barrage of gunfire shot over their heads in warning, the mob began dispersing, but the bullets from this volley had peppered the crowd, and a number of the ruffians were injured by spent balls. Instantly the street was flecked with the wounded. With yells of defeat, the mob surged down the cobbled street, trampling the wounded underfoot.

Mickey's face contorted into an indescribable rage and hate. "Stop!" he screamed. But it was too late. One of the flying stones had struck Daniel.

"Pa.pa" Daniel screamed, unable to get the word out.

Mickey threw his heavy arm around him, catching him before he fell. Like a thunderbolt Mickey snatched the boy up into his arms and broke out in a dead run. A cold, hollow sensation in the pit of his stomach gripped him when he saw the blood streaming down his son's face.

Albert Durant stood staring out the window, shaking his head. He licked his lips nervously. The police had given strict orders to the residents to remain inside. In turn, Albert did likewise, instructing his family to stay in their bedrooms.

"What an evil doing this is," he spat out in a hoarse whisper to himself. He raised his eyebrows at the sight of some of the neighbors standing in defiance, throwing stones at the mobsters who had been bound and determined to lay the blame of the Draft on the upper crust.

Albert's self-control left him and an overpowering explosive emotion overtook him when he saw a young lad in the midst of the melee. "God Almighty," he screeched, "the child's hurt." He flung open the front door and ran down the graveled driveway.

In his desperate effort to protect Daniel from further harm, Mickey crouched behind a large bush with Daniel in his arms. Daniel was crying in a thin frightful wail more from fear than from hurt. Daniel looked up at Mickey through tear-filled eyes. "Am I shot, Papa?" he cried in a shivering voice.

"Naw, ye're not shot," he held a hanker chief to his head. "It's just a scratch from a jagged stone aimed your way."

As Mickey sat there on the ground peering around the bush, Albert Durant approached unnoticed. Mickey's only concern at the moment was to be sure that that mass of senseless humanity was retreating. And that they were like a bunch of snarling animals with their stalkers at their heels.

Sickened from the thought that a man could have such little thought for the safety of a child, Albert Durant stood there looking down at the man and the injured boy. He was sorely perplexed for the man carried no weapon or club and he was dressed too fine to be part of those rowdies.

Albert's expression was grave when he finally spoke, startling Mickey to his feet. "For Christ sake, man, haven't you got the sense you were born with? This is no place for a child," he scolded, bending down to lay a hand on Daniel's forehead to see the extent of the child's injury.

Bitter-faced and furious, Mickey's hand closed in a knotty fist. His smoldering eyes met Albert Durants. "I'll be God damned! I don't need you waggin' your sarcastic tongue at me; you high and mighty know it all. It ain't what you think."

Mickey rushed on with his account of his forced participation. Daniel held onto Mickey's sleeve. "We was snatched from the horsecar by those hoodlums. They wanted a big showy mob, and nothin' I said made a difference. We was forced to march with 'em," he explained.

Albert Durant listened with curious interest, nodding his head. "My apologies, sir," he acknowledged, with a guilty uneasiness. He leaned forward to look more closely at Daniel's wound. Whimpering, Daniel touched his head.

"I trust we best look to that cut, young man," he said, taking Daniel s hand. If you'll follow me up to the house, we'll see to it."

Damn odd for this gent to be so helpful, Mickey thought, but from all appearances he was sincere. He had to admit, it was damn white of him.

Albert Durant hailed the police sergeant, whose men were loading the wounded into the paddy wagons. "Do you think we will have peace and quiet the rest of the night, Sergeant?"

"Yes sir, Mr. Durant," he assured him with a gloating smile of triumph. "Everything's under control. I'll be posting my men about the Avenue." His eyes traveled over the man and boy standing at his side. "These your neighbors, Mr. Durant?

Albert Durant slowly started edging towards the driveway. "Yes of course, Sergeant," he lied.

"Oh, and Sergeant, about this debris?" he pointed, stepping over abandoned clubs and placards, the evidence of the fierce attack.

"To be sure, sir. My men are busy at it."

So this was Albert Durant, Mickey thought to himself. Talk of him had reached his ears. The men of wealth in New York City were well known.

"Well, Sergeant, you and your men did a fine job. I know I speak for my neighbors as well, but I thank you." Albert Durant commented, holding out his hand. "I do hope, however, that, you'll be able to identify these scoundrels and put an end to this rioting."

"To be sure, sir! To be sure!" The Sergeant tipped his hat and went on his way.

Albert Durant turned to Mickey. "I'm sure you'll agree. I had to turn the truth a bit, Mr. ah.?"

"Eagan! Mickey Eagan. And.I thank ya sir." Mickey looked up into the darkening sky. "Looks like rain. We'd best be on our way." Daniel was leaning against him, holding a handkerchief to his bleeding cut.

"I'm afraid, Mr. Eagan, your son's too tuckered out for any walk home, and I'd certainly refrain riding on the horse-car. Let's take care of his cut, and then I'll have Isaiah take you home in the carriage." Sensing Eagan's reluctance, he laid his hand on his shoulder. "Please! I insist. For the boy's sake."

Daniel frowned as Mickey gently removed the handkerchief Daniel held to his head. "It's still bleeding." He looked at Mr. Durant and said without hesitation, "All right then, sir, I believe the cut does need some tending." With a concerned look on his face, he asked, "You all right, Danny boy?"

"Yes Papa," Daniel answered sleepily.

As they walked up the tree-lined driveway, a brisk evening breeze sent the dry, crackling leaves quivering and dancing. By the time they reached the back of the house the sky had swallowed the sun, and the light of day was gone. The heavens suddenly exploded and an eerie, unearthly glow of fiery sparks lit up the sky, and the heady fragrance of a summer rain seeped into the air.

"Come in," Mr. Durant beckoned.

Feeling awkward and out of place, Mickey stepped into the deserted kitchen and gaped around him at the opulence of it. Iron pots hung from the great brick fireplace reaching to the ceiling. He'd never seen the likes of it. Mighty different from his dreary, barren kitchen over the livery stable.

"Looks like cook left a pot of coffee," Mr. Durant said, opening the cupboard door and lifting three cups from the hooks.

"Pour us a cup, Mr. Eagan, while I get something to bandage that cut. And.help yourself to a slice of Nellie's soda bread."

He looked wonderingly at the great coal range, gleaming from spit and polish. He removed the pot and poured coffee into the three cups. He was reflective of his own life when he looked around him. Some day, he thought, I'll buy me a stove like this, and I'll have me a house just like this."

"Isn't it a grand place, Papa?" "That it is. That it is, Daniel."

Carrying a bottle of antiseptic and a torn piece of linen, Mr. Durant returned to the kitchen. "Let's have at it, my boy." He proceeded to tend his cut. At the first dab of antiseptic on the cut, Daniel gasped and his cheeks paled. He knew better than to let out a yell, but by the time Mr. Durant tied the knot in the cloth to hold it in place, his tears were freely spilling over.

"There now, all done. You'll live young man. That's a brave little fellow."

Albert Durant stared at that freckled face that had been partially concealed from him in the shadowy twilight hours. He had an uneasy mixture of feelings, of seeing a resemblance. It was a face familiar. The more he looked at him as he sat down to drink his coffee, the more the cold fingers of curiosity prodded his brain. It was a mystery he could uncover with one question if he chose.but he did not choose.

Suddenly feeling drained and empty and dazed from the pure physical shock of his frightening ordeal, Daniel folded his arms and laid his head down on the table. It was only a few minutes before he fell sound asleep.

Mr. Durant's eyes shifted to Mickey Eagan. "You are Irish, are you not, Mr. Eagan?"

"That I am, sir, and proud of it."

"It's my understanding it's the Irish who are opposing the Draft and rioting for their cause," Albert Durant commented.

"Mind ya now, I've had no part in this rioting, nor will I, or any of my Irish friends. Lot o' nonsense if ya ask me. It's the poor desperate bastards who just sailed over and can't find jobs. They've seen the senseless fighting in Ireland go nowhere, that's what's agin it. They ain't willin' to go to war to free the slaves. I hear they're lashin' out at the blacks in the city."

Albert listened, smiling. "Is that so? If that's the case, they're now at the other end of the same kind of senseless bigotry."

"This here's the first I've seen of the rioting, sir. We've not had any uprising in the bowery. I don't know how far it will go, or how long it will last, but this ain't no way to win a war," Mickey said, slurping the last swallow of coffee in his cup.

"More coffee, Mr. Eagan?" Mr. Durant held the pot over his cup.

"Don't mind if I do." Now, thought Mickey, wouldn't mind if he'd lace the cup with a finger of whiskey or two. He licked his lips thinking about it.

Albert Durant continued the conversation. "You know, you are so right, Mr. Eagan. This is certainly no way to win a war. These riots serve no purpose. My family and I were attacked yesterday," he said, taking out his gold watch to check the time.

"Nobody hurt, I take it?"

"As a matter of fact, Mrs. Durant was injured somewhat the same way as little Daniel here. Unfortunately, it was a serious injury from which she's not recovered. And." he paused thoughtfully, "I must see to her immediately. I've sorely neglected her this evening. She's not at all well. If you are ready to leave, I'll fetch Isaiah." he said. He stood biting his lip. "Do you think, Mr. Eagan, that you could direct Isaiah through some untraveled streets where the rioters are less likely to be found? That is.since much of their wrath is aimed at the Negroes. And for yours and Daniel's safety as well."

"That I can do. To be sure. And I do thank ya, sir. It was right neighborly of ya to help us out the way ya did."

"You're welcome, Mr. Eagan."

It was barely minutes after the departure of Mickey Eagan and his son when Albert Durant stood at the bottom of the stairway to see Dimity in her white linen nightie gingerly picking her way down the dimly lit stairs. Her eyes were quite wide with surprise when she saw him for she knew she was never to leave her bed once the light was out. She hesitated.

To say that he loved this child dearly was a gross understatement. In comparison to his own daughter, who was drowned in a curious, unhappy restlessness, Dimity was a charmer with happy winning ways despite her stark tragedy.

"And what my darling, Dimity, are you doing out of bed?"

Her chin jutted out in a pout. She stood twining a red curl around her finger. "I couldn't sleep cuz my tummy hurt."

He watched her with cool amusement. "Do you think it's because you didn't eat your dinner, and your tummy's hungry?"

She shook her head.

The bronze gas lamp on the newel post flickered, casting a shadow on her face.

Albert knelt on the bottom stair and pulled her into his arms. With a sudden inner clarity, Albert knew he had wronged the child. His rich baritone voice was tender. "We'll have a bite to eat and then to bed. Will that suit you?"

"Yes, Papa," she smiled shyly.

Albert Durant suddenly felt very tired and remorseful. Their looks were too much alike to be coincidental.

On the fourth day of the rioting, the Seventy-fourth Regiment of the New York National Guard was called in. With the troops on guard along the streets, the battered city gradually returned to normal. Stores that had been closed were reopened and the citizens of New York City hurried to purchase groceries and the essentials to go on with their lives. Since the riots began over twelve hundred lives had been lost and over a million dollars worth of property destroyed.

It was on that very day that Jake Trenton stood in front of the New York National Bank amidst a swarm of National Guard troops who were guarding the bank. He'd heard about the rioting and was repulsed to think that able-bodied men would shrink from their patriotic duty and rebel against the Draft Act.

Jake looked up, his eyes following the lines of the tall, formidable gray stone building. It spoke of permanency. It spoke of wealth. Fumbling in his pocket, he pulled out a sealed envelope addressed to the Chairman of the Board. In his hand lay his future.

Having just been discharged only hours before, Jake still wore his Union blues. Clutching a flour sack containing his few meager belongings, he limped inside.

He handed the sealed envelope to the clerk at the counter.

"It's the Bank Chairman you wish to see?" the clerk asked, incredulous that this scruffy young sergeant with hair to his shoulders could have business with the Bank Chairman.

"Yes sir, if you please," Jake said, shifting his weight to his good leg. "That there's a letter of introduction."

"And your name, young man?"

"Jake Trenton."

The clerk disappeared through a door.

Jake looked around at the clerks lined up behind the windows, each engrossed with counting money. More money than Jake had ever seen. Here he was in the home of the rich man's fortunes.

The clerk returned and nodded. "Follow me."

Jake followed him through a corridor lined with polished mahogany doors. The clerk opened the door at the far end and stepped aside. "Mr. Durant is waiting for you."

Jake stood on the threshold. Looking down at his dirty boots and the luxurious carpet, he hesitated to enter.

"Come in, young man," Albert Durant beckoned him in.

Jake stood before him, embarrassed at his sorry state, and wishing he hadn't come. His face tightened with apprehension.

Albert Durant looked into his dark eyes, eyes that held a strained look. The face of the tall, unhealthy looking youth framed by sparse mutton chop whiskers was grave and thoughtful. Undoubtedly, this young man had seen more than his share of misery in his young life.

"And you, Jake Trenton, are the young man Colonel Bryant speaks so highly of?"

Jake drew in a deep breath. "I'm Jake Trenton."

Mr. Durant held the letter up. "Says here you saved his life. Took the bullet intended for him by throwing yourself in front of him. Caught it in your thigh?" he asked, standing.

Sensing the young man was nervous, he quickly put him at ease. Walking around his magnificent oak desk, he put an arm around him. "It's mighty proud I am to meet you, Jake. Have a seat," he said, sitting himself on the corner of his desk. "How is the wound? Healing all right?"

"Yes sir," Jake said, shoving his sack between his legs as he sat with legs spraddled. He could see Mr. Durant was a gentleman of means, being so richly dressed and all.

"A rather rough tour of duty, Jake?" Mr. Durant asked.

Not a boasting lad, Jake answered, "Yes sir, it was a furious hale of bullets and cannon balls aimed at us at times." He paused, reflecting back. "Not a pretty sight;."

Mr. Durant could see that it was still painful for him.

"Now Jake, that's behind you."Is it a job in the bank you'd be interested in?"

"Well sir, Colonel Bryant.he says, you have many interests and many businesses. Wherever you'd have a place for me, I'd be mighty beholden."

"I understand you were Colonel Bryant's aide for the most part and handled his books?" He looked at him intently. "That's a very responsible position."

"Colonel Bryant took the time to teach me, sir." As an afterthought, he added. "I'm a fast learner."

"Well then," Mr. Durant smiled, "I'm thinking along the same lines as my good friend, Jed Bryant."You need to continue with your schooling. You're too bright, Jake, to waste those brains. You'll have a job working for me part of the time, and you'll go back to school."

To find himself treated with such warm cordiality was too good to be true. He had come ill-prepared; not dreaming this stranger would clasp him to his bosom.

Jake beamed. "Thank you, Mr. Durant. It's a dream come true."

Jake Trenton had a sparkling, infectious smile. Albert Durant liked him. If Colonel Jed Bryant could speak of him in such glowing terms, he knew he liked him.

"Any mustering out pay, Jake?"

Yes sir!

"Enough to buy a suit of clothes?"

Jake's face turned red. Knowing he needed money for a room, he doubted he'd have enough.

Seeing Jake's hesitancy, Mr. Durant reached in his pocket, pealed off several bills and handed them to him.

Jake shook his head. "I don't take charity, sir."

Mr. Durant laid his hand genially on his shoulder. "Consider it an advance on your salary, Jake. Now then, I'll see you in the morning. Eight sharp."

Jake left the bank with a glowing look of hope for his future, a future that didn't include crime. For the time being, he had no intention of visiting the Bowery. When he thought of Daniel, however, a swelling of misery filled his chest.

CHAPTER TWELVE

C hristmas vacation gave Dimity the excuse she needed to leave college. Though she dearly loved Mount Holyoke, she had made her decision. It was high time to be master of her own destiny and to take up her rightful place in the Durant household.

Thinking back over the past six years, Dimity gazed out the train window just as the sun took her closing bow and the curtain of darkness opened on another nocturnal drama.

Why must I pay in loneliness and be exiled from my home, she'd asked herself many times. Clarice was to blame for the constant rivalry between us, not I. It was Clarice who was forever breaking into temper fits to touch off one more crises. Clarice was the sole creator of the continuous static and stormy atmosphere that sent Mercedes overwrought and prostrate to her bed, refusing to eat.

When, in a moment of sincere affection, Albert Durant had held her close to him and said, "It's for your own sake as well, Mary Dimity," she understood. Sending her off to Boarding School was the only way he could keep peace in the family. She'd shed her tears in private. It was her way of repaying him. Dimity had to admit she was not regretful. In a way she was thankful for the blessed escape from Clarice's vindictive, hateful ways.

She had served her time away. Now she was going home where she belonged before life slipped away from her.

The scream of the train whistle woke Dimity out of her reverie. Pinned to the seat between two elderly travelers, she waited until the train pulled into the depot before retrieving her portmanteau from the overhead shelf. It was the Hudson River Railroad Depot where she'd stood with her family to watch Lincoln's mourning cortege before his body was boarded on the train to be returned to Springfield, Illinois for burial. That was so long ago it seemed to her.

The train was crowded with Christmas travelers who seemed to plod along at a snail's pace. With mounting impatience and excitement, Dimity elbowed her way through the crowded aisles in a most unladylike fashion.

She breathed a prayer of relief when she saw her father step down from the familiar two-seated closed carriage. Holding the reins of the two prancing bays fitted with their gleaming jangling harnesses was her beloved Isaiah. Though bitter cold, the air was fresh and delicious after the smoky stale air of the train. Dimity drew the velvet collar of her red and black plaid cape up around her neck. It set her to laughing when her black velvet bonnet was lifted off her head by a brisk blustery wind. With her one free hand, she deftly snatched it and forcefully slapped it back on her head of windblown chestnut curls.

With arms opened wide, he greeted her with a wide cheerful smile. "Mary Dimity," he said, relieving her of the portmanteau.

"Dear Papa," she said, standing on tiptoes to kiss the soft whiskered face so dear to her.

Albert Durant was so pleased to have Dimity home, though it was only for two weeks, and he vowed it would be two happy weeks. He studied his daughter's beautiful face full of devotion and loyalty. She had given so much more than she had received.

They walked gingerly to the carriage, over the perilous slipperiness of the snow-packed walk with Dimity lifting her flowing skirts high.

Though her father looked somewhat paunchy since she saw him last, and his brown whiskers were spattered with more gray than she remembered, he looked the same to her.

The loveable gray-haired colored man tipped his high silk hat, holding the carriage door open. "Gud evenin' Miss. Mighty glad to see you home." He held a deep fondness for the young miss as did all the Durant servants.

"Good evening, Isaiah. It's good to be home," she smiled, clutching her billowing skirts as she stepped into the carriage.

Dimity chattered gaily all the way home, but the important news she would keep until later.

Dimity entered the house into the familiar grandeur of the entryway. Looking up the stairway at the garlands and red velvet bows intertwined around the rungs, and the decorated tree laden with lighted candles, she exclaimed, "Oh Papa, it's so festive."

"Yes, isn't it?" Clarice is the artist in resident," he chuckled proudly, removing his top hat and black cape flecked with snow. "Here, dear, let me have your wrap."

Before stepping into the drawing room he put his hand on her arm detaining her. "Mary Dimity, I must warn you of your mother s condition, ' he said, his usual booming voice slowed to a whisper. "I'm afraid she has failed and is quite feeble since you last saw her."

Shocked at his words, she put the palm of her hand on his whiskered cheek. "I am so sorry, Papa. You never mentioned it in your letters."

He shook his head. "No need to worry you, dear." He patted her cheek. "And.Mary Dimity, I neglected to tell you, we have a guest for dinner this evening. Mr. Trenton is a business associate of mine. Indeed, not only is he the Assistant District Attorney, but my lawyer as well."

Out of the corner of her eye Dimity caught a fleeting glimpse of the tall, handsome young man as she bent to kiss her mother gently. "Mama," she said, "how perfectly lovely you look."

Mercedes looked at her with vacant unseeing eyes while fingering the carving of her chair with trembling fingers that were never still. The convulsive working of her thin mouth oozed with slobber. Dimity could see that she was in a world where nothing existed for her.

Their guest quickly rose from his chair to greet Albert. "Good evening, sir."

"Jake," Albert grabbed his hand affectionately. "I'd like you to meet Mary Dimity, who's home from college."

Dimity straightened from her mother's chair to face him.

"I'm pleased to meet your acquaintance, Miss Durant," he said in a heavy bass voice. He couldn't help but stare. She was a vision. Tiny, slim, but voluptuous. The loveliness of her took his breath away. He was struck by the proud upturn of her nose, not pointed like her sister's. It was truly a classic cameo face.

"And I am pleased to welcome you to our home." Her scrutiny of him was brief for discretion's sake. But she was taken with his sparkling, infectious smile and his appearance. She had been too long away from a man's world, but she was sure the pearl-gray worsted wool suit he wore was the latest fashion and the black and silver striped cravat added that dashing touch.

Albert frowned, turning a disapproving face towards his wife. He did not approve of having her present when they entertained guests. He sat down beside her and lifted her cold fingers to his lips. It only served to agitate her.

Jake's dark eyes glowed. I understand you've had a long train ride, Miss Durant."

"Yes indeed, and a bit tiring."

Their conversation broke off at the sound of Clarice's hoarse and demanding voice doling out orders with the air of a sergeant. "Lily, tell cook not to delay dinner any longer. Papa and Mary Dimity are home."

When it was clear all threads of interest had slipped away from Mercedes, Clarice took over as mistress of the Durant household.

"Mary Dimity," Clarice cried, sweeping into the room giving her an air kiss. "It's a pity you do not have time to freshen up before dinner," she said, looking her up and down.

"Good evening, Clarice," Dimity said, knowing it was Clarice's way of saying she looked a mess. And with her sister looking positively regal in that peacock blue gown, Dimity was sure she looked dowdy alongside her. But she was too tired to care.

Jake watched the two young women standing side by side, who greeted each other with such cold politeness. The hollow-ness in their greeting surprised him. It was as though they had an armed truce between them. He regarded the two sisters with a marked curiosity. How different they were. He could see no resemblance whatsoever. Clarice, though not unattractive, had course heavier features contrasted to her sister's which were more delicate. Then he looked over at their mother who looked more like Clarice. The poor woman seemed to be longing for death. In all the years he'd worked for Mr. Durant this was the first time he'd met his daughters, or was invited to his home.

Albert sat holding his wife's hand, speaking to her in soft whispers. "How are you feeling this evening, my dear?"

Mercedes made no response.

He looked up at Clarice who had made no effort to speak a word of welcome to her sister. His face was flushed and his manner nervous for he so wanted Dimity's homecoming to be pleasant.

Rising from his chair, he took his daughter by the arm and spoke to her quietly, "Clarice, your mother prefers to have dinner in her own room."

"Mama," said Clarice, sitting on the edge of a gilt chair, "would you rather have dinner in your room?"

There was no answer. No connection with life.

Dimity wondered why Clarice would direct a question to a woman so uncomprehending.

Albert spoke with a rising intensity. "Clarice, ring for the nurse." He was visibly disturbed that Clarice had gone against his wishes. If the truth were known, he knew it mattered little to Clarice if her mother had her dinner alone in her room. Too often he'd seen Clarice ignore her mother for days without a bout of conscience. He wondered if her act of solicitousness was for Dimity's benefit.

Dimity sighed with relief when Lily appeared in the doorway. Clearing her throat, she announced "Dinner is served.

As Albert directed the seating at the dining room table, Dimity excused herself. I must step into the kitchen for a moment, Papa. I've not had a chance to say hello to Nellie."

"Not too long now, my dear, or dinner will get cold."

With her back to Dimity, Nellie stood at a new shiny gas range Dimity had not seen before. She walked quietly on tiptoes and quickly yanked the strings of Nellie's apron loose.

Dimity giggled.

Overjoyed at the sound of that voice, a screech burst from this huge buxom woman. Dropping her stirring spoon, Nellie twisted around and pulled Dimity into her arms.

"Dimity, lamb," she whooped delightedly, holding her face in her hand to look at her more closely. "Let's see that doll face."

"Oh Nellie," Dimity said excitedly, "it's so good to see you. I've missed you so." This mother figure with the mirthful face was still as warm and gentle as always.

"Mary Dimity!" Albert called, "dinner is waiting."

"Oh Nellie, I have to go now, but wait, up for me. I'll come to your room after our guest leaves."

The conversation picked up when the dessert was served, but at every turn in the conversation, Clarice took the opportunity to babble on about her exciting plans for the Christmas season and the Spring Charity Ball she was chairing. Among high society, Clarice was the height of respectability with her participation in all of New York City's society functions. In reality, it was a mockery and a cover-up for her father's benefit. Her real interest took her to parts of the city that would be forbidden and off limits had he known about it.

"That's quite a responsibility, Miss Durant," Jake remarked.

Clarice smiled. "Sure isss."

Albert eyed his daughter with a flicker of annoyance. After three glasses of wine she was beginning to slur her words. Disturbed, he rose from the table. "Clarice, come with me." He helped her up out of her chair and slowly walked her to the doorway where he paused momentarily.

"Please, finish your dessert. I shall be back shortly."

For Albert the great hope he had of kindling a marriage between Clarice and Jake was dashed. Though Jake Trenton was not a man of great wealth, he was a man of substantial means he accumulated while in his employ. He was a likeable chap and a man of honor. Albert was mortified at Clarice's behavior and knew it would no doubt affect Jake's opinion of her.

All through dinner Dimity's face had been blocked from Jake's view. Moving to Clarice's vacated chair directly across from Dimity, he reached over and slid the tall silver candelabra with its flickering red candles out of the way. "Do you mind?" he asked, sitting on the edge of his chair and leaning his elbows on the table.

Jake was not insensible to the beauty of a woman, but his hunger had not been for the love of a woman, nor was it for wealth. His motivation for living was his dedication to improving the lot of the poor and cleaning up the city. It was a devouring passion for him. Yet, there were times when he'd known the loneliness and emptiness of his life. But if ever he could be seduced by a woman, it was this woman sitting across from him, whose warm hazel eyes reflected the pleasant glow of the candlelight.

"No, of course not." she answered, her cheeks coloring.

"My word, that was a marvelous dinner," he offered, in an attempt to make conversation.

"Yes, indeed, "I'm afraid I ate too much," she agreed, taking the last bite of chocolate cake into her mouth."I truly believe no better cook exists in this world like our Nellie. I assure you," she said, sliding her empty cake plate out of the way, "it's been eons since I've had edible food." She grinned widely. "And it seems eons since I've had my favorite cake. Nothing like this at college."

Knowing that she was a lady of breeding and had been brought up under the most genteel and luxurious surroundings, he marveled at her pure naturalness. Unlike her sister, Dimity was completely without affectations, which was repulsive to him.

"And Miss Durant, do you mean to say we'll only have a short time in which to get acquainted before you return to college?"

She looked at him coyly. Before she realized what she was saying, she blurted out, "But I'll not be returning to college, Mr. Trenton." Touching her white fingertips to her lips as if to stop the words that had already tumbled out, she sighed, "Oh dear! I shouldn't have said that."

He looked at her mischievously. "Ah, and why on earth not?"

At the sound of her father's footsteps, she suddenly appeared uneasy and breathless. In a serious, beseeching voice, she whispered, "Oh please, Mr. Trenton, do not say anything to my father. He knows nothing of my decision."

His spirits soared. This was one thing he knew about this enticing creature that no one else knew. "Of course, of course, ' he said, with a mischievous glint in his eye.

All at once, the dining room door flew open. Beyond hypocrisy, Albert spoke up with open directness, "I'm afraid Clarice imbibed a little too freely this evening. The excitement of Christmas and all."

It was Albert Durant's honesty that Jake Trenton admired the most. Even so, it did not diminish his success in the world of business where unbridled rascality prevailed.

"Shall we have our brandy before you depart, Mr. Trenton?"

"Whatever is your pleasure, sir?"

Albert poured a finger of brandy into the sparkling crystal glasses. Dimity was surprised he included a glass for her.

"So!" Albert Durant said, lifting his glass, "to Jake, this diligent warrior, whose passion for justice and decency took him away from me."

"Not so, Mr. Durant, sir," he disagreed. "I'm still your lawyer and pleased you'll still have me.

I predict a brilliant future for you Jake, my lad."

"Thank you, sir."

Jake's face was suffused with color as he spoke animatedly about his new job as Assistant District Attorney and his hopes for a crime free future of New York City.

They sat talking until the candles burned low. When Jake looked over at Dimity whose eyes were growing heavy, he rose from his chair. "I must say goodnight. I'm afraid I've overstayed my welcome."

"Not at all!" Albert assured him. "I'll have your carriage brought around." He left the room to summon Isaiah.

Jake and Dimity walked to the front door. She handed him his overcoat. "Good night, Mr. Trenton, "Dimity said, smiling at the tall man with intent eyes who was a stranger just a few hours ago.

"Please! Call me Jake. And." he added clumsily, may I call you Mary Dimity?"

"Why yes, do."

Before the courage to say it left him, he blurted out, "Mary Dimity, I would like to see more of you."

She flushed. It was a delicious feeling to have a man interested in her. "That would be lovely,"

There was a new awakening in her for the need of male companionship. She was delighted to have a man in her life. Especially this man.

"Good night." He walked out into the wintery night.

All was excitement and mystery in the Durant household that Christmas morning. No celebration in New York City was touted more than the customary open house held every year at the Durants. It was the highlight of the Christmas Season and for the fourteen years that Dimity was a Durant, some of the happiest times of her life.

At the first sounds of footsteps on the stairs, Dimity flung the covers off and jumped out of bed.

Shivering, she quickly slipped into her dressing gown and drew open the drapes. She smiled for there was all the promise of a clear dry day after yesterday's snowfall. She started for the door, but retraced her steps to the commode where she impatiently splashed cold water on her face.

Mercedes and Albert were already seated at the dining room table when Dimity entered the dining room. "Happy Christmas, Mama," she said, kissing her on her cheek. Mercedes nodded her head. "Happy." she responded.

Albert held out his arms to embrace Dimity. "And you, my dear, the happiest of Christmases."

"Oh it will be, Papa," she said, hugging him, "and Happy Christmas to you."

Clarice came down the stairs humming happily. She burst into the dining room already dressed in her morning dress of fuchsia wool. "Oh Papa, isn't a glorious day for our party?" She kissed Mercedes and Albert. "Happy Christmas" she said, looking towards Dimity. "My, my, Mary Dimity, still not dressed? I should think you could be dressed for our Christmas breakfast." she chided, taking her place, "and at least combed your hair."

Feeling ill at ease at her remark, Dimity quickly tucked a stray lock behind her ear, pinning it in place. "If you prefer, I can go up and change before breakfast," Dimity said, rising from her chair, ready to yield to her wishes. In no way did Dimity care to provide a reason for Clarice's disfavor on this day.

"You'll do no such thing, Mary Dimity," Albert interceded. "Please dear," he motioned, "take your seat and have your breakfast. You can change before we open our presents."

Clarice's eyes narrowed and her lip curled in a cruel smile.

While Lily served the large tray of eggs, ham and potatoes around the table, Lucinda, who had taken over as nurse for Mercedes, sat next to her mistress. "I'll help the Mrs. Mr. Durant, sir."

Albert gave her a grateful look.

"Papa, can't we open our presents now," Clarice asked, excitingly, sliding her half-eaten plate of food off to the side.

"Clarice," he said, pointing his fork, "You've barely touched your food. We'll not be opening one present until you've finished your breakfast." He proceeded to butter a biscuit and handed it to her.

Drawing her plate within reach, she accepted the biscuit without a word. After eating a few bites, she started in again, "But Papa, it's getting late and I have much to do before our guests arrive."

"You have time to eat," he insisted.

Dimity looked over at Mercedes who was smacking her lips with relish. "Mama, are you enjoying your breakfast?" she asked.

Mercedes shook her head stupidly.

Clarice let out a long sigh. An expression of disgust clouded her face. "For the love of God, Mary Dimity, can't you see Mama is confused and beyond carrying on a conversation?"

Dimity looked at her, astonished. How dare she speak as though her mother was not present?

There was something hard in her, as hard as a cut diamond.

Lucinda dabbed at Mercedes mouth with a napkin, and then helped her to her feet. "I think the Missus is ready for her morning nap, sir.

"Yes, Lucinda, I do believe she is."

Dimity rose from her chair to help Lucinda with Mercedes.

For an instant Albert sat facing her with a fixed and searching expression. As soon as they were out of earshot, Albert looked at his daughter with hurt eyes. "Your mother, Clarice, still understands kindness. She might enjoy a kind word from her favorite daughter occasionally."

Clarice was not about to be chastised for her behavior without first speaking out candidly. "Am I the only one in this family who is facing the truth about Mama?" she asked. Before he could answer, she continued. "You know, Papa, she is living in a world of shadows, and it is a puzzle to me why you continue treating her normally, and speaking to her as though she understands. I suppose it's your way of denying that her illness exists. I cannot do that." She paused, knowing her words were hurtful.

He looked at her with sorrow in his eyes. It was as though she no longer possessed any bond of love to her mother. "What you say may be true, but no matter Clarice, for it could be that far down in the depths of your mother's soul she understands and is saddened by your uncaring ways." His voice rose until he was shouting, "As long as your mother lives, young lady, you will show her the respect she so deserves. Is that clear?" He raised a shaking finger.

"Yes Papa," Clarice said softly, "It is clear and I bow to your wishes." She leaned towards him speaking calmly, "but it is not I who persists in closeting her away in her room when we have guests. This only adds to the wagging of tongues, Papa. Not that I care a fig if it does, but we can no longer hide Mama's illness."

"It isn't so much that I'm hiding her away, Clarice. It's entirely for her own sake as she becomes so visibly agitated. It is far better for her to remain in her room when we have guests."

Clarice rose from her chair and put her arms around her father's shoulders. "I am sorry Papa if I've displeased you.

At any rate, the issue is closed and you understand my feelings." He patted her hand resting on his shoulder. Shall we retire to the drawing room and open your presents?"

Dressed in her new smartly-tailored red woolen gown, Dimity was already sitting in wait for them.

"My, you look especially fetching, Mary Dimity," he said, fingering the delicate lace trim at her throat. "Lovely! Just lovely!"

Clarice felt the material between her fingers. "Is this the gown Mrs. Gaylord made for you?"

"Yes! Finished only yesterday, as a matter of fact."

"It is very nice," Clarice commented, her green jealous eyes flashing. "Odd! I did not see it when I picked up my Christmas dress on Tuesday."

Dimity gave Mrs. Gaylord strict orders to keep her dress hidden from Clarice. Too often, she had sneakily copied Dimity's gowns which seemed to have such unusual becoming touches that her own lacked. Adding a bow here or there, a flounce or a colorful piping were special touches that added style and originality to an otherwise plain ordinary gown. You could be a creator of high fashion," Mrs. Gaylord often told her. But Dimity had no desire to make fashion design her life's work.

After whisking the gifts out from under the tree, they returned to the drawing room where the gaily wrapped packages were quickly denuded of their wrappings. No surprises were found in the first round of gifts, just the usual scarves, gloves, books and toiletries.

When Clarice opened the last gift to be handed to her by her father she knew it was her main gift. She opened the black velvet box expectantly. "Oh Papa, how beautiful," she exclaimed, her fingers gently caressing the sparkling diamond and pearl necklace. It was worth a fortune, she knew.

Albert passed a sealed envelope to Dimity bearing her name.

Dimity tore it open eagerly, having no idea of its contents. She slipped a white card out. On the underside of it was pasted a picture of a horse. It was signed, "Happy Christmas, Mary Dimity," Papa.

She looked up into her father's eyes, perplexed.

He smiled widely. "You have a new boarder in the stables, Mary Dimity."

At last comprehending his meaning, Dimity sprang from her chair and threw her arms around him. "Oh Papa, thank you."

She's a fine mare, a good hunter," he chuckled, "just waiting for you to ride her."

Despite the expensive gift that lay in her lap, there was in Clarice's eyes a queer evil look of jealousy.

Pressing a quick kiss on her father's cheek, and with a swish of her skirts, Dimity turned to leave the room but then hesitated for a moment at the doorway. "Her name, Papa. What's her name?"

"Glory!"

"Glory," she repeated to herself as she hurriedly removed her cape from the hall tree. Clad only in thin-soled shoes, she went tearing out the back door to the stables. Albert followed close behind her.

"She'll be a good breeder, Mary Dimity," he said, swinging open the stall door.

"Oh Papa, she's a beauty," Dimity said, stroking the mare's sleek ebony coat. "She has a high and noble head.'

"I knew you'd be pleased with her," he laughed.

"Oh Glory, you're my heart's treasure." Her fingers glided over her lovingly. "Could I ride her now, Papa?' she cried impatiently.

"We've no time today, dear. We must finish packing the food baskets for the poor. Come, we must go." Seeing her disappointment, he assured her, "We'll be riding if it s not too cold in the morning; as soon as the sun is up, we'll be off." He was an excellent horseman and having one of his daughters enjoy the sport as much as he was pure joy.

Dimity gave the horse one last pat on the head. "See you in the morning, Glory."

She loved the stable odors, the musty smell of hay and the pungent scent of newly polished leather, and never had she been squeamish of the manure odor as was Clarice. It was all part of the world of horse flesh and she adored it.

As they walked the flagstone path back to the house, he looked down at Dimity's shoes, which were snow covered. "I'm afraid Nellie will have something to say about your wet feet, Mary Dimity." He reached over to pull her shawl **over** her bare head.

With a surge of affection for him she slipped her mittened hand through his bent arm.

DIMITY AND DANIEL

CHAPTER THIRTEEN

The first hint of the arriving guests was the sound of the tingling sleigh bells as the horse drawn sleighs wound their way up the driveway.

Dimity and Clarice ran down the winding stairway as the sound reached their ears.

"Just remember, Mary Dimity, I'll be greeting the guests in mama's place, not you," Clarice crossly. The thought of her half-sister joining her in the receiving line was an intolerable scenario she could not endure.

Dimity was too happy to have Clarice spoil her day. She looked at her with smiling hazel eyes, and tossing her head in a carefree manner, she retorted, "I don't care a wit about standing at the open door and being chilled to the bone.

Excited guests called greetings to one another as they entered the house anticipating the day's festivities. It was a house of savory, delicious smells of roast goose and roast turkey, of burning hickory logs and evergreens. At first, the children of the rich sat around stuffing their mouths with dried fruits and sweets from the groaning table and boasting of who had the most expensive Christmas present. But finding they were being ignored by the grownups, they soon took to entertaining themselves by playing tag throughout the house.

Surrounded by a circle of well-wishers, Dimity searched the throng of guests. Surely, the whole of New York City was here. Her roving eyes caught the sight of Jake Trenton staring at her. He was leaning against one of the tall columns leading into the drawing room. He was a hulking, solid—shouldered young man and so attractive. He smiled. Just as he started towards her, he was beckoned to Albert's side to meet one of the guests. "Jake Trenton, come here and meet my dear friend, Mr. Morgan and his lovely wife, Frances Louisa."

Jake nodded to Mrs. Morgan. "Ma'am!"

"How do you do, young man?" J. Pierpont Morgan offered his hand. Albert has held you in such high regard. It's a pleasure to meet you. My congratulations on your new position.

Jake tried to think of something interesting to say, but couldn't. "Thank you, sir."

J. Pierpont Morgan was not only a business associate, but a friend who served on the Union League's board of management with Albert. Together they had organized the Metropolitan Museum of Art."

"And how is Mrs. Durant?" Mrs. Morgan asked, eyeing him keenly, knowing that Albert guarded his privacy. For Mercedes was an enigma among his friends.

"I'm afraid not well. She will not be joining us. Oh, by the way, as a contributor, you should know that Jake here will be directing the distribution of the food baskets," he said, changing the subject.

Someone called out over the heads of the throng. "When do we deliver the food baskets, Mr.

Durant?" The crowd joined in. "Yes, when?" "Isn't it time?" another called out.

Albert laughed at their enthusiasm. "As soon as you've collected your wraps. The sleighs are loaded and ready. Jake Trenton here is in charge."

"To your sleighs," Jake shouted, laughing jovially.

At the announcement, an uproar of gaiety arose from the young people who dashed towards the front door to retrieve their cloaks. Chattering and laughing and close to bursting with excitement, the swarming guests gathered in a circle in the center of the foyer.

"Mother, can't we please go?" Arabella Wilson cried, tugging on her mother's skirt nervously.

"Absolutely not, Arabella. Cecilia's barely thirteen."

"But mother. why should she have to tag along?"

"Enough said! Your turn will come soon enough. These young people cannot be looking after you children."

The cold wave of the early part of the week had plummeted the temperatures to zero. The holiday revelers huddled under blankets in the sleigh ride to Tammany Hall. Gliding through the deserted streets, their enthusiastic holiday spirit burst forth with a singsong chant when they came upon a passerby. "Happy Christmas! Happy Christmas to you and yours.

Jake Trenton sat across from Dimity and Clarice, sandwiched between Harley Stokes and

Lem Foster, two would-be suitors of the Durant sisters. Their eyes were bright with admiration for Dimity whose long absence from the social scene made her company all the more inviting. While Clarice sat stiffly and silent with her gloved hands resting awkwardly in her lap, Dimity chatted gaily and waved excitedly to the pedestrians. If it were not for the profound attention given to this event by her peers, Clarice would have no part in it. She had no interest in the poor and their plight.

Dimity's precocious exuberance delighted Jake. His eyes slid over her. Whipped about by the wind, the ribbons of her beaver bonnet had loosened, tossing about the riot of red curls freely about her face. That luxurious head of hair seemed to take on a brighter shade of red against the solid white background of the snow-covered world surrounding them. Jake s face brightened at the sight of her, at her slightly tilted nose, at her creamy skin now flushed to a healthy glow.

Jake was a dashing figure and so masculine. Few ladies had ever resisted his charms. But of all his conquests, they had never stirred in him t he emotions he was feeling for Dimity at this moment.

"My dear," Jake said with a concerned look on his face, "you'll catch your death." He reached over and slipped her bonnet back in place. With deft fingers he tied the black satin ribbons in a bow under her chin. "There!"

How sweet he is! "Thank you Jake," she smiled into his dark eyes. She glanced sideways at Clarice. Unable to hide her growing rage, Clarice momentarily stopped her small talk to give Dimity the evil eye. Dimity took new courage at the thought of Clarice's displeasure. It was a positive personal triumph and Dimity planned to make the most of it.

A silver-haired policeman stood guard at the entrance of the hall calling greetings to the arriving sleighs, "Merry Christmas, and God love ya for ye're generosity."

Jake sprang up; giving orders to the young men of the group as he helped Dimity and Clarice alight from the sleigh.

Above all the voices, Jake yelled out with a lively exuberance, "Men, unload the sleighs and carry in the baskets."

The carefree group bounced out of the sleighs and raced off in a laughing run to remove the precious cargo. Swinging open the doors with their arms full, they stood aside to allow their excited, giggling lady friends to pass through. Entering into the warmth of Tammany Hall, the monument to graft, the atmosphere of the lively bustle of activity, and gay loud voices further enlivened the group's holiday spirit.

A policeman with index finger pointed to the tables lined up against the wall, shouted out instructions, "Place them on the tables, folks. And thank ye."

The annual basket distribution to the poor was one of the most important events of the year in New York City, and organized by none other than Mickey Eagan. In advertising the event, Mickey posted listings of the participants throughout the city. The lists included dozens of prominent New

Yorkers, some of them millionaires, many of them politicians, or just ordinary citizens who made it a point to show up if only to prove their good will. This was the only occasion when Broadway, Fifth Avenue and the Bowery met on the same turf. On this Christmas day, Mickey's son Daniel was left in charge while Mickey returned to his saloon on Catherine Street to pick up an extra barrel of beer.

Dimity's was a life of prosperity, but a whisper of memory of things familiar were awakened when she saw the long lines of New York's ragged poor and unlucky down-and-outs. Dimity, her face suddenly grave, looked upon the homeless children wearing discarded rags, whose faces mirrored their utter hopelessness.

For Jake the sight was humbling. His eyes wandered from one sad face to another. A surly rage at their plight engulfed him. It was a plight in his young life he recalled to his mind. In no way did it salve his troubled civic conscience that his group was providing food for one day to these poor unfortunate souls. They needed far more. This exploitation of them was a ruse the rich used for their own benefit in order to perpetuate their reputation and to prove their sense of civic duty. Albeit once a year. It was pure hypocrisy and it sickened him.

While they stood around, Clarice, in her finery of velvet and furs, stood apart, uninterested, not wanting to be close to the ill-bred, dirty mass of humanity. As her eyes wandered through the hall, she spotted the tall handsome figure that walked around arrogantly, directing the noisy group of volunteers in their feverish activity. He seemed to be in charge. She smiled widely. She had no idea he would be here. She made her way to his side.

Dimity watched as her sister greeted the bold young man with dark auburn hair, whose gaudy mustard-green greatcoat fit tightly across his muscular shoulders, displaying the young virility of him. His demeanor was confident and demanding as he barked orders to several burly men who had interrupted his conversation with Clarice.

Full of silent bewilderment, Dimity stood watching them as Clarice flashed the young man an enthusiastic smile, the like of which Dimity had never seen coming from Clarice. He smiled engagingly while handing her a glass of refreshment. His look of keen interest puzzled Dimity. It was clear they knew one another.

"By all that's holy, is he a friend of Clarice?" Anna Greeley asked as she joined Dimity at her side.

The girl's sudden presence startled Dimity. "Oh Anna! Why, I'm sure I don't know. But then, I can't say I know all of Clarice's acquaintances. Being away and all."

"Quite handsome," Anna chirped.

"Who is he?"

"He's Mickey Eagan's son."

"And pray, who is Mickey Eagan?" Before Anna could answer, a loud commotion arose in the back of the hall. One of the policemen ran in a dead run to speak to Danny Eagan.

"Oh God! No!" he screamed in a tight, choked voice. He turned on his heel and shot out of the hall, leaving Clarice standing there in shock.

Before Dimity and Anna could follow the streaming curious mob out the door, the exit was choked solidly with struggling humanity trying to get through.

Pushing through the tangled mass of bodies, Jake saw the body of Mickey Eagan stripped of his clothes, save for a pair of drawers, lying in the blood spattered snow. Kneeling next to the body was the huddled form of Danny Eagan who was struggling to remove his greatcoat to cover his father.

On either side of him stood Quincy and Ira, the ever-watchful bodyguards who had been ordered by Big Kick to stay at the hall to help Danny.

Quincy laid a hand on Danny's shoulder. "No Danny, put your coat back on," he said flatly, as he covered Mickey Eagan with his own coat.

"Get a doctor, Quincy," Danny cried. "Hurry."

"It's too late, Danny," Ira choked, patting him gently.

Danny looked at him with vacant eyes, and then slowly sagged to the ground. An agonized voice screamed out as Danny shook his fists in a death grip, "You bastards! You dirty rotten bastards."

For several seconds a desperate silence fell over the crowd who cowered in the background.

Disbelieving, in one stunned glimpse, the shock came to Jake like a sledgehammer. It was Danny, the Danny he knew so long ago. Danny who had gone the way of dishonesty and petty thievery, following in the footsteps of the corrupt Mickey

Eagan. It was the life that Jake had chosen to turn his back on, a life without Danny. This was not a new thought for Jake. He'd often despised himself for it.

A worried crease appeared on his face. It was his place to take charge here. This was beyond the limits of the law practice he'd known as legal consul for Albert Durant. With a quick dismay, he realized he was experiencing his formal initiation into the crime world.

It was his troubled civic conscience and his desire to clean up the city that persuaded him to give up his private law practice. Jake Trenton wasn't the young innocent lawyer many thought him to be. He knew about the corruption in the city. He knew that the Irish gangs were not the only gangs, that the Jews and the Italians were also part of the vicious criminal factions, each gang having a recognized privileged territory with a dividing line. Word on the street was that Mickey Eagan had once too often stepped outside his bounds into the expanding Italian quarter springing up west of the Bowery along Mulberry and Mott Streets. It was widely known that Mickey Eagan was buying up property in that area. When Mickey began collecting rent from the Italians, he was crossing over into enemy territory and blatantly flaunting his power in their faces. This was not to be tolerated by this more aggressive Italian gang, many of whom had been groomed in Sicily.

With an air of assurance, Jake walked over to the Sergeant in charge who appeared absently preoccupied in a dizzying sympathy, largely due to his long friendship with Mickey Eagan, who had regularly greased his palm.

"I'm Jake Trenton, Assistant District Attorney," he introduced himself. And your name, Sergeant?

The elderly officer nodded. "Sergeant Tim Donley, sir," he answered, his voice all aquiver.

Jake heard the shrill clanging and the rattling wheels of the police wagon approaching.

"You and your men clear the area," Jake instructed, looking around him. "This is no place for women and children.

At that very moment, Clarice let out a shriek at the sight of the brutally beaten body, whose crushed skull oozed the human debris of brain matter and blood. Her mouth gaped open as blackness closed in on her and she slumped to the ground. Dimity rushed to her side. Slipping to the ground, she cradled Clarice's head in her arms. Opening her eyes slowly, Clarice whimpered, remembering the nightmarish sight. Still shaking from shock, Dimity frowned in sympathy for she, herself, had nearly fainted at the ghastly sight, but had quickly turned away.

As the police officers dispersed the crowd, Jake touched the arm of Daniel. "We'll have to remove the body, Mr. Eagan."

"He'll not be taken away in a paddy wagon," Daniel's rich baritone voice protested. The well-remembered voice of Daniel, the child, was gone. In his agony of mind his sad hazel eyes met Jake's without recognition.

He doesn't remember me, Jake thought. The frightened, lost child had grown into a tall, strong man. Jake had no doubt that Daniel possessed the stamina of soul to see him through this personal tragedy.

Jake stepped back as Quincy covered the battered face of the dead man, then with the help of Ira lifted the body and carried it to the waiting carriage.

Once again Jake put his hand on Daniel's arm. He spoke with an effort. "Mr. Eagan, the police will need to question you if we are to get to the bottom of this killing."

Daniel looked Jake up and down with raised eyebrows. "Be damned to you, mister," he shouted hoarsely. The hate within him rose like a giant. His features contorted in a grimace like an enormous beast ready to pounce on his prey. I don't know who the hell you are and I don't care."

"Assistant District Attorney, sir!"We have only your interest and safety at heart."

Daniel grunted in disgust. "Lies! All lies! Where was that stupid twaddle of protection for Mickey Eagan?"

Heads turned as his shouts went snapping through the cold air. "If that slimy-eyed rat face wants war, he'll get war," his voice boomed.

Jake could see he was not the Daniel he remembered, a little fledgling bird, unwise to the ways of the world. A cold fear shot through him as he watched Daniel turn away with stumbling footsteps. With a daring born of a blooded stallion,

Daniel was as dangerous as any criminal in this world ablaze with hate.

The carriage with Mickey Eagan's body fled down the street. The tragedy they'd witnessed had taken hold. It was a subdued, tamed lot from the gay, wild, party group of a short while ago.

His dark eyes opened wide when Jake realized the sleighs lined up at the curb were waiting for him. Waving his hand, he cleared his throat. "Gentleman, do not wait for me. You must get these ladies home." As he approached the Durant sleigh, he paused, breathless. Harley and Lem were busy tucking the lap robes around Clarice, Dimity and Anna.

But Jake," Dimity said, seeing the proud lift of his chin. "You'll have no way home."

He hung on her words. "I'm afraid my duties will keep me here for a time, Mary Dimity, but Sergeant Donley will see me home." He patted her gloved hand resting on the side of the sleigh. "Off with you now, it's beginning to sleet," he said, looking up into the gray sky as a silver mist of fine sleet began to fall.

Dimity sniffed into a handkerchief, turning beaming eyes on him. "I declare," she whispered to Anna, "he is a take charge sort."

"And handsome, too," Anna said turning her attention to Clarice who showed no spark of interest.

Jake saw Dimity look shyly away as his eyes met hers. With those eyes, and with that face and that charming way about her, Jake frowned thoughtfully; some lecherous young buck is surely bound to snap her up for his wife, unless I beat him to it.

The freezing moisture gathering on the street glistened as the sleighs clattered down the street amidst a clang of sleigh bells. Shivering and white with cold, the passengers bowed their heads against the icy sleet and headed home-ward.

DIMITY AND DANIEL

CHAPTER FOURTEEN

Albert was fuming. "Surely, my ears are deceiving me. What's this?" Albert roared, looking crestfallen. A cold sense of bewilderment swept through him, then anger. He paced back and forth. "You will not quit college," he bellowed. He stopped his pacing to stare at her. "Is that understood?" The veins stood out in his sinewy neck. "What on this earth has gotten into you, Mary Dimity? Have you not seen my disappointment in Clarice's failure to complete her last year in college? As you well know, she's been a great trial to me."

Dimity's heart sank. She cast down her eyes, shrinking back as Albert fumed. She realized in her anxiety that in his eyes she had committed an unpardonable breach of trust by not discussing her decision beforehand. Dimity hoped that his bark was louder than his bite but there was no sign of that soft heart she'd known all her life. She could only hope that he would come around to her way of thinking and understand. It never occurred to her that he would take it so hard.

"I am sorry, Papa," she said in a shaking voice while standing her ground. "I've been carted off away from the family to make Clarice happy for the last time." Nervously, she fingered the tiny gold ring on the chain hung about her neck, knowing she had uttered the unmentionable. "I want to finally take my place in the world and if Clarice is part of it, then so be it."

Albert was restlessly walking back and forth. He halted his pacing to face her. He blushed darkly, stung by her comment, for he knew it was the truth. For now, he chose to ignore it. "And what do you think you are being groomed to do, Mary Dimity?" He did not wait for her answer. "To take your place in the world," he said, studying her, noting the clumsy shyness of the little girl had long transformed into a no-nonsense sophisticated young woman. "It is important to me that you receive the best education available. Indeed! For two young ladies who will inherit a tremendous amount of money, it is vital."

Her big hazel eyes were fixed on him. "But Papa, that is the point." Her face became thoughtful. She needed the right words to give her argument substance. "There is more to life than being a do-nothing socialite and all the other tiresome things associated with that aristocratic life. You know, Papa, a person has to do things for her own soul, and arranging for charity balls and concerts is not a life that appeals to me. Such a life would starve my soul."

"And the status of wife and mother? Is that not in your future plans, Mary Dimity?"

"Of course, Papa," she agreed dutifully. "Some day."

For the first time in her life she was facing up to what she wanted, and a violent longing to do something on her own. "This last year has been a wretched, unhappy year for me," she touched his arm affectionately. "How can I explain?"

His kind touch on her cheek gave her courage to go on.

Gulping back tears, she continued. Her tone was sad. "I feel like a stranger in this house. Except for you. And except for Nellie." She quickly brushed a tear away. "To be honest, when I was little, I wanted to get away from here. From Clarice. I've always underestimated her meanness." She gave a deep sigh. I was hoping against hope Clarice would eventually like me for myself.and Mama too."

Seeing the sadness in her face, Albert's anger was aroused. How could he have allowed this to happen to her? He sat down heavily in his swivel chair.

"My spirit." she hesitated, "it's as though my spirit has been crippled, Papa. I've had no identity."

He saw the honesty in her beautiful, teary eyes. He held out his arms to her.

She bent to kiss him on his whiskered cheek.

He could deny her nothing. As a little girl and as a young woman, she d never once gone against his wishes, nor had she ever asked for anything or ever complained. He hadn't, realized the extent of her unhappiness and loneliness. He was filled with a sick, remorseful feeling. If, Albert thought, this was one way he could make it up to her, he would support her.

His head inclined attentively. "And where, my dear, do you think you want to work?"

"I think," she said, gathering more confidence, "I'd like to work at a newspaper."

"A newspaper?" He burst into uncontrollable laughter.

She looked at him despairingly. Reasons why she wanted to work on a newspaper rose to the surface of Dimity's mind. She averted his eyes. "What better place to learn about the world, Papa, than a newspaper."

Albert raised his eyebrows. "I will tell you this, Mary Dimity; ladies from respectable homes do not work at a newspaper office.

"Oh!" she stammered, "are you worried that you will be exposed to the gossipy prattle of New York s aristocratic old biddies? Do you think my character may be tarnished because I choose to be a part of the real world?"

"I, for one," he said angrily, "have never worried about what people think as far as my business is concerned. When it concerns my family, yes, I admit, I detest the waggling tongues of gossipers." At the sound of a carriage in the driveway, Albert twisted around in his chair to look out the window through the thick transparent icicles trailing past the frosted glass. "There she goes against my wishes," he said, sniffing the cheroot he removed from the humidor on his desk. "Out on a day like this with drifts up to the carriage wheels." His thoughts were pierced by an awareness of the distinct differences between the two girls. Clarice s defiance at his authority had long been a thorn in his side, while Mary Dimity, he thought gazing at her with tenderness, was the joy of his life. And now that quiet heart of hers was aflame with an inner fire. A fire of desire. Dimity's conquest.

"Sit down, my dear," he motioned to the chair beside him. "It seems most improper for a young lady to seek employment at a newspaper where only men work. I m not so sure such worldliness would become you, Kari Dimity.

"It's being a part of the world, Papa. It's a much more important education."

"You know, dear," he said softly, "I would give you anything in the world. If this is what your heart desires, then I'll help you. It so happens I do have connections at the New York Herald." He smiled widely. "I'll see what I can do."

She sprang up from her chair, turning her prettiest smile on him. "Oh Papa," she cried, flinging herself at him. "Thank you, thank you."

He rose and slipped his arms around her. "But.Mary Dimity," he said, cupping her face in his huge hands, "do not deceive yourself. In the business world, men are unaccustomed to working side by side with women. They'll destroy you if you give them a chance. Realizing she did not believe him, he added teasingly, "You'll have scars to prove it."

"Oh Papa, I don't believe that," she laughed, rolling her eyes at him, "and besides, I'll not let that happen." On tiptoes, she gave him a quick kiss and happily spun around in graceful pirouettes, pausing at the door.

"Papa, do you think. I mean would it be possible to go see your friend today?"

"Not today, dear." The expression on her face mirrored her disappointment. "Possibly tomorrow," he chuckled. "Yes, I'm sure I can fit it into my schedule tomorrow."

Dimity giggled, nodding her head. "Tomorrow."

"Yes, tomorrow may be the beginning of your worldly education." He winked.

His reaction to her happiness was infectious. Albert's laughter followed her out the door. Shaking his head, he muttered to himself, she'll land on her feet. I'm sure of it.

Dimity stood on the top stair peering anxiously over the banister to see who had come calling. She leaned up against the railing and smiled. Why, it was Jake Trenton standing in the doorway. Though she listened intently, she could not decipher his muffled words spoken to Lily. If only her heart would stop pounding so, she could hear better. Had he come to see Papa? Surely, he was not calling on Clarice. Dimity proceeded down the stairs.

As she reached the bottom stair, she heard him say her name. I've come to see Kiss Durant."

"Miss Clarice?" Lily asked.

"No, Mary Dimity," he replied. At that moment, he looked across the wide hall to see her coming towards him.

"Mary Dimity," he said, passing his great coat and hat to Lily. "Good afternoon, Ma'am," he bowed.

Her fair coloring darkened with a sudden blush. Pretending she had not heard, she said, "I'm afraid Papa is not at home.

"It is you," he smiled, "I've come to see. He stood rubbing his hands. "It's mighty cold out there today.

"Dear me, forgive me, for my bad manners. This hallway is so dank and cold with all the doors closed. "Shall we sit by the fire in the drawing room?" she asked, drawing her woolen shawl snugly about her shoulders. Dimity shivered. "I fear you are chilled through."

"Yes, the warmth of a fire would be most welcome." His eyes followed her graceful, exquisite figure, her billowing, flowing skirt accenting that tiny waist. He'd thought of her constantly since he'd met her. There was no doubt he was in awe of her beauty, but he wondered what it was about her that fascinated him so. Was it the gentle sweetness of her voice? Or was it her adorable mannerisms? She was not coy or flirtatious like so many women he knew. He admired that about her, that uninhibited naturalness. If he was not mistaken, she seemed interested in him.

There was a secret excitement within her. They were alone. She, Dimity, alone with a man. "Do sit before the fire, Jake. We'll have some tea to warm us," she said, ringing for Lily. She sat down beside him on the settee.

Presently Lily appeared in the doorway. Yes, miss?

"Oh, Lily," she said, feeling ill at ease with the unnaturalness of playing mistress. "We'll have tea here in the drawing room.

"Yes, miss!"

"And Lily," Dimity called to her. "Some of Nellie's little seed cakes."

"How extraordinarily fortunate I have you all to myself.

Where have you been, Mary Dimity, all my life?" He liked seeing the quick color in her cheeks at his remark. Jake's penetrating eyes wandered to her parted lips. "It's one thing that piques my curiosity, Mary Dimity. Never seeing you around when I'm at your father's office. Have you been hidden away all these years?"

Was he teasing her? She felt his dark eyes were looking straight through her. "Yes," she replied sadly, "in a way you might say I was hidden away, away from the family in boarding schools, away at college."

His arm went around the back of the settee. He studied her closely. "However, I must say, I do remember a devilish little girl peaking around the corner at me at the office. Surely, you are not that little girl?" he asked with raised eyebrows.

She burst into a giggle. "Did that little girl have freckles sprinkled all over her face?"

He winked at her. "I'm afraid so."

"Oh bosh! It was me!"

He leaned closer to her, sliding his forefinger across her tilted nose. "No trace of a freckle." He smiled.

She raised her beautiful eyes flecked with gold. Suddenly, his expression grew serious, and the cleft in his square chin was more pronounced.

"About yesterday, Mary Dimity, I am indeed sorry that you were a witness to that horrendous scene."

She shrugged her shoulders. "I admit, Jake, it was most disturbing, and knowing that such violence exists was truly unsettling." That, same sick feeling she felt at the sight of the murdered body once again swept over her.

Seeing her sudden paleness, he grasped her hand. "I am sorry, Mary Dimity, for bringing the subject up. Try to forget it."

She looked at him thoughtfully. "Jake, if you don't mind, would you please call me Dimity? The family insists on calling me Mary Dimity, but I do prefer being called Dimity."

"Dimity," he whispered. The ormolu clock on the mantle ticked loudly as he repeated softly, "Dimity. Yes, of course. I like it."

He could think of nothing but the question in his mind, and the main reason that brought him here. "Dimity," he said, 'as you know I'm investigating yesterday's murder. He hesitated momentarily. "Today I went to question Danny Eagan, and just as I was ushered in, Clarice was leaving." He was deliberately leaving out the important part - their embrace. He had been rattled at the sight of the two of them in each other's arms.

"Are you aware that Clarice and Danny Eagan are friends?"

"Do you mean Mr. Eagan who." she stammered, and then fell silent when

Lily entered the room laden with the tea tray. Dimity gave her a grateful look as she set the tray down on the low squatty table in front of her.

"Thank you, Lily, I'll pour."

Jake waited until the servant closed the door behind her. "I mean Danny Eagan, son of the man killed."

"Why no! Although." she paused, holding the teapot in midair, "I did see Clarice speaking to him just minutes before he ran out the door." She passed him a cup of tea. "And you say you saw her with him today?"

"Yes."

"Did Clarice see you?"

A wave of guilty uneasiness coursed through him. "I'm quite certain she couldn't have missed me."

"But she pretended not to see." Before her thought was out, Clarice burst panting into the drawing room.

She looked questioningly at Jake and then at Dimity. By the look on Dimity's face, Clarice knew Jake had told her. "So." she barked, facing Jake, her eyes glaring, her face red with indignation, "you've told her. You had no right to carry tales back to my family."

"I'm investigating a murder, Clarice. I have every right to ask questions."
Jake set his cup of tea down and rose from the settee.

With extraordinary self-control, he said, "Clarice, if you are involved with Danny Eagan, you are making a very grave mistake."

Dimity remained silent. She could see by the hard set of Clarice's mouth that now that she knew her secret, it would only serve to drive a deeper wedge between them.

Clarice stood there for a moment, hesitating. She needed to gain back her control and time to conjure up a believable explanation. "It's not what you think. A wild piece of nasty gossip. I only paid Mr. Eagan a brief visit to express my condolences. After all, it was the least I could do when he was so kind and helpful at our Christmas Charity Event. The dear man was that grateful. Her voice lifted into a lilting unnatural laugh. "Surely," she shook her head, "you couldn't possibly think it was any more than a casual acquaintance." She couldn't remember if Jake had witnessed their embrace. She didn't believe so. Removing her loden green bonnet and matching cape, she flung it over a chair, and sat down next to Dimity on the settee.

"Ooh, seed cakes," Clarice cried with delight, breaking off a huge piece and stuffing it in her mouth. She then glanced in Dimity's direction. "I do hope Jake didn't make a great to-do about this, Dimity," she choked, gulping down a swallow of cake.

Dimity looked into her step-sister's heathen eyes. What a liar, she thought. She doesn't care a rap what I think.

"Jake mentioned you seemed to know him is all."

"Acquaintance is more the truth," she said nonchalantly, her plain angular face turned towards Jake.

Jake regarded her with disgust. He couldn't help himself. It was beyond understanding how superficial and deceitful she was. So different from Dimity. You wouldn't think they were sisters, he pondered.

"I must say, Clarice, if that is the case, I'm mighty glad to hear it, for this man is part of the criminal faction in the city."

Clarice looked contemptuously at him. "That's purely hearsay."

"Not so, Clarice."

She gave a shrug. Reluctant to continue the conversation, Clarice rose from the settee, retrieved her wraps and marched towards the door where she paused. Turning to face him, she said haughtily, "I'll thank both of you to keep this incident to yourselves. There's no need to discuss this with father." She turned and left the room.

Dimity gave Jake a sorrowful look. She felt wretched. "Do you really believe Clarice has been seeing Mr. Eagan, Jake?" Remembering the couple's animated conversation at the charity event, doubt shadowed her thoughts.

Jake's impulse was to take her in his arms to comfort her. Even though he thought otherwise, he did not wish to cause Dimity further anxiety by telling her the truth.

"Not really, Dimity. He grasped her hand and held it. "I m sure it's as Clarice says. Kind you, you're not to worry your pretty little head about this."

"If you say so, Jake."

The ormolu clock on the mantle struck four o'clock.

"I'm afraid I must be going."

Clarice was standing at the top of the stairs out of sight, straining to hear their conversation as Jake and Dimity stood at the front door. Clarice fiddled nervously with the buttons on the bodice of her dress, unbuttoning, and then rebuttoning the tiny buttons in quick needless, jerking motions. It was near time for Mr. Durant to be home, and she knew her father so well, the master of judging undercurrents of suspicious behavior between herself and Mary Dimity. And with Jake Trenton's damnable honest trait, she was afraid at what might happen if her father should come in at this moment. It was not until the door closed behind Jake did Clarice relax and cease the movement of her unconsciously driven busy fingers. Her head felt light. She was giddy with relief.

DIMITY AND DANIEL

CHAPTER FIFTEEN

Though tucked away quietly in a back room of the New York Herald as a proof reader, Dimity's first few months at the newspaper were exciting. She soon found the newspaper was a mirror of life, arousing in her a sense of reality to the world around her.

From the first day, no friendly hand reached out to her. Hiring women in offices and shops was unheard of, and such snide remarks as "a woman's place is in the home" sent tears rushing to her wide, eager eyes. One day, after weeks of hearing echoes of torturous criticisms about herself, she bounced out of her chair in a fury of defiance. In her aching need for human fellowship, she marched head on into the tumult and upheaval of the outer office.

Huge, drooping gaslight chandeliers hung from the ceiling, lighting the room with a hazy light. The large room crowded with scattered tables and desks was filled with the stale air of smoke and whiskey fumes and the roaring, rowdy laughter added to the abyss of madness.

Dimity looked around her with a sharp distaste, at the old wood flooring spattered with tobacco spit that had missed its mark. The men working at the serious business of getting out a newspaper had the look of wild animals, with faces flushed, and hair and clothes disheveled in a disgraceful, slovenly way, as though possessed by the devil and lost in their wild lust of storytelling.

An audible silence pervaded the room when all eyes followed her to the city editor whose scarred roll-top desk, surrounded by a double row of green steel file cabinets, was heaped with papers, files and ledgers.

"Excuse me," Dimity stammered, standing directly behind the man filling the large swivel chair with his bulk.

Felix Holt, a man of about forty-eight, swung about to face her. "Yes'um little lady," he said, wiping his thick lips on his rolled-up shirt sleeve. "What can I do for you? Need some more work to proof?" He continued chewing loudly.

"No sir, Mr. Holt, I'm not here to ask for more work. My table is filled with two years of work to proof."

He pushed his steel-rimmed spectacles back on his nose. "Well now, that's what you're here for, isn't it?"

A stab of bitterness stung her. On fire with her thoughts, her words rushed out at him. "Am I also here to be ignored and hidden away as though I have a disease? It's only human to expect to be treated with respect, with an ounce of friendliness by your fellow workers. And," she went on breathlessly, "I highly resent being ridiculed by this motley crew who call themselves reporters."

He thought for a moment or two, then rose from his chair. He towered over her. "If my boys here have been disrespectful, I'll see that it stops. They're a lively bunch, but I'm that sure it's not intentional. You know, little lady," he said, scratching his head, "when you work among men, you'll find it's the peculiar way about them. If it's a life's work you can't abide, you're always welcome to leave." This was a girl of whose existence he had scarcely been aware these past months. And here she was standing before him talking her little heart out.

"I shall not be forced to leave, Mr. Holt," she went on with increased boldness. "I've come here to gain experience. I want to write. To be a reporter. And if putting up with bad manners is part of it, I'll do whatever it takes. And". she hesitated, "I'd appreciate it if you'd address me by my name."

His huge body shook with laughter. "You need to be a lawyer to practice law, and you need to be a doctor to practice medicine, and you, Miss Durant, need to be a writer to write." Why, this girl can't be happy rubbing shoulders with the rest of New York's millionaire children is beyond me, he pondered.

"I am a writer," she insisted, reaching in her blue apron pocket for a folded up piece of paper. "I think my writing is just as good as some of the stories I've seen printed. I've written this piece," she said, handing it to him, her burning enthusiasm flashing in her eyes. "It's about the black blight of poverty in this city," she explained. Her heart had ached to write a story about the poor homeless children at the Catholic Center, where she volunteered each Saturday. Since Christmas she and Jake had spent their Saturdays at the Center.

"So what's new about that?" He shrugged. A story in a newspaper's got to be news." He sat back down in his chair perusing her story, his eyes widened in incredulity. He nodded. "Not bad," he said, sliding an apple towards her. "Had your lunch?"

"No sir!"

The mass of russet hair lifted high on her head added to her pertness. He couldn't help himself, but he liked this spunky young woman. He looked up at her. "You don t get no free ride in the newspaper business, Miss Durant," he chided her. "You have to win your way, inch by inch, story by story. An eye for a story, that's what you need," his hardy voice boomed, his bloated face reddened.

Felix Holt's superior scrutiny unnerved her. Dimity could see he was accustomed to having the last word. She dared not show further umbrage towards her employer.

Her ardor, her earnestness broke through his armor. With a clumsy flourish he waved a piece of paper at her.

"A list of social events," he said. "I need a society reporter. That I do." He put his booted foot up on his desk. "Had a feller I thought could do the job, but his liken' for liquor kept him from writen' the story." He lifted a cup to his lips. Gazing over the rim, he watched her. You, Miss Durant, with all your society friends, think you could write the society page?"

A flash of triumph swept through her. "Oh Mr. Holt, yes. Yes, I'm sure I can. Thank you!" she said, taking the paper from him.

"Remember, now, it's a trial I'm givin' you. Do a good job, and it's yours." Waving his hand, he swallowed a great gulp of brown liquid. "Off to work with you."

The rest of the afternoon sped by, and at the end of the day, Dimity threw on her hat and coat and bolted out of the huge building. Her head in the clouds, she clutched her reticule to her breast. Spring was in the evening air. All of earth and sky seemed to sing along as she hummed to herself with joy in her heart.

Overcome by a rush of excitement when she saw Jake waiting for her, she flung herself into his arms. Pleasantly surprised at her show of affection, he slipped his arm around her shoulders. His eyes probed hers.

"Dimity, what is it?"

Her face crimson at her brash show of boldness, she quickly stepped back to regain her composure.

"Oh Jake," she smiled, her eyes dancing, "Mr. Holt: has given me an assignment."

That sweet charming smile of hers melted him. Although he was pleased at her happiness, he wasn't so sure what this meant, and the struggle within him to accept the shocking fact of Dimity's employment had been a strain on him. Especially so, since he intended to ask for her hand in marriage. So far, he'd been able to hide his feelings, but he didn't know how long he could continue that farce.

He helped her into his buggy. Climbing in beside her, he clucked at his red mare. His spirited horse took off galloping at full tilt down the gas lit street. She sat beside him gloating, with a proud lift of her head, her russet curls fluttering in the spring evening breeze.

Glancing sideways at her fondly, Jake smiled. "Tell me all about it when we get to the restaurant."

Dimity broke into a delighted smile. "Oh I will, Jake. I will." Dimity drew in a long breath, feeling content as a tit-fed kitten, sitting beside Jake whose fine handsome profile did strange things to her heart.

The dim gloom of dusk spread across the city as they drove along. Spread before them was a vista of exploding traffic through the streets, of workers going about their business of returning home after day's end. Their buggy mingled in amongst: them at a rapid pace, in sync with the rhythm of the crowded street traffic, alive with the rattle of carriages and drays and tired pedestrians precariously threading their way across the avenues.

Jake couldn't take his eyes off her as they sat across from one another at the Phoenix restaurant. Jake ordered champagne. It was to be a night of celebration. How hauntingly beautiful she was.

Dimity's felt a rush of excitement and her pale hazel eyes flickered with delight when the waiter filled their glasses with champagne. Jake always made her feel so special. "Jake," she whispered, leaning across the table, "what are we celebrating?"

"For one thing, my dear Dimity, our being together."

She grinned.

"And I'm sure before the evening is over we'll have something else to celebrate," he said teasingly, holding up his glass in a toast, "to us." He touched his glass to hers. He smiled at her over the rim of his glass. "Now tell me, Dimity, what is your news?"

"Oh Jake, I've been assigned to report on the social events. Isn't it exciting? I'll be a real reporter."

At first he couldn't answer. He could only worry what this turn of events would do to put a damper on his announcement.

She could see the smile had left his face. "Why Jake, is something wrong? Aren't you happy for me?"

With an effort, he gave her a weak smile, but the congratulatory words would not come freely.

"Jake?" She was confused. Above all, she wanted Jake's approval.

He could see her disappointment. "That's wonderful, Dimity. One more reason to celebrate," he said, halfheartedly.

During dinner, Dimity continued to chatter on excitedly.

After a few more glasses of champagne, Jake gathered up his courage. He took her hand in his, then drew out an envelope from his breast pocket. "Dimity, I have something for you." He handed the envelope to her.

It took every ounce of control to put aside her curiosity and her desire to tear it open, but she followed her feminine instinct to open it in a leisurely, ladylike fashion. She removed the expensive engraved stationery and began reading. She gasped. To Mary Dimity Durant, my dearest love: I, Jake Trenton request your hand in marriage with the approval of your father. Will you share your life with me?

Her mouth dropped open, and the paper slid from her hand. She stared down at the printed words in her lap.

Gently, Jake turned her face towards him. Looking into her lovely face, his eyes softened. "I have loved you since the very first moment I laid eyes on you, my beautiful Dimity."

Oh Jake!" she gasped in sheer delight. It was the moment she had waited for, in fact, longed for. She touched her fingertips to his lips. She nodded. "Yes! Yes! Dearest Jake! I will be your wife."

His features relaxed at her words. He dug into his pocket and drew out a small box and opened it.

Her eyes widened as he slipped a ring on her finger. An emerald encircled in a ring of diamonds.

Suddenly, Jake took her hand in his, and brushed it lightly with his lips. "I want to kiss you. On the mouth," he said breathlessly. "Away from here and prying eyes." Always keeping a tight rein on his passionate feelings for her, he now ached to hold her in his arms. Unknowingly, many a night she had ignited the flames of passion in him, by a look, or by the seductive curl of her lips, or a low-cut gown, only forcing him to exit quickly. His insides aflame, he raced to a local brothel to satisfy his aching lust though only a temporary solace until the day Dimity consented to marry him. But he knew he must not rush such a courtship. For the sake of social decorum, and for the sake of Albert Durant's approval.

Her breath caught in her throat as his gaze moved to her firm full breasts rising enticingly above her lace-trimmed neckline. She knew he wanted her. Never, in all these past months had he held her in his arms. Dearest, dearest Jake. Always so proper.

The restaurant smelled of candle wax, expensive perfumes, heady wines and garlicky roasting meats. They sat there in their new discovery of each other, oblivious of the sounds of laughter and movement about them, separated by the rest of the diners, separated from the rest of the world. Drunk and giddy in their new—found love, they laughed and talked incessantly.

All through the meal, Dimity picked at her food, lifting a forkful of food to her mouth without taking a bite, then putting it down to stare at the sparkling circle on her finger.

Suddenly, Dimity froze. She stared disbelieving at the mirror of herself guiding her half-sister, Clarice, through the open doorway. The devilish handsome man was no other than Danny Eagan. The notorious gang leader.

"Dimity, what is it?" Jake asked, following her gaze to the doorway. "You're as white as."

"It's Clarice."

"Your sister?"

Her eyes narrowed. "My half-sister," she hissed, "with that rogue, Danny Eagan."

He looked at her with a puzzled expression. He was not surprised to see Clarice with Danny Eagan. He had seen Eagan and Clarice together many times. His mistress, he was informed by the detectives who had him under surveillance. Jake was only perplexed at her words. "Your half-sister? I don't understand. You're saying Clarice is adopted?"

She smiled sadly. "I am the adopted daughter." She could see by the startled expression on his face that he did not know. "Surely, Papa mentioned it to you at some time or another."

"No," he shook his head, "Albert never told me."

"As his lawyer, I would have thought."

"My darling Dimity, I'm sure he felt there was no need." Gently, his hand grasped hers across the table. "His love for you is no less than for his own offspring, from my observation, even more so."

Grinning delightedly, she added, "Do you really think so?"

He squeezed her hand. "I know so."

Her thoughts raced as she stared disapprovingly at the couple sitting across the room in a secluded corner. "Do you think Clarice is in love with Danny Eagan?"

He laughed half-heartedly. "I'm sure it's just a passing infatuation for Clarice."

"I hope so," she sighed. "Papa would have an apoplexy.

"Tell me, my darling, about your adoption." He paused, looking into her shining hazel eyes. He so wanted to kiss those parted lips. "Did you come into the Durant household as a tiny baby?"

She inhaled deeply. "I was six years old when Papa took me home with him." She turned away, remembering the loneliness and fear. Remembering the brother she never saw again. A tear escaped down her cheek.

Realizing it was painful for her, Jake touched her cheek, brushing the tear away. "I didn't mean to pry, dearest Dimity," he sputtered, feeling guilty.
She wanted him to hold her in the warmth of his arms. I.

He slowly lifted a finger and placed it on her lips. "Shh! Another time, he said softly, "we can't have you sad on our special evening."

Grateful for the interruption, Dimity nodded. "Yes, another time." She wanted nothing to mar the happiest time of her life.

While Jake settled the bill, Dimity fidgeted in her seat as she strained to see past the palm blocking her view of her half-sister.

"Ready, my dear?"

At the touch of Jake's hand on her arm, she reached into the folds of her skirt for the piece of stationery and carefully placed it in her reticule. A piece of paper she would cherish all her life.

"We'll go out the side door, Dimity," he said, guiding her in that direction.

"No!" She stood erect. "We'll do no such thing. I want Clarice to know that I saw her. And Jake, if she wants to be seen in public with that rogue, then the public will know about it in the newspaper."

Dimity made a turn around the palm and deliberately paused in the aisle to rummage through her reticule. When Dimity looked up, Clarice was staring at her. She gasped. Her fork slipped from her fingers.

Without a word, Dimity walked on with Jake at her side.

"That bitch!" Clarice choked.

Danny Eagan, puzzled at her remark, looked up from his plate of food. "What bitch? Who?

"My half-sister."

"Where?" he said, looking around. "I'd like to meet her." Danny Eagan had never met any member of the Durant family. And for that matter didn't even know she had a sister. Theirs was a clandestine affair and her obvious furtiveness sorely revolted him.

Clarice turned to him, giving him a glaring look. She's gone.

He reached for his half-lit cheroot, inhaled deeply and blew out a cloud of smoke. He leaned towards her. "I'm good enough to bed down with you, Clarry, but not good enough to meet your high falutin family and friends.

Her small blue eyes glinted in anger. Why had she let him talk her into coming here?

"This sister? Why'd she skip out without speaking to you?"

Clarice's face trembled a little for he had looked at her in a most peculiar and threatening way. "Danny, you know what the problem is. We've talked about it. If Papa knew I was seeing you, he'd cut off my inheritance. It was her impetuous nature and hunger for excitement that first drew her to him. She knew full well of Danny Eagan's reputation, of his womanizing, of his ruthless gangster activities, and killings. It didn't matter. With her, he was gentle and loving. She loved his muscular active body, and his good-natured smile in that still boyish face. But she did not miss the hatred that glittered in those hazel eyes of his when he spoke of his enemies, There was no doubt that he was a man with violent animal instincts, those same instincts that had protected him in the streets. He once told her, 'If I have to kill to stay alive, then that's what a man has to do.

It was true at times she was torn between the fear of discovery and his love, but she couldn't control her obsession and need of him. She no longer had control. She could not rid herself of the passionate love she had for him. The only thing that mattered was Danny and being with him. Danny Eagan had the power to corrupt, her mind, and possibly, her soul.

He poured a little more brandy in his glass. "So, you've got a sister," he said, looking at her sharply. "Get this straight, Clarry, I'm not gonna' break down the doors to meet your family, but I'll not run away from them either. I know I'm not one of your ritzy friends. Sure, I'm a little rough on the edges, but I'm not somebody to be ashamed of either." He lifted his glass, swallowed the last drop of brandy, then slammed the glass down on the table.

"Forgive me, Danny," she begged, on the verge of tears, "it's just.oh please, I love you."

"Save the theatrics, Clarry."

She had beguiled him from the beginning. Weary of brothel trollops, in her Danny discovered a species of woman he had not known before. Danny was bewildered that a woman with such unmistakable signs of superior breeding would all but throw herself at him. Considering who she was and what she was, he was pleased by her interest in him. Always intrigued by that mysterious aura of the affluent, he'd yearned to be a part of the lifestyle so off limits for the likes of him. But she had shut him out of her world.

All woman, Clarice Durant had seduced him with her shameless teasing and coaxing, bewitching him with her catlike movements in low cut gowns, allowing glimpses of her over-endowed white breasts. Crossing the threshold of propriety with wild, careless abandon, she was satisfied once she got him in bed. And her hot-blooded sexual appetite kept him there.

But it was her ridiculous rich lady airs that irritated Danny at times, and this was one of them. Love was surely a part of his feelings for Clarice, he told himself, but he was no weakling of a man and no woman would have the upper hand and treat him like some rag-tailed bum she picked up off the street.

Giving her a fierce look, he rose from his chair. His tall lean figure hovered over her. "I reckon you've played your cards to suit yourself.

But Miss High and Mighty, I don't like the hand you dealt me."

She was deathly pale and inwardly trembling as she suppressed the hysterical urge to scream out. But she sat there silent, looking helpless, like the face of a spoiled child who d been scolded.

To her stunned amazement, he turned on his heel and left her sitting there.

Jake's carriage was waiting for them as they left the restaurant. He quickly loosened the leather reins from the hitching post, helped Dimity into the seat, and jumped in beside her. As soon as the carriage moved way, Jake gave her a wide, flashing smile and reached for her hand.

A delicious, thrilling undercurrent of emotions filled her at his touch, but she was still preoccupied with her thoughts of Clarice.

Seeing the thoughtful, perplexed look on her face, he asked, "what is it Dimity? Is it Clarice?"

She shook her head. Accepting the reality of Clarice's disgraceful behavior with the notorious Danny Eagan, Dimity was hot with rage.

"Don't tell me you're concerned about Clarice," he said, tucking the lap robe around her. "Forgive me, but I've seen no great love between the two of you."

"The vixen! Carrying on with a criminal for all eyes to see."

"Good Lord, Dimity," he cried incredulously, "I thought you knew it had gone further than an infatuation.

Turning her soft hazel eyes on him, she hesitated, "No," she replied, "not really, Jake. And you're right; I don't give a rat's ass about Clarice. She's made my life a merry hell." A sad look crossed her face. "It's not her I'm thinking of. It's dear trustful Papa."

"What kind of devilment did you have in mind when you said it would be in the newspapers?" he asked, remembering her words in the restaurant.

At first, it was a beautiful, conniving thought that she would report the shocking news that Clarice Durant was seen dining with Danny Eagan at the Phoenix. But knowing the hurt it would inflict on her Papa, she quickly changed her mind.

Feeling the chill of the night air, Dimity drew her shawl about her. "No Jake. If the news about them gets out, it won't be from me."

"Good," said Jake, her words only confirming what he'd known all along, that there was not a mean bone in her body. Keeping his eyes on his horse as the carriage rattled over the cobblestones, he kept silent for awhile.

"All the same, Dimity," he said, turning to her, "this is an unpleasantness I don't want you burdened with."

She felt a rush of gratitude for Jake's comforting words.

By the time they reached the Fifth Avenue mansion it was late.

"Would it be possible to see your Papa tonight?" he asked as they drove up the winding driveway.

"Oh Jake, I clean forgot. Papa is away on business, but he's due back tomorrow. You can see him tomorrow evening."

"Not soon enough."

Amused at his impatience, Dimity laughed as he lifted her down from the carriage.

"Jake, could we walk back to the stables. I want to check on Glory. She's with foal, you know."

He lifted the lighted lantern off the carriage and took her arm, guiding her in the silence of the night back to the stables.

Jake hung the lantern on the hook outside of Glory's stall and leaned against the post watching her.

There was an air of assurance about Dimity in the surroundings of the stable. Jake saw the sweet softness in her face in the glow of the lantern as she spoke soothingly to Glory. She broke open a sack of oats and filled the mare's empty feed bag. "I'll have to get after Isaiah. He forgets she's eating for two." She gave the mare a pat on the rump and closed the stall door, only to trip over a pitchfork in the darkness. She shrieked helplessly as Jake caught her in his arms.

It was an unguarded moment for both of them. At first his kiss was gentle, capturing her parted lips, then his lips were hot on hers with a driving need. His hands explored the curves of her body. Impatiently, he kicked the pitchfork out of the way, and swept her up into his arms. He carried her to an empty stall, where he laid her on the hay.

She could no longer deny him. She was filled with a physical desire that only he could satisfy. She so wanted to tell him they should wait, but her thoughts were hazy with wanting him, and the words to stop him wouldn't come.

At first when he knelt over her, his mouth brushed hers with a velvety light touch, with a searching tenderness. But quickly his mouth closed on hers hungrily, devouring her, unwilling to let their mouths part. The blood rushed to her face when she felt his passionate arousal against her. She felt his tongue probing and warm in her mouth, and his fingertips probing inside her low cut gown to the thrusting peaks of her breasts, to the tautness of her nipples.

Their desire had been gathering force for too long. She couldn't stop it. He couldn't stop it.

Raising his head, his eyes held hers. His husky voice was urgent, almost pleading. I love you, my darling. I've gone mad with wanting you. Do you want me to make love to you, Dimity?"

Her heart racing, she silenced him with her lips. "Yes, Jake," she whispered against his mouth.

Hastily, he undressed, fumbling at his buttons on his britches, while watching her as she stepped out of her under things. He turned to help her remove her full pleated skirt.

Feeling timid, she quickly averted her eyes at his nakedness. Seeing her trepidation, he gently took her hand guiding it to his swollen member. He wanted her to touch, to feel his manliness.

Her fingers caressed and stroked. And she felt his pulsing desire, hot and hard.

"Lie down, my love," he murmured, lowering her onto the mound of straw. His eyes traveled down the length of her, the vision of her fresh sweetness fixed in his mind. A vision of loveliness. He began exploring, a slow, sensuous touching with his tongue, with his fingertips, to arouse and awaken the secret place within her where ecstasy laid waiting.

She felt no shame, only pleasure, and hunger for the whole of him inside her. Her fingers dug into his back. She gasped as he entered her and began a slow pulsing movement within her. The great pressure of him filled her, breaching through deep inside her. She gave a soft whimper, drawing up her knees. His quickening movements made her shudder with pleasure. Love welled up in her in a convulsive spasm as his seed spilled into her. "My love.my love," he whispered huskily, breathlessly. With eyes glazed over with passion, he caressed her cheek with the palm of his hand. "Oh my dearest love, did I hurt you?"

"Oh Jake," she sighed contentedly, "You touched my very soul. I love you with all my heart."

The world was silent around them while they slept a dreamless short sleep in each other's arms.

Fate was kind to them for they awoke and Jake was off and away, and Dimity was sound asleep in her bed before Clarice returned home.

CHAPTER SIXTEEN

Awakening from a blissful sleep, Dimity raised her arms in a cat-like stretch. A grin started upward. Happily, she reflected sleepily on last night. She touched her bare breasts, and a vestige of enchantment was re-awakened. Staring at the ring on her finger, she said half-aloud to herself, "Mrs. Jake Trenton!"

She lay there nestled in the warmth of the covers, threading her fingers through the thick auburn strands of hair spread out wildly on the pillow. She closed her eyes wishing Jake was lying here with her. Clearly, she envisioned that captivating smile in that handsome sculpted face of his. She stretched out her hand to look at the ring on her finger. She dreaded having to remove it. "But until Jake speaks to Papa."

At the sound of Clarice s gravelly voice outside her door, Dimity covered her ears to block out the sound of her voice. Nothing was going to spoil this day, she told herself. At all costs, she intended to avoid Clarice, leaving by the back stairway, if necessary. A chuckle escaped as she thought of doing that very thing.

With Clarice, Dimity always had to have a game plan. She'd discovered that through the years. It was a delicious feeling when she'd out-witted her half-sister.

As a child, Dimity was never prepared for the meanness aimed at her by Clarice, the adored darling of Mercedes. But Dimity had never allowed herself to fret over it either.

Although Dimity had many girlfriends, mostly her friends at boarding school, she had few lasting friendships with boys. Not because boys weren't interested in her, she remembered with much resentment, but because Clarice made a game of luring them away from her. This practice became an obsession with Clarice. After many heartbreaking times when Clarice deliberately and cleverly seduced a boy with God knows whatever ploy, she finally realized she was only playing into her half-sister's hands. So Dimity changed her course of strategy. It didn't matter how taken Dimity might feel about a certain boy, she simply walked away when he showed the slightest interest in her. By showing little concern, she, thereby, spoiled Clarice's triumphant victory.

Thinking back on it, Dimity realized with Jake it was entirely different. Clarice had obviously been too occupied with Danny Eagan and didn't care to play the old game.

"Mary Dimity," Clarice called in a trembling voice, while banging her fists on the closed door. "Wake up, Mary Dimity. It's Mama."

Dimity sighed and threw her eyes up towards the heavens in disgust. Another one of Clarice's dire emergencies, Dimity thought unsympathetically. When it came to her Mama, Clarice became a skittering, high strung baby, especially when Papa was away.

Not in any hurry to appease Clarice, Dimity sat on the side of the bed and wiggled her toes. Hearing the sounds of hurried footsteps running down the hall, Dimity cracked open the door to see Nellie running up the stairs, wiping her hands on her flour spattered apron.

When Nellie saw Dimity standing in the doorway, she beckoned her to follow her. "It's the Missus," she called over her shoulder.

"She's just fine," Clarice chirped, running her hand over the lace trimmed coverlet. "See," she pointed, "her eyes are open.

It was obvious to everyone in the room that Mercedes Durant was dead.

Dimity's eyes did not leave the dead woman's face. Those sparrow-sharp eyes that had stared at her in such a disagreeable way so often, now stared straight up to the ceiling, lifeless.
"No, Clarice," Nellie took Clarice by the arm and lead her away from the four poster. "Your dear Mama is in the arms of her maker."

Clarice wrenched herself away from Nellie and threw herself on top of the lifeless figure. "No! No! It's not true. Call the doctor, Lucinda," she cried pathetically. "Mama's not dead. She can't be. She just can't be. I ." She wiped her dripping nose on the sleeve of her nightdress. I was so mean to her yesterday," she sobbed. Copious tears escaped her large, heavy-lidded, coffee brown eyes. She looked around the room, seeking agreement. She isn't, is she Lily?"

Lily shook her head. "I'm afraid she is, Miss."

"But I wanted. to tell her I'm sorry." She looked at Dimity. "But Mary Dimity, what shall we do? With Papa away, what.?"

"Papa is coming home today, Clarice, ' Dimity assured her, taking her hand. "He'll take care of everything." Dimity ran an awkward hand over Clarice's arm in comfort. "Go with Lily now, Clarice. She'll help you dress."

Dimity blinked back the tears as Lily and Lucinda left the bedroom with Clarice, who seemed to be comforted by Dimity's words.

"Oh my darlin' child," Nellie said, gathering her into her arms, "After all the meanness aimed at you by the two of 'em, that kind heart of yours still reaches out. Dimity paused and sniffed. "It's just.so sad. Mostly for Papa. Oh Nellie, that's who I care about."

"No sadness there for a Mama who had no room in her heart to let you in? Do you have sadness for her, love?"

Dimity shook her head. "No Nellie, I was sad to see her struck down with that dreaded illness, but the misery and the sadness of it are over."

"And for the adored darling of that Mama?"

Dimity looked at Nellie thoughtfully, her gently curving mouth trembling. "No Nellie, not really," she reflected, "Clarice didn't deserve all the love Mama lavished on her. When she should have paid back that love, when Mama needed her most, Clarice turned away from her in disgust."

Watching Dimity with some interest, Nellie shook her head in agreement, knowing full well of

Clarice's malicious behavior. Towards Dimity, and towards her Mama these past months.

With an affectionate hand, Nellie patted Dimity's cheek. "You best get dressed, dear." Nellie stepped towards the doorway. When Dimity did not follow, Nellie turned to her. "Are you comin' darlin'?"

"In a moment, Nellie. You go on. I'll tidy up a bit."

Dimity stood in the middle of the room, thinking she had to pretend some sadness. Until the funeral at least. With head tilted, Dimity stood staring at the prone, lifeless body. The intensity of those eyes had always scared Dimity. But now, in death, a blessed relief filled Dimity knowing she'd never again have to look into eyes so alive with hate. Hate meant solely for her.

Leaving the smell of death behind, the delicate scent of dried herbs and flower petals filled Dimity's nostrils as she closed her bedroom door behind her.

Jake found her in the stable currying Glory with long, soothing, strokes. The mare nickered as her mistress murmured to her affectionately. "Your foal will be as beautiful as you, Glory love."

Jake stood in the doorway watching her. Grinning to himself, he reflected with tenderness on last night. The sight of her made his insides turn to a hot, piercing longing.

"Dimity!"

She dropped the curry brush and turned to him with a smile. She flung her arms about him and pressed her lips to his. Oh Jake, I m so glad you're here."

He looked down at her lovingly. "Clarice told me. Are you all right, my darling?" He ran the palm of his hand across her cheek.

She leaned against him. "Yes. But it was a shock." Her words were muffled against his chest.
I'd hoped Albert was back from his t. rip." He held her face in his two hands and looked into her eyes. "I love you, my darling, and I've one more piece of business before our engagement is sealed." He paused. "To ask Albert for your hand in marriage." After last night he could readily understand his uncontrollable desire to touch her, to possess her.

Clarice started back to the stables as soon as she heard the carriage wheels. Pausing at the entrance to the stable, she stopped suddenly when she saw Dimity and Jake in each other's arms. She stood there stiffly, unbelieving, listening. Odd, she had never seen such show of affection before. She could see the glint of excitement in Jake's eyes as he spoke of asking for her hand in marriage. Her narrow soul couldn't bear to see such happiness on her half-sister's face.

Her back stiffened as she called out breathlessly, "Dimity, Papa's carriage just drew up. Please. I want you with me when we tell him. "

Jake dropped his arms to his side.

"Of course," Dimity said, closing the door to Glory's stall.

"Please hurry.' Clarice ran off ahead of them.

The two of them walked in silence at a sharp pace up the brick pathway to the house. Before entering the back door, Dimity turned to Jake and gently laid her hand on his arm.

"Jake, I think we should postpone telling Papa about our engagement for now. Until after the funeral."

His response was quiet and understanding. "Yes, by all means. I agree."

Thinking about telling Papa the news, her teeth chattered.

"My darling, you've caught a chill," he said, opening the door.

She paused before entering. "No Jake, it's. it's the dread I have of telling Papa. Mercedes was my mother, But in name only. She never treated me like a daughter. Never! Even when I was little, Nellie was more of a mother to me. She shook her head, remembering the times Mercedes had touched her with a birch switch for some petty failing. She swallowed the lump in her throat and the sorrow that came with it. Like the time she muddied her new patent leather high tops.

"My feelings are not for the loss of her, Jake. But for Papa."

"I understand, dearest," he said in a fervent tone, his gaze detecting the faint flush on her skin.

Nellie was waiting for them when they entered the kitchen. Twisting her apron nervously, Nellie said, Miss Clarice and your Papa are waiting for you in his study." With one chubby hand Nellie reached out to pat Dimity gently on the cheek.

"Thank you, Nellie. Will you prepare tea? I'll ring for you when we're ready."

Dimity paused at the staircase. She ran her hand lovingly over the rough wool of her Papa's coat draped over the heavy wood banister.

"Would you prefer I wait in the parlor, Dimity?"

"No. Please. Come in with me, Jake. I'm sure Papa will need you to help with the funeral arrangements.

She stood for a moment, staring at the paneled door, hoping for inspiration to say the proper words of comfort to her Papa.

They were standing by the fireplace, Clarice dabbing at her eyes with a tiny lace handkerchief and in the faint glow of the firelight Dimity could see the perplexed expression on her Papa s face.

One moment Clarice was happy to see him, and in the next moment her face had clouded over with a dour sadness. But she told him nothing.

He glanced up worriedly under flaring brows. "Dimity! And Jake! How nice to see you, my boy."

"Papa!"

His arms surrounded her as she ran to him.

"I m so glad you're home, Papa."

He looked at her searchingly. His eyes strayed past her to Clarice. Clarice's lips twitched. The visible distress in Dimity's hazel eyes told him something was amiss, and gazing at Jake's face creased with trouble, he was sure of it.

A quiet insistence was in his voice. "Will somebody tell me what is going on?"

Dimity looked to Clarice, whose eyes were downcast. She could see it was up to her. Dimity took a deep breath. "Papa." she began again, "Papa, Mama died in her sleep last night."

There was a quiver at the edge of his mouth, yet his voice was controlled. "In her sleep?"

Clarice finally spoke. "Yes, Papa," she sobbed.

Groping for the comfort of their warmth, he reached out to his daughters and gathered them into the circle of his arms.

His face was solemn. "And she didn't suffer?"

"No, Papa," Dimity choked, "she didn't suffer." Albert released his hold. "I must say goodbye."

I'll come with you, Papa," Clarice stammered.

"No, I'd like to be alone with her." He knew what he wanted. To hold her in his arms once more in the privacy of their bedroom.

He turned to Jake. "I'd like for you to stay, Jake .

"Yes sir. Of course."

Albert slowly made his way up the stairs. The door to their bedroom was slightly ajar. He moved into the room. His gaze lingered over his dead wife for a long while.

He slipped around the bed, and gently lifted the thin frame into his arms. In the guarded atmosphere of death's chamber, Albert felt a sense of resentment that she had been taken from him long before, solely suspended in an illness that destroyed her true self. His characteristic grit lost its hold as tears of grief fell on the still face of his beloved.

The news of Mercedes Durant's death spread rapidly throughout the social world, and over the next few days the house was crowded with well-wishers, mourners, and voluminous sprays of flowers filled every room.

It was during this time of mourning that Clarice admitted to herself that the sick feeling she felt each morning was not part of grieving. And the absence of her menses for the second month was the final proof. She was pregnant. At first she dared not think about it, telling herself that this pregnancy had worked in her favor. A way to get the man she loved. And she saw no problem concerning her father. After all, Papa was the most congenial and tolerant of men and had never deprived her of anything, nor would he now, knowing a grandchild was on the way. As far as her social standing, Clarice relished the thought of the gossip mongers biting their teeth into this bit of gossip. Married to Danny Eagan? Why should she care what they thought when in truth most of the socialites played the old familiar game of hypocrisy and delusion?

Elated at the prospect of telling Danny, Clarice was hard pressed to wait until after the funeral.

On the day of the burial, an anemic sun shown through the trees, forming delicate filigrees of sunlight tendrils as though reaching out from the heavens to touch the gravesite. After attending the Requiem Mass, the entourage of carriages followed in a solemn parade to the Catholic cemetery.

Most were avid with curiosity and more excited at seeing the opulent, stone mausoleum ablaze with the glimmer of gilt erected in three short days. The tallest edifice in the cemetery.

The silent line of mourners passed by the crypt, nodding their heads to the family. They watched with curious eyes the bereaved husband who never took his eyes off of the crypt, and the two lovely young women who stood on either side of him. His daughter, not in birth, the daughter with sensibility and gentleness in her heart, stood calmly on his right, without tears. On the left was Clarice, who with little kindness in her heart portrayed the sweet innocent daughter who appeared to be weighted down in her grief. With trembling shoulders and uncontrollable sobs, she clutched her father's hand.

The bearded faces of bankers, statesmen and business acquaintances, who filed by, in truth, felt no true grief for the aristocratic woman they barely knew. Only the few close women friends whose tear-filled eyes, displayed visible signs of sadness for the friend they had rarely seen in the last few years.

After the priest spoke the final words over the crypt, "May she rest in peace," and the last of the mourners passed on, Albert: turned to Jake who was standing alongside Dimity. "Jake, will you please take the girls home?"

"Why yes sir, but."

"I d like to be alone with my wife for awhile."

Albert gave Clarice a kiss on the cheek, and then turned to Dimity and brushed away the one lone tear. A tear she shed, not for the deceased, but for the father she s aw in pain.

Dimity said in a hushed voice, "Papa, please let me stay with you."

"No, my dear, I need this time."

She nodded. They turned away and left him in his silent misery.

It distressed Dimity that Papa was to be left alone at the gravesite. Not so, Clarice, who felt no need to linger and prolong the ordeal any further.

DIMITY AND DANIEL

CHAPTER SEVENTEEN

D anny heard the rustle of silk behind him before he heard her voice.

"Danny," she said in a high-pitched troubled voice, "what's going on?"

"Didn't Quincy tell you?" he demanded in a hateful tone. "I ain't receiving visitors."

His dark eyes of hate sent, shivers down her spine.

"But that doesn't mean me." Her happiness at contemplating his usual smile of welcome was short-lived.

Ramrod stiff, he rose from the swivel chair at his desk. "Yes that means you, Miss Society Girl."

"But.why? What have I done?"

"Is it too hard for you to get it in your thick head?"

Despite her efforts to stay calm, her lips were quivering. "I know you're angry about something. Tell me. Is it because I've not been here on my usual night? I sent you a note about my mother's funeral. Surely."

"It's over. There's nothing between us."

What was her true heart's desire saying? She stretched out her hand beseechingly to him. "You can't mean it, Danny. We love each other."

He turned away from her and began fingering through piles of papers. "If you'll leave, I'll get on with my work," he said matter-of-factly.

She sped his chair around and dropped to her knees in front of him. "Please, Danny, tell me what's wrong." She uncovered the woolen shawl draped over her shoulders revealing the low cut watered silk black dress. Her white appealing breasts seemed more voluptuous than he remembered. But there was no beguiling him, either by seducing him with her sensual low-cut gown, the fragrance of her perfume, or by fluttering her long lashes at him.

Though he still felt that stubborn persistence in his groin when his eyes followed the rise and fall of her breasts, he resisted his sexual urges.

Despite these nagging urges, he had come to loath her high and mighty airs. The note she sent about her mother's funeral asking him to stay away was the last cruel bit of hypocrisy he would tolerate. His arrogance would not allow such treatment. To his very soul he felt used. At any time she could throw him away at her whim. That wasn't about to happen to Danny Eagan. He would drop her before she had a chance. Admitting that he'd gone into this relationship blindly with his eyes wide open didn't make it any easier, but nothing she could say or do would change his mind.

There was a faint sheen of perspiration on his forehead, for the closeness of her was unsettling. As he slid his chair away from her, she fell forward on the dirt-encrusted floor. He began pacing back and forth, making no attempt to help her up.

Surprised, she uttered a faint cry. She sat there for a moment, collecting herself, before moving. Her fingers tightened on the edge of the desk, but it was an effort to lift herself up. Feeling weak and unsteady, she gave out a sigh as she rose, and then dropped into the empty chair.

"Can't you at least be truthful, Danny, and tell me what it is I've done?" she pleaded. "How can you love me and treat me this way?"

"Love you?" His white teeth flashed a cynical smile. He shrugged his muscle-bound shoulders and gave her a black look and said in a cold, calculating voice meant to hurt, "You can't love a woman who repulses you." He turned to the sideboard and poured himself a brandy.

She had encountered few cruelties in her protected life, and his words were too painful to bear. Without a word, she stood and walked to the door. To leave without telling him about the baby would not have suited her purpose. The most important thing for her right now was to have the last wounding word. Haltingly, she turned to face him. She was determined not to show her pain. Her expression was not tragic as she spoke, but triumphant.

"That's unfortunate, you bastard," she said in a mocking controlled voice. "I came here to tell you that I am carrying your baby."

The stunned stare on his face was the satisfaction she sorely needed.

Before he realized she'd left, he heard her heels clicking on the stairs. The room was hot now and full of her scent. This is a ruse, he told himself. Her way to control and manipulate me. "The bitch," he said out loud, "I don't believe her." He vowed to hold firm to his decision. He wanted no part of her. Baby or not.

Clarice deftly made her way down the stairs. Danny's words drove her to an instant madness with a desire to kill him. At the foot of the stairs she teetered, but caught herself before falling. Dazed and broken, she left the apartment through the back door out into the alleyway where Quincy, Danny's bodyguard was waiting with the carriage.

"The usual place, Miss?" Quincy asked, holding the carriage door open for her.

"Yes," she mumbled, feeling sick.

Looking across the narrow alleyway to the rundown grimy, brick building, her eyes fell on the wooden flashy sign, 'House of Cards'. No, she thought, more like a 'House of Greed'. "How did I end up in that hell hole?" she berated herself. Admitting she was caught in life's trap of curiosity, she had always burned with a desire for adventure, for the unknown, and yes, the forbidden.

Out on the town one night, and bored with their usual haunts, Clarice and her friends, full of a spirit of adventure, found the well-known saloon on Chrystie Street. Touted to be the best gambling house in the Bowery. It was a part of the city Clarice had had never seen before.

Upon entering the saloon, she was at first revolted by the clouds of tobacco smoke and the stale air filled with liquor fumes, and the rowdiness of the patrons. It wasn't long before she became entranced by the excitement of "Eagan's Joint", so-called by the regulars. Clarice and her companions mingled amongst the carefree crowd with money bulging in their pockets.

After a few drinks, the air of festivity spurred them on to try their luck. Keno seemed the least intimidating to Clarice. Each time she displayed her joy at winning by jumping up and down with a fist full of coins ecstatically shouting, "I won, I won," she soon caught the eye of Danny Eagan, who quickly made his way to her side.

After introducing himself as the proprietor, Danny Eagan stood by her, cheering her on, suggesting winning numbers with a nod of the head to the croupier spinning the wheel. Though he did not think her a true beauty, the seductive quality about her attracted him. And there was something rawly innocent about her, a quality he'd rarely seen among his harem of whores.

Deviating from his normal practice, he refrained from reversing the numbers in favor of the house to squelch her winning streak. It was all the inducement Clarice needed to come back night after night. Of course, gambling wasn't her only incentive to return to Danny Eagan's. It was the man himself. His was a life of intense gusto and mystery that intrigued her and it was this fascination that drew her to him like a magnet, and the clandestine affair that followed was inevitable.

As soon as the carriage took off, Clarice buried her face in her hands, gasping out uncontrollable sobs. Tears spilled over her cheeks. Danny's cutting words drove her to an instant madness with a desire to kill. Recalling every word, blind rage and despair swept over her. Clarice wanted to destroy him. Some day, she would, she vowed, dabbing at her eyes with a hanky already wet with tears.

For the first time in her life, Clarice was experiencing the anguish of a human emotion so great, that it threw her into a depression that would last for days.

Deeply distracted, she was standing there waiting for the horsecar when Jake approached the corner in his carriage.

Reining his horse to a stop, he called to her, "Clarice, may I offer you a ride home?"

Surprised, she looked up. "Oh, it's you Jake," she said, appearing agitated, "you startled me."

She held out, her hand to him. "Yes, if you're going my way."

He drew her up onto the seat. "Out shopping?" he asked, though he saw no parcels. He clucked to the horse and they were off.

"No," she lied, "a trip to the dressmaker."

He was puzzled. "Isaiah didn't take you?"

"Yes, of course." Her gloved hands fidgeted in her lap. 'But I sent him home. I love riding the horsecar."

He turned to her. Her face was pale and strained beneath her black velvet bonnet. He turned to her. "I'm afraid your father would not like to hear that, Clarice."

"I don t expect him to hear it," she retorted, curtly in her usual commanding manner. "It's something I enjoy, and I intend to ride the horsecar whenever I please.

Turning into the mansion driveway, Jake nodded. Whatever you wish, Clarice. Have no worry. Your father will not hear it from me."

"Will you be coming in, Jake?"

"No, I've business at the Court House."

Thinking it was Papa's carriage coming up the drive, Dimity raced to the door, only to find it was Clarice and Jake. Puzzled as to why they were together, she stood there in the open doorway bewildered and confused.

As they made the turn in the driveway, Clarice saw Dimity standing there, and instantly, she knew what she must do. The solution to her dilemma was right here for her to grasp.

As they came to a stop, Clarice reached up and kissed Jake on the mouth. Willing her tired brain to blot out her misery, she said gaily in a loud voice.

"Oh Jake, thank you for a wonderful time."

Perplexed at her surprising behavior, Jake stiffened in his seat. He was about to ask what prompted this sudden show of affection, but thought it wise to ignore it as though it meant nothing.

Totally preoccupied, he couldn't get away fast enough. Jake never saw Dimity standing in the doorway.

Dimity drew in her breath, and closed the door softly. A sick feeling swept over her as she ran up the stairs.

Inside the door, Clarice s eyes trailed upward, to the stairway where the last sound of clicking heels could be heard. She laughed to herself. On her cold, white face was an expression of vicious pleasure. Knowing Dimity, she would be tortured by this deception. It was clear to Clarice that she would have to play out this scenario very carefully if she was to be successful.

CHAPTER EIGHTEEN

Dimity wanted order. Order in her head. Order in her life. In a blind sort of way, she was too mixed up to write about the socialites. To report which socialite was seen with whom at the opera seemed so mundane. It held no interest for her now, but she doubted if her managing editor would agree to the list of story ideas she had submitted.

Thankfully, the scene she'd witnessed with Jake and Clarice happened after she'd broken the story of the State Asylum. Realizing the state of her emotions now, she'd have surely botched it.

Even seeing her first big byline, M. D. Durant, in print, didn't help to lift her out of the doldrums, though it was cause for celebration.

Holding the newspaper in her hands, Dimity reread the story splashed across the front page. In spite of her unhappiness, she couldn't deny the excitement and the sight of it did help to whet her appetite to explore and investigate further more of the city's ills, too long kept secret from the public by city officials.

If she had approached him beforehand with the idea, she was sure her managing editor would never have agreed to her writing such an article. But with the story in hand, he was impressed enough to let it go to press.

Dimity had been working late on the particular evening when she heard a soft whimpering coming from the back of the deserted press room.

She found the cleaning woman on her knees, tearfully scrubbing the grimy floor in furious, deliberate motions.

"Mrs. Donovan, what is it? Are you ill?"

She raised her wet, swollen eyes "I've just come from seeing my daughter."

Dimity was confused. "And is that such an unhappy time?"

The woman sat on her heels. The poor woman's jaw twitched as she unfolded the soul wrenching story of her daughter's unlawful confinement in t. he State Asylum. She told of the deplorable, inhumane conditions there.

Dimity listened sympathetically, looking down at the woman on her knees who paused to wipe her hands on her soggy serge dress when she realized she had an interested listener.

"Have you made any attempt to have her released, Mrs. Donovan?"

"Oh yes, many times. I've tried and tried." she choked. "She's not a violent girl." Letting out a sob she shook her head. "Never was."

"Oh Miss, you're that kind to be botherin' with me troubles." She continued to explain how she went to the head man at the asylum and how she called on her Alderman at Tammany Hall.

"It was all a mistake, ya know. They carted me daughter off, thinkin' it was some mad soul. She wasn't mad before they got a hold of 'er, but she is that now."

After that conversation, Dimity was shocked, and it touched off a nagging curiosity to investigate such an injustice and a need to set it right.

It was that curiosity that prompted Dimity to investigate the conditions at the State Asylum. Pretending to be a sister to Trudy Donovan, Dimity was admitted as a visitor. She would see for herself if what Mrs. Donovan told her was true.

When Dimity entered the large room housing close to fifty patient inmates, she was appalled at the skeletal forms of humanity wondering aimlessly in circles. Many of them were half-dressed and filthy, and some were sitting naked on the floor in their own excrement. The soft mutterings of a few drowned out those who ranted and raved at nothing in particular, and those who burst out with ugly, mindless laughter echoed the despair of these haunted, anonymous souls.

In a panic and half-sick from the sight, Dimity was close to running out of the airless room. Not having the faintest idea who Trudy Donovan was, she gave the attendant a sugary smile. "I'm afraid I've been away for a long time, and Mother tells me I may not recognize my sister, Trudy. She says she doesn't look herself.

"Trudy, is it?" The buxom, tough-faced attendant moved towards a pathetically thin, young woman who sat listlessly on an unmade, filthy bed, her eyes staring out of black hollows of fear.

Dimity had no need to worry that the girl would give her away and expose her as a fraud. The girl was far beyond any mental capacity to do so.

Dimity looked around her. She could see that everything Mrs. Donovan told her was true. She was duty bound to expose this inhumanity.

In the flicker of the gas-jet, Dimity reread the black-faced type on the front page of the New York Herald.

Her story began." The Walking Dead Housed in the State Asylum. These poor souls are not dead, but alive, living in deplorable, unsanitary conditions, sitting in their own excrement, eating garbage. Pay a visit to the State Asylum, as I did.

It wasn't Felix Holt's aim to stifle that bravado of pride of any of his reporters, but they could be a ruthless bunch in this cut-throat business of reporting. He could see by their reaction to the lead story in the evening paper that they were anything but happy. That the little Miss was standing toe to toe with them was too bitter a pill for them to swallow. A woman outwitting them with a hot breaking story.

When Casey Grant threw the paper on his desk and shouted, "What the hell is this? Now you're assigning lead stories to Kiss Society? Stories that should go to me?"

"You're a goddamned sniveler, Casey. I didn't assign this story to her. The little lady came to me with a story already written. Yesiree," he grinned, "a story uncovered by none other than herself." He picked up the paper and stood up. Shoving the paper in Casey's face, he said, "None of you slobs lifts a lazy finger to find new stories like this," he said, punching the paper. "Unless I give you the leads, you come up empty handed." Felix didn't want to damage Casey's prima donna ego, but he didn't intend to salve his conscious either.

"Hold it, Felix, you're saying she wrote the story on her own," he asked, disbelieving.

"You're goddamned right." Felix brushed his hand over the stubble of his beard. Knowing that Casey was the leader of the pack, he barked, "And I want, you guys to go to her and congratulate her. And mean it."

He saw the incredulous look on Casey's face. "She deserves your respect, and you damned well better give it to her."

Casey gave a silent nod in agreement.

"I gotta talk to her now. When I'm finished, I want you guys to come on over." He started to turn away, then paused, "And another thing, I don't want anybody telling folks that M. D. Durant is a woman. It's sad to say, but her stories will be more credible if t he-readers think she's a man. Got it?"

"Yeh, sure."

"You tell the rest of 'em."

Remembering his early ambitions and struggles, his understanding eyes rested on her. Felix Holt was feeling puffed up with his own satisfaction for believing in her. If ever I had a daughter, he admitted to himself, I'd want her to be like Dimity Durant.

The last of daylight's rays filtered through the stained-glass window by Dimity's desk. The rays alive with brilliant colors embraced her face, giving her creamy complexion an iridescent glow.

With the feel of his steady gaze upon her, Dimity lifted her eager eyes and smiled into his beefy grinning face. He stood there with the newspaper in his fist.

"Ya did it Dimity Durant," he exclaimed, giving her a wink. "If this don't roust the politicians out of their rat holes, nothing ever will."

She smiled sweetly. "Do you really think so, Mr. Holt?"

"That I do. That I do," he assured her, leaning against her desk. "It's bound to bring about some reform."

"If my writing this story could change things at the Asylum, I can't think of anything more wonderful.

"Believe it, Miss Durant, a story of this magnitude has the power to change such wrongs. The thing that makes a story come alive in the eyes of the reader is the on-sight coverage of real life. Your message came across with a real sincere burning passion. His expression was serious. "I'm right proud to have you on my staff."

His accolades were followed by a chorus of congratulations as the staff of reporters congregated around her desk. It was especially meaningful to her when Casey Grant came up to her and patted her kindly on the shoulder. "Congratulations, Miss Durant. I speak for all of us." The group of congenial, smiling faces standing around him shook their heads in agreement, making comments. "Yeh, swell job. Good story. Ye're one of us, little gal."

"You've reported a story any of us would have given our eye teeth to have written."

The surprise of this bombshell of a story by this greenhorn reporter was at first a thorn in their sides, but they couldn't help but admire her tenacity. The fact that she didn't hang on their necks for help was at the root of their new-found admiration of her.

Casey's words impressed Dimity. He did not speak with his usual indifference, or cold detachment, but with a true sincerity.

"Thank you, Mr. Grant," she said, her eyes misty with tears. "It means so much, coming from you."

Afterwards, Felix handed a paper to her. "You remember this piece on the homeless children?"

"Yes, of course," she said, scanning the paper.

"That's only part of the homeless children's plight. I want you to dig up all the information you can. Think you can do that?"

"Yes sir." Remembering his words to her early in her employment, Dimity looked up at him and smiled. "Have I won my way, Mr. Holt?"

"You sure as hell have, M. D. Durant."

Leaving the building for the day, Dimity felt like a free, wild bird with winged feet as she fled out into the street to the waiting carriage.

"Good evening, Isaiah," she smiled, "isn't it a glorious spring evening?"

"Sure is, Kiss Dimity."

The raucous voices of the newspaper hucksters caught her ear. "Extra! Extra! State Asylum exposed."

Her story. It thrilled her senses. Caught up in the excitement, of her success, her spirits lifted.

"Do you hear that, Isaiah? That's my story."

"You don't say, Kiss Dimity," he chuckled. "My, my, won't your Papa be proud.

"I'm not so sure," she said under her breath.

The newspaper wasn't out on the street an hour, when the newspaper office was mobbed with well-wishers, and curiosity seekers inquiring about this M. D. Durant fellow. Like fire shooting flames into the air, the scandal of the city s neglect leaped from one wagging tongue to another.

The prospect of having a baby was anything but pleasing or appealing to Clarice, and she didn't intend to bring a child into the world without a father. Pacing back and forth in her bedroom at night, sleepless and worried, a flash of revelation came to her and a plan of action took hold. The kiss she gave Jake was the beginning of the role she would play.

On that very evening, without showing any disloyalty to Dimity, she confessed to Albert, with downcast eyes, her growing unhappiness. Papa, while Dimity is busy in the exciting newspaper world, with a goal and a purpose in her life, I am idle with nothing important to do. I know it is thought that I am the empty-headed scatterbrain of your daughters."

Albert, who was sitting at his desk, was thunderstruck. He went immediately to his daughter to sit by her side. He gently drew her into his arms. Albert was taken by surprise at her words and saddened by her degrading self-debasement of herself.

"Why, Clarice, my dear that is not true. What in the world makes you think that? You are known for your accomplishments in the charity work that you do. You run an efficient, household." He brushed the lone tear from her cheek. "Now, now, dear, I don't want to hear such talk."

"But Papa, why is all right for Dimity to be in the business world, and not me?"

Although he didn't wish to criticize Dimity's role as a newspaper woman, he was hard-pressed to approve it. In his eyes, it was unladylike and unbecoming for a young woman to be working side by side with a bunch of rowdy, hard-nosed men, such as reporters.

He gave her a wry, uncomfortable smile. "What is it you propose, my dear?"

"Oh Papa, could I not come to your office and learn all about your business?"

When she saw his perplexed look, she went on, "If you are too busy, couldn't Jake take some time to show me the inner workings of your business."

"My dear, he is far too involved with his political job. He barely has time for me." But he was having second thoughts. It might not be a bad idea for a member of his family to know what his holdings were in case something should happen to him.

She looked at him beseechingly, bright tears filling her eyes. "Please, Papa, please, won't you ask him?"

He squeezed her small hand. "If it's that important to you, my dear, I'll speak to Jake."

"Oh Papa, thank you. Maybe my life will have some meaning now."

Bewildered by the urgency in Albert's voice, Jake consented to tutor Clarice, though reluctantly. His heavy schedule wouldn't allow him that much time with her, but he was duty bound to comply with Albert's wishes.

Dressed in a rich sea foam green velvet dress, trimmed with a flattering lace ruffle about her neck, Clarice looked the part of a society sophisticate. Leaning on the arm of Jake, she came bounding into the dining room aglow with candlelight. Her eyes were sparkling with her too-busy mind actively engaged in her conspiracy plot to seduce Jake.

"Good evening," Jake said, addressing Albert.

With a wide grin on his face, he came across to Dimity, took her hand, bent to kiss it, all the while keeping his eyes on hers.

She did not smile back. "Good evening, Jake."

Albert watched his two daughters who acknowledged one another with a nonchalant nod of the head. His wizened heart stirred. Would their ever present feud never end?

He was saddened to see this, for they seemed so congenial to one another during the funeral.

The conversation was alive and spirited during dinner.

Dimity studied Jake's handsome face all during the meal. There was no guilt or uneasiness that he had done anything wrong. Obviously, he did not: know that she had seen Clarice kiss him. To him, there was nothing clandestine about this arrangement with Clarice, and to him, helping her to learn about Papa's business, was only doing what Albert asked of him. Although, the three of them spoke openly, discussing the details, this was the first. Dimity had heard about it.

"And how is your star pupil, Jake?" Albert asked. "She certainly appears to be enthused."

"Very well, sir. You will be pleased to know that we have a very astute pupil here. Clarice is asking intelligent questions about all your business dealings and investments, and she certainly has absorbed all of the information I've given her to study in the last few days.

"I know she's in capable hands, Jake. He laughed heartily. "If this keeps up, before we know it she may be sitting at my desk one of these days."

Clarice glowed with satisfaction. "Already, I can see what a shrewd business man you are, Papa," she said in a sickening sweet voice.

How did this all come about, Dimity puzzled. Knowing how Papa felt about women in the business world. Dimity was sure that learning about Papa's business didn't come from him. Clarice must have initiated the whole idea. Dimity thought it mighty peculiar for Clarice never did anything she didn't want to do. No doubt, she had touched that core of softness in Papa's heart.

Dimity so wanted to get up and leave the room, but she controlled the urge.

With an air of importance, Clarice looked across the table at Dimity. "And Dimity, my dear sister, what is new in your little world of society reporting?" she asked, goading her with a sardonic smile.

Feeling completely shut out from the dinner table conversation most of the evening, Dimity's poise and composure gave way. She reached for the unread, rolled -up newspaper by Albert's plate. With a very satisfied look on her face, she unrolled the newspaper and spread it out in front of them and pointed to the headlines.

"Not such a little world, Clarice, when the lead story on the front page of the New York Herald is your story," she said proudly.

Albert scrutinized the front page story, then lowered it. "Lord Almighty, Dimity," he cried in a booming voice, "You mean to say you actually set foot in the asylum?"

"Yes, Papa."

"Indeed!" Passing the paper to Clarice, he leaned back in his chair. Studying her closely, he asked once more, "that Godforsaken insane asylum?"

"Yes, Sir." She could see his face was turning crimson and that he was disturbed. She lifted her eyes to him to bravely express her feelings. "It's a very great honor to have your first real story printed on the front page, Papa. This is the most rewarding experience of my life. I'm so very proud of it. I'm envied by every reporter on the paper."

Though he cursed himself inwardly, he didn't have the heart to show his disapproval of the way she obtained the story. He would do that at a later time. He couldn't help it, but her joy swept him along with it.

Dimity felt a rush of gratitude when he reached over and squeezed her arm. "And I'm proud of you, my dear." Albert knew the feeling. Knowing how his success in the business world shaped his whole existence, Albert wondered if Dimity would be affected in the same way.

Dimity commanded Jake's whole attention. With elbows on the table, he rested his chin in his folded hands. "It's an extraordinary accomplishment. Dimity. You have every right to be proud." His tender expression and look of delight did not go unnoticed by Clarice. But Jake wondered where this career would take her. How can she be a wife and mother? What worried him was the carefree, happy person he knew so well seemed burdened with an unfamiliar seriousness.

Dimity was wilted by the look he gave her. There was love in his eyes. So, he still did love her.

"Thank you, Jake."

It was plain to see that Clarice was only interested in the conversation when it concerned her and she had no intention to join in the accolades.

"Why on earth a lady would want to go amongst such creatures is beyond me. I'm sure rumors will fly when all of New York hears that the daughter of Albert Durant is socializing with the crazies at the Insane Asylum."

The bluntness of her words was a disappointment to Albert.

Dimity's jaw tightened. She wanted to scream out her rage. "It was hardly socializing, as you call it, Clarice. And all of New York will not have a clue that the article was written by me. If you had taken the time to notice the byline, you'd see that I am using initials. I doubt that many people, if any, will connect the writer to this family."

Lily stood behind Albert's chair, waiting for a sign from Clarice to clear the table before serving the dessert. "You may clear, Lily," Clarice said, grateful for the interruption.

Lily placed the plates on the dumbwaiter, then passed through the pantry door. As was Nellie's custom, she examined the plates as they came through to the kitchen. "And whose plate might this be?" she asked Lily.

"Ah, that would be Miss Dimity's."

"Barely touched a bite. She'll be fallin' away to a feather weight at this rate," Nellie said with a troubled expression on her face.

Frowning, Albert lifted a hand to Lily as she placed the bread pudding before him. "None for me, Lily. Visibly annoyed, he stood and faced Jake.

Jake flushed with embarrassment. "How can you say that? It isn't true."

"Well then, why didn't you tell her you couldn't see her in the morning? Why didn't you speak up and tell her we ride on Saturday mornings? With an irate swish of her skirt she turned away from him and walked across the room to the window to stare out into the darkness.

Her onrush of feelings left him stunned, and finding the right words to assuage her did not come easily. If he had injured her pride, it had not occurred to him until this moment. But even as he reached her side and put both hands on her rigid shoulders, words failed him.

His silence only enraged her all the more. She twisted her body around and cast her angry eyes on him. "And what of our engagement? When do you propose speaking to Papa?"

"Why, I planned to tell him this evening, dearest, but then he postponed our meeting. It will have to wait until Monday."

Trying to make up for his shortcomings in her eyes, Jake blurted out an apology. "I'm so sorry, my darling." His eyes were fixed on that sensuous mouth. "I never intended to upset you. We'll have our ride tomorrow-afternoon. And." he added hastily, if Albert is home, I'll speak to him then." He wrapped her in the comfort of his arms. "Do you forgive me for being such a thoughtless oaf?

His apology set her mind at ease. How could she ever doubt Jake's word? With eyes downcast, she ran her hands over the satiny brown cloth of his frock coat.

As she looked up, her eyes softened. "You are forgiven," she said, now smiling.

Seeing the crinkles of amusement about her eyes, a flush of pleasure swept over him. His blood pounded in his temples for he wanted her desperately.

"After not seeing you all week, I guess I was jealous of the time you are spending with Clarice."

"Oh, my darling," he said, stroking her hair tenderly, it means nothing." His mouth brushed her lips lightly, then crushed her mouth to his hungrily.

Hearing footsteps, they quickly drew apart.

"Is there anything I can get you, Miss Dimity," Lily asked.

"No nothing, Lily. Mr. Trenton is leaving. Will you see him out?"

"Yes, it's quite late. He smiled broadly, bowing over Dimity's hand. "Tomorrow at one?"

"Yes, she said, catching sight of the twinkle in his eye."At one."

DIMITY AND DANIEL

CHAPTER NINETEEN

L ong before she was ready to awaken, her sleep was broken by her Papa's booming voice, "Dimity, Glory's dropped her foal." She lay there in the darkness of her room, her eyes still closed, not quite awake. He burst into her room. "Are you awake, Dimity?"

"Yes, Papa," she said sitting up with a jerk. "Really? She's had her baby?"

"Sure has. Right on time. I'm told he's a mighty fine specimen." It was clear by the look of pride on his face that he was as proud as a new father. For three weeks they had kept close watch on the mare knowing it could come at anytime. "I'm going down to meet him."

Dimity threw her covers off and shrieked in delight, "Oh Papa, isn't it wonderful? I'm coming too."

He gave her a cross look. "Not in your nightie. You get yourself dressed first."

"Yes, Papa. I'll hurry." She felt a rush of excitement. This was the part of her life Dimity loved, the part Clarice had no part in. Dimity learned at a very young age that Clarice had no great love for the horses. And Dimity couldn't be happier. She cherished those special times she shared alone with Papa, riding through the woods together or sitting by the fire discussing which mare they should breed next. Although Clarice made a great pretense of disinterest when she and Papa rode the Fox Hunt with society's elite, Dimity did not miss the look of regret on Clarice's face when it was clear she ached to be one of society's hunt enthusiasts, if only it didn't mean riding a horse.

By the time Dimity was dressed and about to go out the kitchen door, she could barely contain herself.

"No ye don't, Missy," Nellie called out crisply, grasping hold of her shawl. "Ye'll not be goin' out at five in the mornin' into the cool mornin' air without a cup of hot tea to warm ye're insides."

"But Nellie ."

"No buts."

Seeing Nellie's determined jaw, Dimity knew better than to resist with any sweet talk. Reluctantly, she sat down at the polished oak table.

Nellie set down a steaming cup of tea before her. Dipping in the sugar bowl, she said, "Two teaspoons just the way ye like it darlin'. Her plump face, rosy from the heat of the stove, broke out in a wide smile. With work worn hands, she touched Dimity's face affectionately. "Now won't ye have a bit of breakfast to go with ye're tea? She shook a finger at Dimity. "And sure it's no food ye have in ye're belly a'tal this mornin'. Untouched it 'twas."

"Untouched? What are you talking about, Nellie?"

"Ye're supper plate of food sent back to the kitchen with nary a bite off it."

Dear, dear Nellie. She's always been there, watching out for me. Dimity gave her a warm smile. "Not now, Nellie. I promise to have something later." She sat there stirring the spoon in her cup round and round, allowing it to cool. Close to bursting with the joyful secrets in her heart, Dimity plucked nervously at the few specks of lint on her skirt.

While Nellie's back was turned, Dimity drained the cup of tea. She quickly wrapped her shawl around her shoulders and bolted for the door. Outside the morning air felt damp and cool on her cheeks. In the gray light of the predawn sky she hastened down the pathway to the stable where the familiar whinnying sound broke the silence of the early morning quiet.

When she saw Glory's proud head raised high in greeting to her, Dimity raced to the stall. Anxious to show off her new offspring, Glory seemed to be waiting for her mistress.

"Oh Glory, I wanted to be here with you," Dimity whispered while stroking her tenderly. Dimity peered around her where Papa, Isaiah and Samuel, the new stable hand, were toweling down the new born foal.

She stepped inside the stall and knelt down beside the baby, who stood unsteadily and precariously on trembling weak legs.

A soft moan escaped her throat. "Oh Papa, isn't he beautiful?" She ran her hand over the foal's sleek hindquarters. "Oh, you darling," she cooed. Dimity turned to her father. I've never seen such a beauty.' She moved around the mare to talk to her. "He's just like you, Glory," she said, "You've given us a little prince".

"He is that, Dimity. Just look at the lines of him," Albert said, "a thoroughbred for sure."

"Nice little feller, ain't he?" Samuel said, covering him with a rough horsehair blanket. "Need to keep him warm. Isaiah, whose old legs were almost as wobbly as the foal's, helped Samuel fasten the string ties to keep the blanket in place.

"Not out of his mama's belly long enough, Miss Dimity, to keep his self warm," Isaiah said as he guided the foal to Glory's waiting nipple. "Need to eat, little fella."

Albert lifted the latch of the stall door to leave. "I'm afraid I have a full day's work waiting for me." He stood outside the stall, watching Dimity's attempt to get the foal to accept the nipple." When finally the little foal greedily began suckling, Dimity turned her attention to her father.

"Papa, I think we should name him Prince. What do you think? "

"Perfect! That suits him."

Reluctant to leave, Dimity stayed for awhile longer. Full of wonder of the new life, she felt a giddy intoxication as she scampered up to the house.

While Nellie dished out her breakfast, Dimity hummed happily. "Are you sure ye'll not have your breakfast in the dining room with Miss Clarice?"

"I think not, Nellie. I do not wish to spoil my appetite. Or my day."

Sticking her fork in a fat sausage, she placed it on a buttered biscuit and stuffed it in her mouth. "No eggs, Nellie," she said, her mouthful of food fairly choking her.

"It's no wonder ye've no wish to eat ye're breakfast in the dining room. Shouldn't be allowed to eat in the dining room with such manners," Nellie chided her. "No lady talks with a mouthful of food." Nellie shook her head in disgust.

Knowing this motherly advice coming from Nellie was well-intended, Dimity smiled good-naturedly. "I'm sorry I'm acting like a pig, Nellie, but I'm starved."

"That I can see, Missy." She watched her happily as Dimity devoured every morsel on her plate.

Finishing the last bite, contentment showed on Dimity's face. She sat back in her chair thinking about her plans for the day. Sipping her tea leisurely, she decided she would spend part of the morning in the archives of the newspaper office. And if there was time, she'd do a little shopping. But only if she could do all that and be home by one o'clock.

Jake noticed an unusual exhilaration in Clarice when he picked her up that morning. On the way to Albert's office Jake patiently listened to her infernal chatter. At times when she was drowned out by the traffic sounds, her voice grew loud and shrill. In spite of himself, he couldn't help but be amused at some of the comical stories she told about some of her so-called friends. And his slow easy laughter only served to urge her on. To his surprise, she was bright and witty with a delightful sense of humor, and for the first time since he d known her, he found her a pleasant and entertaining companion.

When they arrived at the three story brick building on Wall Street, the usual week day tumult of the crowded busy street was as dead as a stone and abysmally quiet. All activity had come to an abrupt weekend halt.

Jake stopped the carriage at the front entrance, jumped down and hitched the horse. He smiled, extending a helping hand to Clarice.

They walked through the deserted lobby and down the dim corridor to the first floor office of Albert Durant. Though it was an office rich and opulent, it was tasteful and comfortable.

When they entered his office, he didn't acknowledge their presence. So they stood there quietly. Albert sat at his desk frowning, preparing for his Monday morning manipulation of the stock market. To Jake, this was the dangerous side of Albert Durant's business. To Albert, it was the life-giving excitement that was sorely lacking in his private life.

Finally, he closed the file and looked up.

"Good morning."

"Good morning, Papa," Clarice greeted him in a quiet voice, not wishing to disturb him.

"My dear," he greeted his daughter with a bow of his head.

"Good morning, Sir!"

"Jake, when you get Clarice settled I have something I'd like to discuss with you."

In the outer office, Jake opened a file drawer. "Familiarize yourself with these annual reports," he said, placing the files on the desk. These are a few of your father's enterprises."

Clarice removed her fawn colored cape and sat down behind the desk. After Jake left the room, she tried to concentrate, but all of the figures were one big blur. For the longest time, she stood with her ear to the closed door hoping to hear the conversation going on inside, then finally gave up when not a sound passed through the heavy barricade. Bored to frustration, she sat there gazing out the window.

Albert pointed to a thick sheaf of papers on his desk. "I'd like you to look over these patent papers, Jake. It's a promising steel mill in Philadelphia I'm interested in. They're without the necessary capital they need to forge ahead with their plans for a new blast furnace. I've been there several times in the last six months, and I've come away very impressed with their operation and the promising potential. The future of this mill lies in the continuing expansion of the railroads. I'm confident such an investment would culminate in a veritable gold mine.

No wonder he's so rich and powerful, Jake mused, as he listened to the enthusiasm in his voice. Always thinking. Always planning ahead to a new venture. Or was it the adventure that was so enticing.

"I dare not delay my decision much longer. Study the papers over the weekend. We'll meet Monday night as planned."

"Yes sir!" Jake lifted the file from his desk and started to leave.

"Wait Jake. There's something else. Please! Sit down," Albert waved him to a seat. The muscles in his face twitched as he grew more serious. "I've been meaning to discuss this senseless career you've chosen for yourself. I promised myself that I wouldn't interfere. That I'd give you your head. But

I can't stand by and see a talented young man like yourself waste that talent, in the entanglements of the crooked politics of this city. If you stay honest, as I know you are now, you'll go nowhere. If you choose to join them, you'll end up dishonest like the rest of them."

Jake was caught completely unawares. All that Albert said was true. After he was in the job for several months, it hadn't taken Jake long to realize it.

Albert went on. "You're a good man, Jake. You have the kind of imagination and loyalty I need in an assistant. Trying to keep up two jobs isn't working, Son. I m sure you know that. I want you to be my full time assistant." He moved around his desk to Jake s side. Smiling, he put his arm around him. "I'm sure you know, Jake, I consider you the son I never had. I want you to think about this, and give me your answer Monday."

"Thank you, sir," he said with pure admiration in his eyes, "I'm honored at your offer."

It was past noon when Clarice and Jake left the office. The sun was hidden behind dark clouds and the smell of rain was in the air.

For quite some time he had wondered if he had been remiss in his hesitation to bring up the topic of Danny Eagan to Clarice. If only for Albert's sake, Jake thought it his duty. But not wishing to appear audacious in her eyes, he had waited for the opportune moment.

"Clarice, are you and your friends still spending your evenings at that gambling house?"

Jake took his eyes off the road to see her reaction to his question.

She did not speak for a moment or two. Her expression was somber. "What gambling house are you talking about?"

"Why "The House of Cards". Danny Eagan's place."

A bright flush colored her cheeks. Like a threatened child discovered at some mischief, she cringed, and her expression showed the alarm she was feeling. "No, of course not. Not for months."

"That's good," he said, clucking at the horses to move them along at a faster pace before the thunder-storm struck.

"Why Jake," she laughed half-heartedly, "why in the world did you ask me such a question? It was an amusing pastime, to add a little excitement to our lives."

"Ah, Clarice," he pressed on, "I'm afraid it's a well-known fact that you and Danny Eagan have been seen together socially. He gazed steadily ahead on the street before him. "And you are certainly aware that Dimity and I saw you together at the Phoenix." He went on, determined to get it out into the open. "If we saw you, Clarice, others have also seen you together."

The wheels began spinning in her head. This was her chance to get back at Danny Eagan.

She turned her tear streaked face to him. "Oh Jake, if you only knew the anguish I have suffered," she sobbed. "It is all too humiliating, too painful to talk about. Ah," she sighed, her voice lowered to a whisper, "It was as though I was totally isolated behind the gates of hell with no one to help me."

When she remained silent, Jake was profoundly disappointed that she didn't go on, now that she had piqued his interest. He wondered if she would ever divulge her dreadful secret.

The sky was black by the time they reached the mansion. Jake was grateful they made it before the rain came pelting down. It was the loud clap of thunder and lightening that startled Clarice and caused her to miss her step and turn her ankle. She crumpled to the ground before Jake could catch her.

She sat there on the ground motionless, feigning an injury. "Oh," she cried pathetically, "I believe I've hurt my ankle.

He crouched there beside her. "You poor dear." Seeing she was reluctant to move, he said in a concerned voice, "I don't think you should put any weight on it, Clarice.'

"Oh dear! Whatever shall I do?" she murmured distressfully.

"I'll carry you."

"Her heart soared as a predatory thought flashed before her. Dimity was due home at any moment, and if she were to see Jake carrying her into the house, the sight of her in Jake's arms was certain to fan the flames of doubt in her.

"Oh, could you, Jake?" she murmured distressfully.

Without a word, Jake lifted her up in his arms and carried her into the house.

When he hesitated inside, then moved towards the drawing room, she pleaded pitifully, "Please Jake,' could you carry me to my room?"

"Of course!"

Upstairs, he gently lowered her in her white canopied bed and sat down on the bed beside her. "I'm afraid I was too careless, Clarice. I should have caught you before you fell."

"No, no, Jake, it wasn't your fault," she said, lifting her skirt daintily to look at her right ankle, then quickly lowered it before Jake had a chance to see it. She couldn't very well continue the charade if he should see her supposed injured ankle appeared as normal as the left one.

"It is feeling much better."

"Are you sure, Clarice?"

"Yes. You're not to worry."

Placing her hand affectionately on his sleeve, she started to speak, then gave him a demure look. "I ." she faltered, "I feel." then hesitated again.

"Yes? What is it?"

"This is so difficult for me to talk about." she bit her lower lip, and then looked him boldly in the eye."But I have to tell someone. And I want you to know the truth."

She looked away for a moment. "He was blackmailing me."

"Who was blackmailing you, Clarice?"

"Danny Eagan. I'd lost a large sum of money. He threatened to go to Papa. Oh, Jake, it was a stupid lark I'm not proud of. I was having so much fun, and when Danny persuaded me to keep a tab, it never crossed my mind that I'd end up so deeply in debt."

Being brought up in the genteel life she was accustomed to, Jake was sure this was true.

"I've always thought most people were decent. And when Danny bargained with me to wipe the slate clear, I willingly agreed."

"Bargained with you how?"

"To be his girlfriend."

Jake was startled at her confession.

"I never gave him the slightest encouragement, but he was smitten with me, and wanted me in the worst way. So, when you saw me with him, I was only paying off my debt," she said, assuming a virtuous expression.

Jake wondered how far she had to go to pay off her debt. "How did you finally cut it off, Clarice?"

"I sold some of mother's jewelry. I couldn't go on like that any longer."

He looked at her cheeks wet with tears. "Why that ruthless cad," he said in sympathy. He could plainly see that she had been shocked out of her youthful innocence.

"Come, come," he said lamely, patting her hand, "try to put it out of your mind."

"Will you promise me, Jake, never to speak a word of what I've told you. Not to Papa. Not to Dimity?"

"Yes, of course I promise."

She sat back on her pillows relieved, a shadow of sadness clouding her face, but inwardly, she was as pleased as punch at how resourceful and clever she was in playing the part of a damsel in distress.

In no way did Jake detect the duplicity of her actions. To him, there was something childlike about her that touched his heart and a side of Clarice he had never seen before.

When Clarice heard the front door open downstairs, she sat bolt upright. Closing her eyes, she mopped her brow daintily with a handkerchief. "Heavens, just speaking about it has made me ill. In a vain effort, she tried to loosen the buttons on her high necked dress. Exhausted from the effort, she dropped her arms. "I'm afraid I feel faint," she choked, taking short shallow breaths.

"Oh Jake," she said, twisting herself around, "do you think you could help me unbutton a few of these buttons. I feel as though I'm choking," she sobbed, appearing to struggle for breath.

He patted her shoulder. "Take some deep breaths," he instructed. He nimbly began unbuttoning the long line of buttons down her back, having no qualms about any improprieties. His only thought at the moment was to relieve her obvious discomfort so that she could breathe more freely.

Hearing Jake's voice coming from Clarice's bedroom when she reached the top of the stairs, Dimity made her way down the hall in that direction. She stood in the open doorway and stared, gape-mouthed and bewildered at the scene before her. She looked into Clarice's evil sparkling eyes and knew. Clarice has taken Jake away from me with one of her cunning virulent schemes.

There was mute agony in Dimity's expression when Jake looked up and saw her.

A sick tension rose in Dimity. In her eyes, the man she loved had suddenly changed into a cad who goes from one bed to another. She hid her face in her hands and turned away.

All a twitter, Clarice looked at Jake, "Oh my, what must Dimity think?"

"What the devil." He jumped up to follow her.

A nasty little smile on her face, Clarice was ecstatic with her triumph.

Before Jake could overtake her, Dimity had slammed her bedroom door and locked it. Throwing herself on the bed, she sobbed pitifully into her pillow. The only man I've ever loved, she choked between sobs, and he has degraded me.

Jake knocked on her door lightly. "Dimity, may I come in?" he pleaded. Please, let me explain. It's not what you think."

She put the pillow over her head to shut out his voice. His pleadings fell on deaf ears.

When she refused to open the door and listen to him, real anger flashed in his eyes. With rising irritation, he shook the doorknob violently. Undoubtedly, she was accusing him in her heart of an infidelity he was innocent of. He could not feel guilty when he had no reason to believe he was guilty. "I'll not beg," he shouted in a hoarse voice through the closed door. Though he tried to convince himself she had no cause to behave in this way, in truth, he was completely undone, and despair with a passionate self-reproach gripped him. Slowly then, he descended the stairs and left the house.

For most of the day, Dimity huddled in the comforting warmth of her feather bed. Lying there wide awake in her nightmare, she listened to the exploding sounds of the storm outside and forced herself to face the storm within. As there was no controlling the torrential rain outside, she had no control of the pain in her heart.

Thoughts of him continued to cloud her mind. A life without him loomed before her. This constant thinking would only prolong her inner suffering. She must pull her wits together. She would bury the pain back some place in her memory. "Oh God," she sobbed, "help me."

For a while she managed to stop thinking and the rhythmical patter of raindrops on the window pane lulled her into a fitful sleep.

When Dimity did not appear at dinner, Clarice made the excuse that she had taken to her bed with a headache. Appearing overly solicitous, she instructed Lucinda to take a tray up to her.

Dimity was standing by the window when Clarice entered the room. Clarice was the last, person Dimity wanted to see. Their eyes met in a silent exchange.

"Dimity," Clarice said in a low quiet voice, "I do hope you are feeling better."

Dimity was not fooled by her false concern. Dimity was only too aware of the woman's steely core within.

"I don't wish to disturb you, but I thought." she sighed deeply, pressing her back against the post of the bed, "I beg you; please do not tell Papa what you saw. It's just that Jake has become so amorous of late, with us working so close together, and all." she laughed nervously, "he's so attractive and virile, and so hard to resist."

Remaining silent, Dimity walked with swift, angry steps past her. She stiffened, then turned to face her, "You are welcome to him, Clarice. With my compliments."

Jake darted around the side of the stable when he saw her coming. As Dimity walked into the tack room, an arm closed around her from behind. Her soprano voice rose in a shrill scream. Not knowing who it was she trembled with fear. She kicked and flailed her arms furiously. "Stop! Let me go," she shrieked," trying to free herself from his powerful arms and his hot breath on her face.

Feeling her body alive with a fearful anxiety, he said in firm deep voice, "Don't be frightened, Dimity. It's me, Jake."

Without hesitation, he pulled her down beside him on the wooden bench.

When she saw who it was, her eyes widened in astonishment.

His compelling eyes held hers, but they were cold and hostile.

Not wishing to look at him, she closed her eyes against the image of him making love to Clarice, but could not shut out the remembered light-fingered touch of his lovemaking.

When he gently touched her cheek, she cried out with repugnance in her voice, "Get your dirty hands off of me."

"Dimity, please! It's not what you think." He was speaking to her in a low, soothing voice, but she refused to listen.

Her eyes black with hate, she looked into his smooth, muscular face. "You were making love to Clarice, and you have the nerve to lie about it.

A hurt looked grew in his eyes. Incredulous, he said, "In God's name is that what you think? How can you believe I was making love to Clarice with the door wide open for all eyes to see?"

All she wanted was to escape from his grasp. During her sleepless night, she had convinced herself that he was no loss. Good riddance!

Relaxing his hold on her, he sat back on the bench not believing what he'd heard. His shoulders drooped at her cold bitter look.

Though he still held her there, she wrenched her arm free, and spun away to race up the pathway to the house.

Jake did not try to follow her.

CHAPTER TWENTY

With hands rammed in his pockets, Jake stood by Albert's desk in his study, holding back a fierce desire to beg off from going on this business trip. But a sickening wisdom told him it was no use to believe Dimity would ever change her mind about him. Her deliberate attempt to avoid him, and that steely core of indifference she showed when they did meet should have convinced him that it was no use. It was a realistic acceptance he had failed to face up to until now. Perhaps, this separation was the answer after all.

Sitting at his desk, Albert peered over his spectacles up into Jake's grave face. With that far away look in his eyes, it was clear the young man was visibly troubled. Lately, he had seemed so preoccupied, and it worried Albert.

"Is there a problem, Jake?

Jake looked at him blankly. "Sir?"

Selecting his words carefully, Albert asked him, "Do you have second thoughts about giving up your political career?"

"Oh no, of course not, sir. That was a bad decision on my part. Politics wasn't for me, and I admit it. But it was something I had to get out of my system," he smiled thinly. "You have paid me the highest compliment, Mr. Durant, sir, and I m that proud you want me as your assistant.

Albert looked perplexed. "What then? I hope you don't mind that Clarice will be going to Europe with you."

"Oh no, sir, no problem there."

"I'm glad to hear it. You know, when she overheard our conversation, she was clearly taken with the idea. There was nothing I could say to dissuade her. I'm quite sure she would have thought me an unfeeling father and I would not have survived her barbs of reproach had I refused her. And now with the unexpected turn of events in Philadelphia, there is no way that I can go. I must close the deal as soon as possible." He gave Jake a thoughtful look. "Well then, Jake, is there something else bothering you?"

"Not really," he lied, "it's." he hesitated, trying to think of some excuse for his recent noticeable despondency, realizing he hadn't been too successful in hiding it."I'm afraid I had already become somewhat disillusioned with the game of politics. In some odd way, though, I still have this nagging notion that I was a failure."

"Not a failure, Jake," Albert broke in, "I daresay, it won't be the last wrong turn in the road you'll take in your lifetime. Consider it a valuable lesson. That is," he said kindly, "if you've learned from your mistake."

"Yes sir, but it's the only thing I've ever started and never finished."

"No, my boy, it's only a witless man who cannot turn away from a bad decision. Experience comes with living. Learn by it."

"Since I've already booked passage for three and I cannot talk Dimity into using my ticket, Lucinda will accompany Clarice. I cannot allow Clarice to go to Europe unchaperoned. "It can be very romantic on board ship, you know, Jake, and for a man and woman traveling alone, with so much idle time, who knows." he grinned a knowing grin."No offense, Jake."

"No offense taken, sir," he smiled. "I'll certainly feel more comfortable, knowing she'll have company while I'm occupied with the business at hand."

"Hopefully, I'll be joining you soon."

Albert gathered up the papers and stacked them in a neat pile, and placed them in a leather binder. He moved around his desk, and handed the thick binder to Jake. He laid his hand affectionately on Jake's broad shoulder, then held out an envelope.

"There should be enough money in there to take care of everything. If not, go to our bank in London."

"Thank you, sir."

"Since you've had a chance to study the documents, you do understand what is expected, Jake. You've asked so few questions. Is there anything else you'd like to know?"

The back of Jake's neck prickled with the awesome responsibility he was shouldering. "I think you're briefing covered everything," he paused, "except that I am curious as to how this all came about."

Albert wondered when his young protégé would ask this very question. His genius for disentangling any kind of problem was a sign of a quick inquisitive mind. He had earned Albert's respect for that very quality.

Jake realized he was the target of narrowed and intent eyes. He waited for a protest informing him that that part of the deal was none of his business.

"Jake, my boy, I wondered when you would get around to asking me that very question."

Albert sat on the edge of his desk and gave out a deep audible sigh. "In the strictest of confidence, Jake, Pierpont Morgan, who is my good friend and business associate, as you well know, came to see me several weeks ago. He was inquiring whether I thought some of my English banking acquaintances would be interested in purchasing some railroad stock in America. He told me that William H. Vanderbilt was looking to dispose of 150,000 shares of his New York Central Railroad stock and that he'd prefer to deal with English investors.

"I told Pierpont that the London investors I knew were fit for the plucking."

"But why would Mr. Vanderbilt even consider selling any of his stock? Doesn't he have sole ownership?"

"He does that. Eighty-seven percent to be exact." Albert raised his bushy eyebrows. "It's a fair question you ask, Jake, and there's no man keener for a dollar than William Vanderbilt. But it seems he wants to unload the taxes that go with the ownership of the New York Central. It seems the legislators have taxed him to the hilt."

"But why all the secrecy?"

"Logic, my boy! Pure logic! He doesn't want Wall Street to think the railroad is in trouble. When a multimillionaire sells, people begin to wonder."

"I see," he nodded, "It helps to know the whole story."

"By all means. But I wanted you to be curious enough to inquire. At any rate, my part in it is not only providing the entree to the investors and helping Pierpont in the negotiation of the sale but the plum is my option to purchase as many shares as it takes to sit on the board."

"Shouldn't you be concerned about the exorbitant taxes, sir?"

"Certainly, but I have friends in the legislature and I intend to lobby to get the tax rate changed."

"Why doesn't Mr. Vanderbilt do the same?"

"Although Mr. Vanderbilt is a man of great power and wealth, he has failed to influence the legislators in his behalf. As a matter of fact, I fear he has incurred their wrath in the bullying tactics he's used thus far."

Jake held out his hand. "I appreciate your insight, sir," Jake said with real emotion, "and for believing in me."

Albert studied Jake. "It's you're own doing, son," he said, giving him a paternal look. "You've proven your worth to me many times." He pivoted around to the other side of his desk. "See you in the morning, Jake."

Spring was in the air. Though earth and sky was alive and vivid with the seeds of a new season's birth, a dark cloud of depression hung over Dimity. There was no feeling of renewal for her. The smile had gone from her eyes.

The bitterest barb of all was the news of Clarice traveling to Europe with Jake. When Dimity heard this, she was too violently angry to cry or feel sorry for herself any longer. She only cursed herself for being such a fool.

Thinking everyone was still asleep and anxious to be out of the house before everyone was up, Dimity rushed down the stairway in a furious haste.

She was half-way out the front door when she was startled by the deep voice of her father.

"Dimity, please come back inside."

She closed the door and stood there stiffly with marked attention. His astute look told her he knew what she was up to.

"Dimity, I thought it was understood. I want you there with me to see Jake and your sister off."

If there was one thing she did understand, it was the brusqueness in his voice. Displeasing him was the last thing she wanted. Avoiding his eyes, Dimity nervously fiddled with the buttons on her faille silk jacket. This was the sort of scene she had hoped to avoid. She hardly dared to raise her eyes to look at him. She hated deceiving her father.

Smiling wanly, she began, "Papa, I must finish my assignment. Mr. Holt expects my story to be on his desk by noon today. The ship doesn't leave until two. Papa, I promise you, I'll be there in plenty of time."

Dimity was very nearly at the point of breaking down and divulging her secret. It was almost more than she could bear to see that gloating face on Clarice as she strutted around in such an obvious joyful triumph. It was even more uncomfortable to watch her mooning over Jake in that brazen fashion forgetting those fine fancy manners of hers.

Admittedly, Dimity was tormented in her presence. She was glad Clarice was going.

Albert looked severely at his daughter. "Mind you now, I'll expect to see you at the gate. One o'clock?"

"Yes, Papa! One o'clock!"

With a surprised rapt look Jake s eyes moved slowly from her flushed lovely face, and traveled down to the tiny belted waist, remembering the soft pliant body beneath the folds of material.

"I'm sorry I'm so late," she shouted over the din of the whooping calls of 'bon voyage' from well wishers, the excited laughter from passengers on the promenade deck, and the clanging noise of the ship's bell demanding everyone's attention to board.

The atmosphere was one huge kaleidoscope of euphoria and excitement.

Albert gave Dimity a look of exasperation but remained silent.

As they stood at the foot of the gangplank, behind them loomed the huge luxury liner. Fidgeting from one foot to the other, Clarice, oozing self-importance, and savoring every minute, stood with one hand on the sturdy railing with a red velvet reticule dangling from her wrist. Her white-gloved fingers clutched a large colorful bandbox. Always fashionable, she was wearing an extravagant gray traveling dress piped in a lush color of red velvet, with a perky gray straw bonnet trimmed with the same velvet ribbon. Dimity could see no expense had been spared.

Unmistakably drawn and serious, Jake stood next to her, grasping his valise.

"Dimity," he bowed, without taking her hand. He could not look away from her. Several locks of burnished curls lifted by the lively spring breeze hung limply about her forehead. The adorable look of her left him with an aching longing. In the next moment he was feeling a deep remorse for everything that had happened. It was all so unnatural to be going on a trip with Clarice. Seeing Dimity's resigned acceptance and knowing they were bound to their separate destinies was intolerable for him.

"Jake," she acknowledged him with a painful politeness.

Lucinda had dawdled behind, chatting with the baggage handlers. When she finally joined them, Clarice shoved her bandbox at her.

"Lucinda," Clarice berated her, "upon my soul, what has kept you?"

"Only making sure our trunks was tagged, Miss," she said, her lips trembling in a smile.

Jake's staring eyes on Dimity completely unnerved her, but she faced him with a cool composure she did not feel.

"Do have a pleasant voyage," Dimity said, forcing a smile, all the while feeling empty and lifeless.

"We intend to," Clarice answered impatiently.

At the sound of the final loud blast of horn, Clarice, who wore a beaming expression, cupped her arm in Jake's. "We must board, Jake, it's the last call."

Waving a final goodbye, they made their way up the gangplank.

In those long agonizing few minutes, Dimity thought she would die.

Albert watched anxiously as they departed, his eyes following upwards. "She's a mighty fine ship with a character and grace befitting a lady."

Turning his attention to Dimity, he said regretfully, "What a pity you are not going with them, Dimity."

She breathed a prayer of relief that she was not going with them.

In the days that followed, Dimity shut herself off from the familiar world of New York Society, and the fashionably dressed socialites she'd grown up with. It was one way of shutting out the vision of Clarice.

Before too long, all her bitterness and sense of emptiness was displaced with a hungry eagerness to write more and better stories. Dimity immersed herself in her work, finding it the only semblance of peace of mind in her young life.

Felix Holt had chastised Dimity for the last assignment she had turned in. "Don't make it a sermon," he'd said, "you'll put your readers to sleep." She didn't intend to be preachy with this piece.

Determined to write authentic true life stories and to bring the vision closer to her readers, Dimity felt it was crucial that she submerge herself in the world of the poor who made a meager living sewing garments.

Her pulses throbbed with the excitement of it. Knowing her father would have been horrified if he found out what she was up to, Dimity was thankful that he was away for a week. One week. That's all T need, she thought. But there was still Nellie to deal with. That dear sweet soul who clucked over her like a mother hen. Escaping from her watchful eyes wasn't easy.

Dimity managed to leave very early before Nellie was up. On this warm spring day she didn't mind the walk to the horsecar. Dressed in a shabby dress and broken-down shoes that she bought from a peddler on Hester Street, Dimity boarded the crowded horsecar. The mass of passengers packed into the car were mostly immigrants, who shared a common desire. To improve their lot. Though in coping with America's realities, too quickly they were disenchanted, but their faces all bore a determined look.

She made her way down the cinder-crusted wooden steps to the dark and dingy basement of the tenement.

The man that had hired Dimity the previous day stood at the foot of the steps. His pock-marked face was drawn into a sour sneer. "Ain't gonna last long, sis, if ya can't be here on time." He viewed her with suspicion.

Seeing no lunch sack, he barked, "Ain't got no lunch, ya ain't gonna last no ten hours."

Dimity held up her reticule. "It's in here."

He could see when she spoke; her way of talkin' was educated. Not like the rest of 'em, he thought.

"Over there," he pointed a crooked finger, "ye 're to sit there."

He eyed her with furrowed brows.

Sensing his eyes on her as she moved to the appointed table, Dimity turned to give him stare for stare. She wondered if she would be able to get away with her subterfuge. Looking around the rat-infested cellar, she saw a strange array of foreigners, many of whom Dimity was sure had fled to America with hopes of a decent life.

Dimity settled herself on the wooden bench between a buxom, unkempt woman who ignored her, and a child of ten or twelve who looked at her with a pathetic childish eagerness.

Only the light of the kerosene lamps penetrated the dank, dark basement, and there was little air, if any at all. She couldn't seem to get a deep breath of fresh air into her lungs. A tailoring factory it was called. There was only one man at work besides the bossman, the rest were all women and children.

Those doing piecework seemed most intent and concentrated, their laboring hands working furiously and relentlessly. The women stitching the linings in the caps were less harried. And those few sewing buttons on the shirtwaists, mostly children, unlike the other workers, occasionally looked up from their work to see what was going on. Like soldiers on a battlefield, the workers sat dolefully amid the sewing paraphernalia and cloth remnants in complete acceptance of the intolerable working conditions. The fear of losing their jobs and going hungry was what kept them there. For women there were no other jobs unless they resorted to prostitution.

The only noise was an occasional cough, and the incessant clanking of the treadle on the lone sewing machine in the middle of the room, with its operator perspiring profusely onto the cloth. It was a peculiar apparatus cranking out stitches too perfect, and too fast for human hands. Dimity stared as the tailor lifted a finished tailored jacket from the machine and carefully placed it on the stack of jackets on the table beside him.

At Dimity's table, four women sewed linings into caps, and two children sewed buttons on shirtwaists.

Dimity had seen the woman when she first entered. She was standing by the barrel, holding a long handled community cup of water to her lips; she eyed the new girl disdainfully. She looked much too clean and proper to be one of 'em.

Dimity watched the tall, ungainly creature, called Hannah, coming towards her. Dimity didn't know if those red-lidded eyes were squinting in the dim light because the woman couldn't see, or because it was her way of giving a hard mean look to scare her. When Dimity heard the tone of her manly, mean-sounding voice, there was no doubt she intended to intimidate her.

"Don't be thinkin' ye'll be sittin' on ye're duff without doin', sis," she crowed, shoving a much-fingered, greasy piece of faded material in front of her with a needle and some black thread. "Show some life here," she demanded sharply, "let's see your stitches on this here practice piece.

Obediently, Dimity clumsily drew the thread through the needle with trembling fingers and began stitching. With complete absorption, she slowly slipped the blunt needle through the dirty cloth, leaving black, uneven, unsightly, large stitches. She knew there was no way she could hope to compete with the nimble fingers of the workers who stitched with such speed and dexterity.

To Dimity, it seemed as though the woman stood hovering over her menacingly for the longest time. Finally, she sat across from Dimity, observing her with a superior air, impatiently drumming her fingers on the table. Eyeing her with a critical eye, she shook her massive shaggy head. Her face scarlet with anger, she shouted, "Lord alive, ain't you the worse stitcher I've ever seen. Quick! "Quick!' she demanded, reaching over and cracking Dimity's knuckles with a stick.

All eyes rested on Dimity, who stared at Hannah in stunned silence. Not allowing herself to be provoked, Dimity dropped her eyes and continued stitching.

Restraining her wrath, a hairy hand came from behind and clamped down on the hand holding the afflicting weapon. "Enough, Hanna! Leave her be," the bossman berated her. "Start her on the shirtwaists."

The vindictive woman knew better than to cross her husband. Out of the pile of shirts on the table, she pulled out a thick gray shirt. Throwing it in Dimity's face, she commanded, "Sew on the buttons."

Dimity could see she was an unhappy witch of a woman who took great delight in seeing others in pain. Ordering women and children around suited her.

Leaving the table in a huff, the woman sniffed noisily at a pinch of tobacco she lifted from her soiled apron pocket.

With sensitive fingers, the little girl to Dimity's left touched Dimity's hand shyly. Looking at her, she smiled. Dimity smiled back with an infinite sadness. Why wasn't this child in school? More than likely she'd never seen the inside of a school.

"Lucky, you are, girl," crooned the lady to her right. She's a she-devil. That she is. And may the devil fly away with her," she said in a whisper, leaning close.

No wonder the atmosphere was tense, thought Dimity.

When Dimity opened her mouth to speak, the woman held up a work-worn calloused hand, with torn nails, waving her to silence. "They'll deduct your pay and mine too," she said in a hushed voice.

Dimity instinctively warmed to her. Looking down at her own soft, smooth hands with manicured fingernails she felt a secret guilt. Like a thief she was taking the precious pennies away from some poor soul who needed the money to survive.

At the smell of boiled cabbage and potatoes, pangs of hunger gripped Dimity. With the hint of lunchtime, she questioned the woman next to her, "Is that our lunch they're cooking?"

The woman let out a guffaw. "No dearie, it ain't for us. Sinful ain't it? Eatin' a hot lunch 'afore us."

At the sound of the clanging bell, the place cleared out in a mad race to the backyard privy. As Dimity filed out, she made a mental note. No kindness there, she thought, regarding the couple as they sat with their backs to the boiling pot. The man dunked a piece of folded up bread into his bowl sopping up the juice, and sucked it up hungrily into his mouth.

"I hope the food sticks in his gullet," Dimity said under her breath. Outraged by their lack of compassion, she turned angrily away. The swarm of workers pushed her aside as they sped past her in an energetic frenzy as if their spirits were suddenly released along with their bodies.

Twenty ladies and children stood anxiously in a line, three and four abreast awaiting their turn to use the two-seated privy.

"My name's Dovie, and this here's Sara," she said, her arm linked in the little girl's. "Ye're a pretty little thing. What's ye're name, dearie?"

"Dimity."

A gray wind swirled about choking them with dust and the foul odor of the overflowing privy.

After a long wait, the group gravitated to the front of the tenement where they found a place to sit. Crammed next to the high dirty wall of the tenement, they sat on the pavement which was even harder and less yielding than the wooden bench they'd been sitting on all morning.

Relaxing, Dimity spread her legs out before her. She eyed her shabby shoes disconsolately, the cheap leather about the toes was scuffed off completely, and the heels were nearly worn down to nothing. She smiled to herself thinking, hardly the shoes she could wear to one of her favorite society events. Suddenly, she was overcome with that nagging guilt feeling again when she looked at Dovie's shoes, which were as bad as or worse than the shoes she was pretending with.

Dovie opened a brown paper sack and lifted out a tin container and two spoons. Mother and daughter ate ravenously, their spoons clinking in unison. Dovie paused long enough to look at Dimity who was watching them with a longing for a cup of hot tea to go with her muffin.

Gulping down a mouthful of cold soup, Dovie asked, "Ain't you eatin', dearie?"

"Oh," said Dimity, yes.' She dug into her reticule and pulled out the muffin she'd wrapped in a linen napkin.

Dovie fingered the napkin. "That's a mighty fine piece of cloth, but ya ain't got much to eat," she said suspiciously, taking in the ladylike way of her, with a curiosity burrowed down deep in her.

Brushing that remark aside, Dimity quickly stuffed the napkin back into her reticule, out of sight, then took a bite of her muffin.

"Ya can have a bite of this here soup," Sara said, holding out her used spoon to Dimity. "It's lentil."

Dimity felt a hollow sadness at the generosity of the child who wished to share her meager lunch. "No thank you, Sara," she said, "but that's very kind of you to offer."

After smelling the appetizing soup, it seemed the hunger pains all but exploded in her empty belly. Dimity realized how ill-prepared she was with only a muffin to eat.

"Stop ye're fidgetin,' Sara," Dovie reprimanded her daughter. "She ain't got no summer-weight drawers, and with the days turnin' warm as summer, it's gettin' too hot for them winter woolen drawers she's wearin'. They's itchin' the hide off her."

Feeling a soul-wrenching anguish for the uncomplaining child, Dimity eyed her untidy, straggling hair that looked like it could use a good wash. She wondered if the drawers didn't need a washing as well.

Stoically, the workers marched backed to work at the sound of the bell.

"Ye're doin' right well, sis," he said in a slurred voice. As he bent over her, Dimity could smell his foul smelling breath, reeking of brandy.

"How's about a walk out back while the missus is off to the market," he said thickly, with a lustful gleam in his eye while running his grubby hand over her backside.

Feeling the hardness of him against her, Dimity shivered in disgust.

In a swift, savage jab to his groin with her elbow, she rose from the bench.

"Damme!" he croaked, doubling over, clutching his paunchy pants bursting with his manly parts.

In an instant, Dimity snatched her reticule, and was headed towards the open doorway. She stopped momentarily to see if he was following her. The panic in her gave way to relief when she saw him lying on the floor clutching himself and moaning, his pocked, bloated face crimson down to his powerful bull neck.

Every eye in the place was fastened on him, while they smothered chuckles of satisfaction behind their hands.

"You'll not have another chance to touch me with your dirty roaming hands," Dimity screamed, a glitter of a tear forming in the corner of her eye.

Her legs trembling, Dimity scrambled up the rickety steps.

Dovie followed Dimity out into the street. "Dimity, ya can't leave. Ya got pay comin'."

"It's yours, Dovie. Tell them I said so." she called to her over the clatter of the wagons and drays.

While it was still fresh in her mind, Dimity wrote the story that night. She thought she had prepared herself, but in witnessing life's harsh realities of the garment workers, she had been jolted out of her naivety, and she wanted the citizens of New York City to be jolted out of their complacency.

Dimity launched into a realistic account of the plight of the sweat shop workers, shackled by poverty, who were forced to work for pennies in unhealthy conditions. She wove into her story a realistic fiber of the slum-infested shop. Low pay, long hours, unsanitary conditions, with no water closet indoors. Only a privy outdoors to service twenty to thirty workers. Children are working as many as twelve long wearisome hours a day, she wrote. Why are these children not in school? Where are our city fathers? Is there no social conscience?

Once again, M. D. Durant's byline caught the eye of many politicians who were embarrassed by the story.

DIMITY AND DANIEL

CHAPTER TWENTY-ONE

Ableak, silent drizzle fell on the solemn parade of mourners as they walked to the gravesite. Danny Eagan, supported by two of his henchmen, limped along with halting steps, pausing now and then to give his aching leg a rest. The three men followed close behind the widow who was escorted by Danny's trusted friend, Ira, who once stood erect, was now stooped and hunched over, like the old man he was. Beneath the mound of silver hair, his countenance revealed the sadness he felt for his lifelong friend. Quincy Devlin.

In the midst of a grove of budding poplar trees on a sloping hill above the mourners, stood a stranger. In spite of the misty rain, the slight, attractive lady stood there calmly, observing the scene below. Silvery droplets of rain clung to her green bonnet and gleaming hair.

She watched as the sparse group of men clad in dark suits with black silk bands on their arms, bowed their heads. She could hear the distant rumble of their male voices praying in unison.

Suddenly, the widow pitched forward in a heap on top of the casket, crying in wailful, pitiful animal screams that echoed throughout the graveyard. Danny, forgetting his injured leg, lunged forward in an effort to stop her, but faltered, then fell to his knees. A knot of men surged forward to lift her off of the casket. In a crouched position,

Danny doffed his hat at the slate gray casket that was quickly lowered into the deep carved out pit. "So long, old buddy," he moaned despairingly, thinking how his beloved Quincy, who, in his role of protector, had saved his life. "They ain't gonna get away with it, Quince."

The portly, devout priest stopped to comfort the widow. Impatient and intolerant of the man who made Quincy Devlin a martyr, and who was imperiling his soul by committing such vile and unpardonable crimes, the old priest stalked past Danny Eagan without so much as a word.

Even in the distance, Dimity could see the sadness on the face of the man she knew as Danny Eagan. But in an instant, his expression quickly turned into an angry scowl and a resigned acceptance.

Her thoughts turned to the report of the shooting as she stared at him. Lucky for him, the gunshots that squeezed out the life of his bodyguard barely nicked him.

Dimity wondered why that face inspired such a deep curiosity in her. She did not know the power and scope of Danny Eagan, but recalling that Christmas day when his father was killed, she felt he was ruthless. There was a story here, and she intended to write it. A new sense of excitement nipped at her. Discretely, she turned away and walked out of the cemetery.

A mutinous plan quickly evolved in Danny Eagan's mind, absorbing the whole of his attention. His plan of vengeance became more merciless as the days went by. Though filled with a rebellious misery, he kept his wits about him, purposely postponing his retaliation.

He wouldn't make the same mistake he made when Mickey was killed. At the time, when his father's killers, the Vassallo brothers, were sent to jail, Danny thought that. Vito Scaglione, the man who controlled the Italian gang would have the same fate. But with no proof that he was the brain behind the shooting, and with the brothers' failure to break the code of honor, he was acquitted for lack of evidence. Once again, the law was unable to mete out justice.

When the first wave of Italian immigrants arrived in New York, they found an established underworld of Irish and Jewish gangs. In the beginning, the Italians did not penetrate this underworld and operated within their own circle, though they brought with them a tradition of crime and contempt for the law. Illegality soon became the rule in this country as it had been in Italy.

A liggi e pi ricca, La furca e pri lu poveru, La giustzia pri li fissa: "The law is for the rich, the gallows for the poor, and justice for the fools."

Since Mickey Eagan's death, the Italian gang had advanced into Danny's territory. Although Danny Eagan was powerful enough to bully the Jewish gang, the Italian chieftain proved to be a formidable vicious adversary. Before long, the Italians grew in strength and commanded real power in the Sixth Ward. As Scaglione's prostitution and gambling business expanded, he opened a weapons shop on Elizabeth Street where he sold pistols, brass knuckles, stilettos, and billy clubs with the slug in the end.

Scaglione, the bull-necked, heavy-jowled Italian scored with knife scars, was a real problem for Danny. But Danny's advantage over the Italian faction was his in with the police, and politicians, who turned their heads, when their pockets were lined. Corruption was their companion.

Danny chose the night of the Spring Ball to carry out his plan. The political balls or 'rackets' were the charity events given by the Tammany Hall politicians and friends, or otherwise gang leaders. Danny Eagan gave three rackets a year, with all the proceeds supposedly going to charity, when in reality; he pocketed fifty percent of the booty. Every business owner was shaken down to buy tickets for the poor, even the pushcart peddlers had to buy tickets for these charity events.

It was a night Danny knew the city detective force would be occupied, with all their attention focused on the grand event. And word from his informer, a discontented henchman of the Italian gang, was that the weekly card game was on.

Tammany Hall, the sanctuary of the New York City rulers was stuffed to the doors with the city's assemblymen, judges, policemen and street characters. The crowd overflowed onto the sidewalk. The only citizenry missing were the elements of high society.

Sitting decently with hat in hand next to Danny Eagan was Judge Jeremiah Byrnes who smiled gaily while tapping his cane in time to the music. Across the table was Eddy Cooper, the

Mayor, and to his right was Davie Dawson, the manager of the New York Board of Alderman. The entire table held a weird assortment of characters. All trustees of the city. All there for the benefit of the poor.

Up and down the long hall, the men clustered at the gaming tables banked against the walls trying their hands at the roulette wheels, faro and cards.

The lively music drew the men to the center of the hall where the giggling girls resplendent in dazzling, skimpy dresses and bare shoulders milled around, patiently waiting for a dancing partner.

They were the titillating element of the whole affair, the hand-picked girls Danny Eagan brought from his bawdy houses. His weapons. A sure way to lure the men with their fluttery feminine wiles. After a dance or two, the men were maneuvered to the upstairs hall which opened into a series of dimly lighted and deserted rooms, converted into bedrooms for the night.

When the men finished the hearty meal of chicken and ribs, they settled down to some serious drinking.

"Danny, my boy," the mayor addressed the handsome Irishman with an air of authority, "you've done a fine job." He was well aware of Danny Eagan's criminal activities in the Bowery district. He accepted it, swallowed it whole, and left it there. He was solidly hooked. The fact that, he was beholden to a crook and his paid repeaters for the election, in no way troubled him.

The tall, sallow man, sitting at the end of the table, swilling down one drink after another, had little to say throughout the evening. He was the one man who did not seize the opportunity to line his pockets with graft money. The city's District Attorney, Simon S. Cobb A do-gooder who thought he could change the system. It was plain to see he was ill at ease in the present company.

At the mayor's mention of Danny Eagan ' s good job at arranging the event, and seeing the exaggerated deference paid to one of the city's most notorious crooks, Simon came completely undone. His unbounded faith that he would surely be able to put all the criminals in the city behind bars was proving to be a dream.

Simon looked straight into the eyes of the police chief. "Hasn't he committed some crime you could arrest him for?" he asked in his drunken thick tongue.

Eliciting no reply, he went on. "Thieves helping thieves."

Glaring at him with cold eyes, Danny's face turned purple with rage. He stood up and faced him. "The thieves we got in the Bowery ain't thieves by choice.
They're thieves by necessity. And necessity don't know any law."

Ignoring Danny, Simon turned to the mayor. "Mr. Mayor, what about the Asylum story? And the sweat shop story? Have you and your cronies done anything to change those deplorable conditions?" he asked sarcastically.

"Workin' on it." the Mayor barked, "that M. D. Durant fella better stay out of our hair. We're doin' the best that we can."

Simon had a particular hatred for the man who lived off of the earnings of a lewd woman. Glaring down the table at Danny, he rose from his seat. "Thieve is one thing, but making money off of the misfortune of these girls who are down on their uppers is a disgrace."

Feeling a trifle uneasy, the chief quickly rounded the table and whisked Simon out of his seat and escorted his staggering body out of the hall.

Danny drummed his fingers on the table in a devil's tattoo. It was close to two in the morning when he finally gave his men the signal with a raised hand. With a nod of their heads, they exited quietly to carry out their mandate. In Danny's words, "to cook 'em."

The next morning the headlines rang out with the news of the explosion on Elizabeth Street, killing Vito Scaglione and five of his men.

The day couldn't be sweeter or balmier. The golden, sunlit morning lifted Dimity's spirit. For the first time in days, she thought nothing of Jake and the miserable, dreadful thoughts that had haunted her these past weeks. That Clarice was with him in Europe. In no hurry, Dimity ambled through the double wide door of the New York Herald building.

Preoccupied with a longing to spend this glorious spring day outdoors, she sighed deeply as she climbed the stairs to the second floor. When Dimity threw open the door, her nostrils were assailed with the sharp, mingling odors of mustiness and cigar smoke. She surveyed the group assembled around Felix Holt's desk in quiet conversation. Six men sat with rapt attention, their green eye shades lowered on their foreheads and unused notepads on their laps. Was this the editorial meeting? Dimity wondered. It couldn't be.

At the murmuring rustle of her skirt, the lewd joke telling stopped, but the rumbling, ribald laughter continued for the longest while.

"Ha!" Felix snorted, when he saw her. "Well men, Miss M. D. Durant has finally decided to honor us with her presence." He gave her a disapproving look.

Looking very pretty and demure, she stood there in her fashionable coat of brown wool and matching frock.

"In a cool, confident voice, she retorted, "I beg your pardon, Mr. Holt, but Mr. Grant told me to be here at ten o'clock." She pointed to the large pendulum swinging clock. "My stars!" Her hand went to her mouth. "By that clock it looks to me I'm an hour early." With eyes as big as saucers, she glanced in Casey Grant s direction accusingly.

Casey Grant's mouth fell open at her outspokenness.

So, Dimity thought, she hadn't been mistaken when Casey had turned away without speaking lately. She knew that having two of the latest top stories and beating him at his game had not endeared her to him and it was clear her success was ostracizing her from her cohorts.

A deep whispering murmur ran through the office.

Perplexed, Felix inclined his head towards her. Taken aback, he eyed the peppery, ferret-faced, wiry little man with a tight-lipped scowl. "Mighty peculiar! A right smart gent like you, Casey, tellin' our little Miss here the wrong time?"

The naked expression of disgust on his bosses face told Casey Grant he was caught in an action Felix highly disapproved of. Although, he enjoyed stirring up rows, this was one time when Casey knew it backfired.

"I'm afraid Miss Durant is mistaken," he lied in a flat toneless voice. "No harm done if she is late."

Like a buzzard, he stood with head cocked, defending his territory.

Dimity thought she would choke at his blatant lie. Common sense told her to leave it alone. By the sympathetic look on Felix Holt's face, she was sure he believed her.

From a distant corner, Casey retrieved a chair. With ponderous footsteps, he pushed the chair towards Dimity.

"Have a seat, Miss Durant," he said very proper like as though he was completely innocent of any wrongdoing.

She fixed her vivid eyes on the lank figure. "You would do well to get your stories straight, Mr. Grant."

He could not look at her. With his face hidden from the visor, she could not see the guilt in his eyes.

Dimity stalked off before he could speak. She removed her coat and hung it on the coat rack and then unpinned the monstrance long stabbing hat pin from her sailor hat. Somehow she found comfort in the thought of sticking the weasel with her hat pin right where it hurt the most. Who knows she mused as she settled herself comfortably into the chair, accidents do happen.

In evident perplexity, Felix stroked his whiskers, which were unusually shaggy. Struck by Dimity's crushed look when that bastard told the bold-faced lie, Felix was hard-pressed to assign the story to him. But for her own good, he could not risk her safety. Why he'd be throwing the little lady into the blighted center of crime and the jaws of the devil himself. Although, he had to admit she was a courageous little piece of fluff that didn't do anything by half-measures. Hurling herself with single-minded fury into her assignments had certainly opened his eyes to her potential. He couldn't help but admire her for her spunk, and he liked the way she flowered under a word of praise, but on general principals, it wasn't a job for a lady. Much less, a lady with the privileges of wealth. Plying her away from feature stories wasn't his aim. She was too good. But this one was out of her sphere of investigative stories.

After a perceptible hesitation, and a growing impatience with the snickering men, Felix held up the front page of the morning paper. "Vito Scaglione Killed In Explosion." The headlines struck Dimity like a thunderbolt.

"Casey stumbled upon this story on his way home from the Spring Ball he was covering," Felix continued with his account, "he was about a half a mile away when he-heard the booming echo of the explosion. As luck would have it, we had time to kill the story we had set up for this morning's addition. I expect Casey to follow up on it hammer and tongs."

Casey Grant's story. Disappointment ran through Dimity like an electric shock. Perched uneasily on the edge of her seat, she sat twisting and knotting her handkerchief. Did her past achievements count for nothing? In her passion to expose Danny Eagan and his shady dealings, she had already begun an investigation of sorts. Now, she was all but locked out.

"Mr. Holt," she asked, "where was Danny Eagan when the explosion occurred?"

"Danny Eagan has been completely exonerated. Witnesses told the police he and his men were attending the Spring Ball. "

"That's true," Casey agreed, confirming his statement. "The Eagan gang was still at the Ball when I left at two in the morning. Danny too. In fact, he was whooping it up at the mayor's table with a group of politicians that they can't pin it on him."

"I'm sure," Dimity interjected sarcastically, "that "Danny Eagan did not share one ounce of sorrow for Scaglione's demise." She knew, as did every man in the room, that Danny Eagan was behind the plot to kill the Italian chief.

The rush of talk continued, while Dimity read the story on the front page. She sat silent, inwardly seething at the lack of detail in the story, knowing she could surely do a better job. They broke for lunch to meet at McGurk's, the corner saloon, where the presence of a lady was frowned upon. Usually, Felix brought her back a weighty, two-fisted roast beef sandwich, doused in gravy. Dimity realized she couldn't look into a crystal ball, but one day, she intended to enter that sacrosanct chamber whether it dishonored her or not.

At the end of the day, Felix called her to his desk. He fumbled through the maize of papers spread out before him, pulled out a scribbled sheet of notes and handed it to her with ink-stained fingers. "Some additional information on that story you're working on."

In spite of herself, she couldn't help but like him, knowing he was fair-minded. Not only did she admire him for his sincerity, but she was grateful for the kindness he had shown her. It was his shaking, spontaneous high mirth at times that tickled her. "Thank you, Mr. Holt," she smiled, accepting the paper, not holding her disappointment against him.

Like many men with dirty minds, he couldn't help himself. His eyes lingered over her gracefully curved body as she glided away. She was a jewel of loveliness. Perhaps, he thought that would be her undoing in the newspaper business."

"Oh, and Miss Durant, keep up the good work."

Dinner was the pleasantness part of the day for Dimity, now that she had Papa all to herself. Rather than sitting end to end at the long mahogany table, she sat to her father's side, in Clarice's spot. Dimity reflected on Clarice's choice of maids she'd hired to replace Lucinda. Standing in the middle of the dining room, she watched Eugenia out of the corner of her eye while the girl went about setting the table in her usual frenzy. Already, her white apron was stained, and the ruffled cap on her head was askew. Dimity truly doubted that the girl would work out. Of course, it was only natural for her to be nervous on a new job, but it had been two weeks now, and she still fluttered about, moving too quickly and clumsily, wreaking havoc in her path. If she wasn't pouring water in the crystal glasses to overflowing, she was spilling gravy or soup on the clean white tablecloth. Dimity had tried to put her at ease the night before when she had nearly dumped the platter of cod in her lap.

While Eugenia was occupied, Dimity made her way to the kitchen, where Nellie was bent over a bubbling pot of soup, lifting out a spoonful to taste. Lily was standing beside her grumbling, making reproving remarks about Eugenia "But Nellie, she's near to the clumsiest slip of a girl I've ever seen."

"Give her time, Lily," she said, "think of her as ye're pupil. Like Lucinda done with ye'reself."

Lily shook her head. "She's a poor stupid thing that can't never learn, Nellie."

Thinking it was Eugenia, they were startled as the pantry door swung open, but were quickly relieved when they saw it was Dimity standing there.

"That's what I want to talk to you about, Lily," Dimity said. "I think Eugenia would be happier helping Nellie here in the pantry. I know Mr. Durant would be happier. It seems she causes too much of a disturbance in the dining room. Please see to it, Lily."

"Yes'um," Lily nodded, "I will that."

Nellie waited until Lily left before she put her arms around the only one in this world she cared about. Dimity, luv, ye're lookin' too pale. Work in' too hard ya are with slippin' out of the house before dawn with nothin' warm in ye're belly."

"I'm fine, Nellie," she assured her.

Nellie shook her head.

"No truly. I am."

Sometimes Nellie's frankness was a breath of fresh air. Remembering the child in her who hungered for affection, and that it was Nellie who wiped her nose and dried her tears when she was at the end of Clarice's meanness. Dear, dear Nellie, whose hair was dull and lifeless, and bunched untidily over her head away from a chalk pale face that held an exhausted look. Dimity could see her once enormous frame was not near as fleshy, and the very size of her great soft breasts had shrunk. Concerned, Dimity looked into that ever mirthful face.

"Nellie, are you feeling well?"

She gave a weary sigh and sunk down in a chair. "Och, begor! Don't you be worrin' bout me. Feel in' fine, darlin'. Jest fine. The body's a bit weary with all the work. That's all" She looked into Dimity's eyes sorrowfully. Have to expect a slowin' down at my age, darlin'."

A rush of guilt swept over Dimity. She seized one of her hands and held it. "Oh Nellie! Of course! It's much, too much work for you."

Nellie bobbed her head.

"Papa thinks we should hire another parlor maid, and then you'll have Eugenia to help you in the kitchen."

"What ever the master thinks, luv, is alright with me."

While Dimity sat in the kitchen talking with Nellie, she heard the front door open and close.

As Albert removed his coat, his eyes rested on the familiar coat and hat hanging on the hall tree. "Ah," Albert said to himself, "for once, Dimity is home before me." He was pleased. Whistling happily, he fingered the folded up paper in his pocket as he made his way to the dining room. The surprise of this news had him fairly bursting with good spirits. He couldn't wait to tell Dimity about it. No where on earth did he feel more comfortable, and at ease, than in his own home. He stroked his wiry whiskers thoughtfully. My retreat away from the wild drama of the hectic Wall Street life.

When he lifted her up off of her feet, his usual worldly poise was suddenly lost in his eager exuberance. Dimity could see he was in the best of moods.

"Papa, you must have had a good day," she laughed lightheartedly.

With his jaws locked in a wide, gleeful smile, he handed the cablegram to Dimity. "Jake and I married this morning. Gloriously happy." Signed Clarice.

"It's all that I hoped for," Albert said jubilantly.

Dimity suddenly went white and the cable slipped from her fingers. She gasped sharply and slumped into a chair.

Seeing the color drain from her face, and the torment in her eyes, he frowned. "What is it, Dimity?"

Dimity turned her head to escape his probing eyes.

"Dimity?"

She opened her mouth to say something, but the words were muffled. "I thought." Then the tears, unconstrained, slipped free.

He patted her head gently. Albert eyed her curiously. Had he missed something? Was there some feeling between Dimity and Jake before Clarice entered the picture?

"Please! Dimity, tell me what is wrong?"

She couldn't keep this torment silent within her. "Oh Papa," she sobbed, looking up at him, her eyes brimming with tears. "I've been such a fool. I thought he cared for me."

For the first time, the realization struck him. "Oh my dear," he said in a pained voice, "I had no idea."

He wanted to ask questions, but didn't have the heart.

"I loved him, Papa," she choked. "I was so sure that he loved me." She broke down, sobbing uncontrollably.

"There! There! He stroked her head as he used to when she was a little girl and hurting. His dark eyes narrowed. Had Clarice deliberately snared

Jake away from her? He wondered. What a rotten mess.

Perhaps, some day he would know the truth.

DIMITY AND DANIEL

CHAPTER TWENTY-TWO

The midnight moon cast its silvery light on the loose gravel driveway as the carriage rumbled up to the entrance. They were the perfect portrait of newlyweds. She, the young bride with shining, worshipful eyes, and he, to the casual eye, the solicitous, attentive husband.

"Clarice, I do think you should retire immediately," he pleaded. "You are exhausted, and the baby."

"Nonsense, Jake," she sighed deeply. "Please." she put her forefinger to her lips, "you promised not to say anything."Let me break the news at the proper time."

"Of course, dear, but I'm sure they'll notice how tired you look." Sucking in his breath, he dared not mention her noticeable swollen belly. Her reaction at the mention of it was peculiar. When he remarked about her growing size, a storm of protest broke loose. It is only bloat, she'd protested. In truth, he himself was amazed the baby was developing so rapidly at such an early stage in her pregnancy.

"I know I look frightful, Jake," she said, but now that we're off of the ship and I'm through with that dreadful seasickness, I know I'll feel better."

It was true. Her seasickness had taken its toll. She seemed to be shrinking, except for her wider girth, and her paleness and thinness worried him.

There were moments when she wondered if he actually cared about her. Or did he only tolerate her for the baby he thought was his.

Reining in the horses, Isaiah called out, "Welcome home Miss Clarice and Master Jake."

"Thank you, Isaiah," Clarice smiled, "it's good to be home."

Jake jumped down and glanced over his shoulder at Isaiah who was seeing to the luggage.

"I'll help you with that later, Isaiah," Jake offered, holding his hand out to Clarice.

Clarice reached for his upheld hand, and then hesitated before stepping down. She gripped the side of the carriage to steady her trembling legs.

"Are you all right, Clarice?" he asked, concerned.

"I think so. I seem to be holding on to my sea legs from that blasted ship."

He kept his eyes on her. "I'll carry you in," he said, proceeding to lift her.

"You will do nothing of the sort," she objected, refusing to surrender to her sudden weakness. "I'm quite all right." Relieved the dizziness had passed, her happy mood returned as she climbed down.

"Oh Jake, isn't it truly wonderful to be home?" Seeing no sign of the same happiness on his face, she was puzzled. Tilting her head questioningly, she asked, "Jake, aren't you glad to be home?"

"Of course, I am, Clarice."

"Merciful heavens, where is everybody?"

While Jake helped Isaiah stack the luggage, she cried out her disappointment. "My stars, have they all gone to bed, Isaiah?"

"No Miss Clarice, they'd ."

Before he could say another word, the door flew open and Albert came bounding out to meet them. "Welcome home," he said, gathering Clarice in his arms. "Guess I dozed off in the chair while we waited for you.' Their arrival was anticipated with a mixture of emotions for him.

This was the day that Dimity dreaded. She stood there in the doorway, watching them in the glare of the lamplight.

Breaking into an exuberant show of affection when she saw Dimity, in two quick steps she flung her arms around Dimity in a rare sisterly embrace. "Dear Mary Dimity, it is so good to see you."

"Yes, Clarice," Papa and I are glad you're home," she said wearily, all the while wanting to get away from her touch. Clarice's pretense of the loving sister where no love existed was so out of character. Dimity stood there woodenly, trying to digest this sudden amnesty. There was no amnesty on Clarice's part. Only triumph. Dimity could see it in her flashing eyes. In all her life, Clarice had never made any attempt to hide her dogged hatred for her sister. This was an act for Jake's benefit. Dimity was sure of it. Going through all the motions of this hypocrisy was almost more than Dimity could stand. For Papa's sake, she was bound to make the best of it.

Looking at her curiously, Clarice turned a disapproving eye on her sister. "Well, Mary Dimity, aren't you going to congratulate me? And Jake?"

She was a cheat and a liar, and her love of tormenting, Dimity could see, was ever present. That would never change. So be it, Dimity thought, I can play the game. Going along in a believable pretense, her words became Dimity's own. "Of course, I congratulate you," she said in a composed voice, "and Jake!" Feeling wretched and helpless, there was tightness about her smile as she rushed forth to embrace Jake. She pressed her cheek against his shoulder, unable to bear the thought of feeling his flesh against her flesh. "Jake," she forced herself to speak words that nearly choked her. Welcome to the family." Through her thin dressing gown she felt the caress of his hand glide down her back. At his touch, her heart beat wildly. She kept her head turned away, avoiding his eyes. This was the moment she had dreaded.

"Thank you, Dimity," he said in a soft voice as he held her at arm's length as his eyes probed hers. "You are looking well, Dimity." Though her features were carved in his memory, she looked more beautiful than ever. He wanted to brush away that silken strand of hair freed from its captive net. Before he could fill his eyes with her face, Clarice was clinging to his arm.

Tossing her head in annoyance, Clarice pleaded, "Do let's go in, Jake. I fear I am much too weary to enjoy our homecoming."

In the light of the overhanging chandelier, Albert was shocked when he saw the ghastly paleness of his daughter. He gave her a worried look. "My dear! You do not look well."

"I'm fine, Papa, but very tired."

"Then you must go up to bed immediately."

"It's true, sir. We are both exhausted. It's been a long day." Without pause, he lifted one of the traveling bags, then took Clarice's arm. "Goodnight."

"Goodnight," Clarice's voice trailed off as a wave of dizziness caused her to slip on the stair.

Jake looked over his shoulder as he held onto her. "I'm sure she'll be fine in the morning after she's had a good night's sleep."

"Goodnight," Albert said, shifting his gaze to Dimity. He shook his head. Those large hazel eyes swimming in tears betrayed that trace of bravery she portrayed earlier.

Her eyes ached at the sight of the two of them climbing up the stairs arm in arm. Dimity turned away to block out the sight. She dreaded what lay ahead, living in the same house with him.

The couple's nocturnal return had not only interrupted hours of sleep, but also disrupted the routine of the entire household. Not only did the family miss Mass, but Dimity's usual Sunday morning ride on Glory was delayed until later in the day. So it was on this late summer morning that Albert and Dimity sat having breakfast on the terrace above the spectacle of the rose garden.

Dimity bent over and clipped two yellow rose buds.

"My very favorite," she murmured," sniffing deeply before placing them in a bud vase on the glass top table."

The rainbow aura of color of the luxurious swelling blossoms gave off a pleasant, addictive scent. She clipped off one more rose and held it to her nose, sniffing in the fragrance deeply. "I could smell its sweet nectar all day."

She looked at the roses, freshly sprinkled, with tiny droplets of water still clinging to the blossoms and foliage. She could see that the wilted plants were rejuvenated and reawakened to face the heat of the day. With all her heart, she wished she could be rejuvenated with some hope that life for her could have some meaning without the man she loved.

Albert chuckled as he watched her. "If you're not careful, my sweet, that honeybee buzzing around, will light on your nose." He was happy to see she derived such pleasure from the flowers.

"Ah yes," she agreed, placing the bud in the vase with the others. "I think you are right. Mrs. Honeybee is lingering too close for comfort."

Little did she realize that Jake was standing in the open doorway. He watched her as she crinkled her nose at the pungent scent of the rose she held, and the subtle gesture of a delicate hand smoothing her hair away from her face. The morning sunlight reflected the shimmering highlights of that lush auburn hair of hers.

Remembering the feel of it, and the silken touch of her skin, his insides churned. He had slept little after seeing her last night. God help me. How in this damn world am I going to keep my hands off of her?

His heels clicked noisily on the flagstones as he walked towards them. "Good morning!" His smile rested on her.

"Good morning, Jake," Albert greeted him.

"Good morning!" A smile of cool disinterest passed over her face.

Mopping his brow with a fine linen handkerchief, lie sank into the chair beside Albert. "I'd almost forgotten this appalling heat and how humid the summers could be in New York," he said, rolling up his sleeves, at the same time taking in the lovely, fresh look of Dimity, who was dressed in a fetching, sunshine yellow batiste frock.

She could see the dark curling hairs on his chest as he unfastened the top buttons of his ruffled shirt. Into her memory crept the image of his strong masculine arms embracing her. Her flesh tingled at the thought of his touch. She had to stop this, she told herself. Dragging her eyes away from him, she attempted to eat her breakfast, but each time she'd look up, Jake's eyes were on her, even though he pretended interest; in his father-in-law's conversation.

Jake knew very well why she had her guard up, but he intended, if at all possible, to get back in her good graces. How he planned to do that, he had no idea. He went headlong into involving her in conversation, "Are you planning to breed Glory again, Dimity?"

Albert piped up before Dimity could answer. "She's become quite a clever horse breeder, you know, Jake."

"I'm not at all surprised," he smiled, shifting his eyes to her. "The horsewoman I know has an inbred ability to do just that. She's always taken pride in her horses." He resented his time away from her, the times she rode alone, without him. "What about it? Will you breed her again, Dimity?"

"Possibly," she said, "but not until next spring. I hope to breed her with Ashton's Folly."

"Dimity has a new horse, Jake."

He cocked a dark eyebrow. "Oh? Is it a hunter?"

"No, she's a palomino," she beamed.

He loved that little hint of gold in her hazel eyes when they sparkled with excitement. Talking about her horses never failed to bring joy to her face.

Dimity held the tray of pecan rolls out to him.

"Are these Nellie's famous pecan rolls?" He had a laughing note in his voice. He picked up one of the rolls and began chewing. "Mmmm, just as delicious as I remembered."

"Phew!" Clarice exhaled a deep breath, while fanning herself furiously. She swept out onto the terrace to join them. "Oh dear God, how can I bear this heat?"

Dimity did not at once perceive the change in her sister the night before with her shape hidden under a wide flowing cape. But this morning, there was no disguising the swelling belly beneath her full white linen skirt. Odd, Dimity thought, that those prominent cheekbones seemed to stand out: more than usual, and the thinness of her arms was further proof of a weight loss. It finally dawned on her. She's pregnant.

Kissing Jake good morning, Clarice was breathless and flushed as she sat down in the chair Jake held for her.

"Good morning, my dear," Jake said, "it's high time you're up and about. Did you have a restful sleep?"

"Heavens no," she said with indignation. "Who could sleep in this heat?"

Albert's face was unusually stern and unyielding when his eyes rested on his daughter's figure, taking in the breadth of her.

Jake was in a quandary. He could see by his father-in-law's shocked expression that he knew that his keen eye had not missed the fact that the slenderness was gone from her waist. Jake dabbed at his forehead now glistening with perspiration. Albert deserved an explanation concerning their impromptu marriage.

Albert's hand closed on Jake's sleeve. "After breakfast, I'd like a word with you, Jake."

Clarice had not missed the discerning glances toward her middle. She was in no mood to surrender to the rising tidal wave of curiosity, but she realized there was no point in putting off the inevitable.

"Now that we're all here together," she said, fingering her napkin nervously, "Jake and I have some wonderful news." Gazing at him adoringly, she reached for his hand. Taken by surprise, he dropped his fork, and didn't take his eyes off of her in anticipation of her announcement. She dropped her eyes demurely. "Jake and I are going to have a baby."

There was excitement and confusion at the same time. Albert rose from his chair and kissed Clarice softly on the cheek. "So, I'm to be a grandfather." He held out his hand to Jake. "May I congratulate the proud father-to-be?"

"Thank you, sir." Jake smiled, accepting his hand firmly.

Quietly scrutinizing her, Dimity joined in. "Congratulations to you both," she said in a voice measured and composed. She tried to think of something else to say, but her mind was all in a muddle. What a stupid little fool I was, she told herself, to have given myself to him. The anger of hurt, pride rose in her. Before she could say another word, she'd have to quiet her heart for the words would surely stick in her throat.

Albert couldn't help but admire Dimity's incredible poise, knowing how difficult it must be for her.

Clarice lowered her eyes to the plate Lucy placed before her. Wrinkling up her nose, she pushed the eggs aside with her fork. She forced herself to take a forkful of grits, then nibbled daintily on a buttered biscuit.

"Lucy, what in the world happened to Lucinda last night?" Clarice asked with a mouthful of biscuit.

"It was fearfully late, Miss Clarice," she said, fluttering about clearing away the dirty dishes. "Don't rightly know the time."

Clarice shook her head. "Please ask her to come out here, Lucy."

"I'm afraid she's still asleep, ma'am."

"Well wake her up." Clarice glared at her.

"Yes ma'am," she said, making a mad dash for the door.

"Clarice," Jake said, "the girl must be tired. I told you last night there was no need to have her wait for the other trunks. Surely, they would have sent them on," he said sharply.

"And I told you, Jake," she retorted, "I wasn't about to worry myself silly that my new Paris gowns would be lost or stolen." She stared back at her husband. How dare he talk to me in that tone of voice? She picked up her fan and began fanning herself.

Perspiring profusely, Clarice complained loudly,

"How can you all bear to sit in this sun?" I am truly miserable.

The soft touch of the morning sun was gone as the sun climbed to its noonday perch overhead. No longer were they sitting under the shade of the large oak and with little air stirring, the heat bore down on them.

"I can see it's much too warm for Clarice. Shall we go inside?" Albert suggested, mopping his brow.

Casting a contemptuous glance at Dimity's tiny figure and hating her for it, Clarice addressed her in a poisonously sweet voice, "My! My! Don't you look pretty this morning, Mary Dimity."

"Why, thank you, Clarice." It wasn't real. Dimity knew that Clarice couldn't continue hiding behind that cloak of niceness. She wondered when the charade would end.

The morning had been maddening for Dimity. Despite the heat, she wanted only to be astride Glory right now, away from Clarice. She'd long discovered that a high-spirited ride through the woods was pure nourishment to her soul. She slipped quietly past Clarice's bedroom door.

Although she had always been able to see through her sister's maneuverings, Dimity was puzzled at Clarice's sudden desire to seek her company. Dimity shook her head. She was glad she hadn't submitted to Clarice's urgings to join her for a visit in her room. Dimity's quiet hazel eyes narrowed. Seldom had she ever emerged the victor when it came to Clarice.

There was no feeling of guilt for Dimity when she begged off, feigning a headache, nor did she care if Clarice caught her in her riding habit as she tiptoed down the stairs. Even her delicate condition held no persuasion for Dimity. Clarice had long ago strangled any hope of ever developing a congenial relationship between them.

Knowing she could never trust her, Dimity set her mouth firmly. From this day on, she promised herself, I will avoid her company whenever possible. And Jake, as well.

With soft, light footsteps, and a heart even lighter, she passed through the dim hallway on her way to the stable. When she heard the loud, harsh voice of her father coming from his study, she paused outside the door, which was slightly ajar. She could hear their conversation clearly. It was not Dimity's nature to eavesdrop, but her curiosity held her there. Grateful for the quiet throughout the rest of the household, she stared fixedly at the half-closed door, and listened. She turned a deep scarlet when she heard her father.

"Jake, tell me the truth. Was Clarice pregnant when you married her?"

Jake turned a sickening gray color. He wanted to be frank and open, but to tell him he took advantage of his daughter, would not easily be explained.

"Albert, I've always been honest with you and I do not intend to break that trust." He held his chin high.

Albert could see he labored under a nervous tension.

"Go on, Jake."

He spoke in a flat, spiritless tone. "I mean no disrespect for Clarice, sir, but please understand." he paused."On the first night of the crossing, we were both overly excited, and indulged in much too much wine. That night, between Clarice s passionate abandonment, and my drunken lust and carelessness, we made love." He fidgeted nervously, on one foot, then the other. He gripped the marble mantle for support. He could not tell him that it was she who had been the eager lover, while he was the consenting mistress, so to speak. He had not been that drunk that he didn't know she was the aggressor.

"Believe me, sir, that was the only time. Until she told me in London that she was pregnant."

Albert's eyes searched him questioningly. "All for the sake of honor, you married her?"

"Yes sir!"

"What of love, Jake?"

Outside the door, waiting for his answer, Dimity's heart skipped a beat.

He couldn't dare look at his father-in-law. He held his head down.

"No sir!" A cold inescapable guilt assailed him.

A faint, bright hope dawned on Dimity when she heard these words.

At this extraordinary confession, Albert turned away from the window where he was standing and crossed the room. He clasped Jake's upper arms in his two hands like a vise.

"Jake, to every decent man s regret, he is duty bound to take the responsibility of his one night of passion." His penetrating eyes held his. "You are like the wayward son who sins. Only this time, it's with my daughter.

Albert's heart ached when he saw the grim expression on Jake's face.

"But Jake, you must know, as I certainly know, it takes two consenting adults." He smiled in an approving manner, and then put his arms around him. "Such a single-minded fool to take all the blame," he said, patting him on the back. "I know very well what a devil my daughter is." In Albert's heart, he knew that Jake had been manipulated by his daughter.

A renewed warmth flickered between them.

Hearing all she wanted to hear, Dimity turned away. Her spirits soared. Now she truly believed that Clarice more than likely deliberately seduced Jake.

After the crushing gloom of a loveless marriage forced on him, Jake accepted his fate like a man. The paradox was that his one night's folly held a mighty high price. The cost of losing the love of his life. Dimity.

DIMITY AND DANIEL

CHAPTER TWENTY-THREE

A biting blast of east wind swept across the river harsh and cold, heralding a hint of winter. Dressed lightly, Dimity shivered as she tethered the bey gelding to the hitching post. Today's weather contrasted sharply to the balmy November day of yesterday.

Her eyes followed the man in blue pacing nervously up and down on the pier. Looking out over the North River to the steamer coming in, he wondered when the pier crew would appear to pass its hawsers ashore. He wanted to be long gone before then.

The sensational headlines of the past: few weeks had brought her here. "Corruption in Tammany Hall." When sergeant of police, Denny O'Bannon, sent a note to the reporter known as M. D. Durant to meet him, Dimity was sure he didn't know M. D. Durant was a woman.

Dimity dashed across the pier to where the heavy-set man was standing. His big featured face, embellished with a bushy, dark gray mustache, looked grim as she came towards him.

"Mr. O'Bannon?" she asked, holding out to him the crudely printed note he'd sent.

Deservedly shaken that his note had fallen into the wrong hands, he sucked in his gigantic belly in disbelief.

"Don't know any O'Bannon," he scowled.

"I am M. D. Durant." She could see he was still wary and skeptical. "Would you like to see my press card?" Without waiting for his answer, she whipped it out of her reticule.

Yielding to the persuasion of his own note, and her identification, he finally admitted, "I'm O'Bannon."

"You wanted to see me, Mr. O'Bannon? What can I do for you?" Before coming here to meet him, Dimity had checked him out. The only thing she could find out was that he had been passed over for promotion too many times.

In a state of confusion at finding that M. D. Durant was a woman, he was hesitant to talk. "I didn't know you was a lady.

"I've always been a lady," she smiled engagingly.

His head of silver hair, making him look all of his fifty-five years shook in agreement. "That I can see," he smiled crookedly.

Studying his face, Dimity could see he was unwilling to tell her what he came here to tell M. D. Durant. "If you have information, Mr. O'Bannon, that will help to put an end to this municipal cesspool of crime amongst our politicians, please tell me. I promise you, sir, you will not be named in the story. Believe me; I will not divulge my source. These wrongs need to be righted."

"I thought." he paused, "with the November elections coming up; it would be a good time to.get the goods on some of these politicians and crooks. They're all swimming in the same dirty cesspool together."

"Yes? Go on," she urged.

"It's best if I tell ya a bit 'bout myself. I've been that proud to wear this suit of blue all my life," he said, brushing off the lint from his sleeve thoughtfully. "But it wasn't in me to join in with the rest of the takers."

"Takers?" she asked, perplexed.

"Ya know, the defenders of justice, with their greedy, fat fingers, stuffing graft money into their pockets."

"You mean your fellow police officers?"

"That's right," he said, looking dejected. With downcast eyes, the words spilled out. "Finally, after all these years of refusing to be a part of it, I was forced to be on the take from the District Leader in my ward. If I wanted to keep my job, I had no choice.'

"And who is that?"

"The biggest crook in New York City. Danny Eagan."

She grimaced. A plum for the picking. The plum she'd been aiming for. Is it because of the newspaper articles that you decided to come forth with this information!

"Partly," he said, I ain't hankerin' to be rounded up with the rest of 'em when the Legislature gets their eyes opened. And it looks like that's the way it's aheadin'. Ya got some of the story," he said, gloating, but ya am t got it all.

"Mr. O'Bannon, I feel I must ask you, why did you come to me and not Mayor Cooper or the District Attorney?"

"Know for sure the Mayor's on the take, but don't rightly know if the District Attorney is. This way, if what I know gets in the newspaper, let the Legislature take over the investigation. If the story breaks, the citizens will clamor for justice."

Now in a state of high anxiety, he spewed forth a list of accusations. "Ya know some of the politicians who look the other way, but ya can't even guess all the big shots involved. And the criminals. Like Danny Eagan who killed Vito Scaglione and his men that night on Elizabeth Street. Even though, they was all no-goods."

"You know that for sure?"

He shook his head. "All under the protection of Police Chief McCain. Without taking a breath, he went on "and did ya know that right now they're gettin' ready for the election?"

"What do you mean?"

"Why Danny Eagan's printing fraudulent ballots with phony names and addresses to be doled out to the homeless he's givin' free bed and board to these days. After the election, he'll put 'em all back out on the street again."

Her alert hazel eyes were flashing. This is what I've been looking for, and he's handing it to me on a silver platter.

Wrapped only in her little thin shawl, she was feeling the bite of the wind whipping across the water. She was eager to get the story down on paper. "Under the circumstances, Mr. O'Bannon, you must fear for your life."

"Not to worry," he assured her. "I'm still on the take. They ain't likely to finger me." He looked at her sympathetically. "It's you I m worried about."

"They wouldn't dare hurt a harmless little lady like me," she assured him.

He walked her to her buggy.

"Keep in touch," she called to him as she clucked at the horse.

Puffed up with his importance, Danny Eagan was pleased and proud of himself for the ten additional repeaters his men had rounded up for next week's election. He sat at his usual table in a strategic corner overlooking his customers. There was a degree of respect afforded him when he sat down to dinner and rarely was he disturbed. Whether it was a legitimate reason, either to complain of bad food, or being cheated at the tables, it made no difference, his customers held off until the bossman saw fit to make his rounds to speak to his customers.

Sleeves rolled over his forearms, exposing muscled, hairy arms; he tucked a napkin in his checkered vest. He chewed greedily on pickled pig's knuckles as his eyes squinted through the smoke-filled, crowded saloon. Workers, with wadded-up bills in their fists, were lined up at the bar two deep, and before the night ended, little of their week's pay would be left. Another profitable night. He smothered a chuckle of satisfaction behind his napkin.

Suddenly, the door crashed open and four of Danny's men came bounding across the room. Without a word, Ira shoved the newspaper in front of him. Danny glared venomously at the headlines. A resounding fist punched a hole through the front page. "Instruments of graft are we?" he bellowed. In a voice rough and disapproving, he snapped, "This here's gonna stop." He swung about in his chair, motioning for his men to follow him, which they did unquestioningly. Danny Eagan was their law, and as mercenaries, they killed impersonally for him, without revulsion or remorse, at his command.

Danny attacked the stairs heavily, two at a time, with heavier, pounding steps close on his heels. Parting the gold portieres, he entered the large parlor. To the astute eye, Danny Eagan's living quarters gave the impression of opulence. For a man of his lifestyle, it was most unusual. Not the taste of a virile, gun toting man like Danny Eagan. But then there was nothing gentile or fragile about the expensive mahogany furniture throughout the room. All masculinity was lost, however, in the contrast of the delicate gold wall covering with those deep red rose embossments interspersed throughout. The decor decidedly leaned towards a lady's elegant, feminine taste. More the taste of Clarice Durant.

Feeling the dank chill of the dark, unheated room he waved a bare arm furiously, "No light, no heat," he protested, rolling down his shirt sleeves.

Catching the readable expression on their boss's face and knowing the object of his dark mood, each scurried about to see to his comfort, while Ira handed him a strong drink then sat down beside him on the horsehair sofa. Stumbling over each other in their frenzy to appease him, a fire was quickly lit in the fireplace, and every gaslight lamp in the room was lit in a manner of minutes.

Clutching the drink in his hand, Danny sat staring emptily ahead. He had not been prepared for this bombshell and seeing that story and his name in print was a shock. Thinking reflectively, his train of thought wandered.

He took a swallow of his drink and looked around the room. "Every time I look at that goddamned wall covering I think of her." He glanced over at Ira. "I want that silky shit off my walls. And anything else she talked me into," he pointed to the painting over the fireplace. "That picture."

"Which one, boss?" Ira scanned the walls.

"That goddamned lady by the pond." He waved a fore-finger. "Out!"

"Yeh, boss. I'll take care of it."

Picking up the newspaper, his thoughts returned to the alarming article. It was a threat. And suddenly, he was conscious, as never before, of a gnawing fear that his empire might crumble.

His face was suffused with anger. "Who the hell is this M. D. Durant?"

"Don't know him, boss," Ira said.

Danny untied the shoelace of his left high top shoe. Breathing a heavy sigh, he slipped off his sock and hoisted his foot on top of his knee. He vigorously began scratching the bottom of his foot. After a few minutes, a malignant smile curved his lips as he dropped his foot to the floor.

"Don't need to know him. You only need to get rid of him." The only remedy for M. D. Durant was execution. They nodded. None of his men ever questioned or doubted his motives or decisions. Moving his bare foot back and forth over the thick, luxurious Oriental carpet seemed to soothe his nerves, as well as his foot.

"Got it?"

"Yeh, sure, boss," Ira agreed. "Sure thing."

"Nothin' reckless, mind ya," he said, looking slowly from face to face.

"They ain't hedgin' us out. Ya hear?" He sat fingering the small gold circle attached to his watch fob. "It ain't likely they'll even look for the repeaters, but to be on the safe side, we'll hide 'em 'til after the election. Besides, we got 'em all in our pocket anyways."

Looking up at the painting again, he stiffened as the old familiar longing for the only woman he'd ever loved gripped him in the pit of his stomach. Clarice Durant. Silently, he asked himself, I wonder what's become of her. Was she was with child like she claimed? Suddenly, the name Durant shot out at him. "This Durant fella, do ya think he's any relation to Clarice Durant?"

"Can't say, boss," Ira said.

"A brother?" asked Clyde, second in command, the pugilist, whose muscles had gone to flab since living the good life with Danny Eagan. The force of his fists wasn't enough for him. Under Danny's tutelage, he felt a power of a great cat ready to spring on command. His intent, calculating eyes flashed. "Maybe her father?"

Ira blinked, thinking they were in big trouble if this Durant guy turned out to be a relative.

The table conversation in the Durant household that night was focused on Dimity and the latest political scandal she had disclosed in her latest story.

Albert was the first to berate her. "I think, Dimity, this M. D. Durant thing has gone too far."

The stern look of him as he leaned toward her told her he was clearly out of patience with her. She had seldom seen him so unnerved.

"But Papa ."

Before she could say another word, Jake spoke up.

"I'm afraid, Dimity, you have put yourself in grave danger."

Dimity lowered her eyes to the soup ladled out by Lily. Looking up into his eyes, she shook her head. "I do believe you are exaggerating, Jake."

"Not in the least, Dimity," he assured her, sitting nervously on the edge of his chair. I know these men. Believe me; I know their paths have not been strewn with roses. If you had any idea of the magnitude of the politically damaging evidence you've uncovered, you would flee for your life. What you have done, is a courageous, wonderful thing. But please understand the criminal that you named, I'm afraid, will see to it that you are silenced. Danny Eagan is a ruthless criminal who will stop at nothing."

Clarice cringed at the mention of Danny Eagan's name.

"I urge you, Dimity, to think about leaving the country. Go to Europe until this blows over."

He spoke with an alarming, persuasive intensity. All that he said was probably true, but she couldn't believe they would dare to come after her.

Clarice, silent in her usual moody way, bridled at her husband's anxious attention to Mary Dimity. He acted as though it was his duty to protect her. She waved her slender hand as if to dismiss his words, exchanging a bored glance towards her husband. "How you carry on, Jake. It's all so silly."

Irritated, he snapped back at her, "Have you read the story, Clarice?"

"Why no," she fingered her napkin nervously, "but surely, it couldn't be that serious."

Albert's thin lips quivered. "I assure you, it is serious, Clarice."

With her mouth full of lentil soup, she suddenly bent forward clutching her stomach. Her face was pinched in a painful frown and the color had washed out of it.

Both men jumped to her aid.

"What is it, Clarice? Are you having pain?" Jake asked worriedly.

Looking up at him with the large mournful eyes of a puppy, she whimpered pitifully. "Yes!

Her eyes stealing swiftly across the table to Clarice, then back to Jake, Dimity couldn't help but wish it was herself having his baby. Dimity went to her side. "Is it the baby, Clarice? Should we send for the doctor?"

Panic was in her eyes. She was too afraid to speak. She stiffened as another sudden pain gripped her. She let out a tormented little cry.

The kitchen help rushed through the door in a wave of excited murmurs. The maids stood there nodding to each other knowingly, sympathetically.

"But it's too soon," Albert said, a look of horror on his face.

"Quick," cried Jake excitedly, waving a hand, send for the doctor.

"Ohhh. Clarice moaned.

Jake and Albert carried her upstairs to her bed.

The night passed with an agonizing slowness. The hushed silence of the household was eerie in between bone-crushing screams coming from the upstairs bedroom. Dimity, Jake and Albert sat on the couch in the upstairs sitting room outside the bedroom waiting with eager expectancy while Dr. Pennington and the midwife tended to Clarice. At Albert's insistence, Dimity and Jake acquiesced to his wishes to join him in the celebration of a new life. Through the night he continued to fill their empty wine glasses. To fortify them for the long ordeal, he said. Bound together for moral support, they imbibed in more wine than they were accustomed to and for awhile all worries were forgotten. There was no further talk about Dimity's danger, or of the life-giving scene taking place beyond the closed door. They sat chattering gaily in the glow of the wine. Dimity watched Jake admiringly, his every expression, his every gesture. Her eyes could not drink in enough of him. And he? He had a sudden horrified sense of defeat. Beaten and overwhelmed by his self-made predicament. What a damned fool he'd been. His life with Clarice and the hopelessness inside him was suffocating him. There had been nothing but jealousy and discord between them. He wanted more than anything else in this world to hold Dimity in his arms. Running his eyes over her longingly, he smiled. Albert was too drunk to notice their exchanged glances. When finally a sense of lightheadedness pervaded her, she dropped her head on Jake's shoulder and fell asleep.

At last, as the sun rose, and the low moaning ceased, and the high-pitched screams took over, the baby's head appeared. With one more laboring push from the exhausted mother, the baby boy burst out of the womb, into the world.

When the door opened, the mid-wife presented Jake with his new-born son. "You have a fine baby boy, Mr. Trenton.

Immediately, Jake felt a passionate tenderness towards the red-faced infant, whose tiny face was wrinkled into a continuous squalling cry. He bent to kiss the downy fuzz covered head. At the same time his eyes looked up at Dimity beseeching her to forgive him.

A twinge of jealousy passed over her as she caught his gaze. It took no more than a quick glance to see the baby bore no resemblance to his father.

"Would you like to hold your grandson?" Jake asked, passing the baby to Albert.

With a heart bursting with pride, Albert looked upon the baby. "My grandson!" He unwrapped the blanket to examine the naked newborn. Seeing all was well, he tucked the blanket gently around him and passed him back to the midwife. "We must engage a proper nurse for the child, Jake."

"Yes, of course," Jake agreed.

"He's a darling little dear," Dimity said, timidly reaching out for him. Looking into the little face, she smiled a sweet smile, saying to herself, if only you were mine. She cradled the tiny form close to her, gently rocking him back and forth to quiet him, murmuring soft cooing sounds. "Shhh.little one."

Jake studied Dimity. His heart swelled with love as the little voice quieted to Dimity's soothing words. Jake squeezed his eyes tight to lock the scene in his memory.

Placing the baby in the woman's arms, it suddenly occurred to Dimity that Jake had yet to inquire about Clarice.

Not understanding the husband's indifference towards his wife, the midwife did not conceal her disapproval when she remarked sarcastically, "You have not asked about your wife. Do you not wish to see her, Mr. Trenton?"

"Of course, I wish to see her," he answered, red-faced and ashamed at his oversight. He started towards the closed door.

The midwife reached out a restraining arm. "You'll have to wait, Mr. Trenton, until the doctor comes out."

When the grim-faced doctor came tiptoeing out of the sick room hours later, he sprawled in a chair and stretched out his long, lean legs. Struggling within himself for the proper words, he examined his huge gold watch in an effort to put off the inevitable.

The family was not deceived into thinking all was well when they looked upon his tired, despondent face.

He fixed his eyes on Albert, then on Jake. Shaking his head, he sighed heavily. "I'm afraid the joy of the baby is overshadowed. Your wife, Mr. Trenton, is gravely ill."

A sudden hush fell over the room.

Distraught, Jake's voice came in a hoarse whisper, "She will regain her strength in time, will she not, doctor?"

"It is not possible to know for certain. She has suffered a great loss of blood. It has taken its toll, I'm afraid."

Albert, who sat in his chair, speechless, tried to rise to go to her, then sunk helplessly back in the chair "My God!" He cried. "She cannot die."

Dimity couldn't bear to see him so distraught. She sat on the edge of his chair and put her cheek to his. "Oh, Papa, we must not lose faith," she consoled him, trying to think of comforting words to say. "I'm sure after a few days of rest, she'll begin to improve."

In the next few days, the house was hushed and silent except for the penetrating, intermittent crying of the infant, as yet unnamed. At the breasts of a wet nurse the baby nursed greedily and seemed to flourish, though it was not its mother's milk.

In the intervals when he was not at Clarice's side, Jake spent time with his son, watching him as he slept in his crib, or holding him in the joy of fatherhood.

To his consternation, the dreadful guilt he carried with him all during Clarice's pregnancy, that his son was born of a false love, was soon forgotten. Miraculously, Jake felt that he was redeemed, and it was his vow-that his little son would not bear the black mark of his sin. That he would be dearly loved.

A heavy melancholy settled upon the family when the eminent specialist brought in by Dr. Pennington concurred with him. There was no hope.

The family sat by the dying woman's bedside for hours at a time. Jake was especially attentive, speaking in quiet tones, promising his wife she would soon be well. Nothing seemed to stir her except when Jake held the baby close to her, and at the sound of his cry, her ghostlike expression changed, and she would smile dreamily.

On the last night of November when Jake entered her bedroom, Clarice lifted her head alertly.

"She's been asking for you, Mr. Trenton," the nurse said brightly. "While you're with her, I'll go down to the kitchen for some supper."

"Yes, thank you, Kiss Gleeson."

Swimming in moonlight, the room smelled of wood smoke and death. The hissing sound of the crackling fire was the only sound in the room, except for Clarice's labored breathing. The golden firelight gave her pale face a yellow, sickly tinge.

Jake sat in the shadows of the firelight in the tufted chair beside her bed. Her eyes were closed.

"Clarice?" he whispered, reaching for a feverish hand.

She opened her eyes at the sound of his quiet voice and gazed at him with an unusual intensity. When she spoke, her voice seemed stronger. "Jake, it's you."

"Yes, Clarice." Jake was bewildered at her wakefulness. For days, she had been in a half-conscious, drugged state, fighting the lung fever that had scourged her body. It struck him how curious it was that in this one eager flash of life she had put off dying.

She sat propped up on two heavy pillows, drawing stray hairs through the thick braid resting on her breast.

"What is it, my dear?" He squeezed her hand.

"I want to name the baby," she gasped, breathing heavily.

He smiled, thinking his son would be named after himself. "Yes, my dear. By all means."

Her sunken face came alive. "He is to be named Daniel."

He was fiercely disappointed. "I don't understand." In the dimly lighted room he could see the wild look in her dark eyes. There was no confusion about her. She knew exactly what she said.

"God in heaven, Clarice, he is my son. I want his name to be my name.

"You are a blind fool, Jake," she said, staring at him with mockery and bitterness in her eyes. "He is not your son."

He drew his hand away. "I don't believe you," he said, looking at: her with stunned bewilderment. His handsome face suddenly crimson, he thrust his fingers between his neck and cravat to loosen it. He sat on the edge of his chair. Damn your black heart, he said, his dark eyes fixed with hate. "It can't be."

With the savagery of a tigress, her voice grew sharp and hysterical. "It's true. Danny Eagan is his father." Relieved at confessing her sin, the dying face took on an aura of joyful remembrance at the mention of her lover's name. Her eyes flitted about the room, searching wistfully for someone she would never find again.

He looked upon the emaciated face drawn into a cruel grimace. Was it delirium that forced these hideous words from her lips? A sudden realization began to pierce his brain and his whole being was like a tightly drawn string ready to break.

In an outburst of mad, hysterical laughter, she sat upright, lifted a finger and pointed at him. He's not yours. He'll never be your son," she said with a last measure of strength.

Why this sudden desire to thrust this sharp point of a knife edge hurt into his heart? He tore his eyes away from her. That face. The face of a demon, who had mortgaged her soul to the devil. He sank back wearily in his chair and hid his face in his hands.

Her head fell weakly back on the pillow. She gasped as a ripping pain shot through her. Bright red drops escaped from her parted lips onto the pristine shroud of linen. Her body quivered with a spasm. In the next moment, her race with death was over. She lay staring, sightless.

The nuances of dying had vanished. No more labored breathing. No pitiful groans. No more suffering.

Jake sat there shaken and enraged. His throat knotted painfully as he stared at the dead body, this receptacle of hate. Why?" he mumbled to himself, "why?" He wept. Not for the wife he'd just lost. But for the son that was never his.

The frozen silence in the room was broken by sounds of life. Inside the falling coals rattled in the fireplace, outside the wailing wind drove in a steady pattering of sleet against the window.

Jake sprang to his feet. He had to get away. Away from her. He had always been able to control himself, but now. .he could not. In a daze, he went out into the night, into a heavy torrent of sleety rain, bareheaded, coatless. It was a night of black infinity.

DIMITY AND DANIEL

CHAPTER TWENTY-FOUR

Albert shouted up the stairs at Dimity who was half-way up the staircase. "We found him!" Grabbing up her skirts, she rushed down to greet him.

With the help of Isaiah, Albert guided Jake into the parlor. A horse blanket covered the coatless figure, which moved like a man who had imbibed too much. His black hair was plastered to his head.

Albert lowered the shivering giant of a man into a chair by the fire. Silently, Albert removed his cloak and flung it over a chair. He sat across from his son-in-law.

"Isaiah, bring the decanter."

Isaiah nodded respectfully.

Jake smiled faintly at Dimity who had come into the room. He accepted the glass of brandy Isaiah offered him, gulping it down in one swallow.

Giving him a broad smile, Dimity came towards him. Pushing the thought away that it was his grief that caused his wild flight into the night, she only knew she was relieved that he was all right, and she didn't care if he knew it. "Oh thank God, Jake," she said, her eyes watching him anxiously, "Thank God that you're all right." She tried to compose herself when she looked into his face, at the sweat pouring off of him. How could that be when he was shivering so violently?

Though he could see Jake's unhappiness in his wild-eyed grief, Albert regarded him with a disapproving frown. "God damn it, Jake, what in the world possessed you, my boy?"

It was a reproach Jake couldn't answer. He was contrite and ashamed, but he couldn't tell him the truth that Danny Eagan was the father of Clarice's baby. He couldn't justify his actions by explaining it was the festering poison of his daughter's deathbed confession that drove him to such madness. He could only tell him in his deep grief for his wife his actions were beyond reason.

"I don't know, sir," he choked, clutching the blanket to him, "but when she died I was so overwrought, I felt compelled to run away, away from this house and leave the sadness behind. In all honesty, sir, I didn't know what I was doing." Remembering the violent cold wind and the constant spray of icy sleet in his face, he recoiled, trembling all the more. "I do know," he hesitated, his voice thick and hoarse, "I finally came to my senses in the unbearable cold and found my way back to the stable."

"Oh dear Lord," Dimity cried, her eyes growing misty, "Is that where you found him, Papa?"

"Yes, it was half past five when Isaiah very nearly stepped on him. He was huddled in that blanket in one of the stalls. Lucky for him he did not freeze to death."

Jake felt agonizingly weary and there was a pounding in his head. Slowly heaving himself to his feet, he began to cough in choking gasps for breath. He stumbled, then crashed to the floor.

Hovering over him anxiously, Dimity cried, "Oh Papa, he is ill. We must get him to bed."

Once in bed, while Isaiah and Albert helped him into a clean nightshirt, Dimity sent for Dr. Pennington.

"Plenty of fluids," he instructed, "and bathe him with cool clothes to get that fever down."

"But doctor," Dimity asked, "what is wrong with him?"

"Seasonal influenza," he said, buttoning his greatcoat, and twisting his woolen scarf around his neck tightly. "Like so many of my other patients."

In all the excitement, Dimity had all but forgotten that funeral plans were yet to be made. Her only wish was to take care of Jake, who worsened during the night, but the responsibility of the household was definitely on her shoulders. Fortunately, the wet nurse was taking care of the baby, and the nurse who cared for Clarice was nursing Jake.

"I'll sit with Mr. Trenton while you have your supper Miss Gleeson," Dimity offered, taking the wet cloth from her.

"Thank you, Miss Durant."

"Take your time."

In the hour Dimity sat with Jake, she continued to bathe his hot body with cool clothes. At times, in his delirium, he cried out in a bitter and contemptuous anger, "He's not mine. He's not mine."

"Who, Jake?" Dimity asked, not understanding what he meant.

"The baby."

"Your baby?"

His glazed feverish eyes opened and looked straight at her. "He's not my baby."

"Who?" She prodded. "Who then?"

"Danny Eeeegan.." He fell back into a deep sleep.

"My God," she said aloud, "Danny Eagan is the baby's father." Unbelieving, she stared at the still figure. "Oh my dearest! How you've suffered!" She pressed her face against his feverish bearded cheek.

No matter how her mind fought the human emotion of grief for a sister she had no love for, when the reality of Clarice's death set in, Dimity was overcome with doubts of her real feelings. Possibly, ghostly echoes of Clarice's childish voice came to mind, remembering the times when she and Clarice played together amiably, even though those times were rare. Perhaps, she admitted to herself, it was guilt she felt because of her dancing, happy heart that Jake was set free with her death.

Already, hordes of well-wishers were beginning to appear on the doorstep. Dimity consulted with the undertaker, the parish priest, and the Catholic cemetery. Following Albert's every wish; all was in order when the doors of the Durant mansion were opened to New York's most prominent wealthy families who came to view the remains of Clarice Trenton. She lay in state in the drawing room for three days with a constant stream of mourners. Dimity remained diplomatic and gracious when the sneering remarks reached her ears concerning the absence of Clarice's husband.

After countless explanations of his illness, her patience grew thin. She did not covet Clarice's place in society, but she had no choice. When she looked upon her father's forlorn face, she knew she would manage somehow.

On the scheduled day of the funeral, a gray thick fog descended on the city, and the chaotic jumble of splendid carriages assembled at the church were turned away because of the dangerous road conditions. It was an added sadness for the family that the deceased could not be put to rest. The body was held in the sacristy, and transported, unescorted, to the cemetery two days later.

Like one hypnotized, Dimity watched him as he slept It seemed that a different man lay there in this once powerful body. Exhausted after a restless night, she closed her eyes and rested her head on the pillow tucked behind her, and presently fell asleep. Though her mood soared with joy when she suddenly discovered that Danny Eagan was the baby's father, she felt she was hanging on the edge of uncertainty. Her wakefulness at night was the result of that uncertainty. Until Jake admitted the truth in a moment of lucidity, she could only hope.

When the sun came up and the household began to take on life, she had left her warm bed, dressed quickly and went directly to Jake. Every morning she fed him his breakfast before she left for the newspaper office. It had been ten days since Jake fell ill, and for a time, she feared he would die. Yesterday, in a slow forced determination, he had tried to get out of bed. When he stood on his two leaden feet, he was suddenly overcome with dizziness, and fell back onto the bed. He lay there, dejected, cursing his helplessness. Always strong and healthy, his persistent weakness humiliated him. Dimity thought it was a good sign that he was beginning to show some interest in food when later in the day he sat up in bed and actually finished a bowl of soup.

Slowly, Jake opened his eyes. He felt her presence before he saw her. He looked sideways to where Dimity sat sleeping peacefully. His gaze was fixed on her breasts lifting ever so slightly with each breath. Dressed in a becoming copper colored velvet gown, she looked like an angel. The morning sunlight streaming in the window captured the highlights of that luxurious crown of burnt-taffy hair which she twisted in a coil at the nape of her neck. He loved the appealing wispy little curls framing her lovely face. At the mere sight of her, desire raced through him. He smiled a crooked, knowing smile, grateful that he had not lost his potent male feelings.

Thinking to himself as he watched her sleep, he muttered through tight-pressed lips, "Blast you, Clarice, for destroying my life." His expression was hard and ascetic, knowing he could never have the only woman he'd ever loved. He didn't have the right. He'd caused her too much pain. He swore never to tell the family that Clarice deceived him and that she was carrying Danny Eagan's baby when they married. They will never know, he promised himself.

What was he to do with a child that was not his? What else could he do, but pretend. Heaven help him!

As if his gaze burned into her, she opened her eyes. For one long moment their eyes were fixed on one another. For the first time in ten days, he looked almost human. The color was returning to his face, and the deep dark circles under his eyes were fading. Yes, she thought, he is better.

"Good morning," he said, smiling.

"Good morning!" She bent closer to him. "How are you feeling this morning?"

Without taking his eyes off of her, he didn't respond. He laid there staring at her.

"Jake?

"Better," he said, with a concerned look on his face, "but you, Dimity, are you well? Have you been working too hard? You look tired."

"I'm fine," she smiled. She rose and fluffed up his pillows behind his head, then sat on the edge of the bed. "Oh Jake, you are looking much better."

"Now that Miss Gleeson's ripped that last mustard plaster off me."

"Now Jake, she's worth her weight in gold. She's been an absolute love." She tipped her head thoughtfully. "In a way, she reminds me of Nellie."

It suddenly occurred to him he didn't need a nurse any longer. "I think," said Jake, "there's no need for a nurse, Dimity."

"Jake!' With an anxious expression on her face, she raised her head. "What a queer notion! You are not well enough, Jake."

Watching her smooth his covers, the memory of her teased him. Taunted him.

A thrill ran through her when he reached up and caressed her cheek lovingly with an expression of sweet tenderness.

He drew his hand away and dragged his gaze away.

"I'll go down for your breakfast tray."

"Dimity, has Clarice been buried?" he asked, uncomfortably, realizing he had not inquired about his wife. It seemed an odd question to ask, but he had no knowledge of the funeral. His illness had been the climax of a nightmare he had just awakened from.

A look of sadness crossed Dimity's face at the thought of the delayed burial, but she saw no point in telling Jake that disturbing news. "Yes Jake, in the mausoleum that Papa had built for the family. Where Mama is entombed."

"And Albert?" he asked, looking at her attentively, "how is he?"

Her eyes suddenly filled with tears. "It troubles me to see him so sad," she sighed "He needs you. He needs both of us. If." she paused, "it weren't for the baby; I don't know what would become of him."Oh Jake, he's been drinking. If there's anything that will help him get over his grief, it is the baby. His eyes light up every time he holds his grandson."

"But Dimity, he was always at odds with Clarice."

"That's true, Jake, but she was still his daughter." His pale features grew somber. "And the baby?"

When Dimity thought of him, she couldn't help but smile. "He's so dear," she said, softly, wishing fervently he was hers. "He seems to be thriving with the wet nurse Dr. Pennington hired. And you know he's contented when he hardly ever cries."

"I'm glad he's doing well."

She bit her lip, remembering the haunting sadness in Jake's voice that night he screamed out in his delirium that Danny Eagan was the baby's father. She was certain he had no memory of his frightful confession. It was obvious that Clarice s horrible admission had dominated his sub conscience even in his disoriented state. If he chose not to tell her, she would tell him she knew.

"Has he been baptized?" he asked in a tired voice, preferring to put off discussing the inevitable. The baby's name.

"No Jake. Papa and I wanted to wait until you were well enough to be there." With the funeral and your illness, we felt it was best to delay it." She moved closer to the bed. "But Jake, we should give the little fellow a name. We've been calling him Baby Jake, knowing you will name him after yourself. And knowing it would be Clarice's wish to name him after you." Saying this, she felt hypocritical, but if this would bring the truth to his lips, then that's what was important. Not her deceit.

His face was grim. "I see it is of no use."

"What do you mean?"

For the longest time, he did not answer. "It is not Clarice's wish to name him after me."

More than anything else, she wanted to coax the truth out of him. She continued to play the part well. "Whatever are you saying, Jake? Of course, Clarice wanted to name the baby after you. After his father."

Was it beyond his right to be cleansed of this lie? Or to regain his honor in Dimity's eyes? His instinct told him no. But he had to rid himself of the unrelenting humiliation he'd suffered at Clarice's hands. It was consuming him with hate. Only with Dimity's forgiveness could he resume the long road back to a life of love and trust.

"After his father, yes." He compressed his pale lips. "I am not his father."

Outrage blazoned on her face. She was making an extraordinary effort to hide her relief. He was actually letting go of the secret that was eating away at him. "What?" she cried, mouth agape, pretending disbelief. She watched him with an increasing compassion.

He looked at her beseechingly. "It's quite true, Dimity." Clarice confessed the truth to me on her deathbed. She was like a demon gloating at her deceit towards me. She tricked me. Tricked me into getting drunk that first night of the crossing when we." he dropped his eyes, reluctant to face her. In his desire to convince her, he lifted his eyes with a searching look. "She deceived me into believing she was pregnant with my child when all the while, she was carrying Danny Eagan's baby. She forced me to sacrifice you in the bargain."

His words sent her head reeling, surrendering to hot tears of remorse that she had shown so little trust in him. Knowing Clarice the way she did, she should have known better and listened to him when he'd tried to explain what really happened that day in the bedroom.

"Oh Jake! How cruel!" She clenched her fists in her lap. She wanted to scream out her rage to the dead sister, who had derived so much pleasure in hurting her all her life. This time she had succeeded through the man she loved.

He lifted himself up on an elbow. He frowned as he looked at her. "Can you ever forgive me, Dimity?"

She pressed her fingertips to his lips. "Shhhh. No, Jake! I am to blame. I shut you out. I didn't give you a chance to tell the truth about her advances. It was all for my benefit, you know. It was her way at getting at me. I see that now."

He slipped his arms around her, drinking in the sweet fragrance of her as he brushed his cheek against hers. Sure of her love once again, the veil of hopelessness that had smothered him was blessedly lifted. "Oh my darling Dimity!"

"My dearest! She held fast to him in a long endearing moment of tenderness, remaining in his arms. Silent, in a pledge of her love.

Raising her head, she asked, "Does Papa know?

"No!"

"God help him," she cried, "I'm afraid it would kill him, Jake. He must never know."

"But Dimity.. We don't know whether Clarice ever told Danny Eagan about the baby. The secret can remain with us if he knows nothing about his son. If he knows," he tightened his hold on her, "who knows what he will do."

A chill ran through her. "Oh Jake, you don't think he would claim his baby?"

"The pity of it is, Dimity, I'm not his father. He would have a legal right if he decided to claim him."

With the reality of his words, she silently cursed Clarice. Her heart grew heavy.

Seeing the worried look on her face, he squeezed her hands gently. "We mustn't concern ourselves with that, my love. I don't believe Clarice would have married me if she had told Danny Eagan. She had to consider his character. He's a gangster. Surely, she wouldn't want anyone to know that he had fathered her child."

"But Jake." she said, "Clarice told you."

He felt a knot in his throat. "True," he said, feeling perplexed, "and she wanted the baby named Daniel." He looked at her longingly. "Dimity, we must put this worry aside. And get on with our lives."

"Yes! Oh Yes, Jake," she murmured, looking at him adoringly. "And Jake.as for the baby's name, I think you should name him, Albert. After Papa."

"Yes," he agreed, "the baby shall be named Albert."

From the corner of her eye she saw the door opening slowly. Dimity all but tripped on her billowing skirt in her attempt to bolt from her position on the bed. She stood there fidgeting nervously, trying to regain some semblance of decorum before Miss Gleeson's disapproving eyes, who had wondered about the impropriety of her attentiveness and devotion to her brother-in-law.

The nurse gave Dimity a long narrow look as she placed Jake's breakfast tray on the bedside table.

"I suspect he'll be up a bit more today, Miss Gleeson," Dimity uttered, struggling to straighten her bunched up skirt by smoothing the wrinkles out with the open palm of her hand. "He's feeling so much better this morning. Dimity smiled warmly, gazing down at him.

"Yes indeed!" the nurse agreed. "I can see that sparkle is back in his eyes."

"Will you help Mr. Trenton with his breakfast, Miss Gleeson? I must hurry. I'm afraid I've let the morning slip away."

"Of course, Miss Durant!" she said, helping Jake into a loden green velvet robe. "It'll do you good to sit up and eat this nice hot breakfast Nellie's fixed for you, Mr. Trenton."

Jake held Dimity's gaze as he lowered himself into the chair the nurse held for him. He sighed and wondered how he could have ever gotten along without Dimity. The pain of these past months reflected in his dark eyes. It had all but destroyed him, but now loving warmth closed around his heart. He was actually feeling whole again. Feeling alive. And in love.

Dimity's voice bubbled with a joyful ring, "If you're up to it this evening, Jake, you may wish to come down to dinner," she said excitedly, glancing out of the window. "I see a few snowflakes flying about out there," she said, lifting a woolen shawl off of a chair.

"I'm sure I'll feel up to it," he looked straight into her eyes, wanting to say more. There was so much more he wanted to say to her.

Dimity stood at the door. "Mind you now, Jake, don't overdo," she said, tucking the coffee-bean colored shawl around her. "You'll see to it, won't you Miss Glee son."

"I surely will, Miss."

"Until dinner time," she smiled, and left the room.

DIMITY AND DANIEL

CHAPTER TWENTY-FIVE

The few feathery snowflakes of the morning drifting down to earth's bosom, had gathered momentum through the day, and all too soon had spread the white hand of winter over the city. By evening, when Dimity left the newspaper office, millions of the frozen particles were spilling out of the clouds and flying to earth in a whirling, gale force.

Pausing in the doorway, Dimity peered out into the ghostly moisture-laden grayness. Through the blur of the falling snow, she could barely make out the silhouette of the waiting coach. In the eerie yellow glow of the gaslight lantern, she could see two phantom-like figures hovering in the shadow of the coach. She watched them anxiously for the streets were deserted, but for a few straggling carriages.

Dimity tugged at the brim of her fur lined bonnet, and her gloved fingers clutched at her upturned beaver collar. Turning an uneasy eye to see if the men were still there, she lowered her head, drew in a ragged breath and made a mad dash towards the coach. The snow-flakes touching the warmth of her cheeks disappeared into an icy moisture that trickled down her face.

Suddenly, the intruding footsteps of the two men moved swiftly towards her. While one man held her in place, the other spoke. "Might you be M.

D. Durant?" he mumbled gruffly through the muffler wrapped around his face and mouth.

At first, she did not hear the rough muted voice addressing her as her ears were roaring with the sound of the whistling gale. Rooted to the spot with the force of the stranger's arms, she stood glaring at the two men in outrage.

He repeated his question. "Are you M. D. Durant?"

"I am," she yelled over the din of the howling wind.

Before she could say another word, Clyde cried out, "Heave to!" They hustled her into the coach and Clyde instructed the coachman through the roof hatch. "Off with ya."

In those first few seconds of surprise, Dimity remained fairly calm, but when reality set in, fear turned her heart to ice and she suddenly exploded into a thrashing, gnashing, screaming wildcat. Like a hideous beast in danger, she was driven with an inhuman surge of energy in her desperate frenzy to survive.

Fearing her screams could be heard, Clyde struck her on the chin with a doubled-up fist. Her head slammed against the back of the seat.

Instantly, she plunged into a deep pit of nothingness. She was alone in an empty, invisible space of time.

The coach rumbled along, passing in front of the City Hall, where the usual reckless rush of streaming traffic and humanity had disappeared, out of the winter storm. Off they went, away from the towering office buildings, past the green lamps of the precinct police station to the side streets of the Bowery, and beyond to the wretched poverty district to a tenement building, where all signs of life had vanished on the deserted streets. Thereupon, they slackened their pace and drew up to a rundown tenement.

As the jostling of the coach ceased, Dimity slowly opened her eyes. She sat there dazed and forlorn. Lifelessness enveloped her, but as a degree of wakefulness returned, it occurred to her that it was the stunning force of the man's fist that had put her out.

Clyde kicked open the coach door, and jumped out, while the other man, seeing her awake, gave her a push towards him. He caught her as she stumbled. She could not see their faces in the darkness, but knowing the viciousness of the men, she thought it best to obey. While the one man helped her to her feet, the other man leaned over her waving both hands in annoyance. "You schemin' bitch hidin' behind a man's moniker! Step lively," he snorted out a command with the barest of sympathy.

She felt too tired to care.

Pointing upward, he motioned her to ascend the deeply worn brownstone steps leading to the front door. Still shaky, she followed them in silence into the dirty tenement and up one rickety flight of stairs, where Clyde turned a key into a locked door. They ushered her into the front room.

Sitting at a simple wooden table by a window sat a man of her own age. Although the crack in the window was stuffed with a dirty old rag, the broken slats in t he shabby green blinds beat a tapping serenade with each blast of cold air. Frock-coated in the fashion of the New York politician, he looked less fierce than his two men. She knew at once it was Danny Eagan.

It was then she realized that the two men who brought her were the same two men she had seen earlier in the office speaking to Stewart, the copy boy. Mistakenly, she had thought they'd come to see her when she saw them staring at her. It was true they had asked for the reporter, M. D. Durant, but quickly changed their minds when Stewart, pointed her out to them. At the time, she thought it odd, but then put it out of her mind.

Surprise registered on Danny's face. He gave Clyde a quick inquiring glance.

Keeping a firm grip on Dimity's arm, he said, "We was supposed to fetch this Durant fella like ya said.''But: . but boss," Clyde stammered, "This here's what we come up with. We was told that she's the one. M. D. Durant! He stated guiltily, lowering his eyes.

Expecting a man, he was in shock at the news. His smooth shaven face grew pink with rage and he began pounding on the table in his exasperation. When he finally calmed down, he sat there staring at her with a cold, calculating look. Shrugging in disgust, he muttered under his breath, "I got a goddamned woman crammed down my throat." He rubbed his face thoughtfully. By degrees it dawned on him. Suddenly, he smiled slyly. There was a single-minded stubbornness about him. A woman? This could be even better. They'll surely meet my demands to stop their stories.

A smile of triumph spread across his face. "Take off your coat and hat and have a seat, Miss," he said in a gloating tone.

He watched her as she removed her hat, gave a few quick touches to her hair, and sat down on the filthy, threadbare settee, leisurely sliding her wrap off her shoulders as though she had not a care in the world. Only then did she face him. She was determined not to show any fear.

He opened his lips to speak, closed them, looked at her, then looked at his men. Between gulps of his drink, he said, "So! This is K. D. Durant!

"Yeh, boss!"

"Did ya deliver the note?" Danny asked.

Clyde's thick bushy eyebrows pinched together. "Hey Tony! Did ya leave it?"

The beefy-faced man answered proudly, "Yeh, where ya said."

"In that there 'In Box' asettin' on the counter?"

"Yeh!"

"Anybody see ya?" Naw!

Clyde nodded and flashed a satisfied smile.

Danny Eagan was stripping her bare with his eyes, staring at her as though he was trying to recall where they had met before. A curious expression crossed her face as she looked at his rugged handsome face. Was it a freak of nature that he resembled her? She wondered what it was about him that triggered memories of long ago. To another life. To her childhood. Brushing away those vague memories, she tried to recall the two occasions when she had seen Danny Eagan: the Christmas charity party and that time at the restaurant when he was with Clarice. Those brief glimpses of him had not aroused any remembered recognition. She contemplated her feelings now. She had to admit, there was a deep-seated curiosity in her she could not shake.

Aiming her gaze at him, she shouted in abrupt anger. "You bastard! What is the meaning of this?" Suddenly, it seemed as though the air was sucked from her lungs. His face faded into a blur as she sank back on the sofa in a dead faint.

Danny rose to his feet. All three, men milled around her. A violet discoloration from unseen blood seeping into the skin appeared around her jaw.

"Pour some whiskey in a glass and bring it here." He sat down beside her and fingered the raised bump on her chin with a caressingly soft touch. "Got any idea how she got this?" he asked, looking up at Clyde.

Clyde shook his head solemnly. He spoke in a brisk, clipped tone. "Had to cuff her, boss. She was acting like some kinda she-devil."

Danny drew a white linen handkerchief from his pocket. "Here moisten this," he instructed him as he cradled her head in the crook of his arm.

Clyde accepted the handkerchief, but stood there studying the two of them for a long moment.

"What the hell ya waitin' for? Danny asked, impatiently.

"Yeh boss! Right away!" He quickly moved away. Passing his hand over his mouth, Clyde let out a long breath. His expression showed his dismay at the feature similarities of Danny Eagan and the Durant lady. The same color hair, identical upturned noses, though hers was smaller, and their eyes.compelling eyes, the color of a glass of ale. Awestruck, he glanced over his shoulder for another look. He shook his head in disbelief as he poured water from a pitcher into a tin cup. He dipped the doubled-up piece of linen in the cup, then squeezed it. "I'll be damned," he muttered to himself, "if the two of 'em don't look like brother and sister."

Danny had a miserable sense of clumsiness as his fingers fumbled in his attempt to unfasten the tiny buttons at Dimity s neckline. He hesitated for a moment to look at her. He too saw the resemblance. Curiosity filled his eyes. He was looking at the other half of himself.

Clyde handed him the wet handkerchief. Danny gently touched it to her neck. That's when he saw it. The circle of gold attached to a dainty gold chain. He was staring at the tiny gold ring when Dimity opened her eyes.

A soft whimper escaped from her throat. Dazed, her eyes rested on Danny, who held a glass of brown liquid to her lips. "What is it?"

"Whiskey! Take a sip. You'll feel better."

She took a big swallow, and began coughing as the hot, burning liquid went down. She cleared her throat and took another sip, cupping her hands on the glass. She lowered her eyes away from his steady gaze. Her eyes dropped to the watch fob draped across his vest. The tiny gold ornament dangling on the thick chain caught and locked her eye.

To Dimity's dismay, an image of a little freckle-faced boy invaded her mind. She shivered, not from the cold, but from cold fear.

"Are you cold?" he asked, bending forward to spread her wrap over her shoulders.

Still staring at the gold ring like hers, she nodded.

Danny took the empty glass from her and suddenly stood

"You boys go get us something to eat."

"Sure thing, boss!"

"When you get back, we gotta move her. Why'd you pick this place?"

"We done our duty, boss. Ain't, no other place where there's no people around," he replied resolutely. "And ya said it was okay wid ya."

"Yeh, Yeh."

"Move her where?" Clyde frowned.

"Back to my place."

Clyde's mouth fell open. "But boss, that ain't gonna work."

"That," said Danny, "is for me to worry about," he said gruffly, giving him a granite look.

Clyde bore a look of frustration, but he knew there was no point in getting him all riled up. Both men hustled out the door without another word.

Danny clamped a hand on a chair, dragged it over to the sofa and sat down in front of Dimity. Her eyes widened the moment she gazed upon the gold circle again. She quickly turned away and stared off into space, her thoughts in the past. Dimity remained silent. It was difficult, for her to come to grips with her feelings. Her feelings of hate towards him had suddenly left her. She could not conceive that this Danny could be her long lost brother Danny, who she barely remembered. But the evidence was there before her.

Daniel cast a longing, wistful glance toward the shimmering piece of gold at her neck. His gaze was riveted on it. Something was happening here that went far beyond his wildest imagination. He envisioned his horror as a child when he woke up to find his little sister gone. The scene was indented in his memory. A chill coursed through his blood. This couldn't be he told himself. He was somewhat puzzled at her name.

Dimity's eyes met his. She saw an open warmth in his eyes. Not the look you would give to a hostage.

He felt bad that her delicate features were marred by the lump on her chin. Not of his doing, but he felt responsible for it.

"Are you feeling better?" he asked, sympathetically.

"Yes!"

"Miss Durant, may I ask." he hesitated, then asked hastily, "what is your first name?" He was most concerned with the M. "What does the M stand for?"

"Mary!" she answered in a soft voice.

"And the D?"

"Dime." she paused, thinking that, yes; there is a distinct possibility that he is my long lost brother. She took a deep breath and blurted out, "Dimity."

There was a rise in his chest from breathing hard. Danny fought back the rising feeling of elation, but his suspicions were obviously correct. He leaned forward in his chair, and reached out to touch the infamous gold ring, the only thing that connected their disjointed lives. Smiling with a kind of tenderness, he asked, "And what is this little gold ring?"

She was entranced. "Since I've been old enough to remember, I've had this little ring. When I was very little, it was tied on a string, then Papa bought me the gold chain." Spurred on at remembering, she added, "I do recall another Papa who told me and my brother never to take it off."

"Another Papa?"

"Yes, my first Papa."

"I had a sister named Dimity. What was your brother's name?" he asked, trying to look nonchalant.

"Danny!" she replied anxiously, while she removed the chain and held it out to him. Her eyes darted to his watch fob.

Instantly, he lifted the ring off of the chain. They sat there staring at the two rings.

"There's an inscription in mine. Trying to keep his deep voice calm, he asked, "Is there in yours?"

"I believe so," she said, turning it around in the light. "Two hearts."

"One soul!" Danny grinned. "My God," he shouted in a great state of excitement, "you're my sister. My twin sister."

Tears streamed down her eyes. Momentarily speechless, Dimity nodded her head and smiled.

He took a small knife out of his pocket and pried open one ring, and then the other, then pressed the separate halves together. "Don't you see, Dimity," he held it out to her, "it's our mama's wedding ring."

It was all they both needed to know.

"Yes," she cried out triumphantly, "Oh yes. I see."

What surprised her was the way his face suddenly changed from the stark face of hardness to a loving gentleness. His bright smile bathed her in warmth.

Danny scooted over to the sofa and took her in his arms. His intent eyes met her gaze. The face he saw as he looked at the elegance of her was not the face of an unusually beautiful woman, but of a little girl with a mop of glossy chestnut ringlets, dressed in shabby, patched clothes. A little girl sad and remote, clinging to him. And now at last, brother and sister were reunited. It made no difference to them that their lives were so different, that he was a notorious gangster guilty of unspeakable crimes, and she was a prominent socialite and the reporter he wanted dead. There was no doubt that the deep hurt of their separation through the years laid heavily on their hearts, but it was all too wonderful and exciting that after a lifetime they had found one another.

In her heartsick yearning for her brother all these years, he was suddenly lifted above era in e and mean-ness, and the only thing that mattered was piecing together the mystery of their lives.

The memories of her flooded his senses. For years he never forgot her. "I tried to forget you, Dimity."

"Did you have a hard life, Danny?"

He held her hand. "I will understand if you choose to have nothing to do with me. Afterall, you are a society lady, and in your eyes, I'm a criminal." His face grew somber. "Not only that, but I've kidnapped you. For that, I'm truly sorry." He kissed her hand. "You know, little sister, we are worlds apart."

She smiled. "Let's not talk of that right now, Danny," she urged, "I want to hear what happened when they took you away."

The sadness of that time all returned. "I remember sitting on the steps of a boarding house waiting for our Dada for what seemed like an eternity." He looked at Dimity with a forlorn look. "He never came. That old witch of a landlady told us he was dead. Do you remember that?" The horrible terror of that day was still with him.

For Dimity, some of the memories had dimmed. "Vaguely," she said, her hands trembling when total recall suddenly surfaced. "I remember the Sisters at the orphanage." She looked at him with sorrowful eyes. "For awhile, we were together. But one morning, I remember waking up and you were not sleeping beside me." The tears were streaming from her eyes. "I was alone. The only one

I loved, who cared about me was taken from me. My brother was gone and I was cruelly left with people I didn't know. I was so afraid, Danny. That terror left an open, emotional wound. For days, I was very sick." Her voice broke. "If it hadn't been for dear Nellie, I might have died.

"Nellie?" he asked, feeling the pain she was reliving.

"Nellie was the cook for the Sisters." She brushed the tears away with a linen handkerchief. "And you? Were you awake when they carried you away?"

Danny nodded and squeezed her hand. "No! A priest, Father Nathaniel, carted me off in my sleep to the Jesuit Fathers' Boys' Home. I do remember the one friend I had at the home. A boy named Jake. When Jake was sixteen, he went to work at the livery stable in the Bowery. I followed him, and Mickey Eagan let me stay with him. Jake and I slept in the stable. Then Jake went to war. It was happening all over again. I was being robbed of the only-human being I was close to, who looked after me." He lowered his eyes. "I remember following the parade of soldiers for miles on the day he left. He looked off into space mournfully. "I never saw Jake again."

"Was he killed in the war?"

Remembering that part of his existence was another painful memory. "I guess that's the reason he never came back."

Dimity could see through his impregnable armor. An unassailable shield developed in order to combat any and all emotional feelings. She was sure any show of love, to him, would have been a weakness.

"What happened then, Danny?"

"I went back to the livery stable and Mickey Eagan let me live with him. Later, he adopted me."

"Did you like Mickey Eagan?"

"Yeh, he nodded. He was good to me. He was the father I didn't have. The only man I could trust who wouldn't leave me. He taught me everything I know. How to make a living." He saw the frown on her face. He shrugged. "Before Mickey, the world was a terrible place for me." A deep uneasiness swelled in him. "I had no other choice. It was the only life I knew."

Dimity studied him in silence.

"He taught me how to load a pistol. How to shoot it. In the world I was in, I was safer because of it. I was a young colt wanting to learn, wanting to please."
He treated me fair and square. Before Mickey, I never saw a dollar bill in my life."

"In other words," Dimity offered simply, "he was your teacher in crime."

His tone was stiff with a sharp edge. "It would be utter rot for me to deny it."Yeh, but it goes far beyond teaching me the ropes in crime, as you say. My trust of him was built on respect, and yeh, love. I admit, in the beginning, there was a healthy fear I'd be thrown back out on the street if I didn't prove myself to him. I owed him. Owed him big. To be truthful, Dimity, I liked the challenge Mickey's life gave me. He reached out and touched his sister on the cheek.

You can believe what you want, but Mickey Eagan was a good man in his own way. He brought many a starving waif off of the street, gave 'em a place to sleep, and a job. Sure, he made money off of 'em, but he was doing 'em a favor at the same time." Passion surged in his veins as he spoke. "Do not detest me for what I am. I got no regrets." He stood up and began pacing back and forth. Before she could answer, he added, "Look, Dimity, if it wasn't for Mickey Eagan, I'd be six feet under the sod in paupers' field." He knew his life was a barrier that would stand between their two worlds. Sitting down, he turned around to face her and reached for her hand.

"Remember Dimity, finding you is like a dream come true."

The haunting sadness in his voice filled her with love and tenderness. His words were a grim reality that begged for understanding. She felt a terrible hurt as she studied him in silence. She could see he still suffered the emotional scars of abandonment and of a painful childhood. As did she. Somehow, now that he'd opened the door of his life to give her a glimpse inside, she had to find some way to convince him that it didn't matter to her what he was. Despite the fact that he was a big part of the corruption in the city, she knew in her heart she could not continue to work on the story. She wanted only one thing. To help him. To show him a different life.

"My dearest, Danny, I do not detest you. How could I? You have suffered enough. Certainly, more than I."

Shaking his head, his voice was somewhat surly when he said, "I have not suffered my whole life, Dimity. As a kid, yeh. But with Mickey, I had a good life."

"But Danny, your criminal activities."

"Enough of me."What, of you, Dimity? What happened after I was taken away?"

"It's funny, Danny, but that painful part of my life is nothing but a blur. Like you, I remember sitting on the stoop with you, and strangely, I can still see the ship that seemed to swallow us up." It all seemed to come back to her. Her eyes clouded over. "I remember Mama who slipped away in death. And the words of our Dada when he slid the gold ring on my finger and told me never, never to take it off. She looked at him sadly, "For both of us, his words must have made quite an impression seeing as how we've kept it all these years."

"Yeh, I remember the ship.," he choked, his eyes downcast, "and our dear Mama. The day she died. And nothin' to eat." He watched her mouth tighten at his words.

Thinking back brought, some good memories and it brought back some not so good. Gazing at Danny, she sighed. "In the orphans' home I had dear Nellie. She looked after me. Then Mr. Durant, a man of great wealth, came to the home to help the Sisters. He brought us food every week. He befriended me. Taught me my numbers and how to tell time. After awhile, he adopted me."

"Was that a happy time for you, Dimity?"

She rolled her eyes. If it wasn't for Nellie."

"Did she come to see you in your new home?"

"Oh no, Mr. Durant hired her away from the Sisters. Nellie told me he did that for me."

"Really?"

"Yes," she said, "he was the good part of my life."

"What was the bad part?" he prodded. It still hadn't occurred to him that she was Clarice's sister.

"The bad part was Mrs. Durant, who hated me. And Clarice." she said, waiting for his recognition.

"Clarice is your sister?"

"Was my half-sister."

"Was?" he asked, puzzled, inclining his head. "Is she out of the country?"

"Clarice is dead."

"God Almighty! I ." he choked up. "It can't be." He cringed. His golden eyes darkened. Her words were jostling for a space in his brain. He could not comprehend this. Stunned, he sat there, hunched over, with his head in his hands.

Though his face was hidden in a shadow, there was just enough light from the oil lamp for Dimity to see the glistening tears in his eyes.

He didn't know if Dimity knew about their affair. "She wasn't a stranger to me, ya know."

Her heart skipped a beat at his confession. Dimity nodded. "Yes I know."

"How., how did she die? What happened?" he asked in a bewildered voice, leaning forward.

Seeing the pain in his eyes, Dimity had no objection to telling him the truth about Clarice's death. But what of the baby? Would he expect to claim him? Her expression was grave, and her voice was strained and unsteady when she said, "She died in childbirth."

He shook his head. He sprang to his feet, paced around for a few minutes, then sank back down on the sofa. He put his arm up over his eyes. All toughness and worldliness gone from him. "God! What did I do?" He turned to face her. "I didn't believe her, Dimity." He pressed his hands to his face. "I didn't believe her," he sobbed pathetically.

But was that really true, he asked himself. All these months he had not forgotten the girl he'd loved. The only true love of his life. He was not prepared for the tremendous emotion that took over. His love of her was a spiritual part of him he had not been able to shake He was swept away in a great tidal wave of remorse. A sense of confusion was simmering below the surface. Why, was I so stubborn? Part of it stemmed from the fact that he had come to recognize that Clarice had the power to dominate him. She had surely, but gradually tightened her grip on him. At the time, he thought it was just another ploy to control him. His ego would not allow that. But now, in a tiny corner of his mind, thinking back, he wondered if it hadn't been his way to get back at her. After all, she had treated him as a liability, hiding him away from her world. In truth, he knew there was no angelic innocence about Clarice, but he believed she loved him. And that he was her only lover. Vividly, he remembered her uncontrollable rage when bed professed his disbelief that she was pregnant. It was a game lovers played with each other. Who would give in first? Actually, he believed that she'd be back if it was true that she was carrying his child. When she didn't con tact him, he had thought it was all a lie. Now it was frightening to him that he had turned her away.

He drew a deep breath. "Did the baby live?"

Feeling a deep compassion for him, Dimity nodded.

"Yes."

The words caught in his throat, "A boy or girl?" he choked.

"A boy."

"I would like to see him."

She gave him a wan smile. "Of course!"

It was close to midnight when the door opened.

Danny's gaze darted past her.

The two men hovered in the doorway. There was a silent exchange between them. Afraid to enter, they continued to stand in the open doorway.

Danny lifted his head. "Well, what youse waitin' there for? Lettin' in the cold air. What kept ya?"

A deep exhalation came from Clyde as the door banged shut. "We was stuck in the snow, boss."

Although, they had spent all this time traveling through the snow packed streets, the simplicity of their words did not impress Danny.

"Did ya bring us somethin ' to eat?" he asked, his tone resuming the bark of a boss. "What are ya standin' there gawkin' like a chicken for?"

Cowering with bent head, Tony fumbled in his greatcoat and drew out a knotted-up napkin and handed it to him. "All we could get boss."

His fingers undid the napkin. Danny regarded the dirty little man with a distasteful look. "This is it? Two chicken legs and a piece of bread?" He shook his head in disgust. He hadn't eaten since lunch and he was ravished. He gave a heavy sigh and held out a chicken leg to Dimity.

She waved it away. Leaning forward, she gave him a timid, embarrassed look. "Is there a chamber pot in the back room?" she whispered, blushing profusely.

Her question had touched Danny's sensibilities. Without saying a word, he wrapped the napkin around the chicken set it down, and rose from the sofa to check. He whispered something to Clyde who promptly peered inside the darkened room where the only furniture was a bed, a rickety bedside table, a commode, and a broken down cane chair. Danny brushed past him and opened the bottom compartment of the commode. He removed the chamber pot and set it on the bare floor.

In a jaunty stride, Danny walked to Dimity's side, picked up the oil lamp on the table, and gallantly escorted her into the other room and pointed to the chamber pot as he placed the lamp on the table while the other two men stood in the doorway watching.

Clutching her skirts to her, Dimity glanced around her. Hands falling limply to her sides, her mouth fell open in absolute disgust at the filth. Everything was covered with thick dust and cobwebs. Her nose wrinkled at the offensive smell of mold. She wanted to scream out her frustration at the awful degradation of her predicament. Here she was with three men gaping at her. New-found brother or not, she was too embarrassed to look at him. Dimity bit her lower lip trying to control her tears of frustration.

Danny had learned to harden his heart, but now his heart was reaching out to her in sympathy. A coaxing hand touched her arm. "It's all we have. Dimity," he apologized woodenly.

He hesitated before turning away, then closed the door softly after him.

Both men sported a silly grin. He held up his hand in protest. "As soon as we've eaten, we'll take Miss Durant home."

"But boss." Clyde said, not understanding.

He gave them no explanation. For the time being, there was no need for him to tell them that the lady in that room who was a stranger only hours ago, was the sister stolen from him so long ago.

Facing the loss of Clarice, emptiness swelled within him.

He must forget her. But could he forget his son?

DIMITY AND DANIEL

CHAPTER TWENTY-SIX

Albert parted the Irish lace curtains of the drawing room windows to stare out into the darkness. He stood there drumming his fingers impatiently against the sash, wistfully hoping. Hoping to see his daughter coming up the driveway and that the long agonizing, vigil would be over.

"The snow has stopped," his voice echoed against the pain of frosted glass, his blank eyes still focused on the sea of white.

Across the room, in front of the fire, sat Jake huddled in a robe and blanket. Sitting next to him was Archie Malone, the police officer on the beat.

Still shaky from his illness, Jake's imagination continued to spin unpleasant, scary thoughts of Dimity's demise. "It's Danny Eagan, Albert," he said in a weak, low voice. "I know it." He tried to calm himself but fear radiated from his eyes. His one thought that they may never see her again gripped him.

At his words, Archie Malone nodded.

Albert dropped into a chair across from them. "You too, Officer Malone? Is that what you think?"

"Well sir," he said, twisting his night stick in his hands, "the Sergeant directed a search from the newspaper office to your house. Covered the section that leads through the Bowery. Found no signs of a carriage gone off in a ditch. And Lord knows," he said in a skulking tone, "it's hard enough bein' out in

this weather on a night like this. Streets icy and all."
He knocked his stick against his boots with two
stabbing blows to loosen the snow. "Ain't much
more we can do 'til daylight."

Albert's heart clinched in his chest. "Then
you believe she's been kidnapped?" he asked, barely
able to control his emotions.

"I'm thinkin' all's you told me.the Missy
writin' them there stories 'bout him.," he said, a
thoughtful look on his face. "It could be."

A cold chill crept over Albert. "The man is
evil!" He couldn't shake his sense of despair. "By
God! He'll pay. He'll not get away with this." Albert
did not want to stand around talking about it. He
wanted action and he wanted it now. Ordinarily, he
was able to control any sign of nerves, but he was
beside himself with worry.

"I'll make off now and take me a look see
first thing in the mornin' over at Danny Eagan's
place."He turned up his collar and headed for the
door. His change of shift had long been over and
there was a limit to his authority in the matter. "It's
a mighty grand place ya got here," he said, looking
around him. "One way or t'other, we'll find her."

"See here," Albert said his voice tense with
anger. He reached out to stop him. "You can't mean
you're leaving?"

Jake threw the blanket off his shoulders and
stood up. "Christ Almighty, man, our dear Dimity is
in danger. I demand that you raid Danny Eagan's
place."

The words were barely out of his mouth before the front door flew open. They hurried out into the gloomy foyer.

Dimity closed the door carefully behind her. When she saw Papa and Jake standing there with officer Malone with one eyebrow cocked, she was neither surprised nor dismayed. She knew Papa would be worried.

Jake stepped hastily to her side. "Dimity, are you all right?" he asked, with alarm in his voice.

"Of course, I'm fine." She shook her finger at him. "But you should not be out of bed," she scolded, scrutinizing him, then coaxing him to sit in a side chair. "Why, Jake, you're shaking. You're still very weak."

Knowing she couldn't breathe a word about Danny in front of the officer or for that matter to her father, she managed the deception well by keeping her tone light and carefree. "My, my," she said, casually shedding her gloves one by one, "Officer Ma lone, you surely didn't walk your beat on a night like this?" She smiled sweetly. "Oh," she said discretely, "stopped to have a little nightcap before going home?"

Officer Malone thought about explaining his presence here, but hesitated. He smiled and nodded though his heart was not in it. If she'd be my daughter, he mused, she'd be in for a good tannin'.

Busily, she undid the ties on her bonnet, leisurely lifted it off of her head and brushed off the silvery flakes of crusted snow. She removed her wrap and flung it over the hall tree, and gave her tousled hair a fluff with her fingers. She could not lose control of herself. Strutting across the foyer with a flamboyant carriage, she kissed her father on the cheek.

"Dimity, where."

Twice Albert had opened his mouth to chastise her, but she had quickly interrupted. Besides, he was so glad to see her, it didn't matter.

"Mavis and I had a lovely evening, Papa." Dimity said. She had sense enough not to elaborate on her reason for being late.

Hearing this, Officer Malone was glad he hadn't gone nosing and poking around Danny Eagan's place with her out on the town havin' a good time. He knew how these society girls were. Spoiled and mollycoddled. "Mr. Durant, sir, it's been a long night." He gave a two finger salute. 'I'll be on my way, if ya don t mind."

"Of course! Of course! Albert gave him a simpering sort of grin. "Sorry to have caused you to work overtime," he apologized, tucking a folded-up bill in his hand. "Thank you, Officer Malone."

"Part of the job, sir, Mr. Durant," he said, scratching his ear. "Part of the job."

When the policeman left, Albert took Dimity by the arm and directed her into the drawing room with Jake trailing behind. "Now, young lady, let us have the truth," he said, lowering her into a chair by the fire.

"But Papa, Mavis and I."

He held up a forceful hand to stop her. "Enough of that prattle about Mavis when you and I both know that your friend Mavis and her family are wintering in the South of France with the Astors.

Dimity looked surprised and was visibly shaken for she was unaware that Mavis was abroad. She sat there motionless with her head bowed, her hands folded dutifully in her lap. Never had she lied to Albert. Only in this instance in her reckless attempt to avoid incriminating Danny Eagan had she lied. The stress of it all left her exhausted. It was almost too much for her to think. All too complicated. The fact that Danny was the baby's father. The sudden discovery of a long lost brother, knowing he was the criminal she had wanted jailed, and accepting the fact that they were from two different worlds. She was so tired. So very tired.

Albert, staring beneath frowning brows, said a bit gruffly, "Well?"

Turning it all over in her thoughts, Dimity knew she had to save Papa from the truth. In some wild wonderings of her tired mind, she thought that if the truth were left undisturbed for the time being, it would be easier for him to accept Danny as the father of Clarice's baby later. She began to shiver.

Dragging the blanket off of the sofa, Jake put it around her shoulders and smiled warmly. "You've taken a chill," he said tenderly. Seeing the sweetness in her face, he forgot all the anxiety she'd caused. He felt comforted that she was safe at home. He dropped into a chair beside her.

"Something happened tonight," she said in a hushed voice, her eyes filling with tears, "something I never dreamed could happen." A tear slipped down her cheek. She looked at Jake, then back at Albert.

What mysterious happening could it be? Albert's gaze was insist en t and anxious.

Her face brightened. "I have found my twin brother," she blurted out. She hesitated. The rest of it would not be easy to explain. She worried how they would accept it.

"Oh my dear," Albert bent down and pressed his lips to her forehead. "Who? How?"

She tightened her fingers around the gold ring on the chain around her neck. "Papa, remember when I wore my little gold ring on a string around my neck?"

"Why yes! Of course!"

"You gave me this gold chain. Remember?"

Albert nodded.

She held up the chain for him to see. There were two tiny circles of gold instead of one.

The moment Jake saw the two rings; a childhood memory was set free. He could still see the terrified look on the sad little fella the good fathers brought home to the orphanage. It was wretched the way they separated him from his sister. Jake remembered how he cried for her and how he finally accepted himself as a friend. He also remembered his name was Danny and he wore a little gold ring on his finger. He never took it off. But the memories evoked feelings of guilt. The part he dreaded remembering. That he deserted Danny after the war. Possibly Danny's whole life would have been different if he had gone back to get him when he returned. Jake was ashamed of that.

Pointing to the gold circles, she said, "This one is mine, and this one is my brother's." She glanced at Jake who was sitting beside her, then at Albert. "My brother is Danny Eagan," she said with a tremor in her voice.

Albert sank down onto the sofa. A temporary palsy gripped him. His hands shook. His face was fixed with a terrible grimace. How can this be? How, he wondered, in the common decency of life can there be such a revolt against fate?

The only sound was the blazing fire in the fireplace crackling and exploding into flames.

Jake, not insensible to Albert's shocked expression, reached for her hand. "Dimity, are you quite certain of this?"

The soothing comfort of his hand on hers, gave her the courage to continue. "Yes, with all certainty." She had no intention to mention the fact that he had kidnapped her. It would only make matters worse. I had a meeting with him this evening. When I saw this ring on his watch fob," she said, holding it up, "and.when he saw mine on my gold chain, we knew. Instantly, we knew. The deep attachment we had as siblings resurfaced." She smiled angelically.

Albert studied her. He could see the thrill of her experience was etched on her face. The realization of it was beyond his reach, but; he found he had recovered from shock. "Dimity," he said fondly, "I only hope you realize you cannot fuse together your two lives after all these years.

Dimity forced a smile. "Papa, Danny has no visions of being a member of our family. Nor would I dare to intrude into his life. Although," she said thoughtfully, "you could say I've already done that.

There are too many yesterdays gone from us. The realities of our differences are all too clear. We both know it. We both accept it. To have some stolen times together, is all we ask. I beg you to try and understand what this means to me, Papa. After all, we are brother and sister. We are twins."

The revelation of her words all but redeemed her, and her heartfelt words, bravely delivered, stung at Albert's heart. "My darling daughter, I want only your happiness. I cannot allow you to have clandestine meetings with your only brother. Do not worry. I will welcome Danny Eagan into our home." Abruptly, he stood with both arms outstretched.

The shawl slipping from her shoulders, Dimity flung herself into his arms. "Oh Papa," she cried, her heart lifting, "thank you."

Speculations of what effect it would have on her life wafted through Jake's brain. It was a disquieting thought. Their social distinctions made it an impossible situation. Yet, her new found sense of kinship was too strong and he had the tenderest of compassion when it came to Dimity. "I too, Dimity," Jake joined in, smiling, "will welcome Danny Eagan."

"Now," Albert said, "that we have formed a committee of agreement, I think it is time we get some sleep." Then gently, he pressed her against him and beckoned Jake to follow as they made their way up the stairway.

It was, she knew, inevitable that she resign her position at the newspaper. The other inevitable was to tell Papa that Danny was the baby's father. In time. When the moment was right.

They bade each other goodnight and withdrew to their beds for the night.

He sat there for a long time in his carriage, outside the iron gates of the Durant Mansion, staring fixedly up at the house. Retrieving his large bundle of gaily wrapped packages off of the plush seat, he tapped on the roof to the coachman. "Come back in an hour." Hiring a coach was unfamiliar to him, but this brief visit must be accomplished discreetly. He could not have his men question his business with the Durants. He raised his eyes to survey the opulent three story house all ablaze with lights. With head held high and a devilish expression, he walked up the snow-packed driveway with a vigorous swagger. His footsteps echoed hollowly on the stone steps swept clean of snow as he approached the exquisitely carved door decorated with a holly Christmas wreath. He lifted the heavy brass door knocker, gave it several sharp taps and stood back. While he waited, he gazed down at his black boots, caked with snow hiding the shiny newness. When the door opened, he was lively kicking a boot against the stoop to loosen the snow. He directed his gaze at the colored servant who opened the door.

"Yes sun?"

"Is Miss Durant at home?"

"Step in, please suh!"

"Who is it, Isaiah?" Albert asked, coming up from behind.

Danny lifted his tall brown hat to him and set down his packages. "Danny Eagan! He greeted him. Danny had compromised his usual dandyism style duds by shedding them for a subdued, stylish new wardrobe.

Surprised, Albert could not hide his uneasiness as he looked upon this fine figure of a man whose robust masculinity was enhanced immeasurably by his charming smile. Much like Dimity's. Albert had no discernible dislike for the man personally, but one was lead to believe by the newspaper accounts that he was a barbarian. Setting aside his annoyance at Danny Eagan's sudden intrusion, Albert was conscious of his promise to Dimity. It was only right to greet him amiably. He held out his hand. "Mr. Eagan! Albert Durant!" he said, smiling back at him. "Here to see Dimity?" he asked, helping him with his greatcoat.

"Yeh, to see Dimity." he said, "and my son."

Albert was certain he heard him. "Your son, you say?

"My son!" he repeated, "I understand his name is Albert."

Albert stared at him incredulously, his fists tightly clenched at his sides. "The hell you say! My grandson is not your son," exclaimed Albert passionately.

Danny shrugged. "Oh, but he is, Mr. Durant," he insisted, assuming a coldness and determination. "Clarice and I were lovers. She told me about the baby." He could see Albert Durant didn't believe him. "Ask Dimity. She knows,"

Albert bridled. His words were galling to Albert. He was all too cruel and sadistic. Under the crystal chandelier, perspiration glistened on Albert's forehead.

Damn you! You villainous scoundrel!" He rushed at him. With a loathing and fury, he hit him square in the face with the back of his shaking hand. "You filthy dog!"

Maddened, in one swift movement, Danny's doubled-up fist found its mark on Albert's chin. He fell backwards into a side chair. Feeling suddenly quite ill, he sat there for a long moment to recover himself, then reached in his pocket and drew out a handful of bills and flung them at Danny. "There," he choked, "if it's blackmail you intend, take the money and leave."

Looking down at Albert with murderous eyes, he kicked the bills aside. I ain't here for money. I want to see my son.

White and drawn, Albert became more calm and docile. Knowing he could not advertise Clarice's shame, there was only one thing to do. He's blight on our lives. I can't in all consciousness, he meditated with resolution, allow him to take my grandson. This was the great fear Albert was consumed with. He stiffened and rose from the chair. "If you'll have a seat in the drawing room there, he pointed to the open doorway, "I'll tell Dimity you re here. She will bring your son to you.

Danny looked at him warily. One part of his mind told him the crafty old man was up to something, but the other part told him he was finally accepting the truth. Danny looked at him steadily and nodded, then picked up his bundle and disappeared through the designated doorway.

Upstairs, Dimity was preparing for the quiet informal dinner they'd planned. Still in mourning, the family was not free to attend the many Christmas celebrations going on amongst New York's society elite.

Weary of having to wear the monotonous, dowdy black gowns she'd been wearing of late, Dimity pointed to the midnight blue velvet Lily was pushing aside in her armoire. "No, Lily," she said, "that one."

"This one, Miss?" she asked, holding it up.

"Yes Lily, that one!"

"But Miss." she objected, "this gown is blue."

"I know very well what color it is, Lily," she said, impatiently. "Please leave it. I can manage."

"Yes'um!" she nodded, and left the room.

Leaning out his bedroom door, Jake saw Lily leave Dimity's bedroom. His boots in hand, he closed the door silently behind him.

Gazing down at the gown spread out on the bed, her eye followed the riot of colorful gowns in her armoire. "Oh drats!" she mumbled, her lips forming a pout. What a pity T can't wear this red velvet." She fingered the gown longingly. "I swear I shall wear it on Christmas." She pressed the blue gown to her. Frowning, she stood before the mirror. It's no use. There was absolutely nothing enticing about it. It would do nothing for her figure. Unless, she thought. Her flying fingers began ripping the threads loose holding the ruffled front in place.

"There!" she sighed, her eyes twinkling as she examined her handiwork. "This should show enough of my bosom to catch his eye," she smiled. "Besides, pretending I'm in mourning for a sister who hated me, is hypocritical." Since Jake's illness, he had avoided her like a wary bird. Hungry, but cautious. Cautious because of Papa, Dimity was certain.

On the pretense he needed help to fasten his cravat, Jake emerged from his room and crept past Albert's door. Although he wished to live up to Albert's opinion of him, he found that brooding over his need for Dimity was more than he could stand. He knocked on Dimity's door.

Thinking it was Lily, Dimity opened the door. "I said I could manage, Lily.

Her heart began to beat wildly when she saw the smiling face of Jake who was holding both ends of his cravat in his hands. "Could you help me with this?" he asked sheepishly, his voice cracking when he saw her standing there in her petticoat. The sight of her exquisite figure awoke in him that familiar ache of desire in his groin. An almost unendurable ache. He dragged his gaze away from her swelling breasts, willing the gathering heat in his loins to dissipate.

Bemused at his subterfuge, she released a smile, feeling a sense of relief that he had finally come to her. She took his hand and led him into her bedroom.

His eyes met Dimity's triumphant eyes. His smile was wicked. "Dimity, my love," he said, passionately, crushing her to him in the circle of his arms. "We've been apart so long." He lowered his mouth to hers, kissing her tenderly, coaxing her mouth open with his tongue, while urgently, greedily, he deepened the kiss.

Breathless, Dimity pulled away, shivering with delight. "Oh Jake! At last!" she murmured. "I thought you didn't care."

His mouth silenced her. "Oh my darling! My eyes have followed every movement, very loveable gesture you made. My ears have listened for the sound of your voice and your quick footsteps on the stairs. I've been aware of every breath you take. Every sigh you make. Every smile on your face. Don't you know, Dimity," he gasped, that I love you with my whole heart and soul. I want you, my darling Dimity. I need you."

"Oh yes, Jake! Reveling in his words, she was caught up in the moment of mutual passion and began slipping out of her camisole.

With shaky, impatient fingers he helped her step out of her petticoat. Sitting on the edge of the bed, she continued to undress.

Feeling trapped in the clothes constraining him, he frantically tossed his cravat on the floor and unbuttoned his shirt. Growing impatient at his fumbling fingers, lie removed his pantaloons and drawers. All the while, he kept his eyes on her. Her nakedness was bedeviling him. It seemed to take forever, but finally, he was free of his clothes. He stood there naked before her, his nakedness, exposing his muscular stomach and dark tangle of hair encircling his engorged penis. His eyes were riveted on her, appraising, admiring the exquisiteness of her naked body. He stood her up, bringing her against him. "Let me feel you," he said, his voice ragged and pleading. He stroked her with gentle hands, cupping her delicious breasts, feeling the smooth satin of her skin, discovering the sweet, tantalizing essence of her.

Feeling his arousal, its hardness inviting, she caressed his swollen sex unashamedly with light feathery fingers, stroking and teasing until he stopped the swept, torture of it with his trembling hand. "No more, ray love, or I shall."

In a voice rife with tension, he rasped, with a fierce intensity, "I must have you now." He was clearly wild with desire when he lowered her onto the bed and himself on top of her. His fingers and his lips sought her voluptuous breasts teasing her into mindless sensations of aching need, igniting fires deep inside himself.

On the verge of release, he muttered, "My love, I." Trailing his kisses down the length of her body, he tried giving her the pleasure she craved by ignoring his own urgency.

"I can't wait," he groaned, his anticipation mounting to a feverish pitch. He was powerless to hold off any longer.

She was writhing beneath him when he entered the secret warmth of her. Each thrust sent a torrent of relentless, pleasurable sensations for her and for him, until a blessed shudder of release exploded, catapulting them to the heights of sweet ecstasy.

Jake smiled the smile of the happy lover- as he fell away from her. Tracing his finger over her mouth, he murmured, "My love! You are my life!"

Smiling now herself, she looked at him tenderly. Oh Jake, I love you so."

They laid there in each other's arms, feeling the blessed contentment of sated lovers, impervious to the world beyond, until the sound of gunfire exploded through the house. Not once, but twice. Again! And Again!

Dimity winced. The sounds sent a shiver through her. "What in the world is that?" she exclaimed, sitting up with a start.

Alarmed, in a single movement, Jake leaped out of bed. A worried crease appeared on his face. He shook his head. 'I can't imagine. It sounds like gunshot." Dressing hurriedly, he said, "I'm quite sure it nothing to worry about, darling. But please," he said firmly, "stay here until I've checked downstairs."

"But Jake," she protested, her eyes large and frightened as she began dressing.

He opened the door, then stood there with the door ajar, listening. His eyes quick and darting, he disappeared down the hall to his room, where he loaded a pistol, and headed down the stairs.

A chill coursed through him when he saw Albert standing over the body of a man holding a smoking gun.
It was a man Jake did not recognize.

Jakes first thought was that the man was some sort of a vagrant intruder, but when he gazed down at the lif e less form, he could see he was not dressed shabbily.

"Leave us!" .lake shouted to the servants who were standing around wringing their hands. "I'll take care of this. If I need you, I call you."

Too shocked to do anything but obey, Nellie and Lily and Lucinda dashed back to the kitchen.

Jake faced Albert. "What happened?"

Albert stood there motionless, staring off into space as he spoke. "I couldn't let him defame my dead daughter s name and take my grandson from me."

Now Jake knew. He was peering down at the remains of Danny Eagan. At the moment, Jake's only thought was to make certain he was dead. He knelt down beside the body and felt for a pulse on the bloodied neck. His next concern was to get the body out of the house.

Dimity moved down the stairs quietly and slowly. At the foot of the stairs, she froze. Gasping, she turned her face away from the scene and quickly grabbed hold of the newel post to keep from falling. Her face was chalky white as she forced herself to look. She stared down at the blood spattered body of Danny Eagan, whose sightless eyes stared back. She fought back the rising sick feeling. She fled to her father's side.

"Papa! Oh Papa, what happened?" she sobbed laying a comforting, but trembling hand on his arm.

Distraught, he covered his face with a shaky hand, his bitter rage and fury exhausted. He made no attempt to explain or defend. His face hardened almost cruelly without an ounce of mercy. The deathly stillness was suddenly shattered with his words. "Damn his black heart," he screamed.

Confusion clouding his judgment and reason, he spun away from her grasp and bolted for the front door in a wild flight of escape.

Dimity started after him, but Jake put a firm hand on her arm, restraining her.

"Let him go, dearest." He gathered her in his arms. I'll go after him when he's had a chance to collect himself.

Tears spilling from her eyes, she nodded.

Somehow, this gentle soul had turned violent. One could never tell that his was a life of love and gentleness. Yet, in his quarrel with fate and the world, he had killed a man in the one violent act of his lifetime.

Albert walked away, clumping through the gathering drifts of snow. In the last hour, the snow and the gale force wind had gained momentum. Transformed into a robot of a man with no feeling, or sensations, he was oblivions of the brutal cold and biting wind as he dashed into the night in his nocturnal flight from reality.

DIMITY AND JAKE

CHAPTER TWENTY-SEVEN

Her mind had not taken it in when it happened. It was too raw. Too ugly. A merciful insensibility to all her surroundings was her way of sheltering herself from the incomprehensible tragedy she'd witnessed.

At the time, she did not speak of what she had seen she did not ask questions. She had crept to her room like a wounded child, where she stayed in her bed, abandoning all that she loved. Life itself.

All the while, Jake was dividing his time between running Albert Durant's many businesses and sitting at Dimity's bedside, praying silently, deigning to bargain with God for Dimity's recovery. Prayers were his only weapon against hopelessness and despair.

One day, in early spring, just when Jake had given up all hope that she would ever show any interest in the world around her, she suddenly remembered what she had forgotten and began to speak. "Did you bury Papa?"

Her look was as innocent as a child. He leaned over to kiss her. "Yes, my darling," he whispered hoarsely, trying to recover from the unexpected shock of her question.

Her illness and too little food had severely changed her looks, leaving her with sallow skin, dirty circles about her eyes, and lusterless hair. All telltale signs of her suffering.

Recalling the day he told her that Albert's dead body was discovered, she had shown little recognition that she understood. The thought of that day made him go cold. Now, after all these months, when she finally asked about Albert's funeral, it was as though the gates of her memory suddenly and mysteriously closed, were now opening wide.

Through the past dismal months, the deep emotional wound had been healing, allowing the tide of pain to gradually ebb away. Oh, there was that intangible, fleeting sadness Jake could see in her eyes at times, but for the most part she seemed to be reborn, emerging strong and implacable. Once again she was able to speak about the past. In their exchange of memories, she told Jake, "he never raised his voice to me, or scolded me as he did Clarice. Although, he was not the man that fathered me, he was more my father than my real father."

Jake nodded. "Mine as well!"

"As for Danny." she paused. Slowly and painfully she went on. "I do feel a great sadness for the pitifully brief time we had together. Rut I asked myself when we found each other, whether we would ever be able to recapture those lost years. There was too much separating us." Then she asked, "Can you tell me what happened, Jake? I mean everything I've not wanted to know."

He looked at her sadly. Thinking it would be too much for her, his first impulse was to put off telling her the truth. But on second thought, it may give her peace of mind, knowing her father had not been accused of Danny's murder. "My explanation to the police was accepted unquestioningly."

"And that was?"

"That Danny Eagan came to the house with one thing in mind. To kill M. D. Durant. Because of the stories about him in the newspaper and the indictment of his criminal activities."

"They believed you?"

"Yes! When I found the gun on Danny, it triggered a plausible reason they would believe."

Seeing the sadness in her eyes, he put his arms around her. "Dimity, I couldn't let Albert go to prison for Danny's murder. God help me! I'd have given my soul to keep him from that. If it hadn't been for Albert, I would have ended up like Danny. On the streets! By taking me under his wing, he saved me from a street life, a life of crime, a life I hated and denounced. There is no doubt about it."

"But why would you worry about him going to prison? He was found dead."

"My dear, when the authorities took the body away, I thought Albert was alive. I had no idea we would find him frozen to death, buried in a snowdrift." Seeing her face grow even paler, he stopped abruptly. "I'm sorry, dearest," he said worriedly. "I shouldn't have been so graphic."

"I can't run away from the truth any longer," she murmured, her eyes misting with tears, "the cold may have been his executioner, but I'm quite certain his God forgave him for his moment of madness."

He was moved by her words. And yes, comforted to know she could speak of it.

She looked at him lovingly. "Thank you, Jake. For saving his good name. We both know he was afraid Danny intended to take his grandson away. But Jake," she said, I don't believe that's what Danny intended."

In piecing together the broken fragments of that lost period, a flooding relief and peace freed her from the grief she had blocked out all these months.

Standing on the terrace, beaming with pleasure, Jake watched Dimity who was sitting in the garden playing with the baby. Simply dressed in a white batiste blouse and a soft green linen skirt, she looked lovely, so vibrant! So alive. Since her renewed activity, this was her first outing outdoors. The baby's nurse sat alongside her chatting away. Absorbed in the baby's antics, who was bouncing up and down, squealing with delight, they did not notice Jake coming down the brick steps.

"Good morning, ladies!" he greeted them, tousling the baby's bushy head of brilliant red curls. "He's like a wound-up doll."

"Good morning, Jake."

Wide-eyed and giggly, bouncing happily, the baby held up his chubby arms for Jake to take him.

"Dada!"

Jake squatted down on the grass with the baby on top of him. He gave him a kiss on his cheek, then held him high over his head. "What's my boy been up to today?"

"I would say he's full of energy," Dimity said warmly, feeling a tingle of delight running through her at the scene before her. "But I do think it's time for his lunch and a long nap."

The nurse rose from the bench. "I'll take him, Mr. Trenton."

"Thank you, Miss Gleeson."

They watched her as she made her way up to the house with the baby in her arms.

"I'm mighty glad Miss Gleeson decided to stay on as his nurse." Jake said, sliding in beside Dimity on the stone bench.

Dimity reached out a slender hand to him. "She's an absolute gem. Little Albert adores her."

Jake turned to her, thinking, that tragic figure of only weeks ago was gone. Her cheeks were glowing. Like the colorful roses in full and delicate blooms returning to life, so was she.

"And you my dearest," he whispered, kissing her lightly on the lips, "what have you been doing on this glorious spring day?"

"I spent part of the morning visiting with Glory." Her eyes lit up. "Oh, Jake, she remembered me."

"Of course, she remembered you, my darling."

"And I've had the time of my life playing with the baby." She squeezed his hand tightly. She gazed into his face for the longest time before speaking.

"Dimity?" he frowned, "is there something wrong?"

She smiled. "No dear. Everything is right. I have something of the greatest importance to tell you."

He wasn't smiling. His imagination was running wild. What could it be?

She knew Jake had not noticed her rounded stomach. She, herself, had not noticed her thickened waistline until today when she was unable to fasten the buttons on the skirt she was wearing. If she had worn anything but a loose wrapper lately, she would surely have ripped the seams open. Only in the past few days, when she was finally able to think coherently, was she aware of her tender breasts and the absence of her menses.

"I am going to have your child."

Not fully grasping her words, he said, "What did you say?"

She smiled. "Jake, I am pregnant. Don't *you* understand?"

A flooding relief filled him. His smile broadened. The way he looked at her melted her heart.

He lifted her up in his arms and twirled her around.

"Oh, my adorable kitten!" He could barely contain himself. At the news of this new life within her, he felt a bursting of excitement. He very carefully lowered her back down on the bench. "How do you know? Are you sure? How can it be?"

She giggled. "Believe me, Jake. I know. Mercy! I'm afraid you're going to have to make an honest woman of me and marry me."

"Yes! Yes, of course! We must be married right away." He gathered her in his arms and held her. Smoothing her hair with loving strokes, he whispered in her ear. "My heart is full to overflowing."

"God willed it, Jake. A new life to take the place of the lives taken from us." Her face stained with sentimental tears, she rested her head against him. "And Jake?"

"Yes, my darling!"

"Little Albert is the legacy passed down to me from Danny."

"Your gift to hold on to from the past," he brushed away a tear with a finger.

Feeling the strength of his arms around her, Dimity knew for the rest of her life she could have it all. Jake! His love! His children! The world she had pushed away!

LaVergne, TN USA
11 March 2010
175709LV00003B/1/P

9 781582 752174